R

DATE DUE

P

WHEATON, ILLINOIS

To my family—

more than the ties of blood and kin,

we are held together

by cords of faith and love.

Visit Tyndale's exciting Web site at www.tyndale.com

Scripture quotations are taken from the *Holy Bible,* King James Version.

Edited by Judith Markham

Library of Congress Cataloging-in-Publication Data

Stokes, Penelope J.
    Remembering you / Penelope J. Stokes.
      p. cm. — (Faith on the home front ; 3)
      ISBN 0-8423-0857-1 (softcover)
      I. Title.   II. Series: Stokes, Penelope J.   Faith on the home front ; 3.
    PS3569.T6219R46   1997
    813′.54—dc21   97-15052

Printed in the United States of America

02 01 00 99 98 97
7   6   5   4   3   2   1

CONTENTS

PART THREE
As Time Goes By / AUTUMN 1945

PART FOUR
Till the End of Time / WINTER 1945

ACKNOWLEDGMENTS

My heartfelt thanks to all who played a part in this drama:

First, to my parents, Jim and Betty Stokes, who lived the story and shared it with me;

for their faith in me and their support of my calling;

for my mother's appreciation for literature and my father's sense of humor;

and for their love.

To Dan Balow and Jim Hoff, for sharing invaluable resource materials;

To Judith Markham, my editor, for being a never-ending source of encouragement and expertise;

To Helen and Nancy, friends who inspire me by their lives, their faith, and their wit;

To the memory of Branwyn and the presence of Honeybear, the canine companions who leap into my stories as they have leaped into my life;

And to Cindy, who endures a writer's eccentricities with grace and goodwill.

We are, truly, a family created by God.

Thank you all.

ONE

You'd Be
So Nice to
Come Home To

SPRING 1945

1

Celebration

Paradise Garden Cafe
Eden, Mississippi
May 18, 1945

Willie Coltrain managed a smile as Link Winsom, seated at the table in the middle of the cafe, pushed wedding cake into his bride's mouth and smeared a dollop of white frosting onto her nose. Most of the reception guests had gone home an hour ago, and it was just family and close friends now—Willie's cousin Libba and her new husband, Link, Libba's mother, Olivia, Link's father, Bennett, the Simpsons and the Laportes, and of course Thelma Breckinridge, who owned the cafe, and Ivory Brownlee, who sat at the piano playing everything from Beethoven to blues.

Link, in his dress uniform, looked handsome and relaxed now that the formalities were over and the festivities had begun. Libba—now Libba Coltrain *Winsom*—laughed and leaned down to kiss him.

They seemed so happy, Willie mused. And so they should be. After agonizing months thinking Link was dead, Libba now had him back from the front, more or less healthy and with a new life before them. When Link had finally come home—in a body cast from his chest to his knees—no one knew whether he would ever walk again. But he did walk, the scoundrel, saving that little surprise for the moment when he made his way down the aisle to meet Libba at the altar.

Willie's eyes filled with tears at the memory of Libba's face. For a few tense minutes, the poor girl had actually thought she had been jilted, left standing in the aisle hanging onto the arm of her prospective father-in-law But when Link appeared, almost miraculously, on his feet and aided only by a cane, the whole church had erupted into cheers, tears, and applause.

It had been, without a doubt, the rowdiest, most touching, most unconventional wedding Willie had ever been a part of. And she was trying to be happy for them, honestly she was. It was just that . . .

Couples. Everywhere she went, it seemed, Willie was confronted by couples. Just when she thought she was over the agony of losing Owen Slaughter to the war, the pain would assault her again, triggered by a glance or a song on the radio or the quiet announcement of her sister's pregnancy. At the movies, on the street, even in her own home, she couldn't escape them—laughing together, walking arm in arm, gazing into each other's eyes.

She swallowed down the lump in her throat and looked around at the remnant of wedding guests gathered in the Paradise Garden Cafe. Link gazed adoringly at Libba. Beside them, Willie's brother-in-law Andrew Laporte had one arm wrapped around her sister, Rae. On the surface, they seemed an odd, mismatched couple—Rae with her plump figure and round moonlike face, Drew with his movie-star good looks. But Willie knew they loved one another deeply, a love that would only increase with the birth of the child Rae now carried.

Behind Link and Libba, leaning against the counter, stood Bennett Winsom with his arm linked in the elbow of Thelma Breckinridge. Bennett and Thelma . . . now, nobody would *ever* have dreamed up that match! But Willie had to be happy for them. Thelma's life had been marked by years of selflessness—and no doubt loneliness—and now she had finally been rewarded with a love of her own.

"More food, everybody!" Stork Simpson called as he pushed his lanky form through the swinging door and came out of the kitchen with a fresh pot of coffee and an enormous plate of sandwiches. Close on his heels, his wife, Madge, came bearing their one-year-old son, Mickey.

Everyone surged forward toward the tables, reaching for sandwiches, cake, and coffee. And almost against her will, Willie hung back.

These couples had no idea what they were doing, of course—what bittersweet longing their affection for one another stirred up in Willie's heart. But with every intimate glance, every touch, every familiar intonation of names like *sweetheart, honey,* and *darling,* Willie's sense of isolation increased.

She took a deep breath and shut her eyes, fighting to push back the loneliness that rolled over her like a wave. She couldn't spoil this moment for Link and Libba and the rest of them. She wouldn't.

"Willie? Are you all right?"

Her sister's voice, close at Willie's ear, startled her, and her eyes snapped open. "I-I'm—," she stammered, holding onto the table for support, "I'm fine."

"Well, you don't look fine." Rae cocked her head and narrowed her eyes. "You look pale, and your face is all clammy." She put a hand to Willie's forehead and smiled. "Are you sure I'm the one who's pregnant? Or are you having sympathetic morning sickness . . . in the evening?"

Willie shook her head and forced herself to meet Rae's gaze. "I'm OK," she muttered. "It's just getting hot in here." She averted her eyes. "I think I'll go out and get some fresh air."

Rae gave her a quizzical look. "All right. But don't be too long. Link and Libba are going to open presents pretty soon."

"Just a few minutes." Willie wrenched herself away and fled for the door just as the walls of the cafe began to close in on her.

The warmth of the day had dissipated, and as she pushed open the door of the cafe and escaped from the cloying closeness of the building, a spring breeze wafted the scent of blossoming daffodils and azaleas to her. The wedding had been at three, and the formal reception had lasted until six. Now it was nearly seven. The setting sun had left a fading trail of pink-and-orange clouds in the sky. Willie lifted her face to the cool evening air and took a deep breath.

"Excuse me?"

The hoarse whisper sent a chill coursing through Willie's veins, and she froze. There, in the shadows of the crepe myrtle on the edge of the parking lot, stood the shrouded figure of a man.

★ ★ ★

He peered through the gathering dusk at the woman who stood before him. Taller than he was by a head or more, she was a strapping girl, with strawberry blonde curls and dusky eyes. And she wore the most awful dress he had ever seen—all flounces and ruffles and billowing sleeves. Even from this distance, in this light, he could tell that this was not a woman comfortable with such frippery. She tugged at the neckline of the dress and stared at him.

"Excuse me," he repeated quietly so as not to frighten her. "I'm . . . I'm looking for someone. Perhaps you could help me."

"What-what can I do for you?" The voice was husky and deep, almost as if she had been crying. She sniffed and cleared her throat, then frowned at him. "You're a soldier?"

He ducked his head and ran a hand through his beard. "Looks like it," he said, feeling sheepish. "Except for the beard, of course. I've just been discharged."

"And you're looking for . . ." she prompted.

"The Paradise Garden Cafe. Is this the place?"

The woman pointed to the garish neon sign that proclaimed the name of the cafe in flashing red and blue. For the first time she smiled. "Looks like it."

Then she laughed, a rich, warm sound that sent an unaccountable shiver down his spine. He took a step closer. The hair, the height, the voice—except for the horrible dress, the woman before him looked remarkably like the tiny face in the family picture Charlie had given to him. Maybe he was wrong, but . . .

"Would you, by any chance, happen to be Willie Coltrain?"

The head snapped up and the eyes flashed. She took a step backward, and even in the waning light he could see the look of shock that registered on her face. "I am. But who are—"

"I'm a friend of Charlie's," he said, rushing forward and grabbing her hands. "I can't believe I'm meeting you after all this time—I feel like I've known you for years!"

As soon as he had done it, he realized it was a mistake, blurting everything out like that. The shock was too much for her, and she wavered unsteadily. He took her elbow and led her over to the bus bench outside the cafe.

"Charlie?" the girl said numbly.

"Yes, Charlie, your brother," he said carefully. "If you'll just sit here for a minute and catch your breath, I'll tell you all about it."

"Charlie died in the war."

A lump rose in his throat. "Yes, he did, but not like you might think. He made me promise to come to Eden and tell you in person."

She kept her head lowered, twisting the fabric of the horrible dress between her fingers.

Gently he touched her arm and held her there. "Give me just a few minutes," he pleaded. "I've come so far."

Willie's senses reeled as the bearded stranger in the ill-fitting uniform related a story that boggled her mind. Apparently Charlie, the brother she thought had been killed long ago, had died only recently, in Germany, after escaping from a Nazi prison camp. He was a hero, the man told her. Against all odds Charlie had recovered from severe shell shock after being wounded at Messina. He had gone back to the front and rescued three children in the woods of Normandy, had kept his sergeant alive when they had been ambushed, and then had been taken prisoner by the Nazis when he attempted to find and save a dying soldier's buddy.

"And so, when I was captured, Charlie and I ended up in the same camp." The man's voice came to her as if from a great distance. "I'm not sure what happened to me," he went on. "I came to with a Kraut rifle pointed at my head and no memory of who I was or where I had come from. I only knew my name because of my dog tags." He sighed. "Charlie took me under his wing. He knew what it was like to be thought of as crazy, and he became my friend. My only friend. My link to reality, really."

The soldier reached into his breast pocket, drew out a faded, dog-eared photograph, and handed it to her. Tears welled up in her eyes as she looked at the family—Mama and Daddy, Mabel Rae and herself, and dear Charlie, standing on the front porch of the farmhouse. One of the farmhands had taken the picture on a clear fall afternoon years ago, in better days when Daddy could still work the fields and their life was relatively stable. But everything had changed since then. Everything.

"Charlie shared his memories with me, you see," the bearded soldier said in a choked voice. "Told me all about Eden, about his family. Promised me we'd come here together. Then when he died—"

"How did he die?" Willie interrupted.

The man smiled briefly, and an odd shock ran through her veins—a sense of déja vu, as if she had been here before, hearing this story, sitting on this bench. But the sensation passed as the soldier scratched his beard and continued.

"We escaped from the stalag, and a German woodsman named Fritz Sonntag found us and hid us from the Nazis. But Charlie was pretty sick by then—influenza from exposure and malnutrition. Still, he was a hero. He was burning up with fever and delirious, and when he thought the Germans had come to kill us, he tried to rescue me. Jumped from the barn loft and impaled his shoulder on a bayonet."

An involuntary shudder shook Willie, and the man reached out and patted her hand. "The ironic thing was," he went on, "that the soldiers Charlie 'rescued' me from were there to help us escape across the border to Switzerland." He gave a deep sigh. "Charlie died two days before the liberation."

Willie fingered the photograph in her lap, and the tears began to flow in earnest. She clutched the picture to her and sobbed like a child, her whole body racked with pain and grief.

And then, as the tears began to subside, she felt something else—strong arms around her, holding her, comforting her. The softness of a beard against her own cheek. A murmured whisper in her ear. At first she started to draw back—he was a stranger, after all, and giving herself over to the embrace of a nameless man she had never met certainly wasn't proper. But with a shuddering sigh, she pushed those feelings aside and relaxed against his shoulder. His hand stroked her back, the way a mother might comfort a child. And proper or not, it felt good to be held, to be touched.

At last she sat up and accepted the handkerchief he offered.

"I know it's an inconvenient time," he said, motioning toward the cafe. "Obviously there's a celebration going on, and I don't want to intrude, but I have come a long way, and Charlie told me so much about Eden and his family. I really would like to meet everyone."

"Of course." Willie blew her nose and started to hand him the handkerchief, then thought better of it and gave him a wry grin. "I'll launder it for you before I return it."

"That's very thoughtful of you . . . Willie."

When he said her name, something snapped inside Willie. A fragment of memory, an intonation. For the first time she looked directly into his eyes and saw something that took her breath away. But it couldn't be . . . it just couldn't.

"I think I'd better prepare the others before you come in," she murmured, her heart pounding. "It's likely to be as much of a shock for them as it was for me." She couldn't stop staring at him now, searching his eyes, probing beyond the beard to the contours of the thin, pale prisoner's face. "I'll give them the condensed version, and you can fill in the details," she said, still staring at him. His eyes were blue, so very blue. . . .

"Thanks. I'll wait out here." He helped her to her feet and stood gazing up at her expectantly. "You're going in?"

She blinked. "Oh, yes. Right." She moved toward the door of the cafe, then turned back to look at him one more time. "I'm sorry. I don't believe you told me your name."

He slapped a palm to his head and grinned. "Sorry. Just like me to forget that—I've certainly forgotten everything else." He doffed his cap and offered a grand little bow. "You couldn't prove it by me," he said, "but the dog tags say Slaughter . . . Owen Slaughter."

All the blood rushed from Willie's head, and she ran for the door.

2

Decision

"Willie? What's wrong? You look like you've seen a ghost."

Willie Coltrain collapsed at a table and motioned for her sister, Rae, and the others to give her some breathing space. The cafe was spinning, and she felt as if she might pass out at any moment. *Idiot! You are not going to faint,* she reprimanded herself. *Coltrain women do not faint.*

After a minute or two she had regained her equilibrium and managed a drink of the iced tea Thelma Breckinridge thrust into her hand. Good old Thelma. She believed a glass of tea or a cup of strong coffee would temper the most harrowing crisis.

"What took you so long out there, anyway?" Rae demanded. "I was about to send the troops out after you."

"Well, you didn't need to," Willie sighed. "The troops were already there."

Drew Laporte, her brother-in-law, leaned in. "What are you talking about, Willie?"

"I'm talking about soldiers, Drew," she said impatiently. "To be precise, *one* soldier. Outside, in the parking lot."

"A man?" Drew frowned. "Was he bothering you? I'll get rid of him—"

Drew started for the door, but Willie caught his coattail and jerked him back. "Hold it, Superman," she muttered. "Drop your cape and sit down for a minute. I've got something to tell you—all of you—and it's going to be a little hard to believe." She closed her eyes and took a deep breath. "There's a man in the parking lot. A solider. He says he's a friend of Charlie's, and his name is . . . Owen Slaughter."

"*What?*" Link grabbed Stork and pulled him down in an exuberant bear

9

hug. "Owen's alive? And he's here?" He jerked Stork's arm and headed him for the door. "Well, get him in here! Why is he sitting outside?"

"Wait a minute!" Willie protested. "Sit down, all of you. Now."

Silence descended, and everyone sat. Bennett Winsom cast a significant look at Thelma, and she nodded. "I think we'd better hear what Willie has to say," Bennett said.

Willie cast a grateful glance in his direction. "Thank you, Bennett. Now please, no more interruptions until you know everything—at least everything I know."

★ ★ ★

"You mean he has no memory—none at all?" Link exhaled heavily and sat back against his chair.

"Apparently not." Willie Coltrain shook her head. "Charlie gave him a picture of the family—he said Charlie had 'shared his memories' with him. But he obviously didn't know me, except from the photo. I don't think he knows anything about the past except his name—and he got that from his dog tags."

"We were all there together in France—Owen and Link and me. It must have happened during the explosion at the chateau," Stork Simpson mused. "Everything happened so fast that day—the Kraut ambush, Link getting wounded. Owen took out the ammo supply in that chateau single-handedly, but we never saw him again. We assumed he was dead, and so did the army." An expression of pain and anger settled over Stork's hawkish face, and his wife, Madge, put an arm around him. "We should have gone back for him."

"You didn't have much choice, from what I understand," Link's father said. "Besides, all that's in the past. Owen is alive, and for that we can all be thankful. The question is, what do we do now?"

"What do you mean, what do we do?" Link couldn't believe that his father, normally such an intelligent man, could be so dense. "We go out there and bring him in and tell him what happened, that's what."

"I'm not so sure." His father held up a cautioning hand. "I don't know much about amnesia, but it might be dangerous to overload him with memories before he's ready."

"But Dad, he deserves to know," Link protested. For a long time after the chateau incident, he had dreamed that Owen would show up alive. Now here he was literally at their doorstep, and they were going to treat him like a stranger?

"If we only knew more," Stork said. "If we just understood what was the right thing to do."

From the piano in the corner came a haunting, dissonant blues chord.

"I know."

All eyes turned to see Ivory Brownlee nodding. "I know," he repeated.

Thelma Breckinridge went over to him and put a hand on his shoulder. "What do you know, Ivory?" she asked gently.

"I know all about am-nesia," he said. "Learnt it at the hospital."

Link fought to quell his impatience. Harlan Brownlee, called "Crazy Ivory," was just a washed-up old veteran from the first war who wasn't quite right in the head. Everybody knew it. He was harmless enough, with his piano playing and his talk about his doughboy days. But Sigmund Freud he wasn't.

As if he had read his son's mind, Link's father laid a restraining hand on his arm. "Let's hear what he has to say," he whispered. He motioned to Ivory to come out from behind the piano. "Tell us what you know, Ivory."

Ivory shuffled over to the group and perched on the edge of a table. He puffed his chest out proudly, as if he knew he was in the spotlight and intended to make the most of it. Link sighed and fidgeted in his chair.

"When I was in the war, I got shot—right here." He made a move to pull his shirttail up, and Thelma gently patted his hand. "They might want to see my scar, Thelma. Y'all want to see my scar?"

Thelma shook her head and smiled at him. "Maybe later, Ivory. Go on."

"Well, I got me a Purple Heart and a medal in the Big War. Shot me a officer, right in the head." He grinned, revealing several dark gaps where his teeth were missing.

Link rolled his eyes. He had heard the story before, on the very first day he had ever set foot in Eden. No doubt everyone else in the room had heard it too.

"Anyway," Ivory continued, his smile fading. "I got more than just a coupl'a medals and a trip home. I got shell shock."

Link's head snapped up. "I didn't know that."

"Yes, you did," Thelma corrected softly. "I told you about it a long time ago—that first day you came into this cafe, when Ivory played for you. You just forgot."

Ivory cut a glance at Link. "Most folks would rather forget—they'd rather just think I'm stupid. But I ain't stupid. And I ain't crazy. I got a tremor—" He held up his hand to demonstrate the shake. "But when I play the piano, it don't bother me much."

"So what did you learn in the hospital?" Thelma prompted.

"Oh yeah, the hospital." Ivory swiped a hand across his weathered face as if the memory were still painful to him. "Feller in the bed next to me, he had am-nesia. Got whacked in the head with a cannon barrel, I think. Anyways, when they was gonna let him go home, the doctors warned his wife and family not to push him too hard to remember. Said it'd come naturally, on its own, as he got better and felt like he was in a safe place. But if they tried to get him to remember, like telling him stuff and asking if he remembered it, he might crack worse under the pressure."

Tears welled up in Ivory's rheumy blue eyes and slid down his cheeks. "I 'member one day his wife came to visit—brought their littlest young'un, a boy of mebbe five or six. The little feller climbed up on the bed to give his daddy a big hug, and the man just broke down crying 'cause he couldn't remember his own baby."

The old man looked up with an expression of compassion that shook Link to the core. "You oughta be careful with that boy Owen," he said softly. "Don't want to hurt him no more'n he's already been hurt."

Link felt a lump rise to his throat, and he nodded to his father. "I guess he's right, Dad. We'd better let Owen do his own healing."

His father patted Ivory on the back. "Looks like our best course of action," he said quietly, "is to treat Owen like a friend of Charlie's. If his memory returns, so much the better. If it doesn't, at least he'll have friends who can be here for him—new friends."

Thelma put both hands on Willie's shoulders and leaned down toward her. "Can you do this? Treat Owen as Charlie's friend, I mean, not your long-lost fiancé?"

An expression of unutterable pain flitted across Willie's face; then her expression cleared and she forced a smile.

"Owen's alive, and he's come home," she murmured. "I can do whatever is necessary."

3

Reunion

Outside, Owen Slaughter paced back and forth along the length of the gravel parking lot. On each pass, he peered in through the windows at the group of people gathered around Charlie Coltrain's sister Willie. He couldn't hear their words, but he could see a concerned expression on nearly every face. Willie herself looked pale and shaken—he supposed that was to be expected when a stranger appeared out of nowhere with firsthand news of her brother's recent death.

Clearly, his arrival had cast a pall over the wedding celebration. The woman in the wedding dress—Owen was almost sure she was Charlie's cousin, Libby, the spoiled princess—blotted tears and clung to the arm of a dark, intense-looking soldier. The other young woman, the one with the round face and dark eyes, might be Mabel Rae, the sister Charlie said would probably never get married. But she looked different than he had imagined her—not dumpy and homely like the girl in the picture, but rather attractive, even in that billowy dress just like Willie's. And the man by her side was a broad-shouldered, handsome fellow. If this was Mabel Rae, Charlie had certainly been wrong about her chances for marriage.

As Owen watched, a feeling rose up in him—what people might call homesickness, except that he didn't remember enough to qualify for that particular emotion. What was it, then? A vague wish that he could really be part of this family, the way Charlie had made him feel a part of it? A desire to have a family of his own, a place where he belonged?

Abruptly he turned away, stalked back to the bench, and flung himself down. There was no use getting his hopes up—nothing to be gained by imagining himself a part of the intimate group gathered inside the cafe. He was a stranger, a nobody. He didn't belong anywhere, least of all Eden, Mississippi, which had become his whole world since Charlie Coltrain had befriended him.

He would fulfill his promise to Charlie—tell his story, comfort his family, and be on his way. Why should he set himself up for more pain by trying to live on memories borrowed from his closest friend? Charlie was dead, and any hope of being accepted and welcomed by these people had died with him.

The bell over the cafe door jingled, and Owen looked up to see Willie Coltrain, her eyes red and puffy, standing before him. She fiddled with the fabric of her dress and did not meet his gaze.

"Everyone is very glad you've come," she said formally. "Would you join us inside?"

Owen got to his feet and found that his legs had turned to jelly. His insides knotted with apprehension, and he shook his head to clear his mind. "Thank you," he mumbled.

With a trembling hand he held the door open for Willie and followed her inside.

The Paradise Garden Cafe was just as Charlie had described it—homey and a little decrepit, with a cracked linoleum floor and a pervasive scent of stale grease. Owen's eyes scanned the room and came to rest on a long center table covered with a lace tablecloth and laden with a half-eaten wedding cake, plates of sandwiches, and a litter of coffee cups and monogrammed paper napkins.

All eyes fixed on him expectantly, and he cleared his throat. "I'm sorry to interrupt your celebration," he began. "You don't know me, and you don't have any reason to welcome me here, but my name is Owen Slaughter. I am a friend of Charlie's, and he made me promise to come."

Owen watched as a series of glances went around the room. No one spoke. Then a tall, middle-aged woman with henna-dyed hair and warm brown eyes came forward with a plate of sandwiches and cake and a cup of coffee. "Please sit down and make yourself comfortable, Owen," the woman said as she settled him at a table and placed the food in front of him. "I'm sure you're hungry after such a long trip."

Owen looked into her face as she leaned down over him. "You're Thelma Breckinridge, aren't you? The owner of the Paradise Garden?"

A brief look of confusion flitted across her face.

"Charlie told me about you," he explained hastily. He looked around at the curious faces. "About all of you—or at least most of you." He smiled at the round-faced woman with the dark eyes. "You're the oldest sister, Mabel Rae, right?"

The woman flushed and nodded. "This is my husband, Andrew Laporte," she said, squeezing the arm of the muscular, broad-shouldered man.

"Ha! Well, Charlie was certainly wrong when he said *you'd* never get married!" As soon as the words were out of his mouth, Owen regretted them. How could he be so insensitive to blurt out something like that to a woman he had never met before?

To his profound relief, she threw back her head and laughed out loud. "That's our Charlie! He always did give me a hard time about what he called my 'hopeless chest.'" She gazed up at her handsome husband. "He just didn't know the power of a little hope."

Owen's eyes drifted to the woman in the bridal gown. Auburn hair, pale green eyes. "And you must be Cousin Libby, the Princess."

"Libba," the girl corrected with a chuckle. "But make that Ex-Princess. I've changed a lot since Charlie went away."

The lean, dark man, obviously her new husband, shifted in his chair and leaned forward intently. "And what about me?" he asked, grabbing the arm of a tall blond fellow who stood at his side. "And him?"

Owen studied the two of them—one with dark hair and eyes and olive skin, the other lanky as a crane, with deep-set hazel eyes, a hawkish nose, and a shock of blond hair that fell over his forehead. A flicker of something pushed at his mind but was gone in an instant. He closed his eyes and shook his head.

"I'm sorry. If Charlie told me about you fellows, I can't seem to remember."

★ ★ ★

Link exhaled heavily. When Owen had come in and recognized Thelma and Rae, he had hoped—prayed—that being with them would jog his memory, and everything would come flooding back. He wanted to shout, *Of course you know us, man! We're your best friends. We were there when that chateau blew to kingdom come. If we hadn't been hit, too, we would have moved heaven and earth to find you!*

But he couldn't. Owen's identification of Willie and Mabel Rae and Thelma wasn't recognition at all. He had seen the picture, heard Charlie's stories about the folks in Eden, and pieced the rest together. The poor guy had nothing but memories borrowed from Charlie, and Charlie had never met Link or Stork. The blank, expectant expression on Owen's face told it all—he truly didn't remember. Not even a glimmer.

Link extended his hand and said, "I'm Link Winsom, and this is Stork Simpson." He pointed around the room. "You've met Drew, and that's my father, Bennett Winsom, and my mother-in-law, Olivia Coltrain. The lady behind Stork is his wife, Madge, and the little guy is their son, Mickey. Our piano player here is Harlan Brownlee—people call him Ivory."

Owen got up and shook hands all around, then settled back into his chair. He inhaled the sandwiches and wedding cake like a starving man, and when he was done, drained his coffee cup and said, "I suppose you're all waiting to hear Charlie's story."

We'd rather hear your story, Link thought, but he simply nodded.

And as his best friend began the account of his days as a prisoner of the Reich, Link realized with a sinking feeling that when the tale was done, Owen Slaughter might just disappear from their lives forever.

★ ★ ★

Willie sat on the fringes of the group, watching Owen as he gathered his thoughts and began to relate his story of meeting Charlie in the prison camp. He had grown thin, and behind the curly brown beard, his complexion bore a pale cast, quite different from the ruddy freshness she remembered. But there could be no doubt—it was her Owen, come back from the dead.

Tears made his blue eyes glisten as he told how Charlie had found three little French children huddling in a shed in the woods of Normandy. No one spoke; no one even breathed.

"The smaller of the boys was named Charles," Owen said. "When Charlie told him that was his name, too, the boy kissed him and held onto him and wouldn't let go—not even for a chocolate bar." He paused, wiped his eyes, and looked at Willie with an expression that melted her. "Your brother, Charlie, was a hero," he said quietly. "He went back to the front because he couldn't bear coming home in shame as a victim of shell shock. He didn't want people to think he was crazy."

"I reckon I understand that, all right," Ivory Brownlee murmured.

Owen gave Ivory a compassionate smile and went on. "When I met Charlie, he was the only one in the prison barracks who would have much to do with me. He couldn't really understand what it was to lose your memory, but he sure knew what it was like to be shunned. We took care of each other, and he became my link to a past I couldn't remember."

More than you know, Willie thought with a shuddering sigh.

"A few days before the liberation, we escaped. I didn't know how close the Allied troops were to us—only that Charlie was too sick to stand prison life any longer. In the woods we met Fritz Sonntag, a German who hid us from the Nazis until the end. As Charlie was dying, he made me promise to come back here and meet you all, to tell you in person what had happened."

By the time Owen got finished with his account—adding a lot of details he hadn't told Willie out in the parking lot—Mabel Rae was weeping openly, and most of the others were fighting back tears.

Rae leaned over and put a hand on Owen's arm. "Thank you," she whispered. "Thank you for coming all this way to tell us about our brother . . . to bring him back to us."

Willie couldn't speak, and she hardly dared to look at him for fear of losing control of her emotions. But she found herself envying Rae's freedom to touch him, to make contact. This was the man she had loved, waited for, and spent the better part of a year trying to get over. Now he was home, but he didn't know it was home.

"Well," Owen said at last, "I guess I've taken up enough of your time. I made good on my promise to Charlie, so I guess I'll be on my way."

Be on his way? The reality of the words struck Willie like a physical blow, and she recoiled. It was inconceivable that after all this time he would just walk out of her life and be gone. But it was even more impossible, being this close to him and not being able to love him. Maybe she would be better off letting him go. . . .

She returned to the present just in time to hear him ask, "Is there a hotel or boardinghouse nearby? I won't be able to catch a bus until tomorrow."

"Of course," Thelma answered. "There's Judith Larkins's boarding-house—I'm sure she would have a room available. I'll call if you like, and—"

"No!"

All eyes turned toward Willie, and suddenly she realized how vehemently she had spoken. "I . . . I mean, no, he can't stay at Judith Larkins's. After all, he helped Charlie escape and kept him alive. He's our brother's best friend. He's . . . well, he's practically like family. It would be downright inhospitable of us to let him stay at that rundown old boardinghouse."

"Willie—" The warning tone in Rae's voice was unmistakable, but Willie couldn't stop. She didn't want to stop. She had one chance, just one, and she intended to take it.

"Owen," she said in a rush, "we all appreciate so much what you've done for our brother. And we—well—we'd like to invite you to stay around for a while. Isn't that right, Rae?"

Before Rae had the chance to answer, Willie charged on. "You see, we have this big attic room where Charlie used to stay, and we could really use some help around the place, what with doing renovations for the baby, and—well—I don't quite know how you'd feel about this, but I'm a very good cook and you don't really have anywhere else you have to go, do you? We'd all be disappointed if you didn't stay, at least for a few days. . . ."

Willie sputtered to a conclusion and looked around the cafe. Rae, Drew, and Bennett Winsom were staring at her with incredulous expressions as if to ask, *Have you lost your mind?* Thelma was nodding thoughtfully, and Link and Stork were beaming. Ivory had returned to the piano and was playing "As Time Goes By."

For a moment Owen looked stunned and confused. At last he smiled and ducked his head shyly. "Charlie told me I'd find family here," he said in a voice hoarse with unshed tears. "If it's not too much trouble, I'd very much like to stay for a while. Thank you—all of you."

"You're more than welcome, Owen," Rae said, cutting a glance at Willie that shot daggers. "We'd be honored to have you."

Exhausted from her little outburst and from the emotion of the day, Willie sank into a chair and looked up to see Owen smiling down at her. His blue eyes seemed to penetrate her very soul, and her heart lurched. Did he remember . . . even a little?

If he did, there was no sign. He knelt down by her chair and took her hand in both of his.

"Thanks so much, Willie," he said fervently. "I don't remember having any family, but already I feel as if I've got a sister here in Eden. And that means a lot to me."

Willie fought back a fresh wave of tears. *A sister. He thinks of me as a sister.*

But there was nothing she could do except smile and nod . . . and pretend.

4

Homecoming

"Willie, how could you?" Rae shook her head in desperation. "Invite him to come stay at the farm with us? What are you, some kind of glutton for punishment? The poor man doesn't remember you, you can see that much. You're just making it harder for yourself. And we agreed it would be better not to try to jog his memory. What were you thinking, Willie? Don't you realize this could backfire, and—?"

Willie sighed and gazed out the front window of the cafe. Drew was helping get Owen and his meager burlap bag of personal belongings settled into the bed of the truck. "I know," she murmured. "I just couldn't help it. He seemed so . . ." Her words faded into silence, and she closed her eyes.

"Well, it's done now, so there's nothing more to discuss." A sinking feeling rose in Rae's heart as she watched her sister, eyes shut tight, fighting against the storm of emotions that raged inside her. She softened her tone and laid a hand on Willie's shoulder. "We do have plenty of room, and you're right, we can use the help around the farm."

With obvious effort, Willie opened her eyes and looked at Rae. "If he leaves, I'll never see him again," she choked out. "If he stays, it will be hard, but there's a chance he might regain his memory, and—"

"I understand," Rae soothed, patting her hand.

"No you don't!" Willie shot back. "You've got Drew, and the baby coming, and a future. I've got—" She twisted her face in a grimace. "A *brother.*"

The barb struck home, and Rae winced inwardly. Willie didn't mean to be cruel, but it hurt all the same. She bit back a sharp retort and whispered, "At least he's alive. Charlie isn't."

Willie's face went pale, and she blinked back tears. "I suppose I should be grateful for that."

"I suppose you should," Rae answered. "But I can understand if you're not." She caught herself on the word *understand* and began to backtrack. "I mean, I don't really understand, as you said, but I—"

"It's all right." Willie squeezed her hand and managed a ghost of a smile. "I'll just need a little help to get through this, OK?"

A surge of relief welled up in Rae. "I'll be there." The horn of the truck sounded, and Rae waved through the window to Drew. "I guess they're ready," she said. "Are you?"

"No," Willie replied with a wry grin. "But that doesn't make much difference, does it? Ready or not, we're going home."

★ ★ ★

The familiar countryside warped and twisted, blurred through a sheen of tears as Willie stared out the window. This was what she had hoped for, dreamed of, prayed for—whenever she was able to pray—for nearly a year. Owen Slaughter, alive, and coming home to the farm. With her.

Now the dream was coming true, but the bizarre circumstances of its fulfillment knotted her stomach with apprehension. A lump grew in her throat until she was barely able to swallow.

Charlie was gone. Dead. And in his place, the man she once thought she would share her life with, bear children with, grow old with, had returned— as a stranger. A friend of the family by virtue of his friendship with Charlie. A brother to replace the one who had died.

The tears overflowed and ran down her cheeks as Willie recalled that first rush of emotion when she had realized that the man standing before her in the parking lot of the Paradise Garden Cafe was her Owen, brought back from the grave. Love and longing, followed by sheer panic and then despair.

She was nothing to him. Nothing special. Just Charlie Coltrain's sister, a face in a faded photograph, a borrowed memory.

But how was she supposed to stop loving him after all this time? How could she keep the desire from her eyes so he would not see? How in heaven's name could she hold back, not tell him everything, restrain herself from rushing into his arms and declaring her love for him?

Maybe Rae was right. Maybe she should have let him go. Perhaps it would have been easier if she had said good-bye quietly and let him disappear from her life forever. At least then she could have grieved alone without the constant reminder of the love that had once bound them together.

But she couldn't help herself. She had to ask him to stay, and she wasn't even sure why. The Owen who had come back from the dead wasn't her Owen at all. The shell was the same, but the soul wasn't there anymore.

Choking on her tears, Willie leaned against the window of the truck and fought back a sob. Was this some kind of cruel cosmic joke—a God who answered prayers and then twisted the answer into something unbearable?

It just wasn't fair. If God had done this, then God had a lot to answer for.

★ ★ ★

Owen settled back against the cab of the pickup truck and watched the scenery pass by backward as the truck made its way toward home.

Home. For months now Owen had allowed himself to think of the Coltrain farm that way. Charlie's stories of Eden and the farm and his family seemed so real that Owen could almost believe he had experienced them himself. War had made Charlie his brother, and these people his family. And—miracle of miracles—they had invited him to stay. For a while, at least.

When Owen had arrived at the bus stop in Eden and looked in the doors of the Paradise Garden Cafe for the first time, he had made no plans beyond getting there and finding Charlie's family. What would he have done if they hadn't asked him to stay? Where would he have gone?

The familiar emptiness—the vacuum left by the loss of his memory—crept into his soul. His friendship with Charlie had shored up that hole for a while, given him a foundation, an identity. As long as you had one friend, you were not alone. You could go on, no matter how difficult going on might be. But when Charlie died, the sinkhole had opened up at Owen's feet again.

His heart had nearly broken as he stood at Charlie's graveside and said good-bye. Even the grave gave Owen a kind of anchor, a connection to the only past he knew, and once he left Germany and began the journey back to the States, he felt more isolated than ever.

Then, by some miraculous coincidence, Willie Coltrain walked out the door of the Paradise Garden and into his embrace.

Literally.

Owen closed his eyes and hugged his burlap bag to his chest as he recalled the sensation of holding her in his arms, comforting her. It didn't mean anything to her, of course—she was just distraught over the news of her brother's death. But the feelings it stirred in him took his breath away.

He would have to be careful—very careful—around Willie Coltrain, that was for sure. Those dusky gray eyes and that deep smoky voice would be his undoing if he didn't keep a tight rein on his emotions. There was something special about that girl, and if he intended to be true to Charlie's memory, he would have to treat her with kid gloves. Keep his distance. Be a brother.

Owen breathed deeply and opened his eyes. The scent of wildflowers and springtime came to him on the evening wind, and he smiled. Somehow—he didn't know quite how—this did feel like coming home. He began to imagine that he recognized landmarks along the way: the little country store on the right, the white clapboard church bounded by an ancient cemetery off to the left behind them. Charlie must have described these places, Owen decided, but still he almost felt as if he could have found his way alone.

When the truck turned off the main road and began climbing up a narrow dirt track, Owen stood up in the bed and leaned over the cab for his first glimpse of the Coltrain homestead. He would have known it anywhere, exactly as Charlie had described it. The sprawling two-story farmhouse with peeling white paint and a sagging front porch sat on a hill with rolling pastures behind it to the east, and in front, on the other side of the road, flat farmland stretching to the dark western horizon.

A thrill ran through Owen's veins, a sensation he couldn't quite identify. He didn't remember ever feeling it before, but instinctively he knew its name.

Hope.

5

The Taxman Cometh

Paradise Garden Cafe

Thelma Breckinridge carefully wrapped the top layer of wedding cake and placed it in the electric refrigerator. Everyone except Ivory and Bennett had finally left. It had to be the longest wedding reception on record . . . and the strangest.

Link and Libba had taken Robinson Coltrain's Nash Ambassador—a wedding gift from Libba's mother, Olivia—to Memphis. After what Robinson had done to his daughter—hiding Link's letters and letting her believe Link was dead—Olivia had said that Libba and Link deserved to get something from the estate, and Robinson's precious car seemed the obvious choice. A sudden heart attack had freed them all from Robinson's manipulations, and now Link and Libba were together and on their way to a honeymoon at the Peabody. From Memphis they would go on to Oxford so Link could take his law-school entrance exams and Libba could look for a job.

As Thelma folded the lace tablecloth and began to put the cafe tables back in order, her mind wandered to the wiry little stranger who had appeared bearing the name Owen Slaughter.

When Owen had been reported missing—in the army's terms, "presumed dead"—Thelma had watched helplessly while Willie Coltrain attempted to deal with her grief. It had been so hard for her to admit that Owen was gone, especially when Rae and Drew had turned up married, when Stork Simpson had returned, and when Link finally came home to

Libba. Everyone except Willie seemed to have someone. The closest she had gotten to accepting Owen's death was declaring her intention to be a spinster schoolteacher for the rest of her life.

And now, bless her heart, Willie had a whole new series of trials to face. For Owen to come back like that—without his memories, not knowing her or any of them—had to be as hard as believing he was dead. Maybe harder. Now he would be there every day, reminding her every minute of what she had lost.

Whatever God had in mind this time, Thelma couldn't for the life of her figure it out.

"Thelma!" Bennett called from the booth in the corner, where he and Ivory sat over a sheaf of legal papers. "Could you come join us for a few minutes?"

Thelma smiled at him and nodded. "Shall I bring coffee and cake?"

Ivory looked around, his rheumy blue eyes bright with anticipation, and nodded. Bennett just groaned. "No more food, please. But coffee would be nice."

Thelma loaded a tray with coffee for the three of them and a wedge of wedding cake—his fourth, she thought—for Ivory. When they were all settled at the table, Bennett pushed a handful of papers in her direction.

"Take a look at this."

Thelma scanned the papers and looked up at him, confused. "What am I looking for?"

He pointed a long forefinger at the upper right quadrant of the page. "These are tax records Drew tracked down from counties in three surrounding states. Landowners like Ivory with a history of unpaid taxes and no money to pay them."

Thelma studied the documents. It had been nearly six months since Ivory Brownlee had received the notice that he owed a thousand dollars in back taxes on his land—land that had been in his family since before the War Between the States. There wasn't much left now except for a few hundred acres, a rundown plantation house, and three or four slave shanties—but it was all Ivory had. He couldn't bear to lose it all to the government, so when an offer had come to buy the cropland and let him keep his house and a few surrounding acres, he had jumped at the opportunity.

But Ivory's windfall had proved to be a nightmare. It was a deal "too good to be true," and now he stood to lose everything to a nameless swindler hiding behind a company facade.

Thelma narrowed her eyes. "This one records a foreclosure sale of three hundred acres from an old horse farm in Tennessee." She flipped to the next sheet. "And this one is the same kind of deal—another foreclosure because of back taxes, four hundred acres. Here's one in Arkansas and another from Texas." She looked into Bennett's eyes. "Where did you get these?"

"Tax records are open," he said. "Drew Laporte does his homework."

Thelma nodded. "I guess he does. But what does it mean?"

Bennett handed her a page from another stack and pointed again. "These are the sales records on those same properties—every one purchased within a week of the foreclosure. Here, under purchaser's name. What do you see?"

"Historical Society of Tennessee," she read. "The Arkansas Preservation Foundation. South Texas Archival Interests, Inc." Thelma frowned. "So?"

"The company that gave Ivory the contract on his land called itself the Southern Historical Preservation Society. They *said* they were going to pay his back taxes for him."

Thelma squinted at one page. "You're saying that all these 'historical preservation' companies can be traced back to one person?"

"Maybe not one person. But I'd bet my silk shirt that these tracks converge someplace back down the line. And that's what we've got to find out."

Ivory peered over Bennett's shoulder. "But, Mr. Bennett, even if we do find out who it is, what can we do about it?"

Thelma watched as a brief smile flitted across Bennett's face.

"This kind of activity is right on the borderline of legality," Bennett explained patiently. "If they had paid the taxes, as they promised, they would still be acting unethically, but there wouldn't be much we could do to stop them." He grinned up at Thelma. "But somebody's gotten greedy. Too greedy to shell out the thousand bucks or so for the back taxes and take the land on the purchase agreement."

"But how do you intend to catch up with them?" Thelma asked. "Whoever it is has covered his tracks pretty well so far."

"Yes, but Drew thinks he may be onto something. Besides, we're not going to catch up with him. We're going to snare him in his own trap."

"Excuse me?" Thelma shut her eyes. Surely she hadn't heard him right. "What do you mean, snare him? Bennett, you're not going to do something dangerous, are you?"

Bennett laughed and squeezed her hand. "I just love it when you worry about me, Thelma. But never fear. I'm not talking about anything physically hazardous. Just a little game of cat and mouse."

"I sure hope we're the kitty," Ivory muttered.

"In a manner of speaking we are, Ivory. But we're going to pretend to be the rat—at least for a little while."

★ ★ ★

Bennett watched Thelma's face as he laid out the scheme he and Drew Laporte had concocted. The new law partnership of Winsom and Laporte would set up a "historical society" of their own with some fictitious name and buy Ivory's land as soon as it went into foreclosure. Then they would contact the Southern Historical Preservation Society, extend an offer to join forces and expand their holdings, and sit back and wait. If the plan worked, they would lure the brains behind the scam out into the open.

There was only one problem with the idea. They still had to come up with a thousand dollars by June 15 to pay Ivory's back taxes.

Thelma's expression revealed her skepticism. "But what about the taxes, Bennett? We don't have that kind of money lying around. And that's less than a month away."

"I was rather hoping you wouldn't bring up that point," Bennett said with a grimace. "We'll figure out something. In the meantime, Ivory, I'd like to take a look around your place. Is that all right with you?"

"Well, sure, Mr. Bennett." Ivory gave him a confused look. "Except I don't know why you'd want to see it."

"Call it curiosity. Or research. When we spring our trap on the gentlemen from the 'preservation society,' I'll need to know my way around. Could we go out there first thing in the morning?" He looked at Thelma.

"You want me to go, too?" She scratched her cheek in thought. "I suppose Madge could hold down the fort here for a morning. But what's my part in this little drama?"

Bennett gazed into her warm brown eyes. "I always want you with me," he murmured, and his heart gave a little leap at the flash of love that filled her expression. "But you're right—you do have a part to play. In this case, you're going to be the society woman who fronts for this land-grabbing scheme of ours."

Thelma let out a laugh. "A society woman? Me?"

"Yes, you," Bennett repeated. "You'll be perfect. The rich matron who has her lawyer—that's me, of course—carrying out her underhanded schemes for her. It will make our illegitimate business look a bit more legitimate, if you know what I mean."

Thelma leaned over and squeezed his arm. "So I get to be the cat in this cat-and-mouse game?" She shot a broad smile in Ivory's direction. "This sounds like fun. And it's for a very good cause. There's just one problem."

Bennett's heart sank briefly; then he caught the gleam of mischief in her eye. "What's that?"

"Well, this scam company of ours needs a name, doesn't it? Something elegant and aristocratic."

"I'm two steps ahead of you."

"Why does that not surprise me?" Thelma countered. "And what, pray tell, do we call ourselves?"

Bennett cocked one eyebrow at her. "The most elegant and aristocratic name I know," he said. "We'll call it the Breckinridge Foundation."

6

Slaughter's Dream

The Coltrain Farm
Near Eden, Mississippi

Owen Slaughter opened his eyes and found himself staring into the face of an immense German shepherd. The dog's amber eyes gazed into his; then a long wet tongue snaked out and gave him a slobbery kiss across the cheek.

"Führer!" a heavily accented voice called in a whisper. "Nein! Let the poor man sleep."

Owen raised his head and looked toward the doorway of the humble cottage. Fritz Sonntag's broad shoulders brushed against the sides of the door, and his bearded face cracked in a broad smile. "What can I do?" he chuckled. "He is—how you say—in love with you."

Propping himself onto one elbow, Owen gazed at his surroundings. Germany. He was back in Germany, in Fritz's cabin, in the bed where Charlie Coltrain had died. Pain shot through him at the memory of his friend. Poor Charlie. It was on a morning just like this, with the eastern sun just beginning to fill the cottage with a watery light. . . .

Then another figure appeared in the doorway.

"Are you going to sleep all day, pal? Sun's nearly up, and we're leaving in an hour."

Owen squinted into the shadows. It couldn't be! But it was—Charlie Coltrain, alive and well, and looking better than Owen had ever seen him. All the pallor of the months in prison had disappeared, and Charlie was filled out and healthy, with a ruddiness to his complexion and a flash of fire in his eyes.

"You-you're not dead?" Owen stammered incredulously.

Charlie frowned and shook his head. *"Dead? Of course not. You must have been dreaming again. Come on, man, it's time to get ready. By tomorrow we'll be halfway to Paradise."*

"Paradise?"

"Eden, Slaughter," Charlie said with forced patience. *"Remember? We're going home to Eden. Everybody will be waiting for us. And when Willie finds out you're alive—"*

"Willie?" Owen repeated stupidly, running a hand over his sleep-clouded eyes.

"Yes, Willie. My sister. The girl who has been waiting for you. Now, come on!"

Owen stumbled from the cot and, with Führer trotting at his heels, went to the bathroom to splash cold water on his face. Something was wrong here, something different. This was Fritz's cottage, all right, where he and Charlie had been hidden from the Nazis. But Charlie was alive, not dead, and they were apparently on their way . . . home.

He reached down and stroked the dog's broad head, then knelt down and buried his face in the thick fur.

"What is it, Führer?" he mumbled. *"Something's wrong, but I don't know what it is."*

Führer whined softly and nuzzled his cheek.

"Yeah, I'm going to miss you too, boy," he said. *"I wish you and Fritz could go with us. But I promise—when I get home and get settled, I'm going to get a dog just like you. He can run through the fields and chase rabbits and have a great time. I'll name him after you, and—"*

Suddenly the truth struck Owen, and all the breath went out of his lungs. He remembered! Everything—the farm, the little town of Eden, the look in Willie Coltrain's eyes and the rich deep sound of her voice in his ear. Dancing with her at the USO. Plotting with Link Winsom to get him a dance with his green-eyed girl. Shipping out. Making one last effort to blow up the Nazi ammo supply in that ruined French chateau . . .

These were not Charlie's memories—not just re-creations of his imagination based on the stories his friend had told him about home. They were his memories—all of them, rushing back in a great tidal wave, almost overwhelming him with their force and clarity.

Owen clutched the shepherd tighter and began to sob. Willie—his Willie—was waiting for him, and soon he would be home with her, where he belonged. . . .

Owen jerked awake, his heart pounding. Sweat poured down his face, and he gasped for air. He had been crying.

But where was he? In the shadows of early morning, a pale light coming in the windows revealed a dormer room—an attic, maybe, with a steep slanted roof. His hands gripped the quilt on the old-fashioned brass bed, and a noise above his head made him jump. A ping, then a skittering sound, like an acorn sliding off a tin roof.

He took a deep breath and tried to calm himself. He was in Charlie Coltrain's old room, in the attic of the farmhouse, in Charlie's bed. Eden.

Now he remembered. He had taken a bus to Eden and found Charlie's sisters at the cafe. He had told them all about Charlie, about the prison camp and how their brother had died. They had invited him to come to the farm to stay for a little while. And they had put him in Charlie's attic bedroom.

But there was something else, too. A dream. He closed his eyes and tried to bring it back. It was important, he thought, something he should know. Something he should remember. Vague flashes of the dream flitted through his mind, but nothing he could make any sense of. Führer, Fritz Sonntag's dog, had been there. And Charlie too, he thought. But the rest was a blur. His brain simply couldn't retrieve it.

He smashed a fist down on the bed. The images of the dream were gone, but the emotions remained. A bittersweet pain. Longing. Apprehension. Anticipation.

Maybe if he went back to sleep, he could get it back again. He lay down, drew the patchwork quilt up around his shoulders, and closed his eyes. But it was no good. He was wide awake now, and every little sound invaded his mind and distracted him. A squirrel running across the roof over his head. Birds twittering raucously in the trees outside his window. Why did nature have to be so loud at dawn?

With a sigh he flung back the covers and swung his feet to the floor. He might as well get up. Maybe he could rummage around in the kitchen and find some coffee.

He searched through the bureau drawers until he found a pair of Charlie's jeans and a soft flannel shirt. Charlie wouldn't mind, and Owen was pretty sure it would be all right with his friend's sisters. The jeans were too long, but he could roll them up, and they fit at least as well as the terrible uniform he had been given when he was released from the prison camp. He let the shirttail hang loose and sat on the bed to put on a pair of thick white socks. His army boots would have to do for the time being, he supposed. Maybe in a day or two he could get into town and find something to replace them.

When he was dressed, Owen stood up and surveyed his appearance in the mirror. He could use a haircut, but all things considered, he didn't look too bad. He was filling out a bit and getting some color back. He ran a hand through his thickening beard. He had promised himself he would keep it, in honor of Fritz Sonntag, who had saved his life, but it had never occurred to him to wonder whether Willie would like it. Maybe she would prefer him clean shaven. . . .

What on earth was he thinking? Owen shook his head and brought himself back to reality. Why would Willie Coltrain care? She wasn't his *girl,* for heaven's sake. She was his best friend's *sister.* And she probably hadn't given his beard a second thought—or him either, for that matter.

With a grunt of disgust, he tiptoed down two flights of stairs and headed for the small bathroom off the kitchen.

When he came out of the bathroom, Owen caught a whiff of fresh-brewed coffee. Apparently someone else was up, too, although the house was quiet and still. Gingerly he opened cabinets until he found a coffee mug and poured a steaming cup from the pot on the back of the stove. Then, cup in hand, he went through the living room and opened the screen door onto the front porch.

He saw Willie before she knew he was there. She sat in the swing, wrapped in a blue chenille bathrobe, her feet tucked under her. The porch faced west, and the reddening light from the sunrise behind them cast a glow over the fields and reflected in her hair with a golden hue.

Owen cleared his throat and took a step toward her. "Good morning."

She jerked around, sloshing coffee onto her robe, and gasped.

"I'm sorry. I didn't mean to startle you." *It's probably because I'm wearing Charlie's clothes,* he thought. *I should have asked first.* He gestured with his coffee cup. "I—ah, I found some of Charlie's things in the dresser," he muttered. "I didn't figure he'd mind, but if you do, I'll put my uniform back on."

Willie's expression cleared, and she shook her head. "No, of course not. It was just a shock, that's all."

He took another step in her direction. "You're an early riser, I see."

"I'm a farm girl," she said simply. "Comes with the territory."

"But Drew and Rae—"

"Drew's gone off to Grenada to look for a car. With the family expanding and all, they're going to need something besides Daddy's old pickup." She smiled and shook her head. "Rae's already been up once. Morning sickness. She went back to bed for a while. It was a long day yesterday."

"I guess it was a shock, me showing up the way I did, bringing news of Charlie's death."

A strange expression passed over Willie's face. "You could say that." She pointed at his cup. "I see you found the coffee."

"Yeah. Hope you don't mind me making myself at home. I just . . . well, I don't know. For some reason I feel so comfortable here."

Willie turned her face away and gazed out over the fields. "That's good," she said in a strangled voice.

Owen moved closer. "Do you mind if I sit down? Or if you'd rather be alone . . ."

"Alone?" Willie swiveled her head around and blinked at him. "I'm sorry. I didn't mean to be rude. Of course, come have a seat. I've been alone far too long."

★　★　★

Alone? Willie thought. *No, I don't want to be alone. I've been alone far too long.*

She watched as he came and settled himself on the porch rail directly opposite her. With his face shaded by the porch roof and the light behind him, his familiar form made a shadowy silhouette directly in her line of vision.

This was the kind of scene she had dreamed about when he was gone— one of those ordinary, homey moments, sharing a cup of coffee and watching the sun rise. But in her imagination, the man before her had been her fiancé, her love, not a stranger who had come into her life because he was her brother's best friend.

He peered at her and leaned against the porch post. "I guess it has been lonely, living out here in the country."

She sat up and stared at him. "Excuse me?"

"You said you were tired of being alone."

Did I say that out loud? she wondered. *I'd better be careful, or I'll get myself into more hot water than I can handle.*

"I only meant that I would be happy for you to join me," she hedged, then decided to be a little more honest. "But to tell the truth, it *has* been a bit lonely here—especially before Drew and Rae came back to Eden." She took a sip of her coffee and looked past him to the new growth sprouting up in the fields. "After the news came of Charlie's death—the telegram, I mean, that said he was 'presumed dead'—Mama and Daddy were never the same. Daddy just kept going downhill, and shortly after he died, Mama followed."

Owen winced and shook his head. "That must have been very difficult for you."

"I'll admit that Mama and Daddy weren't much company those last few months. I felt pretty isolated, and I was certain God had forgotten all about me as well. But then Rae and Drew showed up, just in time to see Daddy before he died, and when they told me they were staying, I felt a huge burden lifted from my shoulders."

"You're lucky to have a family like that," he said in a faraway voice. "Charlie told me that he would share all of you with me, that you could be my family too, but—" He stopped suddenly and dropped his eyes. "I shouldn't have said that. Charlie's gone now, so I guess—"

Willie's heart lurched, and her pulse began to pound. Was it possible, even conceivable, that Owen Slaughter might be willing to stay permanently? That they could start over, develop a relationship from scratch, and—?

No. She couldn't let her mind go down that path. Expecting anything in terms of a relationship with Owen would only set her up for more heartbreak. If his memories ever returned, maybe there would be a chance for her. But she would not take advantage of the vacuum in this man's soul. Even if she did know more about him than he knew himself.

"Owen," she said softly, "you're welcome to stay as long as you like. Charlie would want it that way."

He grinned at her, and his blue eyes twinkled. "You know, Charlie dreamed about home a lot, especially right before he died. He told me about it, once in the prison camp and again that last morning."

"What did he say?"

"Well, the one time in the prison camp—it was January, I think. Very cold. He woke me up before dawn and told me he had dreamed about his father coming to him and hugging him, telling him he loved him."

Willie's stomach knotted, and she set her coffee mug on the porch floor. "That doesn't sound like Daddy," she said. "He loved us, but he was never much for saying so."

"That's what Charlie said. But in his dream, it happened. Charlie thought that it meant—" He stopped, shifting uncomfortably. "Charlie thought it meant that he was dead."

"When was this? January, you say?"

"I think so. Why?"

"Because Daddy died in January," Willie whispered, barely able to get the words out. "And right before he died, he said, 'Tell Charlie I love him.' We thought he was delirious, that he thought Charlie was alive and coming home. But maybe he knew something we didn't."

"The last time, right before Charlie died, he became lucid long enough to tell me that he had dreamed about his father again—and this time his father told him that he was proud of all Charlie had done, of his courage. In the dream he said that Charlie's mother was waiting for him, and it was time for him to come home."

A sense of awe rose up in Willie's soul. Even in the prison camp, God had been with Charlie. And God had been in Eden, too—caring for them, watching over them, and in a way she didn't understand, connecting them.

Owen's voice interrupted her thoughts. "Do you believe in dreams, Willie?"

"What do you mean?"

"Do you believe that dreams are significant, important? That God speaks to people in dreams, or that dreams somehow reach into a part of our mind and soul we may not be conscious of?"

"I guess so," Willie said. "I never thought much about it, but the Bible tells about a lot of people who heard God's voice in their dreams. Why?"

He took a deep breath, as if he were nervous about what he was going to say. "Because I had a dream last night. I don't usually dream—I guess a man with no memory doesn't have much to dream about. But last night I did."

"And was it, as you say, significant?" She leaned forward eagerly. If he had dreamed about her, maybe he was beginning to remember something.

"I'm sure it was—important, I mean. Only I can't recall much of it. I keep trying to get it back, to find out what it means. I have this feeling that if I could just get back to it, I'd understand. But all I remember is that I was in Fritz's cottage—in the woods in Germany. Charlie was there, and Fritz's dog Führer. And something was happening." He sighed and shook his head. "I wish I could remember what it was."

Willie felt her spirits deflate. He didn't remember. Maybe he never would.

"But I can't help thinking," he said carefully, "that if I stayed here a little while, maybe some of it would come back to me. It's so peaceful here." He turned to the side and gazed out over the sun-washed fields. "I know what loneliness is," he murmured, half to himself. "Loneliness is not knowing who you are."

Or knowing who you are, Willie added silently, *when the man you love doesn't know who he is.*

"As I said before, Owen," she answered woodenly, "you're welcome to stay as long as you like."

7

⭐ ⭐ ⭐

Blessed Are the Weak

New Orleans, Louisiana
The Laporte Plantation

"I don't care what it takes, just get the job done—or I'll find somebody who can!" Beauregard T. Laporte tugged on his white vest and stuck a fat Havana Royale between his teeth.

"Yes, sir, Colonel, sir," the man stammered.

Beau rolled his eyes and clamped down on the cigar. *Blast!* he thought. Why did his son, the only person he could trust to do this job right, have to up and leave at such an inconvenient time? Andrew would have had this project locked up by now. But no, the boy had to take his homely little wife back home to Mississippi—something about seeing her father before he died. Didn't his own son have any sense of family loyalty? As much as Beau hated to admit it, he needed Andrew by his side. Needed his backbone . . . and his reputation.

This little weasel of a lawyer Clinton Marston had sent down from Memphis was totally useless. Just look at him, cowering in his chair, his eyes flitting around the room for a way of escape. Well, he could look all he wanted. He'd learn, right here and now, that there was no escaping Beauregard T. Laporte's ire.

"What's the matter with you, anyway?" Beau roared.

The little man jumped, and his eyes went wide with terror. "Nothing—nothing, sir. I just—"

"You just what?" Laporte bellowed. "You're not suddenly developing a conscience, are you?"

"No, sir . . . I . . . I mean, I don't think so." He ran a finger between his collar and his skinny neck and gulped. "No conscience. No, sir." Taking a deep breath, he finally met his employer's eyes in a look that was undoubtedly supposed to communicate confidence.

"That's better." Beau pointed his cigar at the little toad's nose. "Because if you're really as good a lawyer as Marston says you are—and I have my doubts about that, boy, believe me I do—your job is to close all the loopholes in this deal. Everything nice and legal, aboveboard. Do we understand one another?"

"Yes, sir, Colonel."

Beau shook his head and leveled an acid gaze on the trembling man. "This project is lining your pockets too—don't forget that. If you let me down, you'll be out on your bony little butt so fast it'll make your head swim." He turned his back and waved an arm. "Now, get out of here. And don't come back until you've got something positive to report."

"Yes, sir." Beau could hear scrambling sounds as the man raced for the door. Then a bump and a crash. Wincing, he turned around to see the man on his hands and knees amid the scattered pieces of a broken vase.

"I-I'm sorry, sir," he stammered. "It was an accident."

"What's your name again, boy?"

The head snapped up. "What?"

"Your name, boy! You do have one, don't you?"

"Uh, Craven, sir. Orris Craven."

"All right, Craven. Get on out of here. The girl will clean it up."

Craven scrambled to his feet and backed toward the door. "Yes, sir. Thank you, sir."

"Don't thank me. It'll come out of your retainer."

The angular face went pale. "Was it—was it expensive, sir?"

Beau Laporte grinned and stuck his cigar back in his mouth. The vase was a moderately priced reproduction, but there was no point in letting this toad know that. "Ming Dynasty," he said with a chuckle. "Craven, my boy, you'll be working for free for a long, long time."

★ ★ ★

For the past ten minutes Beatrice Laporte had been standing outside the door to her husband's study watching his interchange with the new lawyer. The poor boy was absolutely terrified—she could tell that much just from the way he groveled.

What was Clinton Marston thinking, to send a young fellow like this to work with Beauregard T. Laporte? Orris Craven might be a fine lawyer, but he obviously didn't have the fortitude to stand up to Beau. And although her husband might take advantage of such cowardice and use it to his own advantage, he didn't respect it. Poor Orris Craven was in for a rough time—if he didn't lose this job before he ever got started.

Young Craven was a nice enough looking fellow, she mused, although painfully thin. He had blond hair and a light fringe of mustache and rather pleasing hazel eyes. But the suit was a bad choice—tan, double-breasted, meticulously tailored but completely the wrong shade for him. Especially in comparison to her husband's florid face and commanding white-suited presence, the color made Craven seem washed out, a pale shadow of a man.

She couldn't help feeling sorry for him, particularly when he broke the vase. As he dashed out of the room, she caught his sleeve and looked into his eyes. "Don't worry," she whispered. "It wasn't that expensive."

For a fleeting instant a light touched his eyes, and he smiled.

"Stand up to him," she advised. "Make him respect you."

He nodded and looked at the floor. "Yes, ma'am. Thank you."

Then he scuttled down the hallway and out the front door.

Beatrice entered her husband's study and stood in front of his desk, waiting for him to turn around. The room, she mused, was designed for intimidation—tall shelves of books on every wall, an elk's head over the fireplace mantel, and that huge imposing desk with a tall window behind it. When Beau sat in his desk chair, the backlighting from the window made his face almost inscrutable. And the low chair in front of the desk rendered any visitor to the inner sanctum inferior to the man who dominated the room.

Beauregard himself had been carefully fashioned for power as well. A large, handsome man with a florid complexion and a thick head of gray hair, Beau always dressed in the manner of the southern gentleman—white suit and vest, black string tie, shiny black boots. He didn't need to say a word to communicate his authority—he exuded influence like an internal essence, and rarely did anyone question him.

Except Beatrice.

Bea loved her husband, but lately she had begun to wonder if there was very much left of the man she had married in her youth. In the early days, when all Beau had to bring to their marriage was the big Laporte house and his ambition to be a real estate mogul, they had worked together to see the fulfillment of his dreams. They didn't need the money, of course—Beatrice's parents had left her very well off. But Beau needed the challenge. And somewhere along the way, the obsession for more had taken over.

By the time their only son had come home from the war with his bride-to-be, Beau was deeply involved in land deals that demanded the skills of a highly competent lawyer. Andrew, in Beau's mind, fit the bill—with the added benefit of being family. Beau figured he could manipulate Andrew into doing what he wanted, and he almost succeeded.

But he had taken his manipulations a bit too far. To keep Andrew under his thumb, Beau had concocted some crazy story about Beatrice being ill, practically on her deathbed. And when Andrew had discovered the truth, he had packed up and left, taking his wife back to her family farm in Mississippi.

Given his obvious disdain for Orris Craven, Beau was probably at this moment kicking himself for letting Andrew go. But her husband didn't understand their son and probably never would. Andrew had never been motivated by money, and his sense of integrity was an entirely foreign concept to his father. Andrew Laporte might be his father's son in a physical sense, but the comparison stopped there. And Beatrice wondered if anything would ever heal the estrangement between the two men in her life.

She cleared her throat, and Beauregard wheeled around in his chair.

"Bea, honey!" He beamed at her. "And how are you this beautiful spring morning?"

She glanced over her shoulder at the shattered vase near the doorway. "I see *you're* in fine form," she murmured. "You were a bit hard on the new lawyer, don't you think? And why on earth did you tell him that was a Ming vase when it's only worth two hundred dollars?"

He waved a hand through the halo of cigar smoke that encircled his head. "Bah! That little toady had better get himself some backbone if he intends to work for me. And Clint Marston's got some fast explaining to do. What was he thinking of, referring a twit like that for my legal representative?"

Beatrice smiled and raised one eyebrow. "Perhaps he was thinking that a 'twit like that' might seem more credible because he has . . . ah, a bit different image than his employer."

Beau frowned as he considered her words, then brightened. "You know, Bea, you just might have something there. Craven does have a pretty commendable record of legal maneuverings, and he isn't as young or innocent as he seems. Maybe you're right—nobody would ever think that he was up to something, not with that face."

"So you'll keep him on?"

"We'll see how he performs. If he can pull off the job I've given him, he stays." A wistful look passed over Beau's handsome features. "Still, I can't help wishing Andrew hadn't left. If only—"

"If only you hadn't tried to deceive him," Bea interrupted, "he might still be here."

He stubbed out his cigar and shifted in his chair. "You're absolutely right," he blustered. "I misjudged the boy, that's for sure. If I had just played my cards differently—"

Beatrice shook her head. "When will you learn, Beauregard T. Laporte, that you don't deal with people the way you play a poker hand? Especially not your own son! Everything in life isn't about manipulating others to get what you want."

"Isn't it?" He threw back his head and laughed. "Beatrice, darling, you are so naive. Where do you think we'd be without my 'manipulations,' as you so crudely put it?" He pointed with his dead cigar toward the broken vase. "That may not be real, but you could buy a Ming if you wanted to."

"But I don't *want* a real Ming vase," she countered. "I didn't even want the two-hundred-dollar fake. All I've ever wanted is for us to be happy and content. Besides, we would have been just fine. My inheritance would have been more than enough to support us. You didn't have to—"

"Yes, I did have to," he said, flinging the cigar into the ashtray and poking a finger into his breastbone. "For *me*. What kind of man lives off his wife's inheritance?" A cloud passed over his face, and he narrowed his eyes at her. "Besides, this new deal is just about to pay off big—if that bootlicking lawyer isn't too meek to do his job, that is."

"You might be surprised," she said quietly. "Blessed are the meek—"

"For they shall inherit the earth?" he finished. "Oh, no, my dear, you've got it all wrong. Blessed are the *weak,* for somebody stronger shall inherit their part of the earth." He grinned triumphantly and sat back in his chair. "The first beatitude of the land dealer."

Bea sighed and perched on the arm of the low chair across from his desk. There was no arguing with him when he was in one of these moods. No matter what she said, he was always right, always knew better. The next installment of their vast fortune was just around the corner.

"What's that?"

Beau's voice interrupted her thoughts, and she stared at the envelope in her hand.

"It's a letter from Andrew and Rae. From Rae, really—Andrew's too busy these days to write."

"Hah! Probably spending all his time doing good for the poor and needy." The disdain in his voice was palpable, and she cringed. Beatrice was proud of her son—proud of his integrity and his commitment to his beliefs. No doubt Beau would not share her feelings when he found out what was in the letter.

"Something like that," she said softly. "According to Rae, he's struck up a partnership with another lawyer—the father of a friend. And yes, they are working to help people who can't afford legal advice."

"Making a *difference,*" her husband sneered sarcastically. "Wonder when he's going to start making a *living?*"

"They seem to be doing just fine," she went on, ignoring the jab. "They're living on Rae's family farm with her sister, Willie, doing some renovations to the house."

"That girl ought to be doing some renovations to her person," Beau interjected. "How she ever caught a handsome buck like Andrew, I'll never know. She has to be the homeliest, most gosh-awful—"

"Beauregard!" Beatrice interrupted sternly. "That's enough. She is your son's wife and your daughter-in-law. And she is a fine young woman. Besides that, I'd think you'd have a little more respect for the mother of your first grandchild."

Bea hadn't meant for the news to come out so bluntly, but she rather enjoyed seeing the transformation that came over her husband's face. He had his mouth open, about to respond, but no words came out. All the blood drained from his face, and his eyes glazed over. After a moment or two of complete silence, his expression softened.

"A child?" he whispered. "They're going to have a baby?"

"Yes. In November, Rae thinks. Around Thanksgiving."

"They're sure?"

"Absolutely certain."

For a moment more he sat frozen in his chair; then he suddenly leaped up, came around the desk, and caught her up in a wild little dance.

"A grandson!" he shouted as if he himself were somehow responsible for the deed. "My first grandson!" He set Bea on her feet and began pacing back and forth in front of the desk. "A trust fund," he muttered. "We'll set up a trust fund for him immediately. And they'll need money. Andrew can't be making anything, not with his—his scruples." He spat out the word as if it were poison, then continued pacing. "My son may not have any sense about money, but I'll see to it that my grandson never wants for anything. He—"

"Beauregard!"

He turned. "What?"

"You keep saying *he.* What if it's a girl?"

"A girl?" He stared at her as if she had suddenly gone bald. "What do you mean, a girl?"

"In case you've forgotten, babies come in two genders: male and female. There's just as good a chance that it might be a girl."

"A girl? Nonsense. My first grandson will not be a girl."

"And if she is?"

Beau frowned and scratched his head. "Then I hope to heaven she takes after my son and not after that dumpy wife of his. Can you imagine trying to arrange a debutante ball for a girl who looks like that? Nobody would let her come out—they'd all want her to go back in!"

Beatrice opened her mouth to protest, but before she could get the words out, he turned and grinned at her. "Just kidding, my dear."

Then he threw back his head and laughed as she had not seen him laugh in years. And for a brief instant he looked remarkably like the man she had fallen in love with and married so many years ago.

8

Antebellum Catastrophe

The Brownlee Plantation
Eight miles west of Eden, Mississippi

Thelma peered through the windshield of Bennett's Packard and took in a long slow breath. It had been years since she had been out here, and then just in passing. Everybody knew, of course, that the Brownlee place had gone to rack and ruin, but she hadn't expected this.

The double iron gates at the end of the driveway hung from their hinges and sagged against the crumbling brick posts. The center strip of the hard-packed drive was clogged with weeds, and huge honeysuckles reached their long flowered tentacles out toward the car, catching on the bumper as the car slowly made its way up the rutted lane.

Bennett negotiated the ruts the best he could, grunting under his breath every time the axle slammed to the ground. A thornbush close on the driver's side scraped against the door, and Bennett winced at the sound, jerking his arm back just in time to keep from being scratched.

"I'd say the place needs a little sprucing up." Bennett kept his eyes fixed on the pothole in their path, turning his head just enough to give Thelma a grim smile.

"Such a shame," Thelma murmured to herself. "From what I've heard, this plantation was a glory in its day."

"I'm afraid its day is long past." He pointed to the spreading magnolia trees that lined the drive. "How old do you suppose those are?"

"A hundred years or more," Thelma said. "The house itself dates back to

1832." She turned in the seat and gazed at him. "When I was a little girl, I dreamed of having a place like this someday. A big house, lots of land." She ducked her head, feeling sheepish. "Respectability."

Bennett turned and grinned at her. "You are the most respectable woman I've ever met, Thelma Breckinridge."

"But I wasn't always," she countered, "and you know it." She sighed and returned her eyes to the road. "Owning a place like this was a symbol, I suppose. Of social acceptability, of approval. I never had that as a child. We were always . . . well, white trash, I guess."

He pulled the Packard to a stop, reached over, and cradled her chin in one hand. "Trash doesn't have to do with money," he said softly, "or with social status. It has to do with what's inside. And what's inside you is beautiful."

Thelma felt a flush beginning to creep up her cheeks, and she pushed his hand away. "You say the most outlandish things—"

But he wasn't listening. He was staring out the window.

She followed the direction of his gaze. "Oh, my heavens," she breathed.

"Can you believe this?" Bennett turned off the engine, got out of the car, and came around to open Thelma's door.

Before them, gray and weathered but still magnificent, the old home loomed tall and stately, its columns stretching three stories high. A vast porch, shaded by maples and magnolias, spanned the length of the house, and on one end, an ancient wisteria twisted its way around a high trellis and spilled its lush blooms like grape clusters over the edge.

Thelma craned her neck and looked up. "It's incredible. I had no idea."

Bennett tested the porch steps gingerly. "I thought you had been here before."

"Not like this. In the winter you can see it from a distance, from that hill up on the highway." She pointed eastward, back toward town. "I've never been inside the gates."

"Well, let's find out what we have to work with." He extended a hand. "Be careful—the boards are rotted out right here." He helped her across to the massive front doors, carved in walnut with heavy leaded glass windows, and reached for the doorknob.

From behind them came a grinding, clattering sound, and they both turned in time to see Ivory in his dilapidated green pickup truck, roaring up the rutted lane as if the devil himself were in hot pursuit. Ivory hadn't had a driver's license in years, but the local law turned a blind eye to that fact, and everybody in Eden knew enough to keep out of his way. Now he screeched to a halt just inches from the taillights of Bennett's Packard, gave a cheerful honk, and hauled his wiry frame out of the driver's seat.

"Mornin'," he called amiably, ambling toward the porch with his chicken-neck stuck out in front of him. "Beautiful day, ain't it?" He extended his scrawny arms and looked around. "Well, what do y'all think of the old place?"

"Ivory, where have you been?" Thelma asked. "We were just about to go on in without you."

"That'd be OK, I reckon." He stroked his stubbled chin and gave a gap-toothed smile. "Don't suppose you'd be like to steal anything." He cackled at his own joke. "Had to go to town to get me some supplies. I was down to my last can of beans." Then he slapped a hand to his forehead. "I forgot. Left 'em in the truck."

Bennett strode from the porch and went to Ivory's pickup. "I'll get your groceries for you, Ivory," he said, returning with a small bag. Two cans of beans and a package of dry rice stuck out the top.

Thelma exchanged a glance with Bennett. She knew that the old man couldn't pay his taxes and that he often ate for free in the cafe, but beans? She had no idea he was in such dire straits.

"I'm doing all right," he said defensively, taking the bag from Bennett and looking at Thelma as if he had read her mind. "Don't need no charity. I get along just fine."

Suddenly the importance of what they were doing struck her full force. They had to find a way to save Ivory's land. The place might be in ruins and he might be living in a cabin rather than in the fine old house his ancestors had built, but if he lost it, where would he go? What would he do? Not to mention the emotional impact such a loss would have on him. He had lost enough, Thelma vowed. Somehow they would see to it that he didn't lose the rest.

The glance Bennett shot in her direction told her he was thinking the same thing. With a determined look in his eye, he nodded. "Guess we should take a look at our investment, Madame Society Lady," he quipped. "The Breckinridge Foundation has to get prepared for its merger."

"Come on out back first," Ivory said. "I'll show you around a little; then you can go inside."

★ ★ ★

Bennett took Thelma's arm as they followed Ivory around to the back of the house by way of a crumbling brick sidewalk. He loved being close to her, touching her, talking to her, feeling her nearness—and his heart fairly raced when he realized they were thinking alike about Ivory Brownlee. He might be responding like a schoolboy overcome by puppy love, but he didn't care. It had been a long, long time since he had felt this way, and he intended to enjoy it.

Maybe he had orchestrated this little plan to include Thelma just because he wanted her to be with him. But he didn't feel too badly about it. She was obviously enjoying herself, and he had the feeling she would have agreed to almost anything just so she could be included. Playing the part of a money-hungry society matron just sweetened the deal.

Bennett's thoughts were interrupted when they rounded the back of the house and stood in front of a tiny log cabin thirty yards down a well-worn path. To their left stood a wide pasture enclosed by a broken-down split-rail fence. A weathered clapboard stable flanked the near side of the pasture. To their right sat several log structures shaded by giant oak trees.

"That one," Ivory was saying as he pointed with a bony forefinger to the one nearest the house, "was the cookhouse back in the days when they didn't have a kitchen indoors. The next one," he pointed again, "was a smokehouse. Still smells like bacon."

He took a few steps down the path and indicated the smaller cabins that lined the path opposite the pasture. "These were some of the quarters for the slaves—the ones who didn't live in the big house with the family." He went to the door of the first cabin, opening it with a flourish. "And this one is mine."

Ivory stepped back and let Thelma go ahead of him. "Go on in, make yourselves at home. If you want some coffee, I can make it pretty quick. Nearly as good as what you'd get at the Paradise Garden."

Bennett followed, blinking as his eyes adjusted to the dim light inside the cabin. A single window let in a little of the morning light, revealing a room furnished with a sagging sofa, a pine table and two handmade chairs, and a small cast-iron cookstove. Under the window a rough wooden counter held an assortment of mismatched dishes and cups, and a few slanted shelves revealed a meager supply of groceries.

Ivory went over to the counter and unloaded his bag of supplies—four cans of beans, a sack of rice, a bag of dried black-eyed peas, and a small can of coffee. When everything was put in order on the shelves, he folded the paper bag neatly and slid it between the shelf and the wall.

"Do y'all want coffee?" he asked as he went to the stove and lifted one of the iron plates. "I banked the fire this morning—won't take no time at all." Without waiting for an answer, he picked up the coffeepot, took it over to the tin sink, and began to pump water into it with a hand pump.

"No thanks, Ivory—I had my limit at the cafe this morning." Bennett studied the cabin. Although it leaned a bit to the east, in general it seemed strong and sturdy and livable. A faded floral curtain hung at the window, but it was freshly laundered. The hooked rug on the plank floor showed not a trace of mud or dirt. Everything was clean—scrubbed and swept and dusted.

"Mind if I look around?"

Ivory turned from the sink. "'Course not, Mr. Bennett. Help yourself."

Bennett crossed the room in four steps and peered into the next room. An iron bed stood against one wall, neatly made with an old white chenille spread. Except for the bed, a small chest of drawers, and a bedside table bearing a lamp and a tattered Bible, the room had no other furnishings—and in fact could not have accommodated any more. Between the bed and dresser, a rough-hewn door stood partially open, leading to a makeshift bathroom.

"The bathroom lean-to got added some years back," Ivory said when Bennett came back into the main room. "For a few years Daddy had some hired help, and they lived in these cabins." He nodded toward the single bare lightbulb dangling over the table. "Put in 'lectricity, too."

"It's very nice," Thelma said, running a hand over the back of one of the chairs. "Very homey."

"It does for me," he replied simply. "Don't need much." A shadow passed over his weathered face, and he sighed. "But I do need to keep what I got."

Bennett's heart wrenched for this modest, compassionate man, whose only security was in danger of being snatched out from under him. He smiled and clapped Ivory on the shoulder. "We're going to do everything we can," he promised. "Now, I think we'll go take a look at the main house."

"Y'all go on ahead," Ivory murmured. "I got me some things I gotta do." Bennett nodded to Thelma and opened the cabin door for her. He paused for a moment, looking out over the pasture and up to the back of the house. As he turned back to shut the door, he caught a glimpse of Ivory sitting down at his table with a long wooden plank in front of him.

What was he doing?

Then Bennett's eyes focused, and he understood. Painted on the plank was a full piano keyboard in black and white. And Harlan Brownlee, with his head thrown back and his eyes closed, moved his fingers soundlessly over the keys, playing some sonata in his mind.

★ ★ ★

"Did you see that?" Thelma whispered as Bennett closed the door. "He's made himself a piano in that little cabin!"

Bennett nodded. "He's an amazing man. We have to—"

"Find a way to help him," she finished, and they both smiled.

Thelma leaned in toward Bennett as he put his arm around her shoulders. All her life, for as long as she could remember, she had yearned for someone like him. She had known plenty of men in her time—men who took what they wanted without any thought of the damage they might cause, men who left without a word when they were ready to move on. But never a man who loved her, respected her, protected her.

She chuckled to herself. Most people sure wouldn't think of Thelma Breckinridge as the kind of woman who needed to be protected. She was strong, independent, capable. But Bennett didn't represent physical protection for her, someone who would provide for her and take care of her. What he gave her, whether he knew it or not, was a sense of *safety*, the security that came with not having to earn or deserve his love. Their relationship hadn't developed very far, but she was absolutely sure that this was a man who would never knowingly cause her pain. And for all her intentions to "take it slow," to give the relationship time to develop naturally, she felt more certain with every day that Bennett Winsom was the person God had given her to spend the rest of her life with.

Thelma glanced at him out of the corner of her eye as they made their way back around the front of the Brownlee house. He was certainly handsome enough to stop traffic, with those brown eyes and that dark hair with a sweep of gray at the temples. When he laughed, his crow's feet crinkled and a dimple appeared at the left side of his mouth. But there was a lot more to Bennett Winsom than a pretty face. Over the years she had become a pretty fair judge of character, and in Thelma's opinion, this man had a heart as wide open as the Delta.

The look on his face right now proved it. Without his saying a word, Thelma knew that he would do everything in his power to stop the scoundrels who were trying to take this place from Ivory Brownlee. And if his plan worked and they were able to flush out the powers behind the swindle, he might help a lot of other poor folks in the process.

"Watch your step," Bennett said as they reached the porch. "And when we get inside, be careful. There may be loose floor joists or rotten boards to contend with." He turned the knob, and the heavy front door creaked inward.

Thelma nodded and stepped gingerly through the open doorway, then stopped, unable to go any farther.

"What's the matter?" Bennett said over her shoulder.

"Nothing. It's just—well, see for yourself."

She stepped aside and gave him room to enter. Before them, arching up in a wide sweep, a massive stairway rose to a landing and then separated, curving upward on either side. The heavy carved newel posts were covered with dust and cobwebs but were clearly of the finest walnut. In the center of the stairs, an oriental runner in wine and blue was faded and sun streaked but held in place by solid brass anchors.

"Let's look around down here first; then we'll go upstairs."

Thelma turned to the left and pushed back a high carved pocket door to reveal a parlor furnished with an elaborate carved settee. In one corner sat a stout square piano adorned with the most hideous lamp she had ever seen—a bronze miniature of Michelangelo's *David* topped by a pink fringed lampshade.

"This lamp has got to go," Bennett murmured, touching the beaded fringe with the tip of one finger.

"Yes, but look at this!" She stroked a hand along the top of the piano. "Give me your handkerchief."

Without a word he handed it over, and she wiped away a thick layer of filth, then handed it back to him.

"Thank you very much," he said, eyeing the grime distastefully.

"What? Oh, sorry." She smiled at him and batted her eyelashes coyly. "It's for a good cause. Take a look."

Bennett folded the handkerchief and replaced it in his pocket, clean side out, then turned back to her.

"It's inlaid," she said, a sense of wonder rising in her. "Mother of pearl. And look how the detailing goes all the way around—the walnut and mother of pearl inlays against the—what is this? Mahogany?"

"I have no idea. I'm a lawyer, not a carpenter."

"Well, it's absolutely gorgeous, whatever it is." She lifted the lid and placed one hand on the keys. "I wonder why Ivory never plays it." She struck a note. A horrible flat groan emanated from the instrument, and the key stuck fast. "I guess that's why."

"Let's keep going," Bennett said, examining the mantelpiece. "This is all marble—Italian, I'll bet."

Thelma went back across the foyer to a parlor on the other side, identical except for the piano. "These French doors lead to an office of some kind," she called. Her voice echoed off the high ceilings.

Bennett came into the room. "On the far side of this parlor is a big dining room, and adjacent to that, a kitchen, obviously added on." He turned up his nose. "It's awfully musty in here. Ready to go upstairs?"

"I guess so."

"Is something wrong, Thelma? You seem distracted."

She frowned and turned toward him, her mind spinning. "I don't know,

Bennett. There's something about this house—something I can't quite identify."

"Spooky, you mean, because it hasn't been lived in for so long?"

"Maybe, but I don't think so. More like—" She shook her head, trying to clarify what she was feeling. "Like this house is trying to tell us something. Like it has something secret to protect."

"Ooh, a secret," he chuckled.

"Are you making fun of me?" she demanded, trying to be stern. But in spite of herself she began to laugh. He was undoubtedly right—her imagination probably was running away with her.

"Let's check out the upper floors and then get back to town," he suggested. "I need to meet with Drew and find out what he's uncovered."

On the second floor they found several moderate-sized bedrooms, a parlor, and a big empty room with inlaid floors and windows on three sides—a ballroom, Bennett speculated. Thelma rested for a moment on one of the window seats and let her mind conjure up images of a grand ball with women in hoop skirts and an orchestra filling the hall with music.

"You know, the house seems remarkably sound." Bennett's voice interrupted her reverie. "It would take a lot of money to restore it to its former glory, but it's not beyond repair. With some imagination and energy—"

"And a large family of cats," Thelma added, cringing as a mouse skittered across the room.

On the next level they discovered several large bedchambers adjoined by sitting rooms, two bathrooms, and a two-room suite that had probably served as a nursery at one time. A long hallway bisected the third floor, and at the front of the house, a beveled glass door opened onto a large front balcony. A small doorway off the hall led to servants' quarters on the west side of the attic.

"Where's the other balcony?" Thelma went to the far end of the hall and stood frowning at the blank wall.

"What do you mean?"

"Well, look. From everything we can tell, the house is symmetrical—the same in front as in back, except for the kitchen, which was added on. Now these bedroom doors are a good twenty feet back from the end of the hallway."

"So?"

"So, look at it, Bennett. There's no reason to continue this hall all the way down—it just dead-ends down there. There should be another door like that one." She pointed over her shoulder. "And a matching balcony out here."

Bennett crossed into one of the back bedrooms and came back in a minute or two shaking his head. "Nope. I opened a window and stuck my head out. There's a jutted-out place, like where a chimney would go up the side of the house, but no door. No balcony."

"Strange," Thelma murmured.

"I'll tell you what's strange," Bennett responded. "It's strange when a man misses a meeting with his business partner because a hundred-year-old house doesn't happen to be perfectly symmetrical." He flipped out his pocket watch and checked the time. "It's almost noon, Thelma. I really need to go."

Thelma shrugged. "I guess you're right. Besides, Madge will be needing help with the lunch rush. I suppose we should get back."

She tried hard to suppress her impatience, but evidently Bennett read her expression. "We'll come back another time, all right?"

Thelma felt her spirits lift. "Really?"

"Really." He paused and looked into her eyes. "You like this old house, don't you?"

Thelma wanted to say, *This is the kind of place I've dreamed about since I was a child—it makes me feel like Cinderella without a midnight curfew. It gives me hope that there are infinite possibilities in life. And yes, I feel as if this house is trying to say something to me. It's calling to me, and for some reason I'm sure I need to respond.*

But she didn't dare. Instead, she said, "Well, I think it's a pretty interesting old place—don't you?"

9

Curly

The Coltrain Farm
May 24, 1945

Owen Slaughter stood upright and stretched the kinks out of his back. He leaned on his pitchfork, gazing out the high hayloft door toward the house and, beyond that, the western horizon. It was still early enough to be cool, and a breeze ruffled his damp hair and shifted the mist that lay over the fields.

He could never remember feeling this wonderful, this *alive*.

Then he grinned at his own slip of the mind and shook his head. Of course he couldn't remember feeling this good. His only memories were of the prison camp, the terrible loneliness, the deprivation . . . and Charlie.

Yesterday Owen had discovered the chrysalis of a butterfly attached to the fence post on the back side of the pasture. The insect was moving inside, striving to break free. Owen knew better than to help it along. He knew, although he didn't know how he knew, that the struggle for liberty strengthened the butterfly's wings and enabled it to fly. If he helped too much, broke open the cocoon, the beautiful creature would die.

And so he had stood there, watching, resisting the temptation to help, until the tough outer layer split and a magnificent transformation took place. The butterfly emerged, crawled up onto the fence post, and spread its wings to dry in the sun. Within a few minutes it was airborne, and Owen's heart soared with it.

It was amazing, this connection he felt with everything around him—with the blue of the sky and the white clouds sailing by, with the budding fields and the soft rain that watered them. He might not know who he was, but he sensed instinctively that he was more truly himself here than he had ever been.

Maybe he had been a farm boy. The labor seemed to come naturally to him. His body rejoiced in the exercise of his muscles, and his soul responded to the scent of the soil and the pungent fragrance of animal flesh and hay and sweet feed.

But it didn't really matter anymore whether or not this new life was a reflection of the old. It was *his* life, and he was enjoying it thoroughly. At least while it lasted.

The somber thought was an unwelcome intrusion into the joy of the morning. But he had to be realistic, too. He couldn't expect to stay here forever.

He turned from the hayloft door, hung the pitchfork on a post, and slid down the ladder to the barn floor. With both hands he began to scoop up the hay and fill the mangers for the cows that stood waiting in their stalls.

Then suddenly he heard a noise. A whimpering sound, close at his feet. He looked down, and the pile of hay in front of him began to move.

Owen dropped to his knees, thrust both hands into the mound of hay, and felt his fingers close around something soft and warm. It wriggled in his grasp until he freed it from the hay; then it turned its head and licked his hand.

A puppy. Light brown in color, with curly hair and enormous paws, it whined and thrashed until he set it down; then it lunged at him playfully and grabbed his shirttail.

"Oh, you want to play, do you?" Owen took a piece of hay and tickled the dog's nose, then reached out one hand and began to tug at its ears. The puppy responded with a yip and a tiny little growl, threw itself into Owen's lap, and turned belly-up to be petted.

It was a female, two or three months old, he thought. He stroked the dog's pale underside and laughed as she wriggled under his hand and thrust her nose into his palm. Probably wandered away from home. It was a good mile to the nearest farm, but after breakfast he would just have to take her over there and find out who she belonged to.

He got to his feet and finished his chores, then made his way back to the house with the pup at his heels, tugging at the hem of his pants legs and running circles around him. As they reached the porch, Owen scooped her up in one hand, held her behind his back, and knocked on the screen door.

Willie, dressed in dungarees and one of her father's old shirts, came to the door with her hands covered in flour. "Owen? Why on earth are you knocking? Is something wrong?"

He stared at her for a moment, and his heart did a little flip. She looked so young, with those ridiculous shirttails hanging down to her knees and her hair flying out in all directions.

She narrowed her eyes at him. "What's behind your back, Owen?"

He grinned and brought the puppy out with a flourish. "An extra guest for breakfast."

Willie's eyes went soft, and she swiped her hands across the legs of her jeans and reached for the dog. "Oh, he's adorable!"

"She," Owen corrected. "It's a female."

"Well, aren't you just the cutest?" Willie cooed, nuzzling the puppy and receiving a sloppy kiss across the nose in return.

"I found her in the barn. Do you know of any dogs nearby who have recently had pups?"

Willie turned on him and gave him a blistering look. "We *are* going to keep her."

"Well," he hedged. "Maybe. But don't you think we should ask around to see if anybody is missing her?"

Willie's shoulders sagged. "I suppose you're right. What kind is she, do you think?"

"No doubt the offspring of a bored farm girl and a traveling salesman," Owen quipped. A puzzled expression crossed Willie's face. "It's a joke Charlie told me once, about—well, never mind. But if I can't even remember my own past, how do you expect me to know about dogs?"

Willie put a hand under the dog's muzzle and looked at her face. "Spaniel, I'd say, and maybe some terrier. Oh, look—she's got a little white star under her chin."

"If it's OK for me to take the truck, I'll do some checking around after breakfast."

"I guess," Willie sighed. "She probably does belong to someone."

Owen watched as Willie went to the swing and sat down. The puppy, still in her arms, snuggled up to her and licked her chin. And in that moment, Owen admitted to himself that, despite his best intentions, his feelings for Willie went far deeper than appreciation for his best friend's sister.

Whatever it took, that dog would find a home on the Coltrain farm.

The puppy sat in Owen's lap and put her head out the window as the ancient pickup rattled up and down the farm roads of Tullahoma County. Three farms, no luck. Nobody knew anything about a missing puppy. He'd go to one more house, and that was it. If he didn't find anything there, he'd just take the dog home to Willie and forget about it.

Owen pulled into the rutted driveway, hoping against hope that he would come up empty.

Then his heart sank.

As he jolted to a stop between the house and the barn, a wiry old man ambled out to meet him. Close on his heels ran a spaniel surrounded by four pups that looked exactly like the one he held in his lap.

"Hey there, son," the old man said. "What can I do for you?"

Owen fought against the urge to push the puppy under the seat, say he had made a mistake, and take off. But he couldn't. His conscience wouldn't let him.

"I . . . uh, I found a pup in my barn this morning," he began. "And . . . well, I guess now I know where she belongs."

Owen got out of the truck and set the puppy on the ground, and immediately she charged into the pack and began chasing her brothers and sisters. The mother nuzzled and licked her and began herding the litter back toward the barn.

But Owen's puppy wouldn't go. She ran a few steps toward the barn, then came back and circled around him, pulling at his pants legs and whining. At last he bent down and picked her up.

The old man narrowed his eyes at Owen and scratched at his stubbled chin. "Yep, it's mine, all right," he said. "The mama's a pretty good rabbit dog. Treed me a possum once too." He watched as the puppy licked Owen's face and tugged at his beard. "Seems she's a mite attached to you. How long you say you been holdin' her?"

Owen grimaced. "I haven't been 'holding her,' as you put it. She just showed up this morning."

"Been gone a spell," the farmer said. "Nigh onto a week. The mama's been right upset about losin' her baby."

Owen watched as the mother dog went into the barn, followed by the four remaining puppies. "I can see she's just torn up."

"She gets used to it," the old man muttered. "One or two dogs on a farm are all right. But more'n that just gets in the way. Can't afford to go feedin' every stray in the county."

Suddenly it became clear to Owen what the man was saying. Those other puppies—and this one in his arms—would probably be dead by the end of the week. Drowned in the creek in a burlap bag or left on the side of the road to fend for themselves. He clutched the pup closer, and she whimpered.

"See you're kinda partial to that one," the farmer mused. "Suppose we could work somethin' out."

Owen stared into the man's weathered face and saw, just briefly, the flash of greed that flitted across his eyes. "How much?"

The farmer removed his hat and scratched at the bald spot on his head. "I dunno. She's got po-tential, that one. Fine hunting dog."

"I don't hunt," Owen said flatly.

A gnarled hand snaked out and clamped over the puppy. "You won't be wanting her, then."

Owen drew back. "I didn't say that. I asked you a question. How much?"

The farmer smiled, revealing yellow, tobacco-stained teeth. "Ten bucks ought to do it."

"Ten dollars?" Owen gasped. "For a mutt puppy you're just going to drown as soon as my back is turned?"

"You want the dog or not?"

"I'll give you five."

The farmer's grin widened. He had Owen over a barrel—he knew it, and Owen knew it. There was no way Owen was going to leave without this dog. "Eight."

Owen sighed and fished in his pocket, coming up with a five and three ones. Money he had intended to spend on a new pair of boots or some clothes that fit better than Charlie Coltrain's hand-me-downs. "It's all I've got."

The man snatched the money from his hand and gave the puppy a pat on the head. "Son, you just bought yourself a dog." He turned on his heel and ambled back toward the barn, whistling.

"I'm not your son," Owen muttered as he got back in the truck and slammed the door. "And if you have a son, I feel sorry for him. You'd probably sell him, too, if the price was right." He gunned the engine, cranked the wheel, and sped out of the yard in a cloud of dust.

All the way back to the Coltrain farm, the puppy lay beside him on the seat with her chin propped on his leg.

"We're going home," he murmured, scratching her ears with one hand. "And we won't say a word about your brothers and sisters. Agreed?"

The pup grunted contentedly and licked his palm.

Willie came to the screen door and peered down the road. Owen had been gone more than an hour. She had cleared up the kitchen after breakfast, cleaned the vegetables for lunch, and put two loaves of bread to rise. Now she was pacing up and down in the front parlor, rearranging the family pictures on top of the old upright piano.

Why on earth was she so agitated? It was just a puppy, after all.

She went into the kitchen, poured herself the last of the coffee, and took it out to the porch swing.

Owen Slaughter was a good man, she thought, going to all this trouble for a stray puppy. It was the kind of thing she would expect from the old Owen, of course, but when he had showed up at the Paradise Garden with no memory of her or of their past relationship, she had put all her expectations on hold. Now she was discovering that though his memory might be gone, his character was still intact.

The realization gave her hope. Even if he never remembered, there might be a chance for them . . . a chance for something other than friendship.

Willie shook her head, silently reprimanding herself for not controlling her thoughts. If she anticipated too much, she was just likely to be hurt again, disappointed when things didn't turn out the way she dreamed.

But she couldn't resist turning over in her mind the way he looked at her sometimes—as if he remembered, as if something was stirring in his heart that took him beyond his perception of her as Charlie's little sister. *Dear Lord,* she thought, *if only it could be. . . .*

A hot flush crept to Willie's cheeks as she realized how long it had been since she had prayed—truly prayed. For months she had asked God every day to bring Owen back to her, and then, as her parents grew worse and died, loneliness and hopelessness had set in, and she had simply stopped praying. She couldn't think of a thing to say, and nobody seemed to be listening, anyway.

But God had answered her prayer. Owen had come back.

The only problem was, Owen didn't *know* he had come back.

Sometimes Willie wondered what on earth God was thinking. She didn't say this to anyone else, of course. People would think she was a heretic. But in the private recesses of her heart, she couldn't help believing that some divine signals had certainly gotten crossed. And if this was God's idea of a test, some kind of cosmic joke, she didn't appreciate it one bit.

Still, Owen was back. Maybe it was time she quit complaining and started being thankful just to have him here, alive. . . .

A cloud of dust barreling down the road interrupted her thoughts, and she stood up and went to the edge of the porch. It was Daddy's old pickup, all right—she could tell by the peculiar grinding sound the gears made.

She watched as Owen careened up the dirt road and slid to a stop at the side of the house. He opened the door, and the little pup jumped down from the seat and ran, ears flying, straight up the porch steps as if she belonged here.

Willie picked the warm little bundle up and held her close. "What happened?" she asked when Owen got to the steps.

He grinned sheepishly and ran a hand through his curly brown hair. "Happy birthday."

"Excuse me?"

"She's your birthday present," he repeated, reaching out to stroke the dog's head. "When is your birthday, anyway?"

"February," she laughed. "But thanks for the thought."

"I located the owner—a farmer a couple of miles down the road. Had to go to four houses before I found the right one."

"And he let you keep her?" Willie scratched the puppy under the chin.

"Let's just say we came to . . . ah, an agreement."

Willie looked into Owen's blue eyes and felt a rush of love well up in her. "How much did you pay him?" she asked quietly.

He winked at her. "A lady never asks a gentleman how much a gift cost," he chided.

"And I'm no lady. How much?"

Owen reached over and squeezed her arm, and the touch sent a thrill through Willie's veins. She fought against the feelings that rose up in her, but she managed to keep her face expressionless.

"You *are* a lady," he whispered. "And I'm not telling."

With his hand still on her arm, he steered her over to the swing and sat down next to her with the puppy between them.

"Now," he said firmly, "we have to think of a name."

Willie's gaze moved from the pup, with her light brown curly fur and liquid brown eyes, to Owen's dancing expression. The idea that sprang to her mind was outrageous, and might even be dangerous, but she couldn't help herself.

"Curly," she murmured.

His head shot up. "What?"

"Curly," she repeated. "I think we should call her Curly."

As soon as Willie uttered the name, a shock went up Owen's spine and spread into his arms and chest. His heart pumped wildly, and he couldn't get his breath. A flash of awareness passed through his mind, just a flicker of a scene, but it was gone before he could grasp it.

It felt like . . . like a memory. But it couldn't be. Had someone called him Curly a long time ago? His mother, perhaps? Or . . .

A sweetheart?

The idea struck him like a physical blow, and he couldn't believe he hadn't considered it before now. When he got rescued, the army told him the name of his hometown in Iowa, and the fact that both of his parents were dead. Not much more than that. Apparently, the army had been his life.

But he had been so caught up with Charlie, with Charlie's memories of Eden and his family, and more recently with his confusing feelings about Willie, that until this very moment it had never occurred to him that he might have someone the army didn't know about, waiting for him, mourning him. A girl. Someone he had made promises to, back when his memory was intact.

Now here he was, taking up residence in somebody else's life and letting his thoughts about Willie Coltrain run away with him. And with just the utterance of a single word—*Curly*—feelings assaulted him that left him shaken and unsettled. He wanted to push the emotions back down into the darkness, ignore them, hope they would go away. But even with a lost puppy, he had felt compelled to find its rightful owner before he could bring it home to stay. How could he do any less with his own life—or with Willie's?

If there was a chance, even the slimmest possibility, that someone was out there waiting for him, he had to find out before his feelings for Willie Coltrain went any deeper. If he didn't, he would never be at peace. Not here. Not anywhere.

"Owen, are you all right?"

He turned to find Willie staring at him with a worried expression on her face.

"Sure, I'm OK." He avoided her eyes and got up from the swing. "That pasture fence needs fixing. I should go back to work."

"The fence can wait, can't it?" Willie asked. "What about the puppy?"

"What about it?"

"She still needs a name."

"It's your dog; call it what you want," he said, more gruffly than he had intended. "Curly's fine."

Without a backward glance, he strode off the porch and made his way toward the barn.

He didn't know how he was going to do it, but he had to find out who he was and where he belonged. For the sake of his future, he had to discover his past. And quickly, before he ruined not only his own life but Willie's, too.

In the meantime he would keep his distance, even if it killed him.

10

Baby Blues

Paradise Garden Cafe
May 28, 1945

Thelma Breckinridge leaned on the counter and stared into space, lulled by the soft music that was emanating from the piano in the corner. These days, every time she heard Ivory play, her mind conjured up images of him sitting in his dimly lit little cabin, running his fingers over the false keyboard he had created, making music in his mind.

It was too bad the beautiful ornate instrument in the front parlor of the big house was so horribly in need of repair. But Ivory barely had money for groceries. He couldn't pay his taxes, and he certainly couldn't send off to Grenada or Memphis for a piano repairman.

Thelma's mind wandered to the Brownlee mansion. In the week since she and Bennett had gone out there, something happened inside her every time she thought of that house, something she couldn't understand. She felt a longing, a connection with that house that went far beyond admiration for a fine architectural work or a wistful desire to return to bygone days. Ivory's house was calling to her, and she couldn't shake the feeling that it was trying to tell her something important.

But if the house—or God or her own sixth sense—had something to communicate that pertained to Ivory Brownlee's financial situation, she had better get the message soon. In less than three weeks the extension on Ivory's taxes would expire, and the Breckinridge Foundation had to be ready with a thousand dollars to move in and claim the property before the Southern Historical Preservation Society got its hands on the estate.

Maybe she should go back out there, have a look around. Bennett had promised to take her again, but he had been so busy with Drew that he hadn't gotten around to it. She was sure Ivory wouldn't mind. And perhaps in that place, with its history and secrets twining around her like ancient wisteria vines, she would come up with an answer.

Thelma looked up to see Madge Simpson staring curiously at her. "What?"

Madge shrugged. "You look like you're a million miles away, Thelma. Something on your mind?"

"No . . . ," Thelma hedged. "No . . . nothing." She shook her head to clear out the cobwebs and smiled. "Just woolgathering, I reckon."

The bell over the cafe door rang, and Rae Laporte stood in the doorway. "Hey, honey!" Thelma said. "Come on in."

Rae didn't return the smile, but she moved a few steps closer. "Do you have time for a cup of coffee?" she asked, looking directly at Madge. "Or are you too busy?"

Thelma slanted a glance at Madge. Something was bothering Rae, that was obvious. Pain and confusion were written all over her round little face. And clearly she wanted Madge's company—alone.

For a brief instant a stab of jealousy pierced Thelma's heart. Why would Rae specifically ask Madge and not her? Hadn't Thelma always been there for Rae? Hadn't she been the one who had encouraged her to follow her dream—the dream that led her right into the arms of that handsome husband of hers?

But as soon as the emotion registered, Thelma reprimanded herself for it. Rae Laporte was carrying her first child, and no doubt she wanted to talk to another young mother about what she was experiencing.

"Have a seat, Rae, and I'll get the coffee." Thelma smiled at the girl and squeezed her arm, then went behind the counter and poured two cups of coffee. "What brings you into town this beautiful Saturday morning?"

"Drew's working—*again*," Rae said with an emphasis that clearly indicated her displeasure. "So I thought I'd come into town and do a little shopping." She placed a hand on her abdomen and smiled faintly. "You know, for the baby." Her eyes flitted about the cafe, and she lowered her head. "And maybe have a little talk—with Madge."

With Madge. There it was again. Thelma's mind spun, searching for a way to bow out gracefully, to save Rae the embarrassment of asking her to leave. Then she seized on an idea.

"How did you get into town?" she asked abruptly. "Did Drew bring you?"

Rae gave Thelma a baffled look and shook her head. "No. He took the new car—the DeSoto we bought a couple of weeks ago—into Grenada. I brought Daddy's old pickup."

"Are you going to be here long?"

Rae frowned and shrugged. "A couple of hours, anyway. Why?"

"Would you mind if I borrowed the truck for a little while? I've—well, I've got some errands to run. I'd have it back by—" she glanced at the clock— "oh, three o'clock or so."

"Sure, Thelma, help yourself." Rae brightened a little.

Thelma turned to Madge. "You can hold down the fort here for a little while?"

"Of course. Saturday afternoons are usually pretty slow, and Mickey is with his daddy."

"Well, then," Thelma said, "I'll just get my bag and be on my way. You girls have a nice time."

Thelma was on her way out the door when Rae's voice stopped her. "Thelma?"

She turned and looked over her shoulder. "Yes, hon?"

"Can you drive?"

Thelma raised one eyebrow. "Of course I can drive. Where are the keys?"

Rae shook her head. "There are no keys. Just press the starter button. And it tends to jump out of third gear, so keep your hand on the gearshift lever."

"Right." Thelma felt a curious apprehension rising in her, but she pushed it down. The Brownlee estate was calling to her, and if she didn't go now, she might not get another chance. "See you later."

★ ★ ★

Rae watched Thelma's departure with an inward sigh of relief. She loved Thelma, and under ordinary circumstances could talk to her about anything. But these weren't ordinary circumstances. She needed a different perspective—the perspective only another young mother could give.

Madge filled their coffee cups and brought doughnuts from behind the serving counter.

"I . . . I'm glad to get a chance to talk to you," Rae began uncertainly. "Do you think Thelma's feelings were hurt?"

Madge smiled, and Rae was struck by the amazing transformation that had taken place in this woman over the past year. She had first come to the cafe more than a year ago with little Mickey in her arms, running from a life dominated by her mother-in-law's criticism. She had been a pitiful waif of a girl with no home, no friends, no money. Now her husband had returned from the war, her baby had survived scarlet fever, and her mother-in-law had finally abandoned her quest to get her son back. Despite the hardships she had endured, Madge's eyes were filled with hope and love and joy in living.

Rae had felt that way once, too, when she and Drew first met and fell in love. But so many things seemed to be coming between them—the adjustments to their new life in Eden, the baby, and not the least of Rae's worries, Drew's near-obsession with the Ivory Brownlee case.

"I think she understood," Madge was saying, and suddenly Rae realized that she hadn't the foggiest idea what Madge was talking about.

"What?"

"Thelma," Madge repeated, giving her a questioning look. "You asked me if Thelma was offended because you so obviously wanted to talk to me."

"Oh, yes. That."

"Mabel Rae, what's going on?" Madge asked bluntly. "You seem so—well, I don't know. Not here."

Rae shook her head. "I'm sorry, Madge. I was just thinking."

"About what?" Madge tempered her tone a bit and reached out to pat Rae's hand. "You seem to have a lot on your mind."

Rae closed her eyes for a moment, and when she opened them again Madge was peering at her with an intense look. She might as well get it over with before she lost her nerve. Still, it sounded crazy, even in her own mind.

"Madge, how do you do it? I mean, how do you and Stork keep a positive attitude with everything you've been through?"

A flash of pain shot across Madge's face, and Rae realized she had touched an old wound. "Oh, I'm sorry, Madge. That nickname bothers you a lot, doesn't it?"

Madge shrugged. "For a long time, whenever I heard someone call Michael 'Stork,' I was reminded of my own sin—the pregnancy, the hasty wedding, the pain of having to live under Mother Simpson's constant harping. I'm getting used to it now, although I'll probably never be completely comfortable with it. But that's not the point. What are you asking, exactly?"

A shuddering sigh rose in Rae's chest, and she exhaled heavily. This was not going to be easy. "I love Drew," she began hesitantly, "honestly I do. More than anything. But lately, things just haven't been—well—the same."

"You mean because of the baby?" Madge asked. "Sometimes that happens, I've heard. I don't know from experience because my husband wasn't around when I was carrying Mickey. But having a child does change things." She paused. "I know Drew is excited about your baby," she said with conviction. "Thelma says he's ecstatic. But he's probably also a little scared."

Rae fiddled with her coffee spoon. "If it was just that, I wouldn't worry so much. But he's so . . . so preoccupied with the case he's working on, he doesn't have time for much else. Not even me. And that's not like him."

"Preoccupied? How?"

Rae felt her temper flare and struggled to keep her voice level. "It's all he thinks about, Madge. He's obsessed with getting to the truth. He's gone all the time—to Grenada, to Jackson, to Memphis. When I try to talk to him about making preparations for this child, he only half listens. We're supposed to be renovating the house, and Owen Slaughter is out there doing all the work while Drew goes off on his 'research trips.'" She fought back tears. "He doesn't have any idea what I'm feeling because there's never time to talk, and when I try, he doesn't listen."

Madge sat back in her chair. "And what *are* you feeling, Rae?"

The tears flowed in earnest, and Rae swiped at them with the back of her hand. Madge pulled a paper napkin from the holder on the table and handed it to her, waiting while Rae regained control and blew her nose. "I'm sorry," Rae said at last. "I'm just a bundle of nerves, I guess."

"It's OK. You're allowed to cry," Madge assured her, patting her arm. "Believe me, I shed a lot of tears while I was living with Michael's parents."

"But you seem so . . . so strong," Rae faltered. "I don't know if I could do it—raising a child like, like—"

"Like Mickey?"

Rae could have bit her tongue. She hadn't meant it to come out that way, and now she didn't know how to fix it. "I didn't mean—"

"It's all right," Madge soothed. "Now, tell me the rest of it."

Rae took a deep breath and looked into her friend's eyes. "I see you with Mickey—you're so good with him, and he's so adorable. But he—"

"He's deaf," Madge supplied.

Rae nodded miserably. "And as much as I love him, when I'm around him I can't help being scared for my own baby."

"You're afraid something might be wrong with your child?" She gave Rae a reassuring smile. "Mabel Rae, I think that's a perfectly normal reaction. All new mothers go through that—thinking the worst, fearing that their child will be . . . oh, I don't know, not right somehow. But when you hold that baby for the first time and count all his little fingers and toes, you—"

Rae averted her eyes. "It's not just that I'm afraid, Madge. I *know* something is wrong. Don't ask me how I know, but I know." Her throat clogged with tears, and she choked them back. "I need my husband, and he's not here."

"Have you talked to him about this?"

"I tried. But he just says I'm overreacting and that the baby will be fine." She tried unsuccessfully to keep the sarcasm from her voice. "He's got other things on his mind—more important things." She sighed. "That's why I came to you, I guess."

"Because I know what it's like to be the mother of a handicapped child?"

The words were said matter-of-factly, without shame or anger, but nevertheless Rae winced inwardly. "I wouldn't have said it quite like that."

Madge reached out and took both of Rae's hands in her own. "Rae, look at me." Rae lifted her eyes and met her friend's gaze. "I won't try to talk you out of your fear or say you're overreacting. But I will tell you this: If there *is* something wrong with your baby, it won't matter. When I first found out that the scarlet fever had left Mickey deaf, I thought the world had come to an end. But it didn't. He's still my son. I love him, and I will do whatever I have to do to build a good life for him. And that's exactly what you'll do for your child."

"But what if—?"

Madge interrupted with a shake of her head. "No *what if*s. That child in your womb is a product of your love for Drew and his for you. This baby is special." She smiled and squeezed Rae's hands. "And you will be a wonderful mother, no matter what challenges you might face."

Rae gulped and took a deep breath. "Do you really think so?"

"I know so. And Drew will be an equally wonderful father."

"If I can ever get his attention away from his work," Rae sighed. "Right now I feel so . . . so alone."

"You're not alone. You've got all of us—and we love you."

"I know." Rae smiled, amazed at how good it felt. Madge understood, really understood. "Thanks for not trying to talk me out of this."

"Is that why you wanted to talk with me alone, without Thelma?"

Rae sensed a flush creeping up her neck. "I'm embarrassed to say so, but yes. I love Thelma, and I know she loves me, but I just couldn't face the prospect of being told how good God is and how the Lord wouldn't let anything bad happen to my baby."

"You might be surprised," Madge said. "Thelma's not in the habit of giving pat answers. She's been wonderful about Mickey."

"Yes, she has. And maybe I've underestimated her. But somehow I knew that you would be better at helping me deal with this. You've, well—"

"I've been there," Madge supplied. "And I know what it feels like."

Rae nodded.

"But I will tell you one thing that undoubtedly would have come out of Thelma Breckinridge's mouth at a time like this."

Rae looked up. "What's that?"

"We'll pray," Madge said firmly. "Together we will trust God for whatever is in store for you—and for your baby."

11

Antique Secrets

All the way to the Brownlee estate, Thelma's mind bounced back and forth between apprehension over whatever was bothering Rae Laporte and anticipation at what the big old planter house might have in store for her. She was fairly sure that Rae's troubles had to do with the baby and that Madge was, indeed, the best person to help her, so by the time Thelma pulled into the rutted driveway and lurched past the rusted iron gates, she had pretty much put her mind to rest about that.

And once she caught a glimpse of the grand old house between the branches of overhanging trees, all thoughts of Rae Laporte—save for a whispered prayer—deserted her.

The truck shuddered to a stop and Thelma got out, rubbing at the small of her back. She wasn't getting any younger, that was the truth, and driving an old heap like the Coltrains' pickup didn't do her joints any good. But at least it had gotten her here. If she'd had to wait for Bennett to find time to bring her, no telling how long she would have been delayed.

Despite its peeling paint and sagging porch boards, the antebellum home seemed to welcome her as she stepped closer. Its columns wreathed in the late spring sunshine, it stretched heavenward and towered over her like an ancient temple waiting to reveal its mysteries to the one it deemed worthy. The only sounds were the twittering of birds and the scolding of a single squirrel high in the branches of a magnolia tree—that, and the gentle rush of wind through the leaves. And in the one spot right in front where the porch sagged at its worst, she could almost see the image of a smile.

Thelma reached into her purse, withdrew a scarf, and tied it around her hair, then stepped resolutely toward the porch. Since her first visit, the house had been summoning her to return, and it was time to answer the call.

As she made her way into the foyer, Thelma glanced to the right and left at the parlors on either side. For a moment, in her mind's eye, she could see these rooms restored to the splendor they once knew—bright with music and laughter and the sounds of life. What was it about this old place that seemed so compelling to her? Was it the unfulfilled potential, the possibilities? Or was it simply that she had always longed to live in a home like this and that, for an hour or two, alone with its rich history and ruined grandeur, she could pretend that all this belonged to her and bore the stamp of her love and ownership?

Thelma shook her head. What a silly idea. Here she was, a grown woman in her forties, engaging in what her grandmother would have called "play-like" games, letting her imagination run away with her. It was ridiculous, and yet . . .

She had to admit that there was something in this house, some presence, that drew her. Thelma didn't believe in ghosts, of course, and even if she had, what she was feeling didn't seem like a haunting anyway. It seemed more as if God had called her here through her fascination with the place. But for what reason, she couldn't possibly fathom.

When she and Bennett had explored the house, they had gotten up to the third floor, where there were several bedrooms and two bathrooms and that strange hallway with a balcony on one end but not on the other. That hallway still bothered her, but she couldn't figure out why. Bennett was probably right; the matching balcony on the back side of the house had rotted away, and the owners had simply plastered up the doorway rather than gone to the expense of replacing it.

She reached the third-floor landing and stood there for a moment to catch her breath. A dappled light filtered through the trees and danced across the glass door leading to the front balcony, and Thelma followed it. Opening the door, she stood for a few minutes on the balcony, breathing in the sweet clean air laden with springtime scents of azaleas and wisteria and lilies that grew in profusion along the front drive.

Far below, Thelma could see the Coltrains' truck where she had left it, and she could almost reach out and touch the glossy magnolia leaves that hung on heavy branches in front of her. In the distance, from this vantage point, she saw a thin ribbon of silver winding between the hills—the shallow eastern tributary of the Tullahoma River as it drifted southward to dump into Grenada Lake.

Everything looked different from here, Thelma mused. The muddy brown waters of the Tullahoma took on a sheen, as if made of molten precious ore. The sky seemed bluer, the clouds a purer white, the fields an unmarred quilt of deep green velvet.

And she *felt* different somehow. Freer and full of anticipation, as if the treasures of the world were spread out at her feet like a king's ransom for the taking. As if something—something incredible, unexpected—was about to happen.

Dazed with wonder, Thelma went back into the hallway and wandered down to the second bedroom on the right. An ancient four-poster bed, high off the floor, dominated the room, and against the back wall a massive walnut armoire sat with one of its doors slightly ajar. She made a circuit around the room, dreamily wondering what it might be like to awaken in a chamber like this every morning. At last she stood before the armoire and, almost against her will, reached out a hand to stroke the silky finish of the wood. Her sleeve caught on the latch, and as she pulled back to free it, the door opened wider.

Then she saw it. A flash of light.

The wardrobe was empty except for a couple of musty wool coats pressed back against the side. And, oddly enough, at the back wall of the armoire, which should have been solid wood, was a small brass keyhole. She might never have seen it except that the sun, streaming through the clouded window at exactly the right angle, struck the brass and sent back a glimmer.

Thelma reached in and fingered the keyhole. The keyhole cover dangled loose, and when she fitted it back into place, it looked merely like a decorative brad, one of many, that held the back panel of the armoire in place. She poked at the rest of the brads. None of them moved. Only this one was a false cover to hide the keyhole.

But why would there be a keyhole in the back of the wardrobe?

Intrigued, Thelma reached into the armoire with one hand and felt around. To the right of the keyhole, a thin seam ran upward for about three feet, then made a right angle and continued onward.

It was a door. Well hidden, especially if the keyhole cover had been in place and the wardrobe had been full of clothes.

Thelma looked over her shoulder, as if expecting the armoire police to come in at any second and arrest her for breaking and entering. Then, laughing nervously at herself, she wedged her fingers into the seam and pulled.

She hadn't expected it to open so readily, and when it did, she lost her footing and fell backward onto the rug. Panting, she got to her knees and peered in.

It was a door all right, about five feet high and half that wide, leading—where?

She stood up and moved forward, giving her eyes a chance to adjust to the dim light inside the wardrobe and beyond. Then, when she could see a little, she tested the floor of the wardrobe cautiously and stepped through.

Thelma's heart began to pound. She was standing in the attic, under the sloping part of the roof on the back side of the house. A high gabled window, crusted with the dirt of ages, cast a watery light over the cobwebbed room. Obviously no one had been in here in a very long time.

Thelma held her breath. This was no ordinary attic where generations of Brownlees had stored old memorabilia, useless furniture, forgotten toys from children long past. She felt as if she had stumbled into a sanctuary of some kind, a shrine. In one corner stood a dressmaker's dummy clothed in a blue military uniform, complete with gold-trimmed epaulets and a tarnished brass-handled saber. On a sawhorse next to it sat a fancy leather saddle, its flaps embossed with an ornate *US*. And against the back wall under the high window hung a framed portrait of a bearded man, casually seated behind a desk.

As if drawn by a force beyond herself, Thelma moved toward the picture. The glass was grimy and clouded, and she fetched a handkerchief from her purse and rubbed off some of the dirt. She made a face at the filth—that handkerchief would never come clean in a hundred years. But she had wiped away enough of the grime to see the picture more clearly.

It was an old photograph, somewhat faded and brownish in tone, with a cracked seam across the upper left-hand corner. The man in the picture was tall and extremely thin, sitting behind a desk in shirtsleeves with his tie unknotted and the throat of his collar open. One gangly leg was propped up on the corner of the desk, and the chair leaned precariously. The man, obviously caught in an unguarded moment, grinned broadly.

The man's posture and evident humor tugged at Thelma's heart and made her smile. Then she looked more closely at the thin, bearded face, the deep-set eyes and hawkish nose. At the high-backed leather chair, the tall curtained windows behind him, the curve of a round seal of some kind just behind his head.

She blinked once, then again, and squinted at the face. It couldn't be. It just couldn't.

With trembling hands Thelma removed the framed picture from its nail and turned it this way and that to take advantage of the light. It might be, but she couldn't be sure.

Suddenly the frame slipped from her grasp, and she caught it just before it hit the wooden floor. With a sigh of relief she sank down onto an old steamer trunk and clutched the picture to her chest. She'd better put it back and get out of here before she did any permanent damage.

But when she went to replace it, Thelma's eye caught a glimpse of something on the back. Faded handwriting scrawled across the paper backing of the frame.

She tried to read what it said, but the light was too bad. Holding the picture with care, she returned to the doorway and stepped through the armoire back into the bedroom.

Afternoon sunlight filtered through tree branches and in through the bedroom windows; although the light there wasn't really bright, it nearly blinded her. She sank to the floor and leaned against the armoire, waiting until her eyes adjusted.

At last she looked, first at the photograph and then at the paper backing. In ink long since faded, an even hand had written:

> Brady took this one afternoon in the office but promised he would not publish it—it seemed not a dignified enough image. You, however, might appreciate it, as one of the few who laugh appropriately at my "tall tales."
>
> To Major Seth Brownlee, with appreciation for all you have done to further the cause.
>
> A. Lincoln
> August, 1864

Thelma's mind spun. It *was* Lincoln in the picture, although she had never seen a photograph like this one. All the likenesses she had ever seen of the man had been stately, almost stern, and certainly presidential. This picture captured an entirely different side of him—a playful side, a man who, despite the pressures and cares of his office during a tumultuous era of his nation's history, had not lost his sense of humor.

But who was Brady, the man alluded to in the inscription? And more importantly, what was a picture of Abraham Lincoln doing in the attic of Ivory Brownlee's house? The photograph was inscribed to a Major Seth Brownlee—Ivory's grandfather, Thelma presumed. But why? Hadn't Major Brownlee been a *Confederate* officer?

Thelma turned the picture over to read the inscription again. Then, without warning, a shadow fell across the carpet in front of her.

"Thelma?" A low voice, taut with repressed anger, arrested her attention. "What on earth do you think you're doing?"

Thelma's head snapped up. There in the doorway stood Bennett Winsom, his handsome face distorted by a scowl. Behind him, Ivory Brownlee peered over his shoulder.

"Bennett? What are you doing here?"

"What am *I* doing here? The question is, what are *you* doing here?" Bennett, followed by Ivory, came into the room. "I've been half out of my mind with worry. Do you have any idea what time it is?"

Thelma blinked at him and scrambled to her feet. "I'm afraid not. Bennett, you won't believe—"

"After our meeting with Drew, we came back to the cafe," Bennett interrupted with a frown. "Madge was there, and Rae Coltrain. Rae said you had borrowed the truck and gone off somewhere."

"Yes," Thelma began, "I—"

"She said you were only supposed to be gone an hour or two. That was three hours ago. Do you realize we've been driving up and down every road in this county since three o'clock looking for you?"

"Bennett, I—"

"How could you worry us like this? Just disappear, without a word to anyone? I had visions of you being wrecked in a gully somewhere. If Ivory hadn't come up with the idea that you might have come here, there's no telling how long we would have been out searching! Really, Thelma—"

Thelma's temper flared. How dare he treat her like some errant child who has to be watched every minute? She was a grown woman, for heaven's sake—and she had been taking care of herself for a lot of years without any help from the likes of Bennett Winsom. "Would you just hush?" she snapped. "Just for one minute."

He opened his mouth to respond, then shut it again.

Thelma took a deep breath and tried to calm herself. "I'm sorry you were worried, Bennett. I just lost track of time. But," she went on pointedly, "I am not in the habit of answering to other people—even you—as to my where-abouts."

His expression softened a little, and the scowl changed to a frown of confusion. "But why would you come out here poking around by yourself? This house is a death trap. You could have fallen through those rotten boards on the porch, broken a leg, and been lying there bleeding for hours before anyone—"

"Bennett, please!" She held up a hand to stop him. "As you can see with your own eyes if you'll stop raving and just look for a minute, I am perfectly all right—except that you might have scared the life out of me, sneaking up on me like that." She sank down onto the cedar chest at the foot of the bed and sighed.

"All right. I apologize for overreacting. It's just that I was worried."

"I understand that. But if you'll just give me a chance to explain, I—"

"What you got there, Thelma?" Ivory pointed to the picture she still held clutched to her chest.

"That's what I was trying to tell you, if Bennett here can just keep his shirt on for two minutes." She extended the framed photograph in Bennett's direction, and he took it in both hands. "I found this," she pointed toward the armoire, where the hidden door to the attic still stood open, "in there."

Ivory's head swiveled around, and when he saw the door leading through the wardrobe into the attic room, his normally pale face went several shades whiter.

"Did you know about this, Ivory?" Thelma asked. "The attic room, I mean?"

He shook his head. "There was some things said, I guess, when I was a boy, but I never paid much attention."

"What kind of things?" she prodded.

"Somethin' about the family dis-grace, I think they called it. Somebody a long time ago did something real bad, and nobody would ever explain what it was. But no, I never knew about that." He pointed with a gnarled finger toward the armoire, then shuffled over to the door and stuck his head inside. "What's in there?"

"A lot of old things," Thelma said evasively. "That's where I found this picture."

Thelma turned back to Bennett and saw him examining the photograph intently. "I never knew a photograph like this existed," he whispered.

"What do you mean, 'a photograph like this'?"

"Did you read the inscription on the back?"

Thelma nodded. "Do you think it's authentic?"

Bennett raised an eyebrow at her. "I'm no expert, but yes, I'd say so."

Ivory came back to Bennett's side and peered over his shoulder. "Who is it?"

"It's Abraham Lincoln, Ivory. The president of the United States during the War Between the States."

Ivory gave him a scathing look. "I know who Abraham Lincoln is, Mr. Bennett. I ain't stupid."

Bennett flushed and smiled. "I didn't mean to offend you, Ivory. It's a photograph by a very famous photographer of the time, a man named Mathew Brady."

"The 'Brady' referred to in the inscription?" Thelma asked.

Bennett nodded. "A friend of mine, now living in St. Louis, is quite an authority—in an unofficial way—on Civil War photography. Brady was famous for his war photographs—he traveled with the Union army and took thousands of pictures. And he did photographic portraits of most of the society people in New York and Washington, too—congressmen, military leaders, you name it."

"And you think this could really be one of his pictures?"

"We'd have to have it evaluated by an expert, of course, but I'd say there's a good chance. As far as I know, there are no existing photographs of Lincoln like this, in such a candid, obviously unposed setting. And the inscription would bear that out—that after Brady took the shot, Lincoln made him agree not to publish it because it wasn't in keeping with the presidential image."

"So, if it is real, and if that *is* Lincoln's handwriting on the back—"

Bennett grinned. "It might be worth a good deal of money."

Ivory perked up. "Enough to pay my taxes?"

"We can find out," Bennett said. "With your permission, Ivory, I'll send a wire to my friend in St. Louis and ask his advice about it."

"But that leaves one big unanswered question," Thelma said. "Why is it inscribed to—who is this Major Seth Brownlee, Ivory? Your grandfather?"

Ivory nodded. "He died before I was born. Don't know much about him, 'cept that like it says there, he was a officer in the war. Seems I recall when I'd ask my daddy about him, he'd tell me not to talk about it." He frowned. "Ever'body always acted like they were 'shamed of Grandpa Seth. Suppose he was the one who did the bad thing nobody wanted to own up to?"

Bennett shot a glance at Thelma. "Collusion with the enemy, perhaps?"

Ivory's head snapped up. "What does col-collusion mean?"

"It means somebody in a war who spies or helps the opposite side. A traitor."

"You think my granddaddy was a spy?" he asked fiercely. "That he was—was collusionin' with the Yankees?"

"I'm not saying that," Bennett soothed. "Just that it might be a possibility, an explanation for this inscription on the back of the picture."

Ivory's rheumy eyes shifted back and forth as he thought about this. "Yeah," he said at last, "I guess that could explain it. And why my fam'ly was so close-mouthed about Granddaddy Seth." His expression cleared, and he smiled a little. "Well, if my granddaddy was a traitor to the Confederacy," he said at last, "maybe it might turn out to be good for something after all. If collusionin' will pay my taxes and keep my house, I guess it can't be all bad."

Bennett extended a hand to help Thelma to her feet. "Let's go home," he suggested. "I'm hungry, and it's about time we got Rae's truck back to her." He patted Ivory on the shoulder. "Besides, I need to send a telegram to St. Louis. Your grandfather just may turn out to be the tooth fairy in disguise."

12

Ivory's Windfall

June 2, 1945

A soft summer breeze blew in through the open door of the Paradise Garden Cafe, and a sliver of moonlight streamed through the window and fell across the table where Willie sat, watching.

You'd have thought it was another V-E Day, from all the celebrating that was going on. Everybody gathered around Ivory Brownlee, clapping him on the back and congratulating him, raising glasses of punch in salute and laughing while he played rag tunes on the piano.

Willie was happy for Ivory, of course—heaven knows he deserved it. But she had other things on her mind, things that prevented her from entering fully into the festivities.

Her gaze wandered to Owen Slaughter, sitting off to one side in deep conversation with Stork Simpson. It had been only two weeks since Owen had appeared in the parking lot of the cafe during Link and Libba's wedding reception, but it felt like a lifetime to Willie. For the first week or so, he had seemed to be settling in at the farm, enjoying the work—and her company. Against her better judgment, Willie had let herself believe that by some miracle things might work out between them, that Owen would regain his lost past and remember his love for her, or at the very least, that he would come to love her all over again.

She hadn't made it up, she knew. She had felt a connection between them, sensed his attraction to her. He had been so warm, so considerate. He had even spent half a day and who knows how much money to rescue the little spaniel pup, Curly, for her.

That was when things changed, now that she thought about it—abruptly and without warning. As if something snapped inside him. He became withdrawn, distant. Still courteous, but cool. As if . . . well, she wasn't sure. As if he had remembered something that disturbed him deeply and caused him to pull away.

And now he was being so secretive, asking to borrow Daddy's truck without a word about where he was going. Dressing in his uniform and disappearing for hours with no explanation. He still worked hard, of course, taking care of the animals and spending time in the fields with the sharecroppers. He had even taken over a lot of Drew's plans for the house renovation and almost had the plumbing roughed in to make a second bathroom out of the big linen closet upstairs.

But except for doing his work and taking his meals at the big pine table in the kitchen, Owen pretty much kept to himself. He was polite enough, but he kept his eyes averted and talked—when he talked at all—only about the weather and the crops and getting the house ready for Rae and Drew's baby.

Willie couldn't understand it. She had thought things were going so well. Even when she had resigned herself to just being a sister to Owen, at least she had that much. Now suddenly she had . . . well, what did she have? Nothing. Not even a brother. Just a boarder, and a reclusive one at that.

And every time she looked at him, she thought her heart would break all over again. . . .

★　★　★

Thelma Breckinridge, intent upon studying Willie's expression and trying to figure out what was going on with the girl, started when Bennett Winsom stood up next to her and cleared his throat for attention. "All right, everybody, listen up. We've got a big announcement to make."

Ivory waved to him from the piano bench. "Ah, don't, Mr. Bennett. Ever'body already knows about it."

"Maybe they know, Ivory, but this is a night for celebration. And we're going to do this right, with all the proper ceremony. Now, give me an appropriate introduction."

Ivory hit a series of chords that sounded for all the world like a brass fanfare. A few people chuckled and applauded.

Thelma's eyes darted around the room. This was a celebration for Ivory, certainly, but others among them didn't quite look like they were in the mood for a party. Owen Slaughter and Stork Simpson had been carrying on a serious conversation for the last twenty minutes and seemed a little irritated to have their discussion interrupted. Rae Laporte sat next to Drew, and the two of them looked like a study in night and day. Drew, beaming from ear to ear with pride and happiness over Ivory's good fortune, was evidently oblivious to his wife's drawn, pained countenance.

Madge Simpson hadn't disclosed the details of what the two of them had discussed the day Rae showed up at the cafe, but she had asked Thelma, in confidence, to pray for Rae and Drew and the baby. And judging by Madge's expression when she asked for prayer, it was more serious than just first-pregnancy jitters.

Thelma sighed. Did life always have to be like this, one crisis after another? It seemed to her that there ought to be some kind of divine rule about a rest period, a time-out for people who had just gotten through some major upheaval in their lives. But then, she wasn't God—a fact for which she was eternally grateful and figured the rest of the world should be, too. She wasn't omniscient, wasn't equipped to judge what people needed in their lives to draw them closer to the Almighty. All she could do was pray and be there and love them. And trust that God knew what was going on.

God certainly knew what was going on in Ivory's life, that was a fact. Except for Bennett, who still maintained that going out to the plantation alone was a foolish thing to do, everybody had been praising Thelma for finding the Lincoln portrait. But Thelma couldn't take credit for the discovery. Clearly, she had been led, and—

Bennett's voice interrupted Thelma's thoughts and drew her attention back to the celebration at hand. "As you all know, this is a day for rejoicing in Ivory Brownlee's good fortune," he was saying. "You all know about Thelma finding the picture in the attic of the Brownlee place—"

"We know, Bennett, we know—get on with it, will you?" Stork Simpson quipped.

Bennett leveled a glance in Stork's direction and pretended to be miffed. With great flourish he reached into his coat pocket and drew out a telegram, which he unfolded with painstaking care. "Ahem," he began. "I have here a wire from my friend Walter Woodruff in St. Louis. Walter is somewhat of a history buff, particularly concerning Lincoln and the Civil War—" He paused and pursed his lips. "Pardon me, I mean the War Between the States, of course." Everyone laughed, and Bennett grinned and went on. "When I telephoned him about the picture, he wanted to see it immediately, so we sent it up to him. I have here his response."

"Quit stalling, Bennett—read the telegram, will you?"

Bennett waved the telegram in the air and waited until the hubbub quieted. "You people have no sense of high drama," he muttered cheerfully. "All right, here it is. Are you ready?"

"We've been ready for quite a while now, Bennett," Thelma murmured, infusing her tone with sweetness.

He glanced at her and winked, then proceeded to read:

> Dear Bennett,
>
> My friend, the expert from the Smithsonian, was in town over the weekend when Mr. Brownlee's picture arrived. It is, indeed, an authentic Brady, and unlike any other photographs of the president extant today. In its present condition, pending final verification of the signature on the back, estimated value is $5,000. I would be pleased to broker the sale for you and, as soon as I have your authorization, will send a check in that amount.
>
> Congratulations,
> W. Woodruff.

"Five thousand dollars?" Madge said. "That's a small fortune, Ivory! What are you going to do with such wealth?"

"Take care of my taxes first," he said, aiming a gap-toothed grin in Bennett's direction. "Then pay Mr. Bennett and Mr. Drew for their services, and then—" He shrugged. "Don't know. Maybe get me a new stove and a real electric refrigerator."

A great cheer rose up, and Ivory began banging out a raucous chorus of the old twenties' tune "Happy Days Are Here Again" on the piano. Although everyone in the cafe that night applauded Ivory's windfall, not everybody was truly happy. Thelma could see pain behind Willie's smile and near despair on Mabel Rae's countenance.

After a few minutes Rae leaned over and whispered something to Drew, then got up and left the cafe without a word. He jumped to his feet and followed her outside. Thelma cut a glance at Madge, who shook her head and mouthed the single word: *Pray.*

★ ★ ★

"Sweetheart, what's wrong?" Drew could barely keep up with Rae as she stalked back and forth across the parking lot. Obviously, something was bothering her, but he couldn't for the life of him figure out what it was.

"What makes you think anything's wrong?" she snapped as she passed by him on her second loop around the lot.

"Maybe because you're scattering Thelma's gravel all to kingdom come, or maybe because you won't talk to me. Come on, Rae—"

"I won't talk to *you?*" She stopped in front of him and looked up. "Andrew Jackson Laporte, I've been *trying* to talk to you for days—for weeks—but you never hear a word I say."

Drew watched the storm brewing in her dark eyes and shook his head. He had no idea what she was talking about. "Of course I hear you, honey. Just last night you were saying that we needed to get started on the baby's room, and I agreed. As soon as I finish up some work on Ivory's case—"

"That's just the point, Drew," she interrupted.

"What's the point?"

"The baby . . . the renovations . . . me . . . everything!" Her voice began to crack, but she turned away from him when he reached out to her. "The only thing you care about is this case—finding out who's behind this land scam. It's like an obsession to you, Drew. You don't see anything else. Nothing is as important to you as that blessed case—nothing!"

Drew's mind spun as he tried to piece together what she was saying. "You mean you believe this case is more important to me than you are?"

"What am I supposed to believe?" Rae bit out the words. "It's all you think about. You're never home, and—"

"Of course I'm home!" he protested, feeling his temper flare at the unfair accusation. "I'm home every night—except those couple of nights I spent in Jackson and Little Rock doing research."

"But you're not *there.*"

Drew closed his eyes and took a deep breath. He wasn't following this very well, but he sure wasn't going to admit it to Rae. "Explain that, please. What do you mean when you say I'm not there?"

"Your mind—your heart—is somewhere else, all the time," she managed. "Never with me. You agree to plans I make for the baby's room, for the renovations. You nod and say, 'That's fine, dear,' but you're not present. I try to talk to you about things that are . . . bothering me, and you pat me on the shoulder, give me a kiss, and brush it off."

"I do not!"

"Yes, you do, Drew." Her anger had dissipated, and she sounded completely drained. For the first time he noticed dark circles under her eyes and lines of weariness fanning out from the corners. She wasn't even four months along, and yet all the radiance, the glow she had had when she first found out she was pregnant, had vanished. Where had it gone, and when? And why hadn't he noticed?

He took her arm and steered her toward the bench under the awning of the cafe. The moon shone brightly, casting a silvery glow through the trees, and the scent of blooming flowers filled the night air. This could have been a romantic rendezvous, here in the moonlight with springtime budding all around them. But there was no romance in the air this early June night.

"All right, Rae," he said quietly as they sat down. "Talk to me. I'm listening."

Music and laughter from inside the cafe filtered out through the glass door, and without thinking, he turned his head toward the sound. When he turned back, tears were spilling down his wife's round cheeks, glistening tracks illuminated by the moon.

"It won't work, Drew," she said between sniffles. "I can't just pour everything out all at once, like a dog doing tricks on command." She shook her head miserably. "I need you, Drew. And you're not there."

"I'm here," he said. "What is it?"

Rae took a deep breath and exhaled heavily. "All right. I'll try. This may not make any sense to you, Drew, but I'm worried about the baby."

His heart constricted. "Is something wrong? Something you haven't told me? You went to the doctor last week, didn't you?"

She nodded. "According to him, everything is progressing normally. But—"

"Then there's nothing to be concerned about." He patted her hand and smiled. "It's just new-mother jitters, honey—everybody gets them. You'll see, everything will be just fine."

Her expression went blank, and she stared at him. "No, Drew, it's more than that. I—"

"You worry too much, that's all. Talk to Madge; she'll tell you. She probably felt the same way."

Rae nodded woodenly. "Right."

"Now listen." His mind scrambled for a plan, something to make her feel better. "I know I've been busy with this case and all, but we're getting close. It'll only be a few more weeks, you'll see. And then—I promise—I'll spend more time at home, get to work on the baby's room. In the meantime, maybe you and Willie can pick out some wallpaper or something."

"Wallpaper," she repeated dully.

"Yeah, or maybe take a little trip to Memphis for some new clothes. That would lift your spirits, wouldn't it?"

The music grew louder, and he could hear the strains of "I'm in the Mood for Love" with Stork's clear tenor rising above the other voices. They were probably all gathered around the piano by now, wondering—although no one would ask—what was keeping him and Rae from the celebration.

"We should probably go back in," he said with a forced smile. "Don't want to miss the party."

"All right." Without looking at him, Rae got to her feet and headed for the door.

Drew put an arm around her and pulled her to his side, peering down to try to look into her eyes. "Are you OK now, honey?"

"Sure," she whispered. "I'm fine."

She didn't seem fine, but he didn't know what else to do. "The moon is beautiful tonight, isn't it?" he asked. When she didn't answer, he leaned down to give her a quick kiss. She didn't resist, but she didn't respond, either, and before he could say anything else she had opened the door and gone back inside the cafe.

Just new-mother jitters, he assured himself. *What else could it be?*

TWO

You'll Never Know
Just How Much
I Love You

SUMMER 1945

13

The Breckinridge Foundation

Tullahoma County Courthouse
June 18, 1945

At eight o'clock in the morning, Thelma stood on the wide front porch of the Tullahoma County Courthouse, dressed to the nines in a navy suit and hat, with her hair done up in a French twist and Olivia Coltrain's mink wrap around her shoulders. It was too hot for the fur, but Bennett said it gave her the look she needed—a rich society matron who cared more for her image than for the weather.

She fiddled with the white gloves and shifted from one foot to the other. Already her feet hurt, and she wished she could take off these ridiculous heels and get back into the sensible lace-ups that gave her arches some support.

Behind her, Bennett set his briefcase on the courthouse steps and pulled out his pocket watch for the tenth time. "It's three minutes after eight," he grumbled. "Apparently government workers have nothing better to do than drink coffee and eat doughnuts."

Thelma peered through the glass doors and saw a long empty hallway. "I don't see a soul," she murmured. "Where are these folks?"

"Like I said, drinking coffee and eating doughnuts," Bennett responded.

He was getting impatient, and Thelma turned and smoothed his collar. "It'll be fine, Bennett. Friday was the fifteenth, so Ivory's taxes are now officially overdue. It's Monday morning, and we're the first ones here. There'll be no problem."

"I hope not. Our whole plan depends upon getting in there first and taking over Ivory's land under the name of the Breckinridge Foundation."

"Hush," Thelma warned, peering over his shoulder at a small, slight man coming up the sidewalk toward the courthouse. "We've got company."

"Good . . . good morning," the little man stammered as he approached and stood next to them. "Shouldn't they be open already?" He frowned at the closed door and tried the handle.

"Evidently they are a bit late this fine Monday morning," Thelma said in her best imitation of a society lady. "Dreadful, isn't it, how they keep people waiting?" She lifted her head and gave a little sniff.

The man removed his hat and swiped a handkerchief across his forehead. He was a young fellow, Thelma noted, probably in his early thirties, with a sallow complexion and thinning hair the color of dirty dishwater. A sparse fringe of new mustache struggled across his upper lip, and his eyes, a pale hazel, darted this way and that. Here was a man who could be completely invisible if he had a mind to disappear, Thelma mused. Everything about him, from his suit to his shoes, was that same drab tan color, and he looked for all the world as if he could fade into the morning haze and never be seen again.

Just then a harried-looking clerk appeared at the door and turned the lock. Bennett opened the door and ushered Thelma through, and the drab little man trailed along behind them.

"Property tax office?" Thelma inquired of the clerk, looking down her nose at him.

"Yes, ma'am," he stammered. "Down the hall and to your right."

Bennett took her elbow, and they marched down the hall in the direction the clerk had indicated. Out of the corner of her eye, Thelma caught a glimpse of the little man still behind them, shadowing their steps, and she turned.

He stopped in his tracks and shrugged. "I guess we're going to the same place," he said with an apologetic whine.

When they reached the tax office, Thelma and Bennett went directly to the counter. Sure enough, their unwanted companion came in right behind them, but at least he had the consideration to seat himself on a bench next to the wall, out of earshot. Thelma breathed a sigh of relief and turned back to the counter. She had been well briefed in the role she was to play, and she rapped with her knuckles on the counter.

"Excuse me, young man!" she called to the clerk, who had his head in a filing cabinet on the other side of the room.

"Be with you in a minute," he mumbled, not looking around.

Thelma glanced at the clock on the wall and raised her voice. "It is now precisely 8:17. Your office is supposed to open at eight, is it not?"

The clerk craned his neck around. "Yes ma'am. We're just running a little behind, that's all. As I said, I'll be with you in a minute." He opened another drawer and began rummaging through file folders.

Thelma slanted a glance at Bennett and increased the volume another notch. "You know, when I was down in Jackson at the Mansion for dinner last week—the governor's wife has done such a marvelous job making that old place livable, don't you think?—the governor mentioned how difficult it was to keep up with efficiency in government offices. Make a note, Mr. Winsom. I think we might give him a little call later this afternoon." She turned back toward the clerk and peered down her nose at the nameplate that sat on the counter. "Hmmm. Howard Mason, Assistant County Clerk. That's you, I presume?"

The clerk jumped to attention, banging his head on the open file-cabinet drawer, and made a beeline for the counter. His thigh hit the corner of the desk and he reeled, finally righting himself and coming to an abrupt halt directly in front of Thelma. "I apologize, madam," he whispered breathlessly, abject fear filling his eyes. "I had no idea—"

Thelma raised one eyebrow in his direction. "I'm sure you didn't, Mr. Mason," she said sweetly. "And I'm certain that you normally treat *everyone* who comes to your office—even someone like him—" she gestured toward the drab little man in the corner—"with the utmost respect and courtesy."

"Y-yes, ma'am," the clerk stammered. "I mean, I—"

"It's all right, young man," Thelma interrupted magnanimously. "I'm sure it won't happen again. And I'm certain a call to the governor will not be necessary."

"Yes, ma'am—ah, no, ma'am. I mean, it won't. Trust me. It won't."

Thelma adjusted her gloves and slipped the mink stole higher onto one shoulder. "Now," she said, lowering her voice, "I assume we can get on with our business."

"Yes, ma'am. Right away, ma'am." The clerk pushed his glasses up onto his nose and heaved a sigh of relief. "What may I do for you, Mrs. . . . ah—"

"Breckinridge," Thelma supplied. "Aurelia Breckinridge, of the Savannah Breckinridges. This is my attorney, Mr. Winsom, who handles all my accounts."

"Nice to meet you," the clerk said, his eyes fixed on Thelma.

"We are here to pay the back taxes on a foreclosed property and assume ownership," Thelma said, opening her bag and retrieving a lace handkerchief. "The papers, Mr. Winsom?"

Bennett pulled a single sheet of paper from his briefcase and slid it toward the clerk. "Here is the legal description of the property in question," he said quietly. "It is to be registered in the name of the Breckinridge Foundation."

The clerk blinked. "The Breckinridge Foundation?" he repeated stupidly.

Thelma rolled her eyes and gave him a pitying look. "The Breckinridge Foundation," she said with exaggerated patience, "is a historical society founded by my late husband Sterling, rest his soul. We are committed to the preservation of the fine old homes and plantations that represent the heritage of the Deep South. A tribute to his grandfather, Confederate Colonel Bosworth Breckinridge, who passed on heroically in the Battle of Vicksburg." She dabbed at her eyes with the hankie. "Such a loss, the death of the Colonel. He might have made the difference in the outcome of that terrible conflict."

Mason fiddled with the paper and stared at her. "Yes, ma'am. Well, I'll need to look up the record on this property—give me just a minute."

"Take your time, young man," Thelma oozed. When Mason turned his back, she gave Bennett a wink. "How am I doing?" she whispered.

Bennett chuckled. "You missed your calling. You should have been on the stage."

In a minute or two Howard Mason returned with a huge ledger. He slapped it down on the counter and flipped through the pages, finally putting his finger down on one page. "Here it is," he said, scrutinizing the record. Then he pushed his glasses up on his nose and peered at Thelma. "The foreclosure date was Friday at midnight. How did you—?"

"Is there a problem, young man?" Thelma interrupted haughtily.

"Oh, no, ma'am, no problem." He swallowed hard. "The back taxes come to—" he looked again—"one thousand dollars, plus a recording fee of nine dollars and fifty cents."

Bennett withdrew a fat envelope from his briefcase. "You accept cash, I assume."

"Cash?" the clerk gasped. "Well, certainly, sir. A certified check is the more common method of payment, but—"

"Fine." Bennett counted out ten crisp hundred-dollar bills and laid them on the counter, then reached into his pocket and drew out a ten. "Keep the change."

"Oh, no, sir," Mason protested, jerking open the cash drawer and flinging two quarters onto the counter next to Bennett's money. He fixed his eyes on Thelma and forced a smile. "Everything in this office is done strictly by the book."

"Of course it is," Thelma murmured. "I'm sure the governor will be most pleased."

With shaking hands, Mason filled out the transfer of title forms and pushed them toward Thelma. "Your signature here . . . and here, please."

Thelma handed the paper to Bennett. "My attorney is authorized to sign for me."

"Right, right." Mason watched as Bennett signed the forms, then stamped them with the seal of his office. "All done and legal," he muttered. "Keep this copy for your records." He started to hand it to Thelma, then thought better of it and placed the paper in Bennett's outstretched hand. When Bennett slid the form into his briefcase and snapped it shut, Mason looked up from his books with a sigh of relief. "Is there anything else I can do for you?"

"Not a thing, young man," Thelma said, patting his ink-stained fingers with her white-gloved hand. "You've been most helpful." She adjusted her mink and, with a nod to the pale man still seated on the bench in the corner, left the office with a flourish.

Bennett and Thelma were halfway down the hall when they heard an angry voice coming from the clerk's office, shouting, "What do you mean, no longer available? Check your records again, man—that can't be right!"

Thelma linked her arm in Bennett's and gave him a broad smile. "I guess that fella doesn't have an in with the governor," she quipped.

Bennett squeezed her hand. "You were magnificent, Aurelia Breckinridge," he whispered. "Absolutely magnificent."

They descended the steps and headed for Bennett's Packard, where Ivory Brownlee sat waiting in the backseat. "This calls for a celebration," Bennett declared as he opened the door for her. "How about finding a restaurant and getting some breakfast?"

"I'd rather just go home, if you don't mind," Thelma said. "My feet are killing me."

Bennett reached into the backseat, patted Ivory on the shoulder, and came up with a brown paper bag. "For you, milady," he said, handing the package over with a flourish.

Thelma peered into the bag, then began to laugh. She withdrew her comfortable old lace-up shoes and shook one of them in his face. "What is this, Bennett Winsom?"

He leaned over and gave her a kiss on the cheek. "A good attorney anticipates his client's needs."

"All right—breakfast it is." Thelma slipped off the uncomfortable heels and sighed with relief. "But these shoes don't go with the outfit."

"Nobody will notice, as long as you're wearing that mink." Bennett put the car in reverse and began to pull out of the parking space.

"Watch it, Mr. Bennett!" Ivory shouted.

Bennett slammed on the brakes, and Thelma swiveled around to look behind them. The pale drab man in the tan suit dashed by, right on their bumper. For just an instant he looked into the car, and his face was contorted in an expression of fear and frustration. He slammed a fist against the rear fender of the Packard, crossed the street, and flung himself into a dark blue Buick. The last they saw of him was a cloud of oil smoke as he roared off toward the edge of town.

14

Craven's Destiny

New Orleans, Louisiana
June 19, 1945

Orris Craven stood on the front porch of the Laporte plantation house and tried to calm the palpitations of his heart. His stomach churned up acid, and his knees shook. Maybe he should just turn around, get in his car, drive down to the Quarter, and throw himself off the levee. Anything would be better than having to face Beauregard T. Laporte with news of his failure.

He didn't know how it had happened. How could anyone have gotten to that Tullahoma County plantation before him? That elegant rich woman and her lawyer were there ahead of him, of course, but the clerk was adamant that a *company* had purchased the property—some group called the Breckinridge Foundation.

It would have been bad enough if the old geezer who owned the place had come up with the dough and paid his own taxes. Then they might have had a chance of holding him to the original contract, paying up the rest of the money—or some part of it, as little as they could manage—and taking over the land anyway. Surely a poor man, even if he could come up with a thousand dollars for back taxes, would have his head turned by the prospect of an additional five thousand or so in his pocket. And then Laporte's organization—this time it was the Southern Historical Preservation Society—would have their land and no doubt a tidy little profit, once the oil reserves were tapped.

But this was another matter altogether. Somebody powerful had obviously gotten there ahead of him, an under-the-table deal, probably, in some smoky back room at midnight on the fifteenth. Somebody who could bend the rules, not wait for Monday morning to roll around. Apparently this Breckinridge group knew the right strings to pull, the right pockets to line. And a big foundation like that meant big money and big lawyers and no chance in the world of getting that land back. Unless . . .

Of course. Laporte paid him for creative thinking, didn't he? Well, the answer was right in front of his face. Orris would go in, put on a show of being furious at this political maneuvering behind their back, and suggest that they might want to join forces with these Breckinridge people—expand the operation, so to speak, and multiply the profits. Beauregard Laporte was fond of saying that it takes money to make money. A larger funding base would only mean a larger return in the end.

Besides, diversifying wouldn't be a bad idea. If somebody got wind of the operation and threatened to expose them, they could always shift the heat to the Breckinridge Foundation. Orris had the address in his briefcase—a post office box in Grenada. It had to be a cover. And where there was a cover, there was something shady going on, something somebody wanted to keep private. Very private.

Orris took a deep breath. All right, he had a plan. Now all he had to do was convince Laporte that he hadn't failed, not really. That this could turn out better for all of them in the long run.

He straightened his tie and lifted the heavy door knocker.

Beau narrowed his eyes at the little weasel who stood in front of his desk. He should have known that this . . . this Craven character couldn't do a simple job without fouling it up. He would have a word or two for Clinton Marston about recommending him, that much was certain.

"Do you mean to tell me," Beau bellowed, enjoying the way Craven cringed at every word, "that someone else beat us to the punch and took that land right out from under your nose? That you went to the courthouse at eight in the morning on the Monday after a Friday midnight foreclosure, and the property had already been taken over?"

"Yes, sir, but—"

Beau silenced him with a look. Craven stood there for a minute or two, staring at his shoes and shifting from one foot to the other, and then an amazing transformation began to take place. The weasel cleared his throat, met Beau's gaze with a look of fierce determination, and said, "Colonel

Laporte, if you'll just hear me out, I think I can explain this, and I have already devised a plan to rectify the situation."

Beau blinked. A spine? This little invertebrate had a spine? Well, now, this was an interesting twist. He waved his cigar for the boy to continue.

Craven leaned forward and placed his hands on Beau's desk. His pale eyes bored into Beau's, and he spoke in a low, even tone. "It's obvious to me that the organization which purchased the property has some powerful friends in high places—powerful enough to skirt the system and get in ahead of us. They call themselves the Breckinridge Foundation, and it's my guess that they are in the same business we are. If we play our cards right, we could sweeten the deal, both for them and for ourselves." He smiled slyly and stood upright. "And have some insurance in the bargain."

Beau placed his cigar in the ashtray and leaned back, intrigued. Maybe Clinton hadn't been wrong about his recommendation after all. For the first time, he thought this Craven fellow might have potential. "Go on."

"What I propose is to communicate with them in the name of the Southern Historical Preservation Society, to inform them of our knowledge of their purchase, and to indicate our interest in joining forces with them for future purchases of the same nature. A carefully worded letter will cover our tracks and keep us in the clear, so if they're on the up-and-up, they won't suspect a thing. But if they're after the same thing we are, they'll get the message."

"And the insurance you spoke of?" Beau frowned.

"Simple." Craven smiled. "If we do link up with these Breckinridge guys, we'll have that much more capital to work with and that much more information to secure the right properties. But if there's any kind of slipup, and we get caught—"

"We can shift the blame and come out clean as a new baby's bottom!" Beau finished for him and laughed. "Craven, my boy, I'm proud of you, I truly am. Now you're thinking like a lawyer." Then a question occurred to him, and he frowned. "You're sure you can make this work?"

"Yes, sir, Colonel. No doubt about it. We might have lost one individual property here, but we stand to gain a lot more if we join forces with the competition, so to speak."

"And cover our tails in the meantime."

"Yes, sir." Craven picked up his briefcase and squared his shoulders. "If you'll excuse me, sir, I believe I've got work to do."

"Not so fast," Beau said. "Sit down first and have a cigar."

"A cigar?" Craven sank to the chair in front of Beau's desk.

"Havana Royale. Cuba's finest." Beau reached into the humidor and drew one out, then clipped the tip and handed the cigar and his desk lighter across to Craven.

The little man ran the cigar under his nose and twitched a little, then put it in his mouth and lit it. Blue smoke wreathed up around his head, and he coughed. "Fine smoke," he gasped, choking as he puffed.

"Nothing like a good cigar." Beau put his hands behind his head and watched as the weasel's sallow complexion turned a distinct yellowish green. "Report back to me as soon as you hear something."

"Yes, sir." Craven dropped the cigar in the ashtray and fled the room.

★ ★ ★

Out on the front porch, Orris took a deep breath of the humid air and sank weakly into one of the rocking chairs. He felt queasy, as if he might lose his lunch at any moment, and he wasn't sure if it was from the hideous cigar or the pressure of putting on such an act in Beauregard Laporte's presence.

As his stomach settled and the porch quit spinning, Orris smiled to himself. He should have been an actor. Exhausting as it was, he had pulled it off, and finally the Colonel had shown a little faith in him. He had turned disaster into opportunity, and wasn't that what a good lawyer was supposed to do?

Orris walked to his car and slid in behind the wheel. Now he had an even bigger job in front of him—finding out just what this Breckinridge Foundation was up to and whether or not they could strike a deal. He had bought himself some time, a second chance, but if he flubbed this one, he was pretty sure he would be unemployed in a heartbeat.

He just wished he didn't have such mixed feelings about the job. The challenge stimulated him, like a complex puzzle that needed to be worked out. And the sensation of earning Beauregard Laporte's respect was a heady, exhilarating feeling. But sometimes he wondered how far he could stretch, how much pressure he could take without breaking. These days it seemed like every assignment held his future in the balance. One mistake, and he was gone.

Sometimes, too, he recalled his early days in law school, the virtuous causes he had championed, the determination to use his knowledge and expertise for noble ends. All that zeal and enthusiasm had drained away over the years, and what was left now was the practical reality of making a living. Clinton Marston, who had become a kind of mentor for him, had made it clear that idealism had no place in the practice of law, that a good lawyer was one who made it his business to find ways *around* the rules. In the cases Orris handled now, the only challenge was to stay within the bounds of legality while bending the law as far as it could be bent. To find the loophole that would protect himself and his client and get the job done.

Still, there were times Orris missed his idealism. He had lost something, deep in his soul, and although he usually could ignore the gaping hole inside that reminded him of how meaningless it all was, he couldn't rid himself of his conscience altogether. Money might be a poultice that drew out some of the infection, but the wound remained.

Orris shook his head and started the car. He'd do better to leave the philosophy to the priests and sages. A lawyer didn't have time for such nonsense. There was work to do, property to acquire, a merger to propose. More money to make—for Beauregard T. Laporte, and for himself.

And, if all went well, he might just emerge from this deal with a reputation that would land him more clients.

Never mind about his soul. His career was on the line.

15

All or Nothing at All

Camp McCrane, Mississippi
June 20, 1945

Owen Slaughter stood outside the door of Major Mansfield's office and hesitated. He took a deep breath and tried to summon up all his reserves of courage. This just might be his moment of truth. And he wasn't at all sure if he was ready.

At last he opened the door and went inside. Stork Simpson, who was serving out his term of duty as Mansfield's assistant, sat at the desk in front of the major's door, his head down over a file folder. Owen cleared his throat, and Stork looked up.

"Owen!" Stork got up from the desk and came around to shake Owen's hand. "How are you?"

"Fine, I guess," Owen said nervously. "You got anything else for me?"

Stork gave him a peculiar look and averted his eyes. "I'm not sure. Sit down."

Owen took the chair opposite the desk and waited while Stork resumed his position. Finally he couldn't stand it any longer. "What did you find out?"

Stork retrieved a file folder from the basket on his desk and flipped it open. "There's not much here that you don't already know, Owen. You come from North Fork, Iowa, a small town just south of the Minnesota border. Your parents are deceased, and your record mentions no other living relatives." His voice sounded oddly flat, as if he were reciting the information by rote.

"Still, there might be somebody who knows me," Owen interjected, "back . . . back home." The word sounded foreign to him. *Home.*

"There might be," Stork hedged. "But Iowa is a long way to go to find out."

Suddenly a thought struck Owen, and he jumped up. "North Fork is on the Minnesota border, you say? How big is Minnesota?"

"Pretty big, I think." Stork rummaged in the bottom desk drawer and came up with a dog-eared atlas. "Will this help?"

Owen flipped pages until he found what he was looking for. It was a long way between Mississippi and Iowa, that was for sure. But there it was, right on the map. "I found it!"

"Found what?" Stork came around the desk and peered over his shoulder.

"New Ulm, Minnesota." Owen grinned.

"What on earth is in New Ulm, Minnesota?"

"Not what," Owen corrected. *"Who.* Fritz Sonntag's brother, Kurt, and his wife, Leah, that's who. Remember, I told you about Fritz rescuing me and Charlie from the Krauts."

"And this Fritz has a brother in the States?"

Owen nodded. "According to this map, not all that far from my . . . my hometown. When Hitler began to persecute the Jews, Kurt took his wife, who was part Jewish, to the States, and they ended up in this German settlement in Minnesota." He smiled to himself at the memory of his friend Fritz Sonntag, who had been such a godsend to Owen and Charlie. "I promised Fritz that once I got back, I'd contact his brother. So . . ." He sighed and looked down at the floor. "I guess the time has come."

A panicked look passed over Stork's hawkish face. "What time has come?"

"Time for me to go . . . home."

Stork perched on the edge of the desk and looked into Owen's eyes. "You're going to leave? But you can't, Owen. You—"

"I have to," Owen interrupted.

"Why?"

"I have to," he repeated doggedly. Owen felt his neck grow warm. He couldn't tell Stork why—not all the reasons, anyway. Not about his confusing feelings for Willie and his determination not to complicate her life. Not about the sense he had, despite the army's sketchy records, that somebody was out there waiting for him somewhere. "Let's just say I need to do it for myself," he said at last. "To settle my mind and find out whatever I can about who I am."

★ ★ ★

Stork watched Owen's face with a sinking heart. The man was determined to go to this little town in Iowa, that much was obvious. And Stork couldn't do a thing to stop him.

I can tell you who you are! his mind shouted. *I can tell you anything you need to know. I was with you here at this army base and out there, on the front. And I can tell you that the woman you are about to leave behind loves you more than you could possibly imagine. You belong here, Owen Slaughter—in Eden, Mississippi, with the people who care about you. Don't you understand? We're your family!*

But Owen didn't understand, and Stork couldn't tell him. There was no way to predict what an overload like that might do to Owen's balance. It might send him over the edge. Stork wasn't willing to take that chance, to be responsible for what knowing the truth might do to his friend. On the other hand, if he were in Owen's position, wouldn't he want to know?

While Stork was still debating within himself about the right thing to do, the door to the major's office opened, and Major Mansfield stood in the doorway. Stork jumped to attention and waited, following the major's eyes as they settled on Owen.

Major Mansfield had been briefed, of course, about Owen's situation. The CO had even put in a call to the army hospital in Baltimore to discuss the situation with one of the physicians there. The doctor had concurred that it was best not to try to jog Owen's memory or to fill in missing pieces for him, but rather to let the memories return naturally, on their own. Still, this was the first time the major had seen Owen since his return, and the shock registered on his face.

Stork shot a warning glance in the major's direction and said quickly, "Major, I don't believe you've met Owen Slaughter."

The major recovered his composure and nodded toward Owen, who was on his feet and saluting smartly.

"No need for formalities, Sergeant," Major Mansfield said. "I've been told of your heroism. Anyone who has spent time in a Kraut stalag deserves the respect of every man in this army."

Owen nodded humbly. "Thank you, sir, but I didn't do anything heroic—not really."

"That's not what I've heard," the CO countered. "Escaping from the prison camp, taking care of your buddy until his death." He fixed his eyes on Stork but said to Slaughter, "If you ever decide to reenlist, I'd be proud to have you serve here at Camp McCrane under my command."

"I appreciate that, Major, but I doubt that I would make a very good soldier anymore. I—well—I don't know how much you know about me, but—"

"I understand." The major shook his head. "Too bad. You were—"

Stork coughed and cleared his throat.

"That is," Major Mansfield corrected abruptly, "your record is outstanding." He went back into his office and came out with an envelope. "Lieutenant Simpson told me you would be coming by today, so I thought I'd give this to you in person." He handed over the envelope. "Your back pay finally caught up with you."

Owen peered into the envelope and gave a low whistle. "I guess I won't have to hitchhike to Iowa after all."

"Iowa?"

"Yes, sir, North Fork, Iowa. That's where I'm from."

A frown passed over the major's face like a summer storm, vanishing almost as quickly as it appeared. "Right. Lieutenant Simpson here has been tracking down information for you, hasn't he?"

"I trust you don't mind, sir. As a matter of fact, the army seems to have precious little information to offer me. I guess I'll have to find out the rest for myself."

"So you'll be leaving us?"

Owen gave a brief nod. "Right away, sir. There are . . . well, some things I need to know."

Stork watched as the CO swallowed with some difficulty, then came over and gave Owen a slap on the back and a handshake. "Well, good luck, son," he said gruffly. "I hope you find what you're looking for."

All the way back to the Coltrain farm, Owen turned over in his mind what had transpired in Major Mansfield's office. When he had first gone to the base to enlist Stork's help in finding out more about his past, he had hoped for more detail. Something—anything—that would give him a clue to his heritage. Not so much where he had come from because he knew that, at least. But where he *belonged*. Whether there was anyone who might be waiting for him to return.

After this morning he certainly hadn't come away with any more insight about his past than he already had. But he did have one piece of information that helped make his decision easier. North Fork, Iowa, his hometown, was only about sixty miles from New Ulm, Minnesota. And Fritz Sonntag's brother, Kurt, was there. It was a connection—his only connection—to something he knew, someone he actually remembered.

Stork had acted as if Owen's imminent departure was some kind of personal tragedy, and the CO had seemed reluctant, too, to see him leave. But why? Surely they could understand that he had to go, to see for himself what his past held, to try to link up with the brother of his only living friend.

What they didn't know, and couldn't have understood had they known, was that Owen's decision to leave was based at least in part on what he was running *from*. If he stayed here, he would only get more emotionally attached to Willie Coltrain, and that wasn't fair to her . . . or to himself. Not when there might be someone he had left behind, someone who hadn't shown up on the army's records.

Owen wasn't sure there was someone in his past, but he owed it to himself and to Willie to find out. For him, love was an "all or nothing at all" proposition. He couldn't let himself get close to her if he wasn't free to love her. And he didn't know whether he was free or not. All he had to go on was a sense, a *feeling*—that, and the strange dreams he could never remember. Almost every night now he would awaken, aware of having dreamed but unable to get hold of the images that troubled him. Someone whose face he could not see was waiting for him, longing for him, reaching out to him.

And so he was leaving.

Owen tucked his back pay in the breast pocket of his uniform and smiled grimly. He didn't want to go, and that was a fact, but he didn't see that he had any choice. He could never let himself love Willie Coltrain as long as there was the possibility that he had already given his promise to someone else. He would always be wondering, looking over his shoulder. The money was just one more sign that it was time. At least he could take the bus and not have to thumb a ride halfway across the country.

Once he got to Iowa and had a chance to set his mind at ease, he'd go on up to Minnesota and find Fritz's brother, Kurt. He had so many stories to tell the elder Sonntag brother—how Fritz, in rebellion against the Reich, had named his German shepherd *Führer* because, according to Fritz, *"der Führer ist* a dog." How Fritz had trained the shepherd to go wild, snarling and barking whenever anyone said "Heil Hitler." Owen could imagine Kurt throwing back his head and laughing just the way Fritz laughed. Surely Kurt would make him feel at home, like he belonged.

A stack of clean laundry lay neatly folded on the bed. Owen separated his few things from the clothes he had borrowed from Charlie. He replaced Charlie's clothes in the dresser drawer and stuffed his own into his burlap knapsack. This was the hard part—leaving behind this attic bedroom where Charlie had grown up. This house. This farm. Charlie had been his best friend, his brother. And he was trying to do right by Charlie's sister Willie. Why, then, did he feel as if he were betraying the memory of the only person who had ever truly loved him?

"I did my best, pal," he murmured to the photograph on the top of the dresser—a comical picture of Charlie standing on the seat of the old tractor. "I kept my promise, and now I've got to go. Maybe I'll be back . . . someday." He ran a finger over the top of the frame and choked back a sob. For the first time, he felt alone in this room.

Owen picked up the note he had written to Willie, hefted his burlap bag, and went downstairs. He propped the note on the top of the piano in the parlor, against a framed photograph of Willie and Mabel Rae as young girls in matching Easter outfits. His heart broke a little as he looked into Willie's youthful face, but he knew what he had to do.

Behind him, the parlor clock chimed two. The bus came through Eden at two forty-five, and he had to time it just right. If he left soon, he could take the old pickup to town, leave it at the cafe, and catch the afternoon bus to Grenada. From there he would get another one north to Iowa, to his past . . . perhaps to his future as well.

16

Thy Will Be Done

Willie cocked her head and listened as the screen door squeaked open and banged shut again. She heard footsteps across the creaky porch and then the sound of the truck door opening and the engine sputtering to life. Probably Owen going into town for supplies—he had mentioned needing to make a stop at the feed store.

She sighed and pounded both hands into the bread dough she had been kneading. Ever since that man had showed up on the day of Link and Libba's wedding, her emotions had been jerked up and down and around and back worse than the Tilt-A-Whirl at the county fair. One minute she thought he was remembering, or at the very least, experiencing romantic feelings for her, and the next he was as cool and distant as the bottom of the well. She couldn't figure it out for the life of her, and the more she worried about it, the more confused she got.

Willie patted the loaves into place and set them on the back of the stove to rise. She washed her hands, poured herself a glass of lemonade, and wandered through the front parlor onto the porch. Sure enough, the truck was gone. Rae was taking a nap, and Drew was in town with Bennett working on Ivory's case. Maybe the time alone would do her good.

She settled into the porch swing, took a sip of lemonade, and stared out over the fields toward the horizon.

From the direction of the barn, a small brown dynamo came barreling across the yard, ears flying. Curly. Willie smiled as she watched the pup take the porch steps in two awkward jumps and slide to a stop at her feet.

The dog sat there for a minute, beating her tail against the porch boards, then put two feet up on the swing.

Willie scratched her behind the ears, and the puppy whined. "All right, come on up." Curly backed up a couple of steps, twitched her behind, and took a flying leap into the swing. Then, satisfied that she was, for the moment, close enough, she settled next to Willie's hip and laid her head on Willie's leg with a contented sigh.

Rocking gently in the swing and stroking the puppy's head, Willie began to feel a little better. Maybe she just needed to be more like this little stray dog, content in the circumstances of her life and grateful to have a family and a place to call home. After all, she couldn't do anything about Owen, short of sitting him down and telling him to his face that he had once loved her. She would just have to bide her time and wait, trusting that somehow it would all work out in the end.

Trust. The word nagged at her, and she closed her eyes for a minute. She hadn't really been trusting, had she? Not trusting God, certainly, or even trusting Owen to discover the truth for himself. Her only prayers had centered around a plea for Owen's memories to return, for their relationship to pick up where it had left off when he had shipped out for the front. She hadn't been *praying* at all, not really—she had been *telling* God what she wanted and expecting God to agree with her.

Thy will be done. The phrase came into her mind unbidden, and she pushed it away. She didn't *want* to pray, "Thy will be done." She wanted *her* will, and she wanted it on *her* timetable.

The realization shocked Willie, and a deep quivering inside told her that she had stumbled upon an unwelcome truth about herself. In earlier days before Charlie's death, before everything had fallen apart, her mother had always been fond of saying that when you prayed for God's will to be done, what you were really praying for was that you would accept God's will with grace. Mama's words came back to Willie as clearly as if she had been sitting next to her in the swing: *Most times, prayer doesn't change the circumstances of our lives—it changes us and our willingness to adjust to the circumstances.*

Well, Willie didn't want to adjust to these circumstances. She wanted them to change to suit her own vision of how her life would work out. She wanted Owen to retrieve his memories and love her again. She wanted to build a life with him. She wanted . . .

Shame washed over her as she heard her own thoughts. *I want . . . I want . . . I want . . .*

How selfish she had been, and how faithless! Owen was alive—a miraculous answer to her dearest prayer. But she hadn't been grateful to God for his safe return. Instead she had been demanding and petulant, like a child who opens a roomful of beautiful Christmas presents and then whines because she didn't get the one exact gift she had hoped for.

Tears welled up in Willie's eyes, and she sniffed. Of course she wanted Owen to love her, and to be free to love him. God knew her heart. But if she truly believed in divine wisdom as she claimed to, she also had to have faith that God knew what was best at any given moment—both for herself and for Owen.

In a little jolt of insight, Willie suddenly realized she had been *afraid* to pray, "Thy will be done." Afraid that God's will might be different from her will, afraid that the Lord might lay on her shoulders a burden too great for her to bear. But God was not a vindictive, sadistic deity out to make people miserable. The Lord she loved, who loved her, wanted the best for her life. She believed that, but she hadn't been acting as if her belief made any difference.

Curly twitched in her sleep as Willie's hand absently stroked the silky ears. Now here was a study in trust—a helpless little puppy who gave her unconditional devotion to the people who had taken her in and cared for her. Well fed, healthy, and happy, she simply loved Willie and Owen and depended upon their love for her.

That was the way Willie wanted to be—curled up in the Lord's lap, sound asleep, not worrying about what the future held.

She began to pray—truly pray—for her heart to be open to whatever the Lord had in store for her life, for her future, for her relationship with Owen. And as she prayed, the tears fell in earnest. Tears of repentance, cleansing tears that washed away the dust of fear and anxiety that had accumulated on her soul.

Curly stirred and opened her eyes. When she saw her mistress crying, she put her paws up on Willie's chest and licked her face, nuzzling her neck and whining softly.

"I'm all right," Willie murmured, hugging the dog close. "I'll be just fine now."

For a long time Willie sat in the swing with Curly, sipping at her watery lemonade and letting her spirit settle. For the first time in months she felt truly content, comfortable with herself, at peace. It was so simple. Only God knew what the future held, and only God could be trusted to handle it. Why did people have to make faith so complicated?

The screen door squeaked, and she looked up to find a rumpled, sleepy-looking Rae staring at her.

"Have a nice nap?" Willie smiled up at her. "What time is it?"

"About three-thirty, I think," Rae mumbled. "What's going on?"

Willie shrugged. "Nothing. Curly and I have just been having a little heart-to-heart talk."

Rae came over to the swing, squeezed in on the other side of the dog, and stroked her head. "At least you've got somebody to talk to who listens."

"You're still upset with Drew, I take it," Willie murmured.

Rae grimaced. "I go back and forth. On the one hand, I understand why he's so involved with Ivory's case. He's got a good heart, and it's important to him. But I need him to be here for me, Willie. When I've tried to talk to him, he brushes me off. He doesn't mean to, but he's just not listening."

Willie took her sister's hand and squeezed it. "Are you still feeling the same way about the baby?"

"As if something is wrong?" Rae nodded miserably. "More so every day. But you and Madge are the only ones who know about it—and Drew, who isn't paying attention. Maybe it's crazy, Willie, but I can't stop the feeling. Madge, at least, didn't try to talk me out of it, and she told me that it wouldn't matter if the baby was born . . . well, not right. That I'd still love him or her just as much."

"She's right, you know." Willie smiled. "You'll make a great mother."

"Thanks. I just—well, I don't know. It's not like me to be afraid, but I can't seem to shake it."

"That's just what Curly and I were discussing when you came out."

Rae raised one eyebrow at the dog. "She's a good conversationalist, is she? Willie, you've been out in the sun too long."

"Actually, she is," Willie laughed. "She's teaching me a few things about trust."

"Trust?"

Willie nodded. "I realized something today, Rae, that I hadn't been wanting to face. Remember what Mama used to say about praying 'Thy will be done'?"

"You mean that it's really a prayer asking God to let us accept things as they are?"

"Something like that. I got to thinking and realized that I've been afraid to pray 'Thy will be done' about Owen. I didn't want to take the chance that God's will might be different from mine. I wasn't trusting."

Rae thought about this for a minute. "Maybe I've been that way about the baby, too. Not willing to trust God for the outcome of this pregnancy."

"We were raised to believe that God loves us and wants the best for us," Willie added. "But that's easier to do when you're a child. When you're an adult, life just gets so . . . so complicated."

"It's complicated, all right. So what did Curly here teach you about trust?"

Willie grinned. "She was sleeping in my lap, so content, so trusting. Utterly at peace. The way I'd like to be with God."

"Willie, you've always been that way with God. You were always the one who had the most faith."

"Not recently. Since Owen came back, I've been trying to get God to see things my way, to make things happen on my schedule."

"So what's different now?"

"I don't know. I just kind of—well—decided to start trusting. To remind myself that God knows better than I do what the future holds."

Rae leaned over and gave Willie a hug. "I think I need to be reminded of that, too. Maybe we should be more deliberate about praying for each other."

The clock chimed four, and Willie got to her feet. "Want to continue this conversation in the kitchen? I need to get dinner on before Owen gets back."

"Oh!" Rae said suddenly, reaching in her pocket. "Owen left you a note on the piano; you might want to read it before you go to a lot of trouble. Drew will probably get some supper at the cafe, and if Owen's not going to be here for dinner either, the two of us could just have leftovers."

"I thought he had just gone to the feed store," Willie mused, taking the note from Rae's outstretched hand. "I heard him leave, but I didn't see the note. Still, he's been acting so odd lately—"

She sat down again, unfolded the paper, and began to read aloud.

"Dear Willie,

"I'm sorry I've been acting so strange the past couple of weeks. I've had a lot on my mind, and I don't really understand it all. I just know I have to find some answers about myself and my past. I promised Charlie I'd come to Eden and tell you in person about his death, and since that promise has been fulfilled, it's time for me to move on—"

"Oh, Willie, no!" Rae exclaimed, grabbing Willie's arm.

Willie felt a knot forming in her throat. This couldn't be happening, not now when she was just beginning to accept, to trust. . . .

She choked back tears and struggled to read the rest of it.

"I'm catching the bus this afternoon and going up to Iowa to see if anybody is still there who knows me and can help me unravel the mystery about who I am and where I belong. I only hope I can find some kind of family that will be as loving and accepting of me as all you Coltrains have been. I left your daddy's pickup at the cafe and am enclosing a little money to pay you back for your hospitality. My best to Rae and Drew and everybody, and please thank them for being so nice to me. I'll try to keep in touch.

"Love, Owen"

Two crumpled twenty-dollar bills fell out of the note and fluttered to the porch. Willie watched them fall and felt the old emptiness open up in her again, the deep wound that had never quite healed.

"Well," she said in a grim voice, "it looks like the test of my trust has come sooner than I thought."

Then, leaving Rae alone on the porch, she rose shakily to her feet and stumbled blindly through the screen door into the recesses of the house.

17

The Merger

New Orleans, Louisiana
June 25, 1945

Orris Craven leaned back in his squeaky oak chair and read, for the fourth time, the letter that had come in this morning's mail.

> Dear Mr. Craven,
>
> We have received with much interest your letter dated June 19 and believe that it might be to our mutual advantage to discuss the merger you mentioned. The Breckinridge Foundation is committed to preserving the heritage of the Old South, which, as you so articulately expressed, sometimes involves retrieving certain properties in order to protect them from the encroachment of progress. The foundation is not interested in disposing of the property in question, of course, but we would be willing to explore our mutual interest in similar projects.
>
> You should realize, however, that Mrs. Breckinridge is adamant about a face-to-face meeting with the head of the Southern Historical Preservation Society. As soon as you can arrange such a conference with your employers, we would be delighted to entertain any proposal you might wish to offer.
>
> Kindly respond to me at the above address at your earliest convenience.
>
> Sincerely,
> B. Winsom, Attorney-at-Law

Orris smiled and looked around at the dismal, shabby little room that served as his office in New Orleans. It wouldn't be long now, and he could say good-bye to these drab surroundings, to the single window that looked out on a blank brick wall, to the dark alley entrance that always smelled of fish and garlic and gumbo spices. He might be staying in New Orleans indefinitely, but when this deal went through, Beauregard T. Laporte would be paying him enough to have an office in the heart of the Quarter, with a wrought-iron balcony overlooking the park. A place worthy of his position.

First on the agenda, however, was getting Colonel Laporte to agree to a meeting with this Mrs. Breckinridge of the foundation that bore her name.

In her sitting room upstairs, Beatrice Laporte had just begun a letter to Rae and Drew when the maid, Addie, tapped on her door.

"'Scuse me, ma'am," the girl said, "but there's a Mr. Craven downstairs asking for Mr. Laporte."

"Craven?" Bea frowned, trying to recall the name. "What does he look like?"

Addie thought for a minute. "Sort of small, thin, light brown hair, tan suit. Pasty looking." She smiled briefly, a flash of white against her coffee-colored skin. "But I guess all white folks look pasty to me."

Bea laughed, then stacked her papers in order and laid her pen across them. "Is he carrying a briefcase?"

Addie nodded. "Yes'm."

"It must be Mr. Laporte's new lawyer. I'll see to him."

She stopped at the door and patted Addie on the shoulder. "Bring coffee and some of that apple pie to the front parlor," she said, then realized her tone was a bit gruff and added, "Please." The girl had been difficult at first, but she was doing better. Maybe all she needed was a little encouragement. "Addie?"

The girl turned. "Yes'm?"

"I just wanted you to know how much I appreciate all you do around here. You're becoming a real asset to this household." She paused. "And you make the best apple pie I've ever tasted."

A light swept over the brown face, and the brilliant smile returned. "Thank you, Miss Beatrice. I 'preciate that. I surely do." As she reached the stairs, Addie turned. "I'll have your coffee right away, ma'am. And the pie. Right away."

Bea descended the stairs and entered the front parlor. When he caught sight of her, the young lawyer jumped to his feet, nearly upsetting the coffee table. The vase of flowers in the center of the table rocked precariously, and he reached out a hand to steady it.

"Sorry," he mumbled, "I—"

"You don't approve of my taste in vases, I see," she quipped.

Rather than putting him at ease as she had intended, the joke went right over his head. His face turned even paler, and his eyes widened. "Oh, no, ma'am—I mean, yes, ma'am—"

She motioned to him to resume his seat. "Sit down, Mr. Craven, before your knees give out. I'm quite harmless, I assure you."

He dropped to the settee and mopped his brow with the back of his hand.

Bea watched the young man intently. She had seen him only a few times—the day he broke the vase in Beau's office and a couple of other occasions in passing. But something about him intrigued her—something in his eyes, perhaps, or behind them, in his soul.

Addie brought the coffee and pie, and the young lawyer sat cradling his cup as if he were afraid he might break that, too.

"Mr. Laporte should return shortly," Bea assured him when his eyes darted around the room for the third time. "In the meantime, why don't you tell me about yourself?"

"About—about me?" Craven stammered as if the idea were completely out of the question. "Why should you want to know about me?"

"It's a perfectly innocuous question," Bea countered, wondering why he seemed so nervous about talking about himself. "You know, where you attended law school, what your ambitions are, that sort of thing."

"Oh," Craven answered curtly. "University of Tennessee."

"And did you enjoy your time in law school?" she prompted.

He looked away, took a sip of his coffee, and did not answer.

Bea's heart went out to the boy. Clearly he was troubled about something, but she couldn't discern what it might be. Perhaps if she just listened. . . .

Orris's heart leaped into his throat, and he could barely swallow. The hot coffee burned the roof of his mouth and seared his esophagus as it trickled down. He couldn't look her in the eye, this frail, birdlike woman who seemed so curious about him. She was peering at him intently, waiting. What could he possibly find to say to her? What was she trying to find out?

And why did she unnerve him so?

"I don't know why you'd be interested in the likes of me," he blurted out before he could stop himself.

"And why shouldn't I be?" she returned, a smile touching those cool blue eyes. "You seem like a nice young man."

Nice, he thought. Surely she knew that any lawyer who worked for her husband couldn't possibly be a "nice young man." Ruthless, perhaps. Prepared to do almost anything to make his mark in the world. But not nice. No, definitely not nice.

On the other hand, maybe she didn't know. Chances were, she had no idea about her husband's shady dealings—that he was in the process of stripping property out of the hands of poor ignorant people who had no hope of fending for themselves. Many women knew nothing of their husbands' business affairs. They kept the household running, attended society functions, and provided a front for the appearance of propriety.

She was gazing at him, waiting for an answer. And now he couldn't remember what she had asked. Oh yes, a nice young man, she had called him. He wondered briefly what she would think of him—or of her own husband, for that matter—if she knew the truth.

"I just—I just doubt that my life would be very interesting to you," he managed, gesturing vaguely at the opulent parlor where they sat.

An expression of understanding came into her eyes, and she nodded. "I have a son, Mr. Craven. And a daughter-in-law." A faraway look filled her face for a moment; then she returned her attention to him. "My son married—how shall I put this? Society folks would say, 'below his station.' At first I had a difficult time accepting her."

Orris placed his coffee cup on the table and narrowed his eyes at Mrs. Laporte. Why was she telling him this?

"When I finally realized what a lovely young woman my son's fiancée was, I had to face some hard truths about myself. I had let snobbery get in the way of my job as a mother. Supporting my son was more important than clinging to some outdated notions of social acceptability."

Orris nodded, but he couldn't speak. Suddenly, without warning, he missed his own mother. She had been gone for three years now, but he still remembered how she encouraged him through law school, reminding him whenever life got difficult that she believed in him. How she was convinced that he would be a great man, a great lawyer, a servant to the people. How she always told him that his name, his reputation, his honor, were more important than material success.

Sitting here listening to Beatrice Laporte talk about her son and daughter-in-law, Orris Craven found himself ashamed. He hadn't turned into the kind of person his mother envisioned. He had bartered his character for cash, his integrity for a chance to hobnob with the rich and powerful. He had been more concerned about becoming rich and powerful himself than about developing into an honorable man.

"And so," Mrs. Laporte was saying, "I'm terribly proud of Andrew—and of Rae." She leaned forward. "And . . . I'm about to become a grandmother."

Orris averted his eyes and mumbled his congratulations.

"Are you married, Mr. Craven?" she asked.

"No-no, I'm not," he stammered. "Never had time for it, I guess."

Then, to his everlasting surprise, Orris found himself pouring out his heart to Beatrice Laporte, telling her about how his widowed mother had supported him through law school and believed in him, and how he was afraid he wasn't turning out to be the kind of man she had supposed him to be. He left out the part about his present legal maneuverings and the deals he had cut in the past that were not quite on the up-and-up, but he did admit to her that he had once dreamed of doing something noble and wonderful with his life and that practicalities and money and ambition had gotten in the way.

She listened quietly, and when he was finished, she reached over and patted his hand. "Any of us can get sidetracked," she murmured. "The important thing is realizing it before it's too late."

By the time Orris stood in front of Beauregard Laporte's massive desk and rehearsed for the Colonel the conditions under which the Breckinridge Foundation would consider a merger, his earlier enthusiasm had vanished. He considered briefly the prospect of an office overlooking the Quarter, but even that brought him little joy. He kept thinking about his mother and about Mrs. Laporte's words: *Any of us can get sidetracked . . . the important thing is realizing it before it's too late.*

When he looked at Laporte's florid face, at the fat cigar clamped between his teeth, at the fire in his eyes, Orris's heart sank. It was too late already. He was in too deep, and the only thing he could possibly do was to see this through to the end.

"Get back up to Mississippi immediately," the Colonel ordered. "Set up a meeting with this Breckinridge woman and her lawyer, and—"

"But, sir," Orris interrupted, "the attorney made it quite clear that they would not consider a deal without meeting personally with you."

"Then pretend to be me, you little twit! Lie to them, do whatever you have to do, but get me this merger! I'm not going to take the chance of having my whole future snatched out from under me, do you understand?"

"Yes, sir. But couldn't you just—?"

"No, I could not. Don't you get it, Craven? It cannot become public that I'm behind any of this—you knew that from the beginning. Your job is to keep me squeaky clean. Now, can you do that or can't you?"

"I'll do my best, sir." Orris turned to go, his stomach knotting with tension.

"Your best had better get results," Laporte roared, "or you'll be selling pencils in the doorway of some jazz joint on Bourbon Street."

Orris slipped out of the office, shut the door behind him, and came face-to-face with Beatrice Laporte. She smiled at him, her pale blue eyes filled with compassion.

"It'll be all right," she murmured, squeezing his arm.

"Yes, ma'am," Orris replied. But as he headed down the hall and out the massive front doors of the plantation house, he had a sinking feeling that nothing would ever be all right again.

18

A Fork in the Road

North Fork, Iowa

Owen Slaughter stepped off the bus in front of a single row of white clapboard storefronts. A large dog—mostly collie, Owen thought—lay in the middle of the main street, sound asleep and clearly unconcerned about traffic. The bus pulled away, making a wide berth around the dog, turned the corner onto the highway, and shrank into the descending sun.

Owen stepped up onto the sidewalk and surveyed his surroundings. The only buildings taller than two stories were the grain elevator, looming like a protective metal giant over the town, and the water tower, painted like an enormous ear of corn. Main Street consisted of a cafe, a tavern, a garage, and a combination hardware and grocery store. Houses, mostly white, sat in neat rows along square blocks bisected by gravel alleyways. In the distance, beyond the last line of homes, he could see cornfields, green and waving in the wind, all the way to the horizon.

He checked his watch. It was nearly six, and he hadn't the faintest idea what to do next.

Coming here had to be the craziest idea he had ever concocted in his life. The town seemed vaguely familiar, but details escaped him. What did he hope to accomplish by traveling halfway across the country when the army had already told him that his parents were dead and they had no record of any other relatives? It was a fool's errand, and yet . . .

Owen considered his options. The cafe, store, and garage were all closed. That left the tavern. Would anybody there know him, remember his family?

His stomach churned, and he sent up a silent prayer for somebody—anybody—to give him direction. Then he hefted his burlap knapsack and started down the sidewalk.

At the sound of his footsteps, the dog got up, stretched, and looked at him. Then, suddenly, the animal came to life. It bounded over to him, whining and wagging its tail and pushing its nose into Owen's hand to be petted.

In spite of his present uncertainties, Owen couldn't help smiling. He stroked the dog's head, and the dog promptly sat down and held up one paw in greeting. Owen shook the paw solemnly, wondering who would leave such a beautiful animal out in the street on its own. Suddenly a horn blared behind him, and Owen turned. A rust-colored pickup truck skidded up beside him, and the driver—obviously a farmer, Owen thought to himself—rolled down his window and leaned out.

"Need some help, son?"

The man behind the wheel draped a wind-burned elbow over the door, removed his cap, and grinned at Owen. He was beefy and bald, with just a fringe of reddish hair over his ears, and his eyes were a piercing blue.

Owen stepped toward the truck, but before he could speak, the driver slapped his hand against the side of the truck.

"Warren's boy? Well, you could knock me over with a feather, you could. I hardly recognized you with that beard. You finally out of the army, son? How long has it been? You haven't been around these parts since—oh, more'n four years ago." A cloud passed over his amiable features, and he lowered his eyes. "Last time you were here was for the funeral."

Owen approached the pickup on rubbery legs. He couldn't catch his breath, and he felt shaky inside. Was it possible this was someone who actually knew him—knew who he was, who his parents were? Someone who could tell him about his past?

"Yes, sir." Owen held out his hand uncertainly and found it was trembling. "That's right—I mean, I think that's right," he stammered. "My name's Owen Slaughter."

The man narrowed his eyes and gave Owen a curious look. "I know your name, son. And you've never called me 'sir' in your life."

"Who-who are you?" Owen blurted out.

The farmer's ruddy face went pale. "What's the matter with you, Owen? It's me—your Uncle Earl." He closed his eyes for a minute and then reached across the seat to open the passenger's door. "You'd better get in the truck."

Owen went around and got in, then turned and faced the man who called himself Earl. The farmer didn't look at him. He slammed the pickup into gear, swung over to the curb, and shut off the engine. "What happened?" he asked, looking down at the floorboard.

But Owen couldn't answer. The words clogged in his throat, and he croaked out, "Are you really my uncle?"

The farmer looked up at him, his blue eyes filled with compassion. "Yep. Earl Slaughter, your papa's brother. Something bad happened to you over there, didn't it, boy?"

Owen swallowed hard and nodded. "I'm afraid so . . . Uncle Earl." The words felt foreign on his tongue, and yet his heart filled with hope. Quickly, before he choked up again, he sketched out the story—losing his memory, finding himself in a German prisoner-of-war camp, meeting Charlie, going to Eden, Mississippi, to fulfill his best friend's dying request.

"They asked me to stay," he finished, "but I couldn't. Not until I found out who I was and where I came from." He let out a deep sigh. "A man can't have a future when he doesn't know his past."

Earl listened quietly, then put a hand on Owen's shoulder and squeezed. "It's getting late," he said. "Your Aunt Gert will have dinner waiting. Let's go home." He started the truck, backed into the street, and whistled. The collie loped over to the back of the truck and jumped in.

"That's your dog?"

A strange expression passed over Earl's face. "Actually, she's yours. She's probably ten years old now. You found her in a snowstorm one February, frozen near to death. Took her in and nursed her back to health, then named her Valentine. Her nickname's Vallie." He slanted a glance at Owen. "You remember any of this?"

Owen shook his head.

"You were—oh, fourteen or fifteen, I think." He grinned. "Just discovering girls, as I recall. Trained her yourself. Real smart dog."

"She's beautiful."

"She missed you a lot when you went off to college. Didn't eat for a week. Then when your folks died and we moved out to the farm, she just sort of stayed on, adopted us. But she never forgot. You could see that for yourself."

"You think she remembered me? After—how long did you say I've been away—four years?"

Earl turned off the main highway onto a gravel road. "Sure she did. Vallie's always nice and polite to people, but she doesn't take to them the way she took to you."

Owen sat back against the seat and sighed. "And I rescued her, you say?"

"Her and a dozen other creatures. Your mother was always saying you'd be the death of her, bringing home strays the way you did."

Some things don't change, Owen mused, *even if you don't remember them.* He thought of Curly, the brown spaniel he had bought for Willie. For a minute his mind drifted to Eden, to the Coltrain farm, to those dusky gray eyes and that deep, rich voice....

With a shake of the head, Owen pulled himself back to the present. There was no point dwelling on what he had left behind. If Willie had ever felt anything for him, he had probably ruined his chances with her by leaving the way he did. He wouldn't accomplish anything by wishing for what he could never have.

"Up there is Chapel Hill Lutheran Church," Earl was saying, pointing up a rutted dirt road.

Owen looked. At the crest of a small hill stood a picturesque white church, its tall steeple capturing the last rays of the setting sun. The church and the tiny graveyard that surrounded it were bathed in an ethereal light, and a feeling stirred deep in Owen's spirit, almost like ... recognition.

"Are my parents buried there?" he asked suddenly.

Earl nodded. "You remember?"

"No," Owen answered. "Not really. Just a ... a feeling."

"I'll take you up there tomorrow and show it to you," Earl muttered. "If you want to."

They passed the church and went on around a curve until they came to a long driveway on the left. Earl pulled in and stopped just past the cattle gap at the end of the drive. "This is it."

Owen opened the door and stood on the running board, looking up the hill at the house. A white two-story, it faced east overlooking a broad pasture. A tire swing hung from a thick rope in the branches of an enormous oak tree. Behind the house and to the left sat a weathered red barn, its door partly open. Vallie barked, jumped down from the bed of the truck, and ran up the lane toward the house.

"Gert'll sure be surprised," Earl said. "You ready?"

"Ready as I'll ever be." Owen sat down and shut the door, and Earl ground the truck into gear and started up the hill.

★ ★ ★

"And these," Aunt Gert said as she led Owen by the hand around the living room, "are our two children, Bette and Thomas. Bette—her real name is Elizabeth—is married now and lives in Cedar Rapids. Thomas ..." Her voice faded away in a strangled sob.

"Thomas," Earl said huskily, coming into the room behind them, "was a year and a half younger than you."

Owen peered at the photograph of a young man in a navy uniform—a man who bore a remarkable resemblance to the reflection he looked at in the mirror every day. "What happened to him? Was he killed in the war?" As soon as he had said it, he wished he hadn't asked, but the words were out and he couldn't take them back. "I'm sorry. I didn't mean to—"

"It's all right." Earl picked up the framed photograph and stared at it. "He always loved the water, Thomas did. Spent half his life in a fishing boat. You remember that raft you boys made when you were about twelve? Worked on it all summer so you could float down the river like Huck Finn. . . ." His words drifted into silence. "No, I don't suppose you remember that." He cleared his throat. "Thomas always wanted to be like you, Owen. You were his hero. After you signed up, he couldn't wait to join the navy, and then—"

"He died in a training accident," Gert finished softly. "A week before his twentieth birthday."

"I'm sorry," Owen said. And he truly *felt* sorry, too, although he didn't know if it was because somewhere deep inside he remembered his cousin or just because he understood their grief.

He continued to look at the pictures one by one, listening intently to Aunt Gert's commentary about the family. His aunt, a rotund little woman with short-cropped gray hair and a brilliant smile, had only taken about three minutes to adjust to the reality of his situation. She had welcomed him with a motherly hug that made him feel immediately at home, deposited his bag on the steps leading up to "his room," and bustled him off to the kitchen for an enormous meal of pork roast and mashed potatoes. After serving him a second helping of rhubarb pie and a third cup of coffee, she had gotten right to the business at hand—telling him everything he wanted to know about his past.

Now, as Gert talked, Owen's gaze drifted to a photograph of a young couple holding a baby, and his heart stopped. Fighting to catch his breath, he picked it up and stared at it. A short, muscular man with curly hair and an infectious grin stood with his arm around a woman a head taller than himself.

"Your parents," Gert murmured over his shoulder. "Shortly after you were born."

Owen turned toward her, his vision blurred by tears. "Could I keep this?"

"Keep it?" Gert repeated. "Honey, you can keep everything—it's all yours."

"What's mine?"

She smiled at him, her warm eyes glowing. "Sweetie, there's an attic full of your parents' things—and yours. Photograph albums, scrapbooks, all kinds of mementos. Your mother saved everything, and when they died, well, I just couldn't bear to part with any of it."

"An attic?" Owen repeated idiotically.

"Of course." Gert patted his arm. "We'll go up there tomorrow, and I'll help you sort it all out." Her face took on a wistful, faraway expression. "Your mother, rest her soul, saved all your memories for you. Maybe she knew, somehow . . . maybe she knew."

★ ★ ★

Later that night, with the sounds of the country coming in his window and the, collie, Valentine snoring softly at the foot of the bed, Owen lay awake and wondered if his aunt might be right. Was it possible that his mother had known she was going to die and that her son, her only child, would need the memories she had preserved for him?

And what about the "coincidences" of this day—his own dog meeting him when he got off the bus, his uncle driving up just as he was entering the tavern, as if it had all been arranged?

He knew what Charlie would say—that these were no more coincidental than the two of them finding each other in that hellhole of a stalag or stumbling into Fritz Sonntag during their escape. That God had led Owen here to North Fork, Iowa, even as God had led Charlie to go back to the front. Charlie's God had saved him from shame and suicide. Maybe this trip to North Fork was Owen's chance at salvation, to be saved from the rootlessness of a life with no past.

This morning he had nothing but a bus ticket to a tiny Iowa farm town. Now he had an aunt and uncle, a dog who adored him, a house that held the echoes of his boyhood, and an attic full of clues to his past . . . and perhaps to his future as well.

Maybe what people called "salvation" came in a lot of different packages.

19

Cornhusker Sweetheart

Owen awakened the next morning to a wet nose nuzzling against his cheek. He opened his eyes and saw a long narrow face and dark almond-shaped eyes.

"Valentine!" he murmured, stroking the dog's head. Apparently that was all the permission she needed. With a mighty lunge she leaped onto the narrow bed, nearly pushing Owen into the crack between the bed and the wall.

"Take it easy, girl!" he laughed. As he buried his hand in the thick fur of her ruff and petted her, his mind flashed to a different dog, a different room, another narrow bed. Führer. Fritz Sonntag's cottage. The cot where Charlie Coltrain had died.

Those were his memories—his months with Charlie in the prison camp, the weeks in the Black Forest with Fritz and his menagerie of welcoming animals. This room, this house, seemed more foreign to him than a German woodsman's cottage. It felt strange to be here, in North Fork, Iowa, where people knew him but he didn't remember any of them.

Perhaps going through his mother's things would help. Maybe a day in the attic, surrounded by family pictures and memorabilia, would jar his memory and give him back what he had lost. If it didn't, at least he could begin building some understanding of his heritage from the ground up.

Owen nudged Vallie to the floor and got up. From downstairs, the smell of coffee and sausage drifted to his nostrils, and his stomach rumbled. He could use a good hearty breakfast of eggs and biscuits and grits . . . no, they wouldn't have grits, not in Iowa. Potatoes, probably. Whatever the menu, it smelled wonderful.

The collie followed him, step for step, as he hurried to the bathroom, brushed his teeth and dressed, and then took the stairs two at a time. Aunt Gert fluttered around the big farmhouse kitchen, humming to herself as she took biscuits from the oven and broke eggs into a bowl.

"Good morning."

Gert turned her beaming smile on him and came over to give him a kiss on the cheek. "Good morning, Owen. Your timing is perfect. Help yourself to coffee."

He poured a mug and sipped at it, then seated himself at the pine table. "Where's . . . Uncle Earl?" The name still sounded strange on his lips, but he was determined to get used to it.

"He had to go into town. Arnie Krupp, down at the elevator, called to tell him some supplies he had ordered came in. He'll be back soon." She scooped the biscuits onto a plate. "Let Vallie out, will you?"

Owen looked around. The dog was sitting patiently in the back entry, staring intently at the doorknob. When he got up and opened the door for her, she rose to her feet, licked his hand politely as if to say thank you, and trotted outside.

"She's a wonderful dog," he said as he resumed his seat.

"She should be—you trained her." Gert smiled over her shoulder at him. "I assume she slept with you last night?"

Owen nodded. "At the foot of the bed. Until this morning, when she demanded a little more room." He chuckled. "That bed's not big enough for both of us."

Gert placed a platter of scrambled eggs and sausage in front of him and went back to the stove for fried potatoes and the biscuits. "Every night since you went away, that dog has slept in the hallway right outside the door to your room."

"Really?" For some reason Owen couldn't quite understand, the idea gave him a warm feeling inside. A sense of being loved, of belonging. Someone *had* been waiting for him, after all.

"When your parents died, you stayed here for a couple of weeks, getting all the arrangements made. You don't remember that, of course, but Vallie remembers. We took care of her after that, even before we moved into this house. But she was always restless until we brought her back here."

The back door opened and Vallie came into the kitchen, followed by Uncle Earl. He removed his cap and hung it on a peg, then seated himself across the table from Owen. "Morning, son. You sleep all right?"

"Just fine, Uncle Earl." Owen sneaked a piece of sausage to Vallie, who had settled herself beside his knee. "Aunt Gert was just telling me about how Vallie always sleeps outside the door of . . . my room."

"Yep. Regular as clockwork."

Gert sat down in the chair adjacent to Earl, took his hand, and extended the other one to Owen. "Would you like to say grace, Owen?"

In a panic Owen bowed his head and stumbled through a prayer, thanking the Almighty for the food, for the hands that had prepared it, and for his aunt and uncle's hospitality. "And thanks for bringing me home. Amen."

"That was nice, honey. Real nice." Aunt Gert spread her napkin in her lap and passed the biscuits to Owen.

"Thank you," he mumbled, busying himself with buttering a biscuit. He *was* thankful for the food and for his aunt and uncle, but he felt distinctly uncomfortable praying out loud. It wasn't that he had lied exactly—except for the part about being home, because he didn't really feel at home yet. It was just that he didn't have a clear picture of who he was praying *to*. He felt like a hypocrite, a fraud. Charlie would tell him that God had most certainly brought him here, but that was Charlie's belief, not his own. He couldn't borrow Charlie's faith, any more than he could live on Charlie's memories.

Owen was halfway through a second helping of sausage and eggs when he realized that back in Mississippi, working on the Coltrain farm, he had felt at home, in his element. Suddenly he knew why. He *was* a farm boy. The idea hit him like a splash of cold water. This was his *home*. His heritage. And here, if anywhere, he could find out what his life before Germany had been like.

"Owen?"

He looked up to find both Gert and Earl staring at him with curious expressions.

"What?"

"Are you all right? Your hand is shaking."

Owen's eyes dropped to the table. The knife he held in his right hand was trembling, clattering against the side of the plate and making a horrible racket. With a deliberate movement he set it down and took a deep breath. "Sorry. I was just . . . thinking. This is all so strange, you know."

"It's all right." Gert patted his hand and smiled. "I'm sure it must be overwhelming to you, after losing your memory like that."

"Arnie said he'd heard about somebody else who had amnesia from the war," Earl put in. "Took him awhile, but he got his memories back. Arnie said it happened a little at a time."

Owen stared at Uncle Earl. "You told this . . . this Arnie . . . about me?"

"Sure. Arnie Krupp's known you since you were in diapers. Nearly everybody in this town has. They're all concerned about you."

"All?" Owen got a sinking feeling in his stomach, as if some well-guarded family shame had just been revealed for all the world to see.

"I sorta stopped in to the cafe for a cup of coffee after I left Arnie's. Seems people already knew you were back—somebody must have seen you when you got off the bus."

Owen shook his head. Great. Just what he needed—a whole town full of well-meaning people regarding him as some sort of freak, a curiosity of nature.

"This is a small town," Earl went on. "Can't keep anything quiet for long around here."

"Well, I guess it was inevitable," Owen sighed. "I just didn't think it would happen so soon." His appetite had vanished, and he laid his fork down across his plate. "Thank you for the wonderful breakfast, Aunt Gert."

"You're welcome, honey. Now let me just get these plates in the sink, and we'll get ourselves up to the attic and have a look around."

Owen could hardly believe all the things his mother had saved. Aunt Gert was right; she had preserved the family memories for him. Whether she had known she was going to die, had some sixth sense about it the way people did sometimes, Owen had no clue. But he did have clues to other things—hints of who he had been and what kind of man he promised to become, shadows and signs to lead him in the right direction.

He found a blue high school jacket with the letters *NF* emblazoned on the sleeve. A faded photograph of himself and a young woman in a rakish pose against the fender of a black sedan. A picture of his father and mother—he recognized them from Aunt Gert's photo downstairs—on a beach with waves in the background. A battered football and a leather bag full of marbles. Ticket stubs from a theater in Algona, Iowa. A high school diploma bearing the name *Owen Warren Slaughter.*

Cartons and trunks and hatboxes full of fragments from the past, things he knew instinctively were important. But he could not *remember* any of it.

Frustrated, Owen leaned back on his elbows on the dusty attic floor and sighed. He had hoped—prayed, even, with his limited experience in prayer—that somehow these remnants of life his mother had treasured might stir something inside him, some glimpse into the dark recesses of his own mind. At least now he knew he had a past, knew where he had come from. But it was nearly impossible to claim these mementos as his own when his mind didn't attach any particular significance to them.

Owen got to his knees and returned his attention to the half-emptied trunk in front of him. More clothes. A dried rosebud in brown paper. An old worship bulletin from the Chapel Hill Lutheran Church. It was no use. There was nothing here for him, nothing that would have any meaning until he got his memories back and understood why these items had been saved in the first place.

He replaced the clothes, shut the trunk, and sat for a moment looking at the newspaper his Aunt Gert had given to him. It was the *Algona Gazette,* dated March 15, 1941. On the lower portion of the front page, a dark photograph showed a mangled car on the side of the road. The caption read:

NORTH FORK COUPLE DIES IN COLLISION

Yesterday's blizzard claimed yet two more lives as a North Fork man and his wife, less than a mile from home, failed to yield to a train at the crossing on Highway 42. The accident occurred at approximately 6:30 P.M., during the worst of the storm. Residents of North Fork report that visibility at that time was near zero, with heavy snow and winds in excess of forty miles per hour. The sheriff's report concludes that the driver of the vehicle was unable to see the crossing or the oncoming train. Dead on arrival at the county hospital were Warren Slaughter and his wife, Edith, life-long residents of North Fork.

He flipped to the back of the paper and read the obituaries.

Warren Slaughter, age 44, and Mary Edith Slaughter, age 41. Services and interment at Chapel Hill Lutheran Church. Survived by one son, Owen Warren Slaughter, age 21.

Owen shook his head sadly. Over four years ago, his parents' lives had been cut short by a split-second twist of fate. Half a minute more or less, and they would have crossed the tracks safely and made it home, blizzard or no blizzard. Now they were dead, he was alone, and—worst of all—he had no feeling at all about their deaths except the pity one might feel for a stranger. He didn't even remember the funeral.

"Owen!" Aunt Gert's voice called up to him, interrupting his thoughts. He laid the paper aside and went to the top of the stairs.

"Yes?"

"There's a telephone call for you. Can you come down?"

"I'll be right there." Owen dusted off his pants and took the steps two at a time. A telephone call? Who on earth could be calling him?

His first thought was of Willie Coltrain, and his heart leaped with anticipation. But, no, she had no idea where he was, and she was probably so mad at him that she wouldn't call him if her life depended upon it.

"Who is it?" he asked in a low voice as his aunt handed him the receiver. She shrugged and raised her eyebrows. "A girl. She didn't give her name."

Owen's stomach lurched, and he took the telephone. "Hello?"

"Is this Owen Slaughter?" asked a sultry female voice on the other end of the line.

"Yes," Owen croaked out. "Who is this, please?"

"Oh, Owen, I'm disappointed. I had hoped you'd at least remember *me*. But then, they say you don't remember much of anything."

"Who says?" Owen's mind flashed an image of the photograph he had seen of himself and the young woman. "And who is this?"

"Why, it's me, Owen. JoLynn. JoLynn Ferber." She gave a deep, rich laugh.

"Do I know you?"

"Of course you know me, silly boy," she said. "Or at least you used to."

"I . . . I don't understand," Owen stammered. "Why are you calling me?"

"Well, you're back in town for the first time in more than four years," the woman replied. "I assume, since they say you have amnesia, that you're here to find out about yourself. Your past. Is that a correct assumption?"

"Yes," Owen hedged. "But what does that have to do with you?"

"Come to see me, and you'll find out," JoLynn said. "I'll be home all afternoon. Your uncle can tell you how to get here." With a gentle click, the line went dead.

Owen stood there for a minute with the receiver in his hand, then replaced it in its cradle. He turned to find Gert and Earl standing in the hallway behind him, staring at him.

"Who is JoLynn Ferber?" Owen asked bluntly.

His aunt and uncle exchanged a significant glance but said nothing.

"Who?" Owen demanded.

Earl patted Gert's shoulder and sighed. "He might as well know, I guess." He turned to Owen. "JoLynn Ferber is a girl you used to know in high school."

"The one in the picture I found? The girl leaning against the car?"

"I'm not sure which picture you're referring to," Aunt Gert said, "but it's most likely her."

Owen's heart pounded. "Was I—was I in love with her?"

"I wouldn't call it love, exactly," Uncle Earl muttered. "But yes, you two were . . . an item. A long time ago."

"She wants to see me," Owen said. "She says she can help me find out about myself."

Gert sighed. "I guess it was bound to happen sooner or later. Let's have some lunch, and Earl can run you over there in the truck."

Uncle Earl drew Gert aside and whispered something in her ear. Tears came to her eyes, and she blinked them back, but she nodded.

"We'll do better than that," Earl said firmly. "Gert and I want you to have Thomas's car."

Owen gaped at them. "What did you say?"

"Before Thomas signed up with the navy, he bought a car—a '39 Chevy convertible. We didn't have the heart to sell it, but we'd like to give it to you. In memory of Thomas."

"It's on blocks in the barn," Gert added. "Earl has taken real good care of it."

"Yep. After lunch I'll gas it up for you, and it should suit you just fine." He paused and gave Owen a weak smile. "I get extra gas for my tractor, but I can spare a tankful for you. Thomas would have wanted you to have it."

A lump rose to Owen's throat as he sat down to lunch, and he could barely swallow. He might not remember these people and this home he had left behind, but they were offering him more than he could ever have expected. Not just the car, but their acceptance. Their generosity. And he fervently hoped that whatever it was that made his aunt and uncle so noble and unselfish, it hadn't deserted him when he had lost his memory. *Let me live up to the Slaughter name,* he prayed to whoever might be listening. *Let me truly belong in this family.*

At 1:45, Owen pulled up to the curb in front of a tiny green house at the very edge of town, half a block removed from its nearest neighbor. Weeds grew up around the single tree in the front yard, and the grass needed cutting. But the house itself looked neat enough, with a rocking chair on the porch and a small plant hanging in the window.

He could have been here thirty minutes sooner, but he had enjoyed driving the Chevy up and down the gravel back roads between the cornfields. It was a beautiful day, bright and sunny, and he had put the top down and let the wind blow through his hair. He wasn't sure he could accept

Thomas's car as a gift from his aunt and uncle, but they seemed so happy about giving it to him that he didn't have the heart to refuse.

And it was a beauty, too—dark blue with white seats and top and a radio and wide, white-sidewall tires. From everything he could tell, poor Cousin Thomas hadn't had the chance to drive it much before he had gone off to the navy and gotten himself killed. It wasn't new, but it had been lovingly cared for, and it had roared to life as soon as Uncle Earl turned the key.

Reluctantly, Owen slid out of the driver's seat and shut the door behind him. He squinted at the bright blue sky. Not a cloud anywhere; he could leave the top down without worrying. Pocketing the keys, he slowly made his way up to the door.

This had to be the right place. North Fork wasn't exactly the kind of town you could get lost in. Laid out in a precise square, the streets that ran north and south were numbered, and the east-west ones named after trees, in alphabetical order. Give a person your address—the corner of first and Elm—and anyone who had ever been to town once could find it without any trouble. Still, Owen double-checked the address twice before he knocked.

He wasn't sure why he was so apprehensive about meeting this girl he supposedly had known in high school. Maybe it had to do with the strange looks that passed between his aunt and uncle at the mention of her name. But it couldn't hurt to see her just once. If she had information that would help him, he wanted to know about it.

Steadying himself with a deep breath, Owen raised his hand and knocked twice. The door opened while his knuckles were still in midair.

Owen didn't remember much about women his age—only Willie and her sister, Rae, Stork Simpson's wife, Madge, and that one introduction to Cousin Libba at her wedding reception. But this woman had to be the most ravishing creature he had ever seen, memory or no memory. She was tall and shapely, with long blonde hair, blue eyes, and full, luscious lips. His heart skipped a beat, and he heard himself say, "JoLynn Ferber?"

"Owen," she purred, "I was hoping you'd come." She put a hand on his arm and drew him inside, and as soon as the door was shut behind him, she twined her arms around him and kissed him full on the mouth.

Owen tried to pull away, but she pressed against him until his back was up against the door with the doorknob pressing painfully into his spine. She continued to kiss him ardently, stroking the hair at the back of his neck. Almost against his will, Owen's knees buckled and a fire shot through him. When she finally drew away and looked into his eyes, he found himself breathless and a little shaky.

"I'm sorry, miss," he began, but his voice came out in a squeak, and he had to clear his throat and start again. "I apologize if this is embarrassing for either of us, but I really don't remember you."

She took his hand and led him over to the sofa. "I know, Owen," she said softly. "I could tell by the way you kissed me—or rather, didn't kiss me." She smiled sadly and sat down beside him. "I was hoping that I could, well, stimulate your memory a bit."

Owen stared at her, not at all certain that it was his memory she had intended to stimulate. "I have coffee ready in the kitchen," she said, rising to her feet and moving toward the doorway. "Would you like pie as well? It's coconut custard."

He nodded. "Sure. That's fine. But—"

"I'll be right back."

While she was gone, Owen took the opportunity to look around the tiny house and regain some of his lost composure. He withdrew a handkerchief from his pocket and wiped the lipstick off his face, then settled back on the sofa cushions and studied the room. The furniture was obviously second-hand. Nothing matched. The coffee table was scarred and battered, but everything looked clean, and there were bright touches of color from scarves and decorative pillows. A small brick fireplace in the far wall was neatly laid with logs and kindling, and a framed landscape print over the mantel lent a homey atmosphere to the place. Not much money, Owen concluded, but enough style to make something out of nothing.

By the time she returned with the coffee and pie, Owen's initial impression of JoLynn Ferber had tempered somewhat. Evidently there had been something between them at one time; it had to be hard for her, too, to discover that he didn't even know her. But if she had been, as Uncle Earl and Aunt Gert had implied, a friend of his—or even a girlfriend—in high school, what connection did she have with him now? And why was she so sure she could help him in his quest to discover himself?

"Sugar?" she asked, lifting her eyebrows at him.

"No thanks." He took a bite of the pie and a sip of the coffee, then leaned back and looked at her. She was pretty, that much was certain, although she had spent a little too much time, perhaps, in the cosmetics department. "What do you do for a living, JoLynn?" he asked, taking refuge in small talk. "Or perhaps you are married?"

She gave him a curious look and said, "No, I'm not married. I wait tables at the cafe six days a week. And four nights a week at the tavern."

"So that's how you knew I was in town. Uncle Earl—"

"A person has to work hard to keep a secret in this town," she said cryptically, as if she knew what she was talking about. "I was working last night and saw you get off the bus. As soon as Vallie came up to you, I knew who you were." She reached out a slim hand and stroked his beard. "Even with this hiding your face."

"I'm not hiding," he protested. "Don't you like it?"

Owen could have kicked himself. Why had he said such a thing to a woman he had just met? Had her kiss affected him that much?

She shifted her hand to his knee and squeezed. "Yes, I believe I do like it. It's . . . curly, like your hair."

Curly. Owen's stomach lurched, and his mind flashed back to the day he had bought the pup for Willie. When she named the dog Curly, it set off a whole series of unexplained feelings in him, emotions he couldn't identify. He had wondered, in that moment, whether he had once had a sweetheart who had called him by that name, someone who was still waiting for him, hoping he was alive. And he had been determined to find out, one way or another.

Was it possible that this woman, this JoLynn Ferber, was the one? That his relationship with her had been more than just a high school infatuation?

Owen sat up straight and removed her hand from his knee. He had to know, whether he remembered anything or not, if he had made some kind of promise to this girl. Something that would prevent him from allowing himself to love Willie Coltrain. Something that would bind him here, rather than giving him the freedom to go. . . .

Home.

The thought shocked him. How had he come to think of Eden, Mississippi, as home, rather than here, where he had blood kin and a family homestead and a history? And how could he make himself feel differently if it turned out that he was obligated to stay in North Fork, Iowa?

Owen turned to JoLynn and forced himself to meet her gaze. "I'm sorry if this seems blunt," he said, "but I have to know. Exactly what was our relationship, if you don't mind my asking? Uncle Earl said we knew one another in high school, but—"

Just then the front door flew open and a boy about six years of age barreled into the room. He skidded to a stop in front of JoLynn, tossed a baseball glove into her lap, and eyed Owen's half-eaten slice of coconut pie. "Is there any more pie?" he demanded. "I'm starving."

JoLynn grasped him firmly by the shoulders and raised one eyebrow. "Where are your manners, Buddy Ferber?" she said. "We have a guest."

She turned the boy around to face Owen. He was a ruddy-faced lad with mischievous brown eyes, a sprinkling of freckles across his turned-up nose, and a wild mop of curly blondish hair. "Buddy, this gentleman is Owen Slaughter."

Buddy grinned at Owen and gave him a firm handshake. "Nice to meet you," he said politely.

"Owen, I'd like you to meet Buddy. Your son."

20

Breckinridge & Company

Grenada, Mississippi
June 30, 1945

Orris Craven entered the opulent foyer of the Jefferson House Hotel feeling
for all the world like a country hick come to town for the first time. He
craned his neck and looked up at the massive chandelier, then down at the
two inches of plush pile under his shoes. He didn't know what was wrong
with him—after all, he had hobnobbed at the Peabody with the most
influential and powerful men in the South. This meeting with the legal
representative of the Breckinridge Foundation, however, had him as agitated as a wet cat. Maybe it was because his job was on the line.

Colonel Laporte had flatly refused to meet with Mrs. Breckinridge. He
wanted to keep a low profile, he insisted, ordering Orris to do whatever was
necessary—even pretend to be Laporte—in order to get the job done.

Orris hadn't always been scrupulous about the truth, of course. In this
business, a man did what he had to do to get ahead, especially if that man's
mentor and supporter was Clinton Marston. But lately Orris's conscience
had been nagging at him. He kept thinking about his mother, about all she
had sacrificed to send him to law school, about how she believed he would
do something honorable and noble with his life. And try as he might, Orris
couldn't get her out of his mind.

It was all that Laporte woman's fault. She reminded him too much of
Mother, with her gentle probing, her interest in his life, her obvious pride
in her own son. Irrational as it might be, he felt like the second son, being

held up for comparison with Andrew the Golden Boy. His conversation with Mrs. Laporte had resurrected the memory of his mother, and now he couldn't rid himself of the aggravating voice of his conscience. He felt— what was it? Shame. And he wished he had never met the woman.

Suddenly Orris felt a presence behind him, and he turned to face a tall, black-suited maître d' with a crisp white towel folded over one arm.

"May I help you, sir?" The maître d' looked down his long nose with an expression that said clearly that Orris didn't belong here.

Orris tugged at his tie. "Yes," he began with a squeak, then cleared his throat and tried again. "Yes," he repeated in his best professional voice. "I am meeting some . . . business associates. A Mr. Winsom and a Mrs. Breckinridge."

The waiter gave him another condescending look and extended one arm. "Right this way, sir."

Orris kept his eyes on the ramrod-straight back of the maître d' as they went down a long hallway and turned into a small private dining room on the left. "Your party, sir," the man said formally, then disappeared.

Orris squinted, trying to get his eyes to adjust to the softly lit room. At a table in one corner sat three people—a middle-aged man and woman, and a second gentleman about his own age. He took a step or two forward, and the older man rose and approached him.

"Mr. Craven, I presume," the man said, shaking his hand and giving him a curious look.

Orris faltered. Of course they would assume he was Craven. He had written the letter, set up the appointment. He'd never get away with trying to pretend to be Beauregard Laporte. He might as well not try. Nervous as he was, he would probably make some kind of stupid mistake and give himself away, anyway.

"Yes," he answered. "And you are—"

"Bennett Winsom, attorney for the Breckinridge Foundation." Mr. Winsom frowned at him. "You're alone? I thought I made it clear in my letter that your employer was also expected to attend this meeting."

Orris's insides twisted. "Mr. —uh, my employer had other matters to attend to," he stammered. "I am fully empowered to negotiate on his behalf."

"Certainly," the lawyer said smoothly. "I suppose we can at least do some preliminary work until he becomes available."

Mr. Winsom led Orris to the table and stood with one hand on his elbow. "Mr. Craven, I'd like you to meet Aurelia Breckinridge, founder and chairwoman of the Breckinridge Foundation."

Orris found himself looking into the warm brown eyes of a gracious, red-haired woman who extended one gloved hand toward him. She looked vaguely familiar, but he couldn't place her. He shook her hand formally. "I'm very pleased to meet you, Mrs. Breckinridge. Your . . . ah, reputation as a benefactress . . . is well known."

A hint of a smile touched the woman's lips. "Indeed," she murmured. "Do sit down, Mr. Craven."

Just as Orris was about to sit, Mr. Winsom pulled the chair out for him, and he nearly ended up on the floor. *Wonderful,* he thought grimly. *I'm supposed to be making a good impression, and I put on a slapstick act like the Keystone Kops.* He righted himself and tugged at the lapels of his suit coat.

"I'm Drew." The young man across the table stood up and extended his hand. "Mr. Winsom's assistant."

"Mr. Winsom's partner," the older man corrected.

"Mr. Drew," Orris acknowledged. "Craven. Orris Craven."

Mr. Winsom resumed his seat and motioned toward the doorway. Instantly a waiter appeared with a tray of appetizers and four glasses of iced tea. "I thought perhaps we could have dinner first and get to know each other a little," he said. "Then we'll get down to business."

★ ★ ★

All during dinner, Thelma watched the thin, pale young lawyer with a mixture of pity and amusement. She had seen him before, but when? Then it came to her—the angry young man at the courthouse. Of course. He had been there, intending to take over Ivory's property, and had been furious when they had bested him. Did he recognize her and Bennett? Evidently not, or if he did, he gave no sign of it.

The poor fellow shifted uncomfortably, picking at his food and tugging at the knot of his necktie. He stumbled through basic conversation, obviously overwhelmed at the prospect of being in the presence of a great and wealthy lady such as herself.

Then, somewhere between the entree and the dessert, Thelma began to have a nagging unrest in her spirit about Orris Craven. Something was bothering him, something more than just this deal. He avoided her eyes, and when she caught his glance a time or two, she saw an expression she could only define as guilt. She had said little to him other than the perfunctory small talk over the meal, and yet she sensed a deep need in him, something she couldn't quite put her finger on.

Pray for him, a voice inside her urged.

Pray? For a little rat of a lawyer whose sole purpose in life was to cheat innocent people out of what was rightfully theirs? Pray for a man who apparently had no concept of right and wrong . . . or didn't care?

Thelma continued with her dinner, resisting the urge to offer Orris Craven—and whatever was disturbing him so—to the Almighty. Bennett had been right about setting up the meeting here at the Jefferson House. The surroundings were perfect for her facade as a wealthy widow. The food was fabulous. And Orris Craven was already on the defensive. It was money well spent.

She looked down at her plate and picked a last forkful of fish away from the bone. The skeleton lay across her plate, its glassy eye staring up at her, with one small piece of baked potato skin lodged between the ribs.

It looks like Jonah, she thought, *captured in the belly of the great fish.*

Suddenly the image sprang to life in her mind. Jonah, refusing to do God's bidding and preach salvation to the people of Nineveh for fear they might hear and repent. Jonah didn't think the Ninevites deserved the Lord's grace and mercy. He had the chance to be part of a miraculous work of God's Spirit, but he resisted the call.

As conversation hummed around her, Thelma smiled and nodded and pretended to be interested, but her mind was on Orris Craven, the pain she had seen in his eyes, the nudging in her spirit to pray for him. It didn't matter if he was a sinner or a saint. He was a person who evidently needed prayer.

And so Thelma prayed. On the outside she continued to smile and nod and carry on polite small talk, but on the inside, she was asking God to touch this young man and meet his needs, to work in the midst of the guilt and pain she had seen, to reconcile him to the Almighty. And as she prayed, Thelma reached into the fish's ribs with her fork, released the baked-potato Jonah, and set him safely on the side of her plate.

★ ★ ★

As dinner drew to a close, Orris Craven found himself relaxing a little. They seemed like genuinely nice people, and he wondered briefly if he could have made a mistake about their operation. But, no, the letter Mr. Winsom had sent to him was quite clear. They would be able to do business. And it would be on Orris's terms.

He could deal with the two lawyers just fine. But Mrs. Aurelia Breckinridge was another matter. Every time she looked at him, he got the feeling she was looking *into* him, seeing his soul. The idea made him distinctly uneasy, and he avoided her gaze whenever possible.

At last the dessert plates had been cleared away, and the waiter brought more coffee. It was time, in Mr. Winsom's words, to "get down to business."

Orris reached into his briefcase and drew out a file folder labeled Southern Historical Preservation Society. He flipped through the papers and pulled out the contracts he had already prepared—a merger between the SHPS and the Breckinridge Foundation, specifying that all information about "appropriate properties" should come directly to him before any purchases were made. What Winsom and his cohorts didn't know was that a good many of those properties would be bought up by Laporte's other corporations before the Breckinridge Foundation had a chance at them. Not enough of them to arouse suspicion, but enough—the choicest selections—to line Laporte's pockets and his own for years to come. In return, Orris would shift a few properties of lesser value to the Breckinridge Foundation, just to keep up the appearance of equality.

Orris was in his element now. Briefly and with businesslike precision, he outlined the terms of the contract and then slid the copies in Bennett Winsom's direction. "All you need to do is sign here," he said with a smile, "and we'll be all set."

Mr. Winsom picked up the contract and scanned it. "Yes," he murmured, nodding. "This all seems to be in order. There's just one other little matter we need to discuss."

He shot a glance at his young associate, Mr. Drew, who reached down into his briefcase, came up with two thick folders full of papers, and slammed them onto the table so heavily that Orris's coffee sloshed into the saucer.

"What's all this?" Orris asked, frantically mopping up the coffee with his napkin.

"All this," Mr. Drew said with a crafty smile, "is the record of activities from your other corporations." He flipped through the papers and read at random: "Historical Society of Tennessee, three-hundred-acre horse farm. Arkansas Preservation Society, four hundred acres and a river-bluff mansion. South Texas Archival Interests, Inc. —" He flashed a crooked grin at Orris. "Shall I go on?"

A cold sweat broke out on Orris's forehead, and his hand began to shake. "I-I don't know what you're talking about."

The young lawyer's smile never wavered. "Of course you do. I'm talking about a dozen or more 'historical societies' just like the SHPS, all under the ownership and control of a single organization." He pulled out a copy of a purchase agreement and held it in midair over the table. "Your signature, Mr. Craven. As representative of the North Georgia Trust. Some of the others are signed by a Clinton Marston of Memphis, Tennessee." He lifted one eyebrow. "Shouldn't be too difficult to find the connection between yourself and Mr. Marston, I would guess."

Mr. Winsom leaned in close and said in a low voice, "A paper trail like this would not be tolerated by the Breckinridge Foundation, Mr. Craven. Sloppy work. Totally unacceptable. Do we understand each other?"

In his mind's eye, Orris could see the furious expression on Beauregard Laporte's florid face when he heard this bit of news. He would be fired for sure—not only fired but blackballed. Laporte's prophecy would be fulfilled. Orris would end up working the graveyard shift, sweeping peanut shells and broken whiskey bottles out of some sleazy all-night jazz joint on Bourbon Street.

"What-what are our options?" he managed in a shaky voice.

Winsom leaned back in his chair and crossed his arms. "Options?" He turned to Mrs. Breckinridge and laughed. "He wants to talk about options."

Until this moment, the elegant lady had let her attorneys do all the talking. Now she straightened her back and leveled her gaze on Orris. "Perhaps we need to return to our original request—the one which has not yet been fulfilled."

"Request?" Orris squeaked. "What request?"

Mr. Winsom planted both hands squarely on the table. "A face-to-face conference with your employer," he said. "Mrs. Breckinridge does not like to do business with anonymous partners."

"But-but—"

"But your employer does not wish to reveal himself," Winsom interrupted. "Fine. You may relay this message to him: Either he deals with us directly, on our terms, or all the information we have on your so-called historical preservation corporations will be turned over to the authorities."

In spite of himself, Orris laughed. "You won't do that. You'd be calling attention to your own operation."

Winsom froze him with a scathing look. "I have already told you, Mr. Craven, that the Breckinridge Foundation leaves no paper trail. Our organization is completely clean. If you don't believe that, I challenge you to find the kind of information we have on you."

Orris looked into Winsom's eyes and knew he was telling the truth. They had him, and there was nothing he could do about it. He was beaten.

"All right," he said wearily. "What do you want?"

Mr. Winsom glanced at his associate, who handed a list across to Orris. "Full disclosure of all your business dealings. Contact names, purchases, financial records. Mining and mineral reports."

Orris shook his head. They knew. They knew everything. He was dead in the water.

"Lists of prospective acquisitions," Mr. Drew continued. "And a merger contract that includes every one of your corporate organizations, not just the Southern Historical Preservation Society."

"One company's holdings in exchange for a dozen?" Orris repeated incredulously. "That doesn't sound like a very fair deal to me."

"I doubt that 'fair deal' is a concept you're very familiar with," Mr. Winsom snapped. "Your only other option is to be shut down completely, and we'll find out the other information about your prospective purchases on our own. It will just take a little extra legwork."

"I-I'll need some time."

Winsom nodded. "Sixty days. If we don't have an agreement by September one—"

"I know, I know!" Orris snatched the contract off the table and stuffed it back in his briefcase. He couldn't breathe, his heart was palpitating, and his stomach was churning wildly. He had to get out of here. Now. Before he lost his expensive dinner.

"I'll be in touch," he muttered, lurching to his feet and tipping the chair over.

"We'll look forward to hearing from you," Aurelia Breckinridge said sweetly as he headed for the door. "And to meeting your employer."

★ ★ ★

"I thought he was going to faint!" Drew shouted when the pale young lawyer was gone. "We did it—we really did it!"

"Well, we've started the process, anyway," Bennett said. "But we won't do any permanent good until we've flushed out the man who holds the reins."

"He admitted that all these corporations were just fronts for the one organization." Drew hefted one of the folders. "The information we've got here is enough to shut them down."

"But not enough to put the brakes on the big boss," Bennett countered. "If he gets away, he'll just do it again, only he'll be smarter next time and harder to catch."

Thelma stripped off her gloves and sighed. Playing the part of a rich society matron exhausted her, and the niggling concern about Orris Craven's spiritual condition hadn't gone away. But they had done the right thing, she was sure of that. If there was a way to put these people out of business, they had to do it before other innocent people like Ivory Brownlee fell prey to their schemes.

"I'm worried about him."

Bennett turned to her with an incredulous expression. "About whom?"

"About that Craven boy. He's so young, and—"

"He's a snake, Thelma. He may look innocent and naive, but he's obviously been doing this for some time."

"He's in pain. I think his conscience is bothering him, and—"

"If he has a conscience, it *should* be bothering him," Bennett interrupted. "But what makes you so sure he's bothered by anything—except maybe the prospect of losing his job?"

"I could see it in his eyes," Thelma mused. "He's troubled."

"He's *in* trouble, you mean," Drew said.

Thelma shook her head. They hadn't seen it, hadn't sensed what she had from that poor misguided boy. "I felt as if God wanted me to pray for him," she said quietly. "And I resisted at first. But when I finally did pray, I knew there was something in him, something better than what he is now." She looked at Bennett and felt tears stinging her eyes. "Everybody's got the potential to be honorable, you know. It may be buried deep inside him, so deep he doesn't even realize it himself, but God can bring it out."

"Like the Lord did with you?" Bennett asked quietly, sitting down beside her and taking her hand.

"I guess so. I just know that no one is beyond redemption, with the right kind of support."

Bennett seemed to think about this for a minute, and his countenance softened. "Do you want us to give this up?"

Thelma shook her head vehemently. "No. This is important. And it might just be the catalyst to bring that boy back to himself." She squeezed Bennett's hand, suddenly thankful for what God had done to turn her life around, to prepare her for a man like this. "I just want us to pray for him," she whispered.

"All right, sweetheart." Bennett leaned over and kissed her on the cheek. "We'll pray. And we'll trust God to bring some good out of this for Orris Craven."

Thelma sagged against him for a moment, drawing strength from his presence. If God could rescue her from her sordid past, renew her, and give her a love like Bennett Winsom, then surely God's grace was sufficient to bring someone like Orris Craven back to the fold.

She would pray. God would do the rest.

21

Independence Day

Eden, Mississippi
July 4, 1945

As Libba turned the Nash Ambassador off the main highway onto the state road that ran into Eden, she felt her heart surge with anticipation, and she reached out and squeezed Link's hand.

"Nervous?" he asked, stroking her hand and giving her a tender smile.

"Just excited." She paused and glanced at him. "It seems like we've been away a long time, doesn't it?"

"It's only been a few weeks," he mused. "But we've been so busy. I never dreamed it would take so much time to take my entrance tests, find you a job, arrange for an apartment, and all. Of course, we lost two weeks in Memphis." He raised his eyebrows in a rakish expression.

"I wouldn't call our honeymoon lost time exactly," she quipped. "And you did spend a number of those days at the hospital in physical therapy."

"Ah, yes," he sighed melodramatically. "Now, *that* was lost time. While I was being poked and prodded and stretched, we could have been back in our room at the Peabody, doing our own range-of-motion exercises and—"

Libba felt a warm flush rise to her cheeks, and she slapped his hand. "Link! Behave yourself!"

"There's no one here but us," he protested, leaning across the seat to kiss her on the neck.

"Us and a couple of police cars, if you make me run off the road." She gave him a playful shove back toward his seat.

"All right, all right." He settled back and patted the cane that sat propped between them. "I must admit, however, that the physical therapy is helping. Pretty soon I should be able to drive, and it won't be long before I won't even need this anymore."

Libba's eyes rested on the wooden cane. In an odd, backward way, it represented the fulfillment of all her hopes and desires. For most people, walking with a cane would be an inconvenience, a disadvantage. For Link, it was a victory. For him—and for her, for their life together—it meant liberty, the freedom to live out their dreams. Link was walking with more strength and confidence every day. Now they had an apartment of their own, she had landed a job in the library, and Link had been admitted to law school. They were on their way.

"I was just thinking," Link mused as he leaned his head back against the seat, "what a funny honeymoon we've had."

Libba cut a wry glance at him. "What a romantic thing to say, sweetheart. You really know how to charm a girl."

"I didn't mean it like that," he laughed. "But think about it. We spent three days alone at the Peabody, and then for the past five and a half weeks we've bounced from your Aunt Mag's and the hospital in Memphis to Freddy Sturgis's house in Oxford." He straightened up and grinned at her. "Believe me, darling, if anyone had told me I'd spend half my honeymoon as a guest of my wife's old boyfriend, I would have said they were crazy."

"Aunt Mag loved having us. I think she got used to me staying with her while you were hospitalized at Kennedy General, and she's been lonely since I left. As for Freddy, he's just a friend, and you know it. Besides, his offer was a godsend. We never could have afforded the necessary time in Oxford if we'd been paying for a hotel. And he was very sweet, you'll have to admit."

"Yes, he was nice," Link agreed reluctantly. "I just hope he doesn't have any ideas about—"

"Freddy's only 'ideas' are about his painting, Link. Not about me. There was never anything between me and Freddy—nothing serious, anyway. He couldn't be happier for us."

Link narrowed his eyes at her. "Well, if you say so. And he is turning into a pretty good artist. That portrait he did of us for your Christmas present was something else, wasn't it?"

Libba nodded. "I think that was the first time I knew—really knew—that everything was going to be all right between us. Freddy helped me understand why you would do what you did—tell me you didn't love me and send me away. . . ."

Her words drifted into silence as she thought about that difficult time, and an old leftover pain wrenched at her heart. Only God's grace and Freddy's support had gotten her through that lonely Christmas, separated from the man she loved both by distance and by misunderstanding.

"I'm sorry for that, Libba," Link said softly. "I didn't mean to hurt you."

Tears stung her eyes, and she blinked them back. "I know, sweetheart. It's all in the past." She looked over at him, and the expression of love on his face melted her. "I don't think I ever told you what happened to me when Freddy gave me the portrait."

He shook his head. "Tell me now."

"I felt as if I had been transported fifty years into the future," she whispered, keeping her eyes on the road ahead. "I could see us together, celebrating our anniversary, with Freddy's portrait behind us. In spite of all the struggles we were going through at the time, I saw it so clearly, and I knew at that moment that somehow everything would work out."

Link captured her hand and kissed it tenderly on the palm. "I promise," he said in a husky voice, "that I will do everything in my power not to hurt you like that again."

She stroked his cheek, and a lump formed in her throat. "If I hadn't known that," she said, "I wouldn't have married you."

★ ★ ★

Thelma went to the door of the cafe and stood with one hand over her eyes, peering down the road. Link and Libba had promised to be here by three, and it was two-thirty now.

She hadn't told them on the phone how badly their presence was needed—only that they had planned a big Independence Day celebration, that everyone was going to gather at the cafe, drive to Grenada Lake for a late-afternoon picnic, and then watch the fireworks over the lake. Stork and Madge and Mickey had already left, promising to save a good spot for the picnic. If Link and Libba got here on time, Thelma should have a good hour with them before the others arrived.

She didn't see any point in worrying them unnecessarily, but she needed some time alone to fill them in on recent developments. They didn't know yet that Owen was gone, and they would undoubtedly be shocked at the change in Mabel Rae. The poor girl was physically well enough, Thelma supposed—or so her doctor said. But emotionally she was in terrible shape. She hardly ever smiled, and she seemed to have no joy at all in the prospect of motherhood.

Thelma didn't know for sure, but she suspected that part of the problem was Drew. The boy was an inveterate worker, and when he wasn't on the road to Jackson or Memphis or Little Rock, he was bent over his desk burning the midnight oil in the new offices of Winsom & Laporte on Main Street. Thelma loved Drew, and she appreciated his tireless labor on Ivory's behalf, but he was so involved in this case that he couldn't see what was right in front of him. His wife.

Thelma had overheard one conversation between the two of them here in the cafe—Rae trying to tell Drew about everything that needed to be done at home to get ready for the baby, and Drew half-listening, nodding, with one eye on the clock and the other on the file in front of him. It wasn't her business to get involved in anybody's marriage, but Thelma had to restrain herself from going over and shaking Drew by the shoulders to wake him up. He kept assuring Rae that it would all get done as soon as he was finished with this case. But he wasn't listening. He wasn't seeing. Even from a distance Thelma couldn't miss the look of despair on Mabel Rae's face, the plaintive tone in her voice. About everything else, Drew was bright and alert and flawless. But when it came to his own wife, he was deaf and blind.

And Willie! When Thelma heard about Owen leaving a note for Willie and just disappearing, she felt the pain in her own heart. How many years had it been since she found the note from Robert Raintree pinned to her screen door? Yet she remembered like it was yesterday the hurt, the despair, the feeling that nothing would ever be right again. And what could she say to Willie? Wait twenty years, and the right man will come along? Just have faith, trust God?

Willie deserved better than that. It was bad enough losing the person you loved when you only had to go through it once. Willie had endured it three times—once when she thought Owen was dead, once when he came back but didn't remember her, and now, when he had left again to "find himself." Only God knew what he would find, and whether his search would ever bring him back to Willie Coltrain. In the meantime, what were her friends supposed to do to support and comfort her?

The only comfort Willie seemed to find these days was in the dog Owen had bought for her—the little brown spaniel. Willie had named her Curly, and all of them knew why. It had been Willie's nickname for Owen when they had first met. That dog never left her side. She slept on the foot of Willie's bed and followed her everywhere, almost as if she knew Willie needed a friend who wouldn't let her down.

That's why it was so important to Thelma that Link and Libba get here for this Independence Day picnic. Rae and Willie were both so caught up in their own struggles that they couldn't be much help to each other. Thelma couldn't seem to do anything either . . . except pray. But maybe Libba, who had been like a sister to both of them, might be able to break through those walls and bring some comfort and encouragement. Thelma was counting on it.

She was just about to go back inside and check to make sure everything was packed and ready to go when she heard a horn in the distance. She held her breath and waited, then sighed with relief when a car came into view and slid to a stop in front of the cafe.

Libba jumped out of the driver's seat and ran toward Thelma, her auburn curls glinting in the afternoon sun. She caught Thelma up in an enormous hug and laughed out loud. "I am so glad to be here!"

"Welcome home, honey," Thelma said, blinking back tears and holding her tightly. *Here, at least, was one prayer answered.*

Libba sat on the bank of Grenada Lake and stretched her legs out in front of her. The sun was setting, and the high clouds caught the last rays of pink and purple and spangled a glorious show of light and color across the sky and down into the water. One star glimmered faintly on the eastern horizon. One star.

The sight of it, hanging there against a patch of deepening blue, brought an image unbidden to Libba's mind—the small star banner that had hung in the window of the Coltrain farmhouse through all those difficult months. Charlie's star. In her mind, it had been Link's star too, and Owen's. Three men, thought to be dead on the battlefields of Europe. Three women, mourning the loss of their lovers, their brother, their cousin, their friends.

Yet they had been alive all that time. Link in a hospital ward, writing letters to her that she never received. Charlie and Owen, miraculously drawn together in a German prison camp.

There was a fine line between death and life, Libba mused as she looked across the bank and saw Willie staring into the calm waters. A person could be technically alive, still breathing and eating and going about the daily business of existence, without any purpose for it, any significance to the routine. Libba wondered if this final loss of Owen Slaughter might not be the last straw on the back of Willie's hope, the thing that broke her spirit once and for all.

She fervently hoped not. She prayed that her cousin would rebound as she had always done, taking the difficulties and uncertainties of life in stride. Willie had so much life, so much joy and vitality inside her, but it had been buried under an avalanche of sorrow and defeat. While everyone around her was moving on with life—developing relationships, having babies, making plans—Willie was stuck in the past. How many times could she let herself love Owen Slaughter, only to lose him, without completely losing faith in life itself? Once perhaps, or even twice, a person as strong as Willie might regain her equilibrium from such a blow. Three times seemed too much to ask.

Libba caught a movement out of the corner of her eye and turned to look. Mabel Rae was pacing back and forth on the top of the hill, peering down the road into the distance. She had gone up there right after supper, looking for Drew to come and join them as he had promised. But it was nearly dark now, and there was no sign of him. In the dim light, against the backdrop of sky and sunset, Libba could see Rae's shoulders drooping in disappointment.

From what Thelma had told them, Rae, too, was having a hard time. The combination of Drew's preoccupation with his work and Rae's fear for the health and safety of her baby had dealt a one-two punch to her dream of the perfect marriage with the perfect man. Rae had confided in Madge, and to some extent in Thelma, and both of them were praying for her and supporting her, but she still seemed terribly alone and afraid.

Libba heaved a sigh. She wanted to help her cousins, but what could she do? She wouldn't be in Eden for long—she and Link were making the eighty-mile trip back to Oxford on Monday to set up housekeeping in their apartment, and her job in the library began a week later. She couldn't be here for them.

But God could. The realization came suddenly, followed by a second thought: *And they can be here for each other.*

Breathing a quick prayer for guidance, Libba jumped to her feet and went down the bank to where Willie still sat, staring. She stood behind her cousin for a minute, then plopped down on the grass beside her. Willie did not look up.

"It's nearly dark. The fireworks will be starting soon," Libba began.

"Uh-huh," Willie muttered.

"Should be a big celebration, with the war in Europe over now."

"Uh-huh."

"If only the fighting would end in the Pacific, too. Then we could *really* celebrate."

"Uh-huh."

Libba put an arm around her cousin's shoulders. "Are you all right, Willie?"

"All right?" Willie turned and gave her a vicious look. "Sure, Libba, I'm just fine and dandy. Perfect. Life is wonderful." Her tone was as sarcastic as her expression.

"Stupid question," Libba said.

"I'm sorry." Willie's voice softened, and she turned her face away. "You didn't deserve that." She shook her head. "It's just that—well, I don't know how much more of this I can take. I feel like a yo-yo being snatched up and down. First Owen's here, then he's gone. Then he's dead, now he's alive, but he's gone again." She shifted toward Libba and sighed. "I know you mean well, Libba, but you can't understand what I'm going through. Nobody can. Look around at this little group of ours. Thelma and Bennett have eyes only for each other. Ditto for Madge and Stork. You've just come back from your honeymoon, for heaven's sake. Mabel Rae is married to her dream man and about to give birth to her first child—"

Libba held up a hand. "Mabel Rae's dream isn't what it once was."

"I know. She's having a hard time right now. Forgive me if I don't fall down with compassion because she and her husband are having a little tiff. At least she's got a husband. And a baby. And a future."

Libba waited while Willie blew off steam. When the tirade had wound down to its conclusion, she said softly, "Rae needs you."

"Rae doesn't need me," Willie countered. "Rae doesn't even talk to me anymore."

"Maybe she doesn't know how."

Willie considered this for a minute, then frowned at Libba. "What do you mean?"

"Well, look at the situation. She's upset and afraid and probably lonely. I don't know all the details, but I know enough to see that she's hurting. She needs family—she needs you. Her dream isn't turning out like she hoped. But how can she talk to you about her fears and confusion when you're going through so much yourself?"

Libba could see tears welling up in Willie's eyes, glistening in the fading light. "I can't be strong for her right now, Libba. I just can't."

"I know you can't. You don't have to be strong. Just be there. Love her. Let her love you. Be her sister."

A tear tracked down Willie's cheek, and she swiped it away. "I need her, too."

"Yes, you do. You can help each other get through this, if only—" Libba stopped suddenly, not sure how to continue.

"If only we can set our own problems aside long enough to care about each other's," Willie finished.

"Something like that. Don't you see, Willie, you don't have to be a rock all the time, to solve Rae's problems or anyone else's." Libba remembered the advice Aunt Mag had given her when she was in Memphis searching for Link, and she smiled to herself. It was good advice then, and true for Willie as well. "Just be there and let her do her own healing. And let her be there for you."

Willie nodded, then craned her neck toward the top of the bank, where Rae continued to pace back and forth. "She's still waiting for Drew?"

"Yes."

"I'll go talk to her."

"Let me go first," Libba said, getting to her feet. "I'll be back in a minute."

Willie watched the two silhouettes on the top of the bank, lit from behind by the last rays of sunset. Libba was right, and she knew it. It was like their situation more than a year ago when the fellows had shipped out, and later when they thought that Owen and Link were both dead. The only thing that kept them all from being consumed by their grief and sorrow was the sense of family that they shared, the realization that they were not alone.

Willie's eyes rested on the familiar round figure of her sister, and deep inside her soul love welled up, and longing. Rae was her family—the closest kin she had left in the world. With Mama and Daddy and Charlie gone, all they had was each other. And they had almost lost that by letting their differences come between them.

They had always been so close, sharing each other's secrets, knowing each other's heart. When had they drifted apart?

In a flash of insight Willie saw a series of mental images that answered her question. Mabel Rae, keeping her love for Drew hidden because she didn't want to hurt Willie and Libba, who were mourning the loss of Owen and Link. Herself, angry and isolated at the farm, tending to Mama and Daddy all alone. That terrible moment when she found out Rae had gotten married in New Orleans, with none of her own family present, and Willie's dream of sharing her sister's wedding came crashing down.

A sliver, here and there, of anger and mistrust and even well-meaning pretense, had combined to create a wedge that had driven them into their private worlds. Under the same roof, sharing the same meals, both of them had been orphans, alone in the universe, with no family to help bear the burden of their sorrows.

With tears clouding her vision, Willie looked up to see Rae and Libba coming down the bank toward her. She leaped to her feet and ran toward her sister, who met her halfway with arms outstretched and tears staining her own cheeks.

She caught Rae in a desperate embrace and held on tight. "I'm sorry," she murmured over and over into her sister's ear. "I'm so sorry."

Willie didn't know how long they stood there like that, awkwardly trying to keep their footing on the sloping bank, weeping on each other's shoulders. But it was a cleansing moment, when all their differences were washed away and they were, once more, sisters—not just in blood but in heart and soul and mind.

At last Willie took a shuddering breath and stepped back. With one hand she wiped the tears from Rae's cheeks and gave her a twisted smile. "You look pretty awful, Sister."

Rae laughed. "And you look awful pretty." She wrapped an arm around Willie's waist and looked up at her. "I love you, you know."

"I know. Me, too," Willie said. "First thing tomorrow we'll go into Grenada and look for wallpaper for the baby's room. Have a nice long lunch, just the two of us. Would you like that?"

"I'd love it."

Together they walked down the bank and sat down beside Libba, who had joined the rest of the group. Thelma looked over her shoulder and smiled, then turned and whispered something in Bennett Winsom's ear.

Willie didn't need to know what it was. She was pretty sure Thelma had been praying mightily for both of them. And maybe her prayers were beginning to be answered.

Then suddenly the black sky was ablaze with light and color, and the ground shuddered beneath them with the noise of the explosions. Above them in the air and below them in the water, bright fireworks lit the night with celebration

Willie felt Rae lean against her shoulder, and she smiled.

22

Dependence Day

North Fork, Iowa
July 4, 1945

Owen Slaughter sat at the kitchen table with his head in his hands, watching as Aunt Gert packed a basket full of fried chicken, potato salad, and thick slices of homemade bread. It should have looked delicious, but his stomach churned like a cement mixer, and Gert's cheerful chatter was beginning to irritate him.

Finally he looked up at her and made a face. "Aunt Gert, talk to me."

"That's what I thought I was doing, sweetie," she responded. "Do you want chocolate cake or strawberry-rhubarb pie? I've got both. Or I could give you some of each."

"I don't care," he snapped. "I want you—or somebody—to tell me what to do."

Gert stopped flitting around the room, wiped her hands on her apron, and came to sit across from him. She took his hands in hers and looked him directly in the eye. "Owen, no one else can tell you what to do. You have to follow your own heart."

Owen sighed. She was right, but that particular truth was the last thing he wanted to hear at the moment. "Is it possible, Aunt Gert, that I could have a son? A six-year-old son? And not even remember *that?*"

Gert smiled sadly at him and patted his hand. "Exactly what did JoLynn Ferber tell you?"

"She said Buddy was my son."

"I know that much, sweetie. What else?"

"Apparently he was born in January of 1939 in Minneapolis. JoLynn was just barely eighteen and went to live with her older sister."

Aunt Gert nodded. "I remember when she left. It was shortly after you had graduated from high school and moved down to Des Moines."

"What was I doing in Des Moines?"

"You worked nights and went to college part-time. Came home for holidays, as I recall, when you could get a ride. Everybody thought it was a little strange, JoLynn up and leaving like that when she still had a year to graduation."

"And when she returned?"

"She just arrived in town one day—oh, about four years ago—with the little guy in tow. Took a job waitressing, and her mama watched the baby for her while she worked. People were curious, of course, but she never breathed a word about who the father was. Until now."

"Did people . . . treat her badly when she came back?"

Gert shrugged. "For a while there was a good bit of gossiping behind her back—speculating about the father, calling her a tramp, that kind of thing. A few people shunned her, and once a group from Wayside Baptist went down to her house to try to get her to repent. But folks lose interest in other people's troubles after a while. Eventually she and her son just became fixtures, part of the landscape of North Fork. Nobody thinks about it anymore."

"They'll think about it now," Owen said miserably.

"I suppose you're right," Gert mused. "Do you think there's any chance the girl might be wrong? Or lying?"

"You said yourself JoLynn and I were dating that spring. And she sure seemed to know me . . . ah, pretty intimately . . . when I went to see her."

Owen fell silent, thinking for a while about his first meeting with JoLynn Ferber. She was so pretty, so full of life, so young. And that house was so tiny. The knees of Buddy's dungarees were patched, he had noticed, but the boy was clean and polite and well brought up. It must have been hard for her, raising a child alone like that. Working two jobs trying to make ends meet.

He had gone back twice after that, trying to piece together the fragments of the story. When he had left Eden bound for North Fork, he had hoped to find some link to his past, some clues about who he was and where he belonged. He hadn't expected to find a ready-made family waiting for him.

"I've tried to find loopholes," he said half to himself. "Reasons to deny that her story is true."

"And what have you come up with?" Gert prompted.

"Nothing." He gave a deep sigh. "I came here, Aunt Gert, because I felt compelled to, as if there was something I needed to know. I had this sense—don't ask me how—that someone, somewhere, was waiting for me. And I couldn't go on with my life until I knew the truth. I didn't expect this, of course, but I have to admit that I . . . well, I experienced something . . . when I was with her."

"A memory?"

"Not exactly. More like—oh, I don't know." He shook his head and gave up in despair. After a while he said, "Gert, I have to do right by her."

His aunt gave him a curious look. "And that means, exactly—?"

"Apparently I made some promises to her. The fact that I don't remember any of it doesn't matter. I've got to sort out my obligation in all this."

"This is a small town, Owen. You won't be able to keep this quiet, and people will talk. Your reputation—"

"My reputation," he interrupted, "is not nearly as important as my responsibility."

Gert leaned over and kissed him on the cheek. "You may have lost your memories, Owen Slaughter, but you haven't lost your integrity. Whatever you decide to do, your Uncle Earl and I will support you."

"Thank you," Owen said. A wave of gratitude washed over him, and he squeezed her hand. "I can't tell you how much that means."

"Just two words of advice," Aunt Gert added. "First, make sure you're getting your guidance from the right place." She lifted her eyes heavenward, then fixed them on him again. "And second, try not to get honor confused with guilt. Or pity." She rose from her seat and retrieved the picnic basket from the counter. "Now, you'd better get going or you'll keep them waiting."

★ ★ ★

Owen drove slowly down the back roads toward town with one hand on the steering wheel and the other on Vallie's thick ruff. The dog loved to ride, especially with the top down. She lolled her head over the side of the car, grinning and barking occasionally at a rabbit in the road or a cow in a nearby pasture.

"Keep your nose out of the fried chicken," he warned when she began to investigate the picnic basket between them on the front seat. "There's something in there for you, but you can't have it until we all eat."

As if she had understood every word, the collie straightened up and cocked her head at him, then lay down on the seat and crossed her paws.

If only all relationships were this simple, Owen thought wistfully. Then he wouldn't have this eternal knot in his stomach and a pain at the base of his skull from trying to figure everything out.

They were waiting for him on the front stoop of the little green house, JoLynn with a basket of her own and Buddy with his baseball and glove. As soon as the boy caught sight of the dog, he ran to the curb and threw his arms around her neck. "Is this your dog?" he asked, stroking her fur.

"Yep. Her name is Valentine because I found her in a blizzard one February. Vallie for short."

"She's beautiful. Can she play with me?"

"I bet she'd love it." Owen smiled as the dog leaped over the side of the car onto the grass and began a game of tag with the child. Within a minute or two boy and dog were wrestling on the ground together; then Vallie caught sight of the baseball lying in the grass. She grabbed it, ran over to Owen, and plopped it at his feet.

Buddy sat up and gasped for air. "What's she doing?"

"She wants to play fetch." Owen tossed the ball in the boy's direction. "Throw it out there." He pointed toward the long backyard that butted up against a cornfield.

Buddy threw it, Vallie went after it, and the game was on.

"He's a nice kid." Owen took the basket from JoLynn's hands and placed it on the backseat.

"Yes, he is." Her eyes followed her son as he threw the ball again, and she smiled, an expression of love filling her eyes. "I'm very proud of him."

"You should be proud of yourself, too," Owen added. "You've done a wonderful job with him."

"Well, he's all boy, and he can be a handful sometimes, but I've never regretted having him. From the first time I held him—" She paused and turned her wide blue eyes on Owen. "You probably don't want to hear all this."

"Sure I do," Owen said lightly. "Go on."

Her expression softened and took on a faraway look. "That was a difficult time for me, those months I carried him. Being away from home and all. My mother wanted me to go, said it would be easier not to be in this gossipy little town. And maybe it was easier in some ways to be anonymous. But it was also very lonely."

"I'm . . . I'm sorry I wasn't there," Owen said awkwardly.

A strange look passed over her face, like a cloud crossing the sun, and then was gone. "Everybody tried to tell me what to do," she continued. "My sister, especially. She was determined that I would give the baby up, and I considered it. But I wouldn't sign the papers before he was born. And after that—well—as soon as I held him for the first time, I knew I couldn't do it. I didn't feel lonely anymore."

The pathos in her voice tugged at Owen's heart. He knew what it was like to feel utterly alone, to be separated from everything you knew—or in his case, everything he could no longer remember. It was a black hole that would suck you in and smother you unless you had something to hang on to. He'd had Charlie Coltrain. JoLynn Ferber had her son. *Their* son.

Buddy and Vallie came racing toward them, both panting with their tongues hanging out.

"She's great, Mr. Slaughter!" he shouted. "Can she be my friend?"

"Of course she can, Buddy." Owen ruffled the blond head. "Looks like she is already." He squatted down to the child's level and looked into his brown twinkling eyes. "And I'd like to be your friend too, Buddy. Do you think you could call me Owen?"

Buddy blinked at him, then looked to his mother. "Is that all right?"

"If he says so."

"All right . . . Owen," Buddy said awkwardly. Then without warning he threw his arms around Owen's neck and hugged him hard. "Are you . . . are you really my father?"

Tears clogged Owen's throat, so he couldn't speak. At last JoLynn said, "All right, boys, let's get this show on the road. I don't know about anybody else, but I'm hungry!"

Owen swung Buddy off his feet and settled him in the backseat, then whistled for Vallie. She jumped in and sat beside the boy, smiling her doggy smile as they set off toward the river.

The wind blowing through Owen's hair made him feel awake and alive. He turned slightly and caught a glimpse of Buddy and Vallie in the rearview mirror. The boy had his eyes shut and his arm around the dog, grinning wide enough to make his face break.

Reputation be hanged. Owen would fulfill his responsibility to this little family. And it might not be so difficult after all.

★ ★ ★

JoLynn sat on the riverbank amid the litter of their picnic and took a long drink of the iced tea she had brought in a mayonnaise jar. Down at the water's edge, Owen and Buddy were fishing with makeshift poles cut from willow branches, using safety pins for hooks and slivers of chicken for bait.

Her son was in heaven, that much was obvious. She had never seen him laugh with such abandon or have such a good time. Vallie bounded back and forth between them on the bank, barking as Buddy lifted his hook and came up with a tiny fish.

"I got one! Look, Mom! I got one!"

JoLynn waved and blew him a kiss.

She had never known love like the devotion she felt for her son—hadn't even known she was capable of it until she had held him in her arms. Now she knew the truth about motherhood. She would do anything for that boy. Anything.

But there was a limit to what she could do. She didn't want him growing up in poverty, always having to scratch out a meager living and eating potatoes and beans when her tips were bad. She wanted a better life for him—Christmas presents under a lighted tree, a dog to play with, a big house with a broad front porch and a room of his own. A mother he didn't have to be ashamed of.

And a father.

She watched as Owen caught him up in a hug, clapping him on the back and congratulating him for his fine catch. What a wonderful man to be the father of her son! A noble man, a man of integrity and honor. She had always known he'd turn out like this. Maybe that's why, even as a teenager, she had always been a little bit in love with him.

JoLynn had never been sure that God answered the prayers of a girl like her until that Monday evening when she saw Owen Slaughter get off the bus, and the following morning when his Uncle Earl had come into the cafe telling the amazing story of his amnesia. That's when she knew. God had listened.

It was her one chance, and she intended to take it. For herself and for her son.

She had seen the look in Owen's eyes when Buddy had asked, "Are you really my father?" She couldn't have planned it better if she had prompted the child. Owen needed a family, a place to belong. JoLynn needed him. It was a perfect solution for both of them. He was almost hooked, the way that little river trout was hooked.

All she had to do was bide her time. He would reel himself in.

23

A Voice from the Past

Eden, Mississippi
July 16, 1945

Waves of heat shimmered up from the cotton fields and blurred the forms of the sharecroppers as they bent their backs over the rows. It was barely seven, and already Willie's shirt stuck to her shoulder blades. How could anyone manage field labor in such heat? Willie herself could barely breathe in the heavy, muggy air, and the idea of doing anything other than taking a cool bath exhausted her. But the men worked on, as field-workers had for a hundred years, sweating and hoeing, seemingly oblivious to the blistering summer sun.

Curly wandered up onto the porch and jumped into the swing beside her. The dog's dripping tongue hung out, and Willie fished into her tea glass and offered the pup an ice cube. Curly took it, propped it between her paws, and began to lick it until it was no more than a sliver. Willie gave her another one.

"Didn't you make coffee this morning?"

Willie looked up. Rae stood at the screen door in a thin cotton robe, her swelling abdomen stretching against the fabric.

"If you want coffee, bring the pot out here," Willie said. "You could boil it on the sidewalk."

Rae came out onto the porch and squeezed into the swing next to the dog. "I guess you're right. Iced tea does make more sense in weather like this." She sighed and rubbed at her back. "I didn't plan this pregnancy very well, that's for sure. Being pregnant in this heat is awful."

"Just existing in this heat is awful," Willie corrected.

"We've lived in Mississippi all our lives, Sister," Rae muttered. "Don't you think we should have adjusted to this by now?"

"The human body doesn't adjust to conditions like this." Willie lifted one eyebrow. "You just endure it." She leaned back and handed her tea glass to Rae, who took a sip. "I've heard rumors that humidity rots the brain cells. Maybe that's why southerners talk slow."

"Talk slow, move slow, *think* slow," Rae added. "Yeah, we're just walkin' stereotypes." She drew out the last word in an exaggerated drawl, and Willie laughed.

"No, we're *sittin'* stereotypes. It's too hot to walk." They both dissolved in a fit of mirth, doubling over and howling until the tears came. It felt good, Willie thought, to laugh like this again. Like old times.

"What's so funny?"

Startled, Willie and Rae both jerked upright. Drew stood at the edge of the porch with a bewildered expression on his face. "What?" Willie demanded.

"I asked what was so funny," he repeated.

"The heat."

Drew frowned, and a whole series of expressions flashed across his face. Clearly he thought that both his wife and his sister-in-law had lost their minds. Willie started laughing again and couldn't stop, and before long Rae was giggling too.

"I give up," he said. "I'm going to town. Obviously someone in this family has to keep a grip on sanity, or they'll come and take us all away." He leaned down and kissed Rae on the cheek. "Don't wait dinner for me. I might be late."

"So what else is new?" Rae muttered, flashing daggers at his departing back. But she didn't stay angry for long. One look at Willie, and she began to smile again. "Whew! I haven't laughed that way in—oh, I don't know how long."

Willie narrowed her eyes. "Remember the night Libba brought Freddy Sturgis home?"

"Hah!" Rae said. "That was a good one. We laughed so hard we cried." She wiped at her eyes. "I didn't think Libba would ever forgive us for that."

"I didn't think *we* would ever forgive *her.* She could have gotten us evicted from the apartment, bringing a soldier in like that."

Rae nodded. "It's a good thing our esteemed landlady, Charity Grevis, never found out, or we would have been sleeping on the street."

Willie sat back in the swing and stroked Curly's ears. The dog shifted her eyes toward Willie and grunted with contentment. "Libba's certainly changed, hasn't she? Whatever happened to Her Royal Highness, the Queen of the Universe?"

"I think she grew up," Rae answered.

"Yeah. What she did for us the other night at the lake was certainly not the old Libba." Willie thought for a moment about how Libba had managed to get her and Rae talking to each other again. The results had been remarkable. She and Rae still had their individual struggles and heartaches, of course, but just sharing them with someone else made all the difference. "I never thanked her for that," Willie mused. "But I'm sure grateful to have my sister back."

Rae reached over and squeezed Willie's hand. "Me too. These last couple of weeks have been much better for me, just because I don't feel so . . . so alone." She paused for a minute and then shifted to look Willie square in the eye. "Are you doing all right with this, Willie—I mean, with Owen being gone?"

Willie nodded and sighed. How could she answer such a question? She was adjusting, if that's what Rae meant, to Owen's absence. She didn't feel quite so much like a yo-yo. She was going on with her life, trying to trust God in the midst of a very painful and confusing situation. Yes, she supposed she was doing "all right."

"I've thought a lot about it," she said after a while. "About Owen leaving, I mean. And the more I think about it, the more convinced I am that Owen belongs here with me. But there's nothing I can do to make that happen. I just have to trust God and wait. I guess I'm coming to realize that if I really love Owen, I have to let him do what he feels called to do, even if it means letting him go. And if he never comes back—" She swallowed hard, determined not to cry. "If he never comes back, well, I'll just deal with that when the time comes."

Rae touched Willie's arm lightly. "I'm proud of you, Sister. I truly am."

"Thank you. But I have to admit I'm not waiting very patiently to see the outcome of all this. Not on the inside."

"And you haven't heard from him at all?"

"Not a word. But I'm trying not to expect it. The only way I'll get through this with any semblance of faith is one day at a time." She shut her eyes and sighed. "Maybe it's for the best. If he wrote or called, I might be tempted to say something I shouldn't say."

"Such as?"

Willie looked at Rae and shook her head. The girl could be so dense sometimes. "If it were you and Drew, what would *you* say?"

Rae thought about this for a minute and then gave a crooked grin. "I might say, 'Don't come back until you can get your mind and your heart in the same place your body is.'"

Willie chuckled. "Good point. But are you talking about Owen or about Drew?"

Rae threw back her head and laughed. "Take your pick."

★ ★ ★

Rae followed Willie into the house and sat at the kitchen table while Willie made breakfast. It was a pure relief to have things back to normal and not have to tiptoe around her sister like she was avoiding broken glass.

Willie set a plate of scrambled eggs and toast in front of Rae and sat down. "I thought I'd take that chicken we had left from Sunday dinner and pull it off the bone for chicken salad," she said. "There's no point in heating up the kitchen fixing a big meal, especially if Drew isn't going to be here."

"Uh-huh," Rae answered, only half-listening.

"Yoo-hoo. Are you in there?"

"What? Oh, sorry, Willie. I was just looking through the mail."

"Anything interesting?"

"Mostly bills. But here's a letter from—oh my gosh, Willie!" Rae tore open the envelope and scanned the contents. After all this time! She couldn't believe it.

"Who's it from?" Willie leaned across the table and peered at the discarded envelope. "Frost, Minnesota?"

"It's from Ardyce Hanson." Rae continued to read. "Hold on a second and I'll read it to you."

"Who's Ardyce Hanson?"

"You remember—my old pen pal, the army nurse. I started writing to her about the same time I was writing to Drew, and . . . well, I guess I just got caught up with things and lost track of her."

"Got caught up in Drew, you mean," Willie quipped. "You fell in *love.*"

Willie emphasized the last word, *luuuvvv,* and Rae felt herself blush. "I guess so. Anyway, I lost contact with her. Now she's back in her old hometown and working at the little county clinic in a larger town nearby, a place called Blue Earth. Funny name, Blue Earth."

"Not nearly as funny as Frost. Up there in Minnesota, they probably have frost year-round."

Rae looked up from the letter and smiled. "I can't believe I didn't keep up correspondence with her. You'd like her, Willie. She's intelligent and witty and always seemed to understand exactly what I was thinking and feeling."

"Sounds like me."

"Intelligent, witty, or understanding?"

"All of the above. Now, go on—what does she say?"

"When she came back to the States, she was assigned to the army hospital in Minneapolis. She was discharged six months ago and wanted to stay in the Cities—that's what they call Minneapolis/St. Paul—and go to medical school. But—oh, Willie, it's so sad. Her mother got cancer, and Ardyce came home to help nurse her. She died last month."

"That's too bad."

"Anyway, she says she'd really like to get back in touch with me and wants me to write to her. Apparently she's got a good job and enjoys her work, but there aren't many people our age in Frost, and she doesn't have many friends. Lots of relatives, but nobody she really connects with."

"So you're going to write to her?"

"You think I should?"

"Why not?"

Rae searched Willie's eyes and found no trace of duplicity, but she had to ask the question anyway. "I don't know. I just . . . well, if I start corresponding with her, I wouldn't want you to feel . . . you know, left out."

"Don't be silly," Willie answered immediately. "Why on earth would I be jealous of her? This is somebody you like and want to have a friendship with. Besides, she's a nurse. She might be able to help reassure you about the baby."

"I didn't say you were jealous."

"No, but that's what you meant. It's ridiculous."

"But we've had our difficulties in the past few months. You're my sister, Willie, and I love you. I don't ever want you to feel—"

"As if somebody else is taking my place? Nonsense. It sounds like she needs a friend." Willie smiled. "Besides, you said I'd like her. And we know she'd like me. What's not to like?"

Rae grinned and slapped Willie lightly on the wrist. "And you're so humble, too."

"I am," Willie agreed modestly. "Where is this Frostbite place, anyway?"

"Frost," Rae corrected. "It's in southern Minnesota, right on the border of Iowa."

"Iowa?" she repeated the word slowly, deliberately, and Rae looked up. All the color had drained out of Willie's face, and her eyes had taken on a faraway look. Suddenly an idea came to Rae, a good idea. If Willie would agree to it, it might help settle her mind about Owen.

"Willie, listen. Owen is in Iowa, right?"

Willie nodded. "A place called North Fork."

"Well, let me write to Ardyce and ask her where North Fork is. If it's not far away, maybe she can find out some word about Owen—whether he's still there, if he's all right. Not to meddle, of course, simply to get some information."

"Do you think she might be able to do that?" Light returned to Willie's eyes, a spark of hope. "I guess I would like to know . . . just for myself."

"I'll write her today," Rae promised, "with your permission."

"Tell her anything you like," Willie whispered. "As long as she won't interfere."

Rae folded the letter and took a bite of her toast. This was perfect timing. Perfect. She could renew an old friendship and have someone else to talk to, and perhaps that old friend could help Willie as well. For both of them, Ardyce Hanson represented fresh hope.

Maybe God was still at work in this after all.

24

Summer Dreams

North Fork, Iowa
August 15, 1945

Owen awoke with a start. His T-shirt and shorts were soaked with sweat, and the sheets felt damp and clammy. Outside his open window, the noise of crickets and tree frogs filled the summer night air. A faint breeze stirred the curtains, and a chill snaked up his spine.

He had dreamed again.

The same dream over and over: himself in uniform, beardless, hefting a duffel bag over his shoulder and walking toward a train. Behind him, as he turned, he caught a glimpse of a female form, shrouded in shadow, waving. He could see glistening streaks of tears on her cheeks but could never make out her face. She was calling to him, sobbing, crying, "Be careful, Owen. Come back to me."

Owen shook his head and tried to clear his mind. From the foot of the narrow bed Vallie edged up closer, whining softly and licking his hand.

"I'm all right, girl," he murmured absently.

He closed his eyes and tried to concentrate. Maybe if he just thought hard enough, the rest of it would come to him—the identity of the woman in the shadows, what her face looked like. Was this a memory, something stirred up from his subconscious when his conscious mind was at rest? A recollection, perhaps, of the day he shipped out? Or simply a distorted dream image, taunting him?

He swung his legs over the edge of the bed and took a drink of the watery lemonade that sat on the nightstand beside him. It was infuriating, not knowing, not remembering. He had gone through every bit of memorabilia in his aunt's attic and had pieced together a picture of himself and his family and his past life here in North Fork. But still he didn't remember any of it. He stored it all away as if cramming for a final exam, as if his very existence depended upon the information. He knew all the facts—the names, dates, places, faces. But still he felt like an imposter taking on another man's identity.

Owen ran a hand through Vallie's thick ruff and sighed. "What am I going to do, girl?" he whispered. "Where am I going to find the answers?"

The dog nuzzled her long nose against his beard and licked his face. He smiled and stroked her ears. Here, at least, was someone who seemed to understand his dilemma—or at least someone who loved him and stood by him, whoever he was. A guy couldn't ask for much more than that. Owen had the feeling that if Vallie could talk, she might give him some pretty sound advice.

But she couldn't. He was on his own. Aunt Gert and Uncle Earl loved him, he was sure of that, but they wouldn't tell him what to do. They just kept saying that he had to make his own decisions and live with the consequences.

And, barring some miraculous intervention from on high, the present decision Owen had to make was what to do about JoLynn Ferber and her son, Buddy.

He had been here almost two months. In that time he had spent most of his Saturdays and Sundays with them and some evenings with JoLynn alone. Tongues were wagging in town, especially after they had shown up in church together, but that couldn't be helped. He had told his aunt that his responsibility was more important than his reputation, and he meant it.

Only this week, American planes had dropped atomic bombs on two Japanese cities. From the news reports, it appeared that the destruction was horrendous, but the government was expecting the Japanese to surrender at any minute.

Owen groaned under his breath. The parallels were all too obvious. He had already surrendered, and he was about to drop his own bomb. He was going to ask JoLynn Ferber to marry him.

He closed his eyes and heaved a sigh. Like the decision to set off the A-bombs, it was a radical step. But if it resulted in peace, maybe the destruction would be worth it in the long run. He fervently hoped so.

Owen knew what he had to do. He had just been postponing the final decision. And all things considered, it probably wouldn't be that bad.

JoLynn wasn't exactly "his type," but then how did a man with no memory even know what his type was? She was a hard worker and a devoted mother. She was attractive and appealing, and now that he thought about it, she *had* stirred something in him that first day. He could learn to love her, he thought, given time. And little Buddy, with his freckled nose and bright brown eyes, had won Owen's heart weeks ago, that Fourth of July afternoon when he had thrown his arms around Owen's neck and asked, "Are you really my father?" What man wouldn't be proud to have such a son?

A home. A family. A place to belong. People who loved him and needed him. It was all so perfect, except . . .

Except for Willie Coltrain.

Owen tried to push the thought of Willie out of his mind, as he had done so often over the past six weeks. True, he didn't have the same kind of yearning for JoLynn Ferber as he had for Willie, but what difference did that make? He had a responsibility here. Eventually his heart would let go of those dreams, of the fantasy that Charlie's sister harbored the same desire for him. Sooner or later, he would be free. He would forget. Or if he didn't forget, he would be able to relegate those dusky gray eyes and that low smoky voice to his past—the bittersweet memory of a love that never happened.

In all the weeks he had been here, Owen had not communicated with Willie at all—not one note, not a single telephone call. What could he say to her? How could he make her understand his need to find himself? And especially now that JoLynn was in the picture, how on earth could he tell her that what he had found was a high school sweetheart—and a six-year-old son—of whom he had no memories at all?

At some point, of course, he would have to write to Willie. But not now. Not yet. He would postpone the inevitable as long as he could. Still, he regretted the price of this peace, the lives and dreams of innocent people caught in the crossfire.

Ardyce Hanson sat at the desk in the study of her parents' big old Victorian house, staring at the blank sheet of paper in front of her. The house, with its high ceilings and open rooms, always stayed cool, even during the dog days of summer—a welcome respite from the August heat. Summer in Minnesota arrived late and didn't last very long, but when it came, it came with a vengeance. In another week or two, autumn would push the heat and humidity aside, turn the leaves to brilliant hues, and send the gnats and mosquitoes back down south where they belonged. In the meantime everyone just waited, with varying degrees of patience, for summer to be over. Once it was done, they would begin the process of complaining about the frigid winter temperatures and longing for summer to return.

Ardyce sighed and scratched her head. In the past few weeks she had exchanged several letters with Mabel Rae Coltrain—now Rae Laporte. Rae's letters had been full of news: an account of her wedding in New Orleans, a detailed description of her new husband. The sad news of her parents' deaths and her return to Eden to live on the family farm, and joyful tidings of a baby on the way. Rae had questions, too: Where, in relation to Frost, was North Fork, Iowa? Had Ardyce heard anything of the return of a man named Owen Slaughter, a soldier who had sustained amnesia during the war and been imprisoned in a German stalag?

Frost was, in fact, only fifteen miles or so from North Fork, just across the state line. But Scandinavians were a reticent people. She wasn't about to march herself down there and start asking questions. One day in the clinic, however, she had overheard a conversation about the son of one Warren Slaughter who had returned from the war not knowing who he was. Summoning up all her courage, Ardyce asked who they were talking about.

She learned more than she bargained for.

Inveterate gossips, the two old women in the waiting room pounced on her like a cougar on fresh meat. This young man, Owen Slaughter, you see, had returned to North Fork, oh, about six weeks ago. Handsome young fellow, short and muscular with a nice beard and those startling blue eyes that all the Slaughter men were blessed with. Didn't remember a thing—not who he was or who his people were or even the gruesome auto accident that claimed his parents' lives when he was only twenty-one. And then, to everyone's surprise, he took up with the town hussy, a girl with a—well, a reputation. A six-year-old son, you know, and no father in sight. Rumor had it that young Slaughter himself might be the papa, but no one was saying. Still, he sure kept company often enough with that girl and her little boy. It was too bad, too. His Aunt Gert still had to show her face around town, and he was shaming them all.

Ardyce sighed and crumpled up yet another sheet of stationery. Rae hadn't said a lot about Owen Slaughter, only that he was her brother Charlie's friend, had saved Charlie's life, helped him escape from the Germans, and stood with him at his deathbed. But clearly Rae—and especially her sister, Willie—worried about him, and Ardyce surmised that it was probably more than just a friendly concern.

The question now was, how much should she tell Rae? Ardyce had no patience for rumors and gossip, in most cases flatly refused to listen to such nonsense, and certainly never passed it on. But this situation presented a definite dilemma. If, as she suspected, Rae's sister, Willie, was more than casually interested in this Owen Slaughter, the news of his involvement with this woman would no doubt hurt her. She might be wounded more in the long run, however, if she *didn't* know.

Ardyce picked up her pen once more and began to write:

> Dear Rae,
>
> I appreciated so much your last letter and certainly understand your fears for the health of your baby. Be assured I will be praying for you and hoping for the best. If I can do anything to help, please let me know.
>
> In the meantime, I want to respond to some of the questions you've been asking. Frost is less than twenty miles from North Fork, just across the border. We do get people from North Fork in our clinic once in a while, and last week I spoke with a couple of women who were able to give me a little information on your friend Owen Slaughter. . . .

Ardyce reread what she had written. So far so good. Now for the hard part:

> From everything these ladies told me, Owen is in town and is doing well. He is living with his aunt and uncle on the family farm, which they took over after the death of Owen's parents. I don't know much detail about his progress in regaining his memories, but he seems to be settling in and making friends. . . .

She grimaced at the last line. *Making friends?* That was an interesting euphemism for—well—for whatever Owen Slaughter was up to. But it was sufficient. There was no point in spreading unconfirmed rumors, especially when they might hurt her friend's sister. Whatever was going on in this man's life, it was his story to tell, not hers. Only God knew what was in Owen Slaughter's past and what was in his heart today, and only God was capable of making judgments about it.

> I don't know much else, except that according to the women at the clinic, he seems to be healthy and doing fine. I've never liked to meddle, so I won't make contact with him unless you specifically want me to. But if there's any message you'd like me to communicate to him, I'll be happy to do that. Or you could probably reach him directly simply by writing c/o the post

office in North Fork. It's a small town, much like Frost, where everybody knows everybody. . . .

And where everybody knows everybody's business, Ardyce wanted to add. But she didn't.

★ ★ ★

When Owen finally left, JoLynn Ferber sank to the couch with a contented sigh. Buddy had gone off to bed, reluctantly, an hour ago, leaving her and Owen alone. The man had seemed nervous, so distracted that it made her jumpy just to watch him. He picked at his dessert, and his hands shook so badly that he sloshed coffee all over the napkin in his lap. At last he got up and paced around the room a couple of times, then turned to face her.

"I-I need to talk to you about something," he had said.

"All right, Owen. I'm listening."

"W-well," he stammered, "I've been spending quite a bit of time with you and Buddy, and you know how attached I've grown to him. And he likes me too, I believe—and especially Vallie. Every boy should have a dog, don't you think?"

By this time JoLynn had suspected what was coming, but she held her peace, tried to calm her racing heart, and let him ramble on some more. At last he got to the point.

"What I'm trying to say, I guess, is that . . . well, I think we should think about getting married. For Buddy's sake, that is. I mean, a boy needs a father. And I guess I'm it."

It wasn't the romantic proposal JoLynn had dreamed of as a young girl, but it was good enough, given her circumstances. It had taken him so long to get around to asking her that she was about to run out of time and patience, and she had begun to wonder if she had taken the wrong approach. Maybe she should have been a little more aggressive with him, put a little more pressure on him. He might have been different than the other men she had known—more honorable, more principled—but he was a man, after all. And JoLynn knew from experience exactly what it took to wrap a man around her little finger.

Fortunately, she hadn't had to resort to those old techniques. And she was glad. Not only was she attracted to Owen, and had been since her hormones had asserted themselves in the seventh grade, she genuinely liked him. He was a nice guy. It was better this way—him thinking the marriage was all his idea.

She knew he didn't love her, of course. She wasn't a brain surgeon, but she was smart enough to see that much. Still, he obviously cared for Buddy, and he would be a good husband and father. He wouldn't beat her or desert her or make life miserable for her. He'd be a good provider and an interesting person to have around. And maybe, with a little maneuvering, he'd find a way to take his parents' place back from that aunt and uncle of his. She had always wanted a big house with a pasture and a barn and maybe a horse for Buddy.

Real love would have been too much to ask. JoLynn didn't want to press her luck.

Her mind began to spin with the possibilities. A small ceremony, but in the church with a preacher—like respectable people. Before God and witnesses, that's how it should be. But soon, as soon as it could be arranged. Owen Slaughter was too confounded moral to be talked into a honeymoon before the wedding.

And the honeymoon was the most important part of JoLynn's plan.

THREE

*As Time
Goes By*

AUTUMN 1945

25

Pete

Thelma Breckinridge stood behind the counter at the Paradise Garden Cafe with her chin propped in her hands. September always stirred up a nostalgic feeling in her, memories of new notebooks and fresh unsharpened pencils and the chance to start over. It had been more than twenty-five years since she had seen the inside of a classroom; in a month she would celebrate her forty-fourth birthday. But every year, when the first hint of fall began to creep in around the edges of the summer heat, she could have been twelve again. Twelve, with her whole life ahead of her, new worlds to explore, and infinite possibilities on the horizon.

She probably wasn't the only person who felt this way—especially this year, with all the boys coming home. The Japanese had finally surrendered last month, after that terrible bombing, and everyone was celebrating the end of the war and the beginning of a new era. The whole country, it seemed, was starting over.

This morning, however, the new world that invaded her imagination was closer than it had ever been.

Ivory Brownlee's place.

Try as she might, Thelma could not keep herself from daydreaming about the grand old house that sat like a tarnished jewel in the center of what once had been the Brownlee plantation. She had not been back out there since that Saturday three months ago when she had discovered the

Lincoln photograph, but she couldn't seem to get the place out of her mind. In idle moments, in daydreams, her thoughts drifted to it like iron filings to a magnet. And always in her mind's eye she saw it not as it was, but as it could be, restored to the glory days before the War Between the States and before time and neglect had taken their toll.

Thelma had never been a mercenary woman, never longed for wealth or status or material possessions. For most of her adult life, especially in the past year or two, she had been content with her lot, happy with the friends and loved ones who surrounded her like a large and cheerful family. She had a good business, a stable income, and the promise of a future with a man who was everything she had ever dreamed of. Why, then, did she feel this gnawing restlessness?

She rejected outright the idea that she might be growing discontent in her middle years. Thelma was not the kind of person who kept looking for something better, for greener pastures in some other field. God had been gracious to her, and she knew the value of counting her blessings. But Ivory's big house, with all its vast potential, still fascinated her, and she couldn't shake the feeling that it held mysteries yet undiscovered, secrets that would be revealed in their own time. And she couldn't help wondering what it would be like to live in a fine house like that. . . .

The bell over the door interrupted her reverie, and Thelma looked up to see Bennett coming through the doorway, followed by Drew and Ivory. Bennett caught Thelma up in an exuberant hug, and over his shoulder Thelma caught sight of Drew waving a cream-colored envelope.

"What's all this?" Thelma asked.

Bennett leaned down and kissed her before answering. "This," he said when he let her go, "is the first of September."

"If this is the kind of greeting I get on the first day of every month," she answered, her voice husky with the emotion his embrace had stirred, "I'll never complain about paying bills again."

Bennett threw back his head and laughed. "It's the deadline for our little cat-and-mouse game, remember? And young Drew has in his hand a letter from the mouse."

"The rat, you mean," Drew corrected.

"What does it say?"

Bennett sat down at one of the tables and motioned for the others to do the same. "We haven't opened it yet."

"Well, let's hear it!" Thelma plopped into a chair at Bennett's side.

Drew slit the envelope with a table knife and pulled out a single sheet of paper. He scanned the letter quickly, then began to read aloud:

"Dear Mr. Winsom:

"I have had some lengthy discussions with my employer about the situation we encountered on my last visit. He is, as you might imagine, less than pleased at the demands your organization is placing upon him and feels that your proposal is grossly inequitable, but he is willing to negotiate.

"My business has held me in New Orleans longer than I had expected, so I will need an additional two weeks to prepare for our conference. I trust this will be acceptable to you and you will not take any action against us until we have the opportunity to settle this matter.

"I will be in touch with you to arrange a time and place for our meeting. Until then, I remain,

"Sincerely yours,
"Orris Craven, Attorney-at-Law"

"I don't get it," Ivory said when Drew put the letter aside. "What's it mean?"

"It means they're delaying us, hoping we're greedy enough not to take our evidence to the authorities," Bennett answered. "They're counting on us wanting this merger enough to hold off on reporting them. My guess is that the big boss, whoever he is, isn't going to give in so easily."

Thelma felt a knot forming in her stomach. "So what do we do?"

"We put a little pressure on Craven," Drew suggested. "Insist upon a second meeting immediately, and give him an ultimatum."

"In other words, we bluff," Bennett added. "If we want to put an end to this once and for all, we need to flush this boss out of hiding. If they call our bluff and refuse, we've still got enough evidence to shut them down, but we can't guarantee that he won't start his operation up again somewhere else."

Thelma watched Bennett's face and saw there a mixture of passion and determination. "I know you're concerned about other people like Ivory that this fellow might take advantage of," she said softly. "And that's admirable. But is there something else, Bennett? Something more . . . personal . . . involved?"

He gave her a sharp look, then shook his head miserably. "When I was just a boy, I had a friend—an old gentleman named Pete, about the age my grandfather would have been. My own grandfather died before I was born, and Pete, a friend of our family's, took me on as his own. He didn't have much, but he was always generous with what little he did have. Then an unscrupulous lawyer charmed him into sinking his meager savings into a scam—a plan that would supposedly give him security for the rest of his life. They took everything he had." Bennett paused and swiped at his eyes. "On the day Pete's little house was to be sold, I went over to see him. He wasn't there, so I went looking in all our favorite places. I found Pete's body hanging from the rafters in the attic."

Thelma felt a chill run up her spine, and tears sprang to her eyes. "Oh, Bennett, no!"

He nodded. "I was only ten, but I remember it like it was yesterday. At that age I didn't know much about what lawyers did—I only knew that a lawyer had killed my friend. And I decided that somehow I would spend my life trying to help people like Pete, to make sure something that horrible never happened again."

"We'll get him," Drew said quietly. "Whatever it takes, we'll get him."

Thelma watched from behind the counter as Bennett and Drew went over their paperwork for the third time. Ivory played softly in the background, and as the strains of "Moonlight Serenade" drifted through her consciousness, Thelma prayed.

She prayed for God's intervention in their plan, that somehow they would be able to get to the man who was responsible for so much misery. She prayed for Drew, that he would see the light and turn his attention back to his wife and their baby. She prayed for Bennett, that his heart would be healed.

And she prayed for herself. Somehow Bennett's story about Pete put everything into perspective for her. She understood, finally, what made Bennett the man he was, why he had given his life to helping those who could not help themselves. Suddenly she knew that if she married this man—as certainly she would—they would never be wealthy or live in a fine house like Ivory Brownlee's family home.

And it didn't matter.

All the money or status in the world wasn't worth a dime compared to such nobility of soul and generosity of heart.

Thelma Breckinridge was a woman blessed with riches beyond her wildest dreams. And his name was Bennett Winsom.

26

Clinical Analysis

Eden, Mississippi
September 1, 1945

Willie felt a tug at the hem of her jeans and looked down from the kitchen counter. Curly sat next to her foot, gazing up expectantly at the stew beef she had cut.

"Oh, no. You can just forget about it. You're not getting my meat ration, and that's final." In spite of herself, Willie smiled as the spaniel flopped to the kitchen floor and put her head on her paws. If she hadn't known better, Willie would have sworn that dog understood every word she said.

"Oh, all right. You can have this." Willie offered the pup a small bone end with a little meat still on it. Curly took it daintily between her front teeth and wagged her tail. "But take it out on the porch. I just mopped this floor, and I don't want bone mess all over it."

Following the direction Willie pointed, Curly trotted through the parlor with her treasure and pushed the screen door open.

Willie tossed the meat into the stew pot with the vegetables and set it on the back of the stove to simmer. The marrow in that bone would have added extra flavor to the stew, but Curly was a member of the family, too, and deserved a treat now and then.

After she had wiped off the countertops and put bread to rise, Willie went out on the porch and sat in the swing, idly watching as Curly gnawed contentedly on her bone. She should be cleaning the bedrooms, but it was all she could do to bring herself to go upstairs. The house held reminders of Owen at every turn—the half-finished bathroom, the markings on the wall where the door would be cut between Drew and Rae's room and the nursery.

It would all get done eventually, Willie supposed. Drew kept promising Rae that as soon as Ivory's case was settled, he would devote himself to finishing the renovations. It wouldn't take long, he insisted, as soon as he could get to it. Meanwhile, Willie lived every day with the painful reminders of Owen's sudden departure.

Rae's friend Ardyce Hanson had written with the news that Owen was in North Fork, Iowa, living with his aunt and uncle and doing well. Willie couldn't help feeling as if there were something Ardyce *wasn't* saying, but that was probably just her imagination running away with her. Owen was gone, finding his past, making a life for himself. She ought to wish him well, she supposed, and get on with her own life.

But the ability to let go graciously was, in Willie's estimation, a highly overrated virtue, and certainly not one she possessed. Besides, it just wasn't that easy.

Let go, everyone told her. But her heart said, *Hold on.*

The problem was, she had only two truths to hold on to: that God somehow would bring good out of this and that once in her life she had experienced true love.

A bittersweet longing welled up in Willie's soul, and she fought back tears. She reminded herself that love was never wasted, not really. At the very least, loving someone the way she loved Owen deepened her and made her a better person. Surely she could learn something from this pain, something that would uplift and ennoble her and strengthen her faith.

All the pat answers sounded so good. But another part of her, a more honest part, thought it was a pretty rotten deal. Losing the love of your life—three times—was a high price to pay for an object lesson in trust.

★ ★ ★

Minn-Iowa Community Clinic
Blue Earth, Minnesota

Ardyce Hanson looked at the appointment list and sighed. These Saturday morning schedules were always crowded and harried. All the people who somehow couldn't manage to get in during the week appeared on the doorstep at seven on Saturday. The clinic was only supposed to be open from eight until noon, but you couldn't turn away a farmer who was bleeding or a mother with a feverish child. It was usually well past two by the time they got everyone treated and sent home.

She looked at her watch. Twelve forty-five, with one patient to go. Maybe no last-minute emergencies would show up, and they would get out of here at a decent hour. Ardyce didn't have any big plans for Saturday afternoon—just a walk in the woods down along the river. But it was a beautiful autumn day, the leaves were beginning to turn, and she preferred the scent of wood smoke to the smell of antiseptic.

Ardyce looked out into the waiting room. An attractive young blonde sat next to the door, twirling her hair and absently paging through a six-month-old magazine.

"Come in, please," Ardyce said. The young woman looked up and smiled brightly, then got to her feet and followed Ardyce back to the examining room. "Have a seat," Ardyce told her. "I'll be right back."

While the girl waited, Ardyce went back to the waiting room, locked the door, and turned the sign so it said CLOSED. Anybody who had a real emergency would ring the bell. The others could just wait until Monday.

When she returned to the examination room, Ardyce took the girl's chart and sat down across from her. She flipped open the folder and scanned the record of the girl's last visit, a little over a week ago.

"I see that . . . ah, congratulations are in order?" Ardyce began cautiously. Given the girl's youth, she wasn't at all sure that this would come as joyful news, but there was no way around it.

"The rabbit died?" The young woman's blue eyes sparkled. "Not that I had any doubt. My symptoms are the same as last time."

"Last time?" Ardyce worked hard to keep the look of disbelief off her face. "This is your second pregnancy?"

The girl nodded and gave a light laugh. "I'm not as young as I look, Miss—" she peered at Ardyce's name tag—"Miss Hanson." She pointed to the folder. "Check the chart. I'm twenty-four."

Ardyce checked. Just as she said, twenty-four. "I also see here that you're not—"

"Married?" The girl shrugged. "I'm engaged."

Ardyce jotted a few notes in the girl's chart. "Your first child is how old?"

"Six. His name is Buddy. Want to see a picture?" She dug through her handbag and came up with a photo. "He's a great kid."

A quick mental computation put the girl at just barely eighteen when her first child was born. Ardyce took the photograph and examined it—a candid shot of a dungaree-clad child with a baseball bat on his shoulder, blond curls, and dark, intense eyes.

"His daddy recently got back from the war," the girl explained. "I was a little bit worried about it since Owen had never seen his son, but they hit it off just fine. Owen adores Buddy, and Buddy worships the ground he walks on."

An alarm went off in Ardyce's mind, and she busied herself with the chart. Name: JoLynn Ferber, age 24. Address: Box 37, North Fork, Iowa.

North Fork. A soldier named Owen, just back from the war. Coincidence? Ardyce didn't think so.

"Father's name?" she prompted.

"Owen W. Slaughter," the girl said. "That's S-l-a-u-g-h-t-e-r."

A sick feeling rose up in Ardyce's throat. Owen Slaughter. The "friend" Mabel Rae Coltrain had asked her to find out about. And, unless Ardyce's instincts were extremely rusty, more than a friend to Rae's sister, Willie.

So the old gossips had been right after all. Remarkably accurate, given the usually unreliable nature of the rumor mill. Owen Slaughter, returning to North Fork after an extended absence, taking up with a young woman of questionable repute. The possibility that he might be the father of her six-year-old child . . .

Still, something didn't seem quite right to Ardyce. From what Rae had told her, this Owen Slaughter just didn't seem the type to—well—to take advantage of such a situation.

She forced herself to speak in a calm, professionally distant tone of voice. "And how far along are you, do you think?"

"About three months. Maybe a little more." JoLynn gazed toward the ceiling and calculated. "My last cycle was the end of May. And I started having morning sickness and stuff like that sometime in June."

Ardyce nodded and kept her eyes averted. "According to the doctor's report you're as healthy as can be. Keep an eye on your diet, and I'll schedule you for a checkup a month from now."

"I'll be here." The young woman jumped down from the examining table and grinned. "Am I done?"

"You are." Ardyce watched as JoLynn Ferber went through the waiting room and shut the door behind her. When she was gone, Ardyce sank down on one of the shabby chairs in the waiting room and sighed.

What on earth was she going to do now?

Ardyce had told Mabel Rae that she wasn't given to meddling, and she meant it. But something was terribly wrong here. If Owen Slaughter was indeed the father of JoLynn Ferber's baby—and of her six-year-old son as well—Mabel Rae and her sister, Willie, had to know. They needed to be told that Owen had found his past, however checkered it might have been, and that he wasn't coming back to Mississippi. Not now. Not ever.

But Ardyce had absolutely no experience in matters of romance. She had enjoyed a brief relationship or two in her time, moonlit walks and evenings by the fire and a few kisses shared with some nice young man. But nothing serious. Nothing that equipped her to deal with a situation like this. Most of her adult life had been taken up with her schooling, and after that, the war. Only once, during her stint at an army hospital in Europe, had she even come close to falling in love, with a handsome young surgeon who had a rather charming and compelling bedside manner. But she found out soon enough that she wasn't the only nurse who occupied his attentions—and that he had a wife and baby daughter waiting for him in the States.

Her heart had never been broken, not even then, for she had never given herself fully to anything but her career. Every decision in Ardyce's life had to be filtered through a rigorous analysis governed by her call to medicine. Her friends accused her of being calculating at best, at worst obsessed. But if she ever intended to fulfill her dream of attending medical school and becoming a doctor, everything else had to take second place.

She couldn't even imagine what it would be like to be in Willie Coltrain's shoes—hopelessly in love, as Rae's letters implied, with a man who had once loved her but had lost his memory. A man who, to all appearances, had made some pretty serious mistakes in his past and now might be about to confirm them for all time.

For a brief moment Ardyce wished she had never heard of the Coltrains from Eden, Mississippi. This predicament was far too complicated. Still, she valued her long-distance friendship with Rae, and she had a responsibility, like it or not.

Well, she didn't like it. But her lifelong pattern of analyzing a situation before she got involved in it would probably serve her well in this instance, too. The one thing she couldn't do—wouldn't do—was relate any of this information, or any of her suspicions, to Mabel Rae. Not until she found out the facts. And the only place to get the real story was from the source.

So much for her peaceful Saturday stroll in the woods. The unanswered questions would nag at her until she had settled this once and for all.

And the sooner the better.

Owen threw the rubber ball in a high arc across the front yard, and Vallie tore after it full speed. She loved this game; he could almost see her smiling as she came toward him with the ball in her mouth, her long hair streaming in the breeze.

Victoriously she trotted up to him, plopped down on her haunches, and dropped the ball at his feet as if to say, *See how smart I am?*

"Yeah, you're a genius," he goaded, feigning a throw. Vallie jerked around as if to go after the ball, then turned back and barked. "I can't fool you, can I?" He tossed the ball up and down, and she barked again.

"All right, all right." He threw it for real this time, and she flew down the hill, catching it on the second bounce. But she didn't return right away. Instead she looked toward the road and gave a muffled woof.

"Hey, Einstein!" Owen called. "You can't bark with a ball in your mouth. Come on, bring it back."

Just as she wheeled to come to him, Owen saw a cloud of dust coming up the road. The car slowed to a crawl as it passed the mailbox, then turned in and proceeded up the driveway.

It was a late-model Buick, pale yellow. Nobody in North Fork had a car like that, Owen thought, then scolded himself silently for the reaction. He was beginning to sound like everyone else in this town, speculating about any stranger who drove down Main Street in an unfamiliar vehicle. *Not from around here,* the old-timers would say with a sage nod, as if they had offered some profound gem of wisdom.

Owen stood at the fence post and waited while the car made its way to a stop and a woman got out. She was a stranger, that much was certain—very tall and willowy, in her early thirties, he thought, with her hair pulled back from her face. Not unattractive, especially when she smiled in his direction and revealed two deep dimples on either side of her mouth.

"Can I help you?" Owen asked. Probably lost, he thought, and stopping for directions.

She came toward him with one hand extended. "Owen Slaughter, I presume?"

Taken aback, Owen nodded mutely.

"And who is this?" The woman knelt at Vallie's side and ran a hand through her long ruff. Vallie lifted a paw in greeting, and the woman shook it solemnly. "She's beautiful."

"Her name is Valentine. Vallie for short."

"Well, hello, Vallie. It's nice to meet you." She gave the dog a final pat on the shoulder and rose. "I'm Ardyce Hanson. I'd like to talk with you. Do you have a few minutes?"

"Well, uh, I guess so," Owen stammered. She was scrutinizing him as if he were some kind of bug under a microscope, and he had the uneasy feeling that he didn't quite measure up to her expectations.

"Can we sit?" She pointed toward a wooden picnic table at the side of the house. Her no-nonsense manner unnerved him, and with some hesitation he settled himself on the bench across from her.

At last Owen remembered his manners and found his tongue. "Would you like coffee, Mrs. Hanson? It's already made, and it's a little chilly out here—"

"Not Mrs.," she corrected. "Miss. But I'd prefer it if you'd call me Ardyce."

"All right—"

"And yes, I'd appreciate coffee. Black, with a little sugar."

Owen went into the house and came back with two cups of coffee and a plate of homemade cookies. "Aunt Gert insisted I bring these, too," he said as he set them on the table. "She's pretty curious about you."

"And I suppose you are, too," Ardyce countered. "Well, I'll get right to the point. I am a friend of Mabel Rae Coltrain—she's Rae Laporte now, of course."

At the mention of the name Coltrain, Owen's stomach lurched and his hand began to shake. Images of Willie leaped unbidden to his mind—Willie in that soft blue chenille robe, sitting in the porch swing at sunrise . . . that deep, low voice and velvety laugh . . . her dusky gray eyes . . .

"Mr. Slaughter? Owen?"

The voice jerked him back to the present, and he blinked.

"I asked if you knew Mabel Rae—and her sister, Willie."

"Y-yes, of course," he stammered. "My best friend, Charlie, from the war. They're his sisters. But how—?"

"Rae and I have been friends for over a year. We met through correspondence, when I was serving in Europe. I was an army nurse."

Owen nodded, and a sudden panic seized him. "Is everything all right at home—I mean, in Eden? Is Willie—?"

"Everything's fine," she said in a low voice. "Rae mentioned you in one of her letters and told me you were here in North Fork, and I—well, I just thought I'd pay a visit and see how you're doing."

His confusion growing by the minute, Owen frowned at her. "You're from around here?"

She smiled suddenly, and her dimples appeared. "I'm sorry. I can be, well, rather blunt at times. I'm from Frost, just over the state line in Minnesota."

"I've heard of it," he said. "Never been there."

"I recently met a friend of yours. A JoLynn Ferber."

"You know JoLynn?" Owen had no idea what this woman was doing here, sitting in his yard drinking coffee and eating peanut-butter cookies, but he wished she would get to the point.

He didn't have to wait long to get his wish fulfilled.

★ ★ ★

Ardyce watched Owen Slaughter closely. He seemed like a nice young man, a bit naive perhaps, but genuine enough. She noticed how his hand shook when she mentioned the name of Coltrain, and his eyes gave away more of his feelings than he was probably aware. Such unusual eyes, too—such a startling bright blue . . .

Ardyce had always considered herself a good judge of character, less by instinct than by analysis. What she saw in Owen's expression was a mixture of pain and anxiety, confusion and longing. Especially when she mentioned Mabel Rae's sister, the longing surfaced. He might be engaged to JoLynn Ferber, but he was definitely in love with Willie Coltrain.

She wouldn't tell him what she knew, of course, or betray Mabel Rae's confidence. She would simply wait and see what he had to say.

"I recently met JoLynn at the clinic where I work," she said. "She seems very excited about the wedding."

"Wedding?" Owen's brow furrowed. "Oh, yes. The wedding."

"I suppose Mabel Rae and Willie are very happy for you. I'd love to meet Rae in person—I've never seen her, you know. Will they be coming up for the ceremony?"

His eyes went wide, and his jaw dropped. "No . . . no," he stammered. "I—uh, I haven't told them I'm getting—ah, married."

"So they don't know about your impending fatherhood, either."

Owen gave her a puzzled look. "You mean Buddy?"

"Buddy, of course. But the baby as well. It must be quite an adjustment for you—"

"Baby?" Owen interrupted. "What baby?"

A chill snaked up Ardyce's spine. JoLynn hadn't told him about the baby. "I'm sorry. I thought you knew."

"Knew what?" He leaned over the picnic table, sloshing coffee into the cookie platter. "What's this about a baby?"

Ardyce closed her eyes for a minute to shut out the expression on his face. It wasn't surprise or even guilt. It was more like . . . betrayal.

When she opened them again, the poor man had his head in his hands. "I apologize for breaking the news to you like this, Owen. It should have come from JoLynn, not from me."

He raised his head, and his blue eyes flashed. "Unless you believe in another Immaculate Conception," he countered, "nobody should be breaking this news to anybody."

Ardyce reached across the table and placed her hand on his trembling fingers. "JoLynn listed you as the father of the child," she said softly. "Are you telling me—?"

"You're a nurse; you figure it out," he snapped.

"Then you haven't—?"

"No. I haven't."

She believed him without question, and her heart went out to him. "Why would she say such a thing?"

Owen sighed. "Buddy is my son," he said. "I don't remember any of it—of course, you probably know that, being a friend of Rae's—but whether I remember it or not, I will do right by my child. And his mother."

"Even if his mother is—?"

Owen looked up at her with an expression of utter misery. "I don't suppose it matters much who the father is," he whispered. "Or that she tried to deceive me." He ran his hands through his hair. "It all makes sense. Of course she wouldn't tell me, not until after we were married. And then it would be too late."

"It's not too late now."

"Yes, it is. I've got Buddy to consider." He gave her an anguished look. "How long?"

"What do you mean?"

"How far along is she?"

"About three months, she thinks."

Ardyce could see the wheels turning in Owen's mind. "That would make it early June," he muttered. "Shortly before I came."

"If she already knew she was pregnant, or suspected, she may have thought she could entice you into an . . . ah, an intimate relationship. Then nobody would ever know."

Owen shook his head. "Is that what you came here to tell me? That my fiancée is pregnant with some other man's baby? What gives you the right—?"

"Owen," Ardyce interrupted, "believe me, it was not my intention to meddle in your life. I just—well, I'm Rae's friend, and once I knew you were engaged to JoLynn, I guess I thought she and her sister should know that you wouldn't be coming back. But it wasn't my place to tell them—it needed to come from you. I didn't know how long you'd been in North Fork. I just took JoLynn's word for it that this was your baby. I never meant to hurt you. Or JoLynn. Or anybody."

"I believe you," Owen sighed. "We never mean to hurt people, do we?"

Ardyce couldn't think of a thing to say, so she waited for him to go on.

"Take JoLynn," Owen continued. "I doubt that she meant to hurt me, either. She was probably pretty desperate, and when I came back home, well, I was the logical solution to her problem. Buddy's father, reappearing as if from the grave, to take up his responsibilities." He paused and shook his head. "I'm not stupid—or blind. I know what people say about JoLynn. But she's a good mother, a loving mother. She's just trying to do what's best for her son. And right now she doesn't have a lot of options."

When Owen said, *She's just trying to do what's best for her son,* a memory of that photograph—that dark-eyed, dungaree-clad urchin—snapped into focus in Ardyce's mind. The nagging feeling that she was missing something crystallized, and she looked deep into Owen's eyes. Blue eyes. Of course.

"Buddy is not your son," she said with intensity.

"What are you talking about? You don't even know him."

"I've never met him, that's true. But I have met JoLynn. And you."

"What does that have to do with anything?"

"Humor me," Ardyce answered. "Describe JoLynn."

"She's a few inches taller than I am," Owen recited dully. "Pretty, I'd say. Blonde hair, blue eyes, nice figure—"

"And what about Buddy?"

"He's just a boy. Freckles across his nose. Blond hair the color of his mother's, but curly like mine."

"And his eyes?"

"Brown."

"That's it!"

"What's it?"

Ardyce's mind spun. How could she explain it to him? "Do you know anything about genetics, Owen? Cross breeding cattle, maybe, or corn?"

Owen shook his head. "I might have, once. But if I did, it's buried somewhere with the rest of my memories. What's this all about?"

She pulled three cookies off the plate and broke one in half. "OK. The round cookies represent dominant genes. The half cookies represent recessive genes. Do you know what that means?"

Owen nodded. "I think so. The dominant characteristics come out over the recessive ones."

"Right. Say you have a brown cow with a brown gene, which is dominant, and a white gene, which is recessive." She laid down one of the whole cookies and one half. "She mates with a bull who has only brown dominant genes. What color is the calf?"

"Brown," Owen said.

"And what if both the bull and the cow have one of each gene?"

"The bull and the cow will both be brown because the brown gene is dominant, but they could have a white calf if the two recessive genes combined."

"Exactly."

"Exactly what?" Owen demanded. "What do brown and white genes in cattle have to do with me?"

Ardyce held her breath. "Blue eye coloring is recessive, not dominant."

"Is this some kind of riddle you learned in nursing school?" Owen challenged, clearly frustrated. "I don't understand—" He paused; then his expression changed as the reality of the situation began to dawn on him. "Buddy has brown eyes."

Ardyce nodded.

"And you're saying it's genetically impossible for two blue-eyed parents to have a brown-eyed child."

"I'm afraid so. Owen, I'm so sorry, I truly am—"

"Sorry for helping me see the truth?" His words sounded brave, but an expression of utter misery filled his countenance.

"It wasn't my intention—"

"I know it wasn't. But you did it just the same. I should thank you."

"I'd guess you don't feel very grateful right now."

He shook his head. "My Aunt Gert warned me not to confuse honor with pity. I should have listened."

"You're a good man, Owen Slaughter. Now I understand—" She had been about to say *why Willie Coltrain is in love with you,* but she stopped herself in time. Instead she asked, "What are you going to do now?"

Owen ducked his head. "I'm not sure. First I have to figure out the gentlest way to break a six-year-old boy's heart." He looked up at her, and a single tear tracked down his cheek into his beard. "And how to put mine back together again."

27

I'll Walk Alone

On the road to New Ulm
September 3, 1945

Autumn colors streamed by in a blur of red and green and gold as Owen sped northward between Mankato, Minnesota, and the little town of St. Peter. To his right, the river bottom stretched low and muddy, and to his left, high rock bluffs reflected the light of the morning sun. According to the talkative waitress at the little cafe where he stopped for coffee, Jesse James had used the caves in these bluffs as a hideout before he was captured by the authorities.

"A hideout," he muttered. "Sounds like a good idea to me."

Beside him, Vallie whined and licked his hand.

The morning was chilly, but Owen couldn't resist the freedom of having the top down, so he burrowed a little deeper into his coat. Cousin Thomas's coat, actually. Cousin Thomas's convertible. And he had left just after breakfast to the sight of Cousin Thomas's parents, his Aunt Gert and Uncle Earl, shivering on the porch as they waved good-bye.

He would be back, of course, to visit. In the few weeks he had been in North Fork, Owen had grown remarkably attached to them and to the old family farmstead. As much as any place could feel like home, he guessed, that place did.

But he couldn't face the ridicule he was bound to get from the townspeople when word got out of how he had been deceived. Owen supposed it was better to be taken for a fool than to have people believing he was a lowlife who would run away from his responsibilities as a father. Still, it wasn't much of a choice. And even though he knew what he had to do, he still felt pretty miserable about it.

Facing Buddy was the worst. The moment Owen showed up on the doorstep on Sunday morning, JoLynn took one look at his face and knew that he knew. She had confessed everything—privately, of course—and begged him to let Buddy down easy.

But it was the hardest thing Owen had ever done, gazing into those trusting brown eyes and telling Buddy Ferber that he was not, in fact, his father. And that he would be going away.

A lump rose in Owen's throat as he remembered the bewildered look on the child's face. "Your mother and I—well—we made a mistake," he had forced himself to say. "I'm so sorry, Buddy. I never meant to hurt you—"

Then he had completely broken down as the boy's tears fell on his shoulder. "Couldn't you just—stay—anyway?" Buddy had asked desperately. "Nobody would have to know."

"I'm afraid I'd know," Owen responded, hating how he felt but knowing he had to be honest with the child. "And your mother would know. I have to leave, Buddy. I know you can't understand it, but try to trust me. It's better this way."

It was a stupid thing to say, and of course the boy knew it. "It's not better," he countered. Then he looked into Owen's eyes and whispered, "Will you be all right?"

The intensity in the child's voice shook Owen to the core. "What-what do you mean?"

"You need us, too," Buddy said quietly. "You need a family. I'm worried about you, being all alone."

Pain knifed through Owen's chest at the memory. "I want you to take good care of your mother," he had managed to say. "She'll need your help."

Buddy nodded and wrapped his arms around Owen's neck. "You'll always be my daddy," he said in a choked voice. "No matter what anyone says."

It had taken all of Owen's willpower to get into the car and drive away. Buddy was right. It wasn't the best choice. It was only the lesser of two terrible options.

★ ★ ★

Gradually, as the miles rolled by under his tires, the ache in Owen's heart subsided a little, and he was able to enjoy the freedom of being on the road. The sunshine warmed his face, and Vallie, in the passenger's seat, lolled her head over the side of the car and drank in the wind.

She was enjoying this outing immensely, and Owen had to admit that he was glad to have her along. He didn't remember having the company of a dog in his former life, of course, and he couldn't have imagined how people could talk to dogs as if they were human and treat them like a member of the family. Then he had met Fritz and Führer. And when Vallie came into his life—or *back* into his life—she helped fill a void he never knew was there.

He reached across the seat and stroked her long fur, and she swiveled her head toward him. "We'll be there soon, girl," he murmured. "I hope they like dogs."

Vallie gave him a disdainful look as if to say, *What's not to like?* and then turned back to watch the road.

Owen flipped the radio on and fiddled with the tuning knob until a station came in. "I'll walk alone," a female voice—Dinah Shore, he thought—was singing. "They'll ask me why, and I'll tell them I'd rather . . . there are dreams I must gather. . . ."

He hummed along with the music, letting the words wash over him in a soothing wave. It wasn't so bad to be alone—not like it had been back in the prison camp when he didn't know anything about who he was. Now, at least, pieces of his past fit together like the image in a jigsaw puzzle. Some pieces were missing, to be sure, but he had an overall picture. And the dark void, the gaping hole that had tormented his spirit for so long, was gone.

When had that happened, and how? When had the emptiness subsided? Even though he didn't feel emotionally attached to what he knew about himself, he now realized with some surprise that he *felt* like Owen Slaughter. As if he finally had an identity.

Maybe belonging, having a place to call *home,* had more to do with internal geography than with a fixed address. Perhaps this was the need that drove Owen to leave Eden and go to North Fork, Iowa, and beyond— not someone *else* waiting for him, longing for his return, but *himself* out there somewhere, urging him to come home.

"I'll always be near you, wherever you are . . . so close your eyes, and I'll be there. . . ." the voice on the radio sang. And almost against his will, Owen thought about Willie Coltrain. Was she waiting for him, hoping he would come back again? Or had she forgotten him, relegated him to the past, and gone on with her life?

Dinah Shore's voice tugged at his heartstrings. Even when he was planning to marry JoLynn Ferber, to do his duty and take up his role as husband and father, Willie had been with him, always in the back of his mind. For the moment he had to walk alone, but his dreams—the dreams he had not even dared to speak—still gathered in his soul. Dreams for . . . someday.

Caught up in his reverie, Owen had almost missed the turnoff to New Ulm. Now, driving down the main street, he felt as if he had been transported back in time, to Germany. But it was a gentler Germany than the one he had known in the war. Here people smiled and chatted to one another on the sidewalks, and a few turned and waved at the unusual sight of a man in a convertible driving with a large collie in the front seat. He almost expected to see Fritz Sonntag and Führer standing on the street corner.

Owen pulled into a parking space in front of the post office and got out. "Stay," he told Vallie. "I won't be long."

The postmistress, a square, heavyset woman with pink cheeks and a broad smile, nodded vehemently when he asked if she knew the where-abouts of one Kurt Sonntag and his wife, Leah. *"Ja, ja!"* She patted him on his bearded cheek. "Herr Sonntag *ist* very fine man. Very fine. And that Leah, what a lovely frau!"

"The address?" Owen prompted.

"Just down the street—four, maybe five blocks. Sixth Avenue—you turn right, *ja?* Two more blocks, house on the left. Nice white house with green trim and a big red maple tree in the front yard."

"Thanks so much," Owen said, turning to go.

"One moment, please." When Owen looked back, the postmistress had a look of concern on her face. "You not bring bad news, I hope?"

"Bad news?"

"Kurt and Leah, they worry a great deal about their brother back in Deutschland."

Owen grinned at her. "No. No bad news. Good news, I hope."

"Das ist gut." Her head bounced up and down in affirmation. "You go now."

Owen returned to the car to find several towheaded children clustered around Vallie.

"I hope you don't mind, mister," one of the older girls said politely. "We just wanted to pet her."

"Of course not. She loves attention."

"What's her name?"

"Valentine," Owen answered. "I call her Vallie."

"We tried to call her out of the car," the girl admitted. "But she wouldn't budge."

Owen grinned. "That's because I told her to stay." He looked at Vallie. "It's all right, girl. You can get out if you want to."

The collie leaped over the door of the convertible and sat down in the middle of the crowd of admiring children. She charmed them all by offering to shake hands and submitted to being petted and pulled at. Owen smiled as he watched the dog's gentleness with the little ones. Even when a tiny child of about three tugged on her ears, she made no move to retaliate.

"I'm afraid I have to go now," he said at last. "Vallie, come."

Vallie stood and shook herself, then jumped back into the car and sat down.

As Owen backed out of the parking space and headed off down the street, the children waved and Vallie barked. Before he knew it, he was turning onto Sixth Avenue and pulling up in front of the white house with the big red maple.

Owen's stomach churned. He probably should have told them he was coming. The idea of the visit had been in the back of his mind all along, but until he found out about JoLynn, he hadn't made any firm plans. He could only hope that Kurt Sonntag shared his brother's gift of hospitality.

With Vallie at his side, he went up the walk to the front door and knocked. After a moment or two, a woman answered the door. "Ja?"

"Are you—are you Leah Sonntag?" Owen stared at her. She had ash-blonde hair and rather angular features, with large dark eyes and a large full mouth. Not beautiful by conventional standards, but very striking and rather exotic.

A look of suspicion flitted briefly across her face and was gone. "And you are—?"

"Oh, I'm-I'm sorry," he stammered, holding out his hand. "My name is Owen Slaughter, and I'm a friend of—"

He never got to finish his introduction. The woman's expression cleared, and an amazing transformation took place. Her eyes lit up with some inner light, and she smiled. "Fritz's friend from the prison camp! He wrote all about you and your—" She paused, and her face clouded. "I am so sorry about the death of your friend. Fritz said he was a good man, a hero."

"Yes, he was." An image of Charlie rose up in Owen's mind, and he shook his head. "I still miss him a great deal."

"Please, come in," she said, standing aside.

"I should have called or written, but—"

"Certainly not." Her voice was warm, welcoming. "You are family, and family is always welcome in the home of Kurt Sonntag."

Owen looked down at Vallie, who sat quietly on the stoop beside him.

"This is Valentine, my dog. If you'd rather she didn't come into the house, she—"

But his concern was obviously misdirected. Leah Sonntag was on her knees on the front porch, stroking Vallie's fur and accepting the paw the collie offered in greeting. "She is lovely," Leah murmured, "and very well mannered. Of course she is welcome too."

They went into the house—a small Cape Cod with lace curtains at the windows and handmade rag rugs on the hardwood floors. In the living room, a small child sat in a wooden playpen arranging blocks. As soon as she caught a glimpse of the dog, she was on her feet reaching over the rails. "Pup-py!"

Leah laughed and picked her up. "Our daughter, Stephanie. Steffie, this is Mr. Slaughter. Can you say 'Mr. Slaughter'?"

"Pup-py!" Steffie squirmed and reached down toward the collie.

"It's all right," Owen assured her. "Vallie is very gentle with children."

Leah set Steffie on her feet, and the girl ran immediately and threw her pudgy arms around Vallie's neck. "Pup-py," she murmured into the soft, thick fur. "Nice puppy."

"Kurt should be home soon," Leah said, glancing at the clock as she led Owen into the kitchen. "I was just about to prepare lunch for him." She turned and gave Owen a plaintive look. "You will stay for a while?"

"I don't know. I guess I hadn't made any . . . firm plans."

"We have an extra room, and you are most welcome. Kurt will be eager for firsthand news of his brother and the . . . situation . . . in Germany."

She didn't mention her own people, Owen noticed. But he supposed that if his family had been slaughtered in a Nazi death camp, he wouldn't want to talk about it either.

"You said Fritz had written about me?"

Leah opened the refrigerator and pulled out a covered dish. "Hasenpfef-fer," she explained. "Kurt likes it cold, but I will heat some for you if you wish."

Owen remembered the way Fritz made the traditional German dish, and his mouth began to water. "Hot or cold, it doesn't matter. I love it."

She smiled in his direction. "Anyone who lived with Fritz for more than two days would have to love it—or starve to death."

"That and squirrel stew," Owen added, recalling the rich thick concoction that had put meat back on his bones during their stay in the Black Forest.

Leah wrinkled her nose. "Kurt is always—what is the word?—pestering me to make some for him."

"You don't like it?"

"I am a city girl," she said. "I grew up in Heidelberg, then moved to Baden-Baden when I was twenty. I never became accustomed to eating from the forest."

"Except for rabbits." Owen pointed at the hasenpfeffer.

"All Germans eat rabbit," she countered. "It is not kosher, but I gave up keeping a kosher diet long before I married Kurt."

Owen sat down at the table and watched as she prepared the meal. "Do you find life in the States very different?"

"Different?" She shrugged. "Ja. More peaceful and less frightening. I think our—our adjustment—would have been more difficult if we had not come here to New Ulm. There are so many of our countrymen here that it is almost like being at home." A shudder passed over her thin frame. "Without the Nazis."

"Your English is very good," Owen commented. "Am I right in assuming that you plan to stay now that the war is over? That you've found . . . a home?"

Leah paused in her work and smiled up at him. "Danke. Kurt and I work very hard at speaking well. And yes, we see no point in returning to Germany. My family—" She stopped suddenly and turned away from him.

"I know," Owen said gently. "Fritz told me what happened to them. I'm so sorry."

"Thousands died," she murmured quietly. "Perhaps millions—who knows? But one thing I do know—Hitler's ideas did not die with him. I can never go home again. Many will try to resurrect that terrible dream; many will keep on working to see the Jews, and all 'undesirables,' eradicated."

"And many more, like Kurt's brother, Fritz, are determined to see that it never happens again." Owen saw the expression of disbelief on her face, and he sighed. He knew all too well what it was like to feel homeless and disconnected, cut off from your heritage. "The war in Europe is over, Leah. Maybe the time will come when you can go back. After all, you don't look Jewish. You could pass—"

She turned toward him, her eyes smoldering. "Do you have any idea what it is like, Owen Slaughter, to be forced by your own society, your own people, to live a lie—to pretend to be something you are not? To survive each day haunted by the knowledge that if they found out who you really were, they would reject you, even kill you? Do you know what the Nazis call Jews? *Untermenschen*—less than human." She shook her head. "No, Owen, I will not go back to that. Not ever. It is like trying to exist in a coffin. We are making a life for ourselves here, a life where Steffie can have the benefit of light and air and opportunity. We miss Fritz, of course. But we cannot return."

Owen walked to the kitchen doorway and looked into the living room. Little Steffie lay sound asleep on the rug with her head on Vallie's haunches. The dog looked up at him with liquid eyes but did not move.

"You see," Leah said softly, coming up behind him, "there is peace for my daughter in this new land. 'The wolf shall lie down with the lamb . . . and a little child shall lead them.'"

He turned. "That sounds familiar—what is it?"

Leah smiled. "It is from the writing of Isaiah, part of the prophecy of the Messiah."

"The Messiah?"

"Yes," she responded simply, "the Anointed One, who was sent as the Sacrifice Lamb. The One whose coming was foretold by the prophets."

Owen shook his head. Charlie—and Fritz too, for that matter—would say without hesitation that the Messiah had already come. Leah seemed to accept that truth without question. But how was it possible to see what she had seen and believe in a Savior, a Messiah?

As if she had read his mind, Leah touched him gently on the shoulder. "Some terrors cannot be explained," she said softly. "But they should not be blamed on God."

Just then the front door opened, and Owen caught a glimpse of a tall man in the entryway. Steffie awoke and bounded to her feet. "Papa!"

"Hello, my little *liebchen!*" he boomed, swinging her up and bouncing her on his hip. "We have a visitor, I see. A visitor with a topless car about to get soaked."

"Uh-oh!" Owen ran to the door just in time to see the clouds open up in a downpour.

"Do not worry, my friend. I took the liberty of putting the top up and closing the windows."

"Thank you." Owen turned from the doorway and, for the first time, looked carefully at Kurt Sonntag. Except for being clean shaven, Kurt could have been Fritz's twin—the same brawny build, the same light brown hair thinning in front, the same twinkling eyes.

A rush of emotion assailed Owen. Suddenly he missed Fritz—and Charlie—more than he thought possible. But one was dead and the other was thousands of miles away . . . yet here stood his mirror image, right in front of Owen.

"Kurt, we are honored by the presence of Owen Slaughter," Leah said quietly.

"Owen Slaughter? The man Fritz—?"

Leah nodded.

Apparently what Owen had heard about German reticence had been grossly exaggerated, for in two strides Kurt crossed the room and swept Owen into an enormous bear hug, pounding him on the back. "You are my brother's brother," he boomed with a deep laugh. "Welcome! Welcome!"

Owen's mind told him this was Kurt, but it was Fritz's voice he heard, Fritz's laugh. His heart surged with warmth, with the memory of those weeks in the Black Forest. Fritz Sonntag had saved his life, and now his brother was giving him something equally valuable.

Belonging.

28

Turning Leaves

Paradise Garden Cafe
September 10, 1945

Orris Craven stood outside the door of the Paradise Garden Cafe and peered in. In a last-ditch effort to get this mess with the Breckinridge Foundation straightened out to Colonel Laporte's satisfaction, he had decided to go straight to the horse's mouth, so to speak—to confront Harlan Brownlee, former owner of the land in question, and find out what he knew. Poor people could usually be bullied and intimidated into giving you the information they needed.

Orris had never met Harlan Brownlee, but according to Clinton Marston's sources in Memphis, the old geezer spent most of his time in the little one-horse town of Eden, playing the piano and living on handouts. If he had any information at all on the Breckinridge operation, he was sure to be upset about losing his land and ready to talk. Orris would play up to Brownlee, gain his trust, pretend to be on his side.

It should be easy enough: a hot meal, a little pressure . . .

The problem was, Orris was losing his taste for tactics like this. He didn't *enjoy* it anymore. For the first time in years, his conscience had started bothering him, and he had begun to lie awake nights wondering—and worrying—about the people involved in these foreclosure deals. Where were they, and how were they living? Were little children going hungry or cold because of him? His imagination conjured up a horde of gaunt faces that invaded his dreams and haunted his waking thoughts.

This wasn't like Orris—at least not like he had been in the past few years. He kept thinking about Beauregard Laporte's wife, that frail, birdlike woman who spoke in such glowing terms about her noble and self-sacrificing son. And thoughts of Mrs. Laporte led inevitably to memories of his own mother, her dreams of greatness for him, her belief in him, in his . . . his character. Now he found himself wanting to be the man his mother had envisioned, a man of integrity. A man like Mrs. Laporte's son, Andrew.

Laporte—and Clinton Marston, too, for that matter—would say that character was a liability in a lawyer, that integrity was a luxury a good attorney couldn't afford. And maybe they were right.

But right or wrong, Orris didn't have much choice at this point. He was scheduled to meet with that rich Breckinridge woman and her lawyers on Saturday in Grenada, and if he hadn't come up with something by then, Laporte was sure to give him the boot.

Straightening his tie and summoning his courage, Orris pushed the door open and entered the Paradise Garden Cafe.

The cafe, on this Monday morning, was all but empty. The room smelled of onions and grease and stale cigarette smoke, and Orris looked around in dismay. If this was someone's idea of Paradise, the Almighty had played a wicked practical joke on the universe.

The strains of piano music reached his ears, and Orris's gaze drifted to the far corner of the room, where a wiry old man played a rickety upright, his rounded shoulders bent over the keyboard. This must be his target, Harlan Brownlee. Behind the counter, a waitress with henna-dyed hair sat with her nose buried in the newspaper. The only customers were two men, a young fellow and an older man who could have been his father, drinking coffee in the back booth.

Orris took a step forward, and the waitress lowered the paper. A look of recognition flashed in her brown eyes, and suddenly the bottom dropped out of his stomach. It was her—that Breckinridge society woman! Or someone enough like her to be her twin sister. But what was she doing here in a shabby small-town cafe, impersonating a waitress?

His eyes drifted to the two men and fixed on the older one. Dark hair with a sweep of gray at the temples. The attorney, Mr. Winsom—and his assistant, Mr. Drew!

A chill ran up Orris's spine. He didn't know how or why, but somehow . . . He had been set up.

Thelma felt a jolt run through her whole body when the bell over the door sounded and she looked up to see Orris Craven standing in the doorway.

They weren't supposed to meet him until Saturday, and that was at the Jefferson House in Grenada. Then the truth hit her.

He wouldn't be here unless he knew everything. The jig was up.

Panicked, she caught Bennett's eye and flashed him a warning glance, then motioned with her head toward the door. Bennett caught sight of Craven and jumped to his feet with Drew right behind him.

"Mr. Craven," Bennett said as he approached the lawyer, "this is . . . ah, unexpected. We didn't anticipate seeing you until Saturday in Grenada."

Craven gave him an odd look and shook his hand cautiously. "Mr. Winsom." He paused, then narrowed his eyes at Thelma. "Just what is going on here? What is Mrs. Breckinridge doing masquerading as a waitress in a place like this?" He wrinkled his nose in disdain.

The condescending expression on his face and the way he said *a place like this* made Thelma want to throttle him, but she restrained herself. She glanced first at Drew and then at Bennett.

Drew took a step forward. "The question is, what are *you* doing here?"

Craven's eyes drifted toward Ivory, who had stopped playing and was gaping at them with his mouth open. "I have business with Mr. Brownlee."

Thelma saw the anger rising in Drew's eyes, but before she could intervene, Bennett laid a restraining hand on Drew's arm and shook his head. Drew stepped back, and Bennett said, "Mr. Brownlee has no business with you."

"What right do you have to speak for Mr. Brownlee?" Craven flared.

"The right of an attorney to protect his client's interests." Bennett spoke in a low, controlled tone, but Thelma could hear the underlying determination in his voice.

Craven's face hardened and his brow furrowed. Then, as if all the pieces had suddenly fallen into place, his expression cleared. "I see." He turned to Thelma. "There is no Breckinridge Foundation, is there?"

She shook her head.

"So you are—?"

Thelma looked toward Bennett, and he nodded. "Thelma Breckinridge, owner of this cafe."

Craven's lips turned up in a cynical smile. "You were good, you know. Almost had me convinced." He turned toward Drew. "And you, Mr. Drew. You really did your homework. You could be very successful at this, if you set your mind to it."

"Your definition of success doesn't interest me," Drew snapped. "Not in the least."

For a moment a bewildered expression crossed Craven's face, then his eyes cleared. "Why?" he asked. "Why this elaborate charade? What's in it for you?"

"I suppose we should sit down and discuss it," Bennett said. He motioned to a table and pulled out a chair for Craven. "Thelma, could you bring us some coffee? This is likely to take a little while."

Thelma shut her eyes and sighed, but even behind her closed eyelids the image of Bennett's face remained etched in her memory—an expression of frustration and defeat.

They had come all this way, only to lose in the final round.

★ ★ ★

Orris sat sipping his coffee and listening to the story Bennett Winsom was telling. The three of them had concocted this scheme to get to him, setting up the fictitious Breckinridge Foundation and buying Harlan Brownlee's land out from under his nose. If he had been paying more attention that day at the courthouse, he might have recognized Winsom and the woman when they met in Grenada. But he had been so angry at losing the deal that he couldn't see beyond the threat to his own position.

Now his position, such as it was, was secure. He had won. Beauregard Laporte would be proud of him, probably give him a raise and that office he coveted in the Quarter.

Still, his victory gave him no joy.

"You managed to take over the Brownlee property so Mr. Brownlee wouldn't lose his land," Orris summarized, wanting to make sure he had all this clear.

Bennett nodded.

"But that wasn't enough. You set up this scheme, this phony foundation, to catch my employer and put him out of business? Why? What did you hope to get out of it?"

The younger lawyer, Drew, raised one eyebrow. "You might not be capable of understanding this," he said in a scathing tone, "but the only thing we wanted to 'get out of it,' as you put it, was the satisfaction of helping a lot of people who were powerless to help themselves."

Orris's mind churned, trying to sort it all out. These three people had spent countless hours researching and working, with no hope of compensation, to help a broken old man they called their friend—and a bunch of people they had never even met? It didn't make any sense at all, and yet . . .

Suddenly, even as his mind was trying to wrap around the concept, something in his soul snapped. Mr. Winsom, intelligent and capable as he was, probably could have been a superior court judge by now, but here he was giving his life away to people like Harlan Brownlee. And Mr. Drew—well, he could have been the son Mrs. Laporte was so proud of, a young attorney who, even starting out, already had his priorities in order and his heart in the right place. He wasn't quite sure what Thelma Breckinridge's connection was in all this, but clearly she cared, not only about Brownlee, but about all the other "little people" Orris's employers had cheated. Even, Orris realized with a start, about him.

As if seeing them for the first time, Orris looked from one face to another. Honest faces. Noble faces. People of . . . of integrity.

Other faces rose in his memory: Beauregard Laporte's sneering, power-glutted countenance; Mrs. Laporte's wistful expression when she talked about her son; his own mother's trusting gaze, full of confidence that her boy would make her proud.

Without even thinking about it consciously, Orris knew that he was at a turning point in his life and career, a moment of truth. He could turn his back, return to New Orleans in victory, enjoy the admiration and approval of a man like Beauregard T. Laporte, and go on to line his own pockets deceiving people like Harlan Brownlee. It would be so easy.

But could he live with himself if he did? That part wouldn't be easy, nor would it be a simple matter to erase these faces from his memory. It was one thing to take advantage of an anonymous target on a legal contract, but quite another to face living, breathing human beings, look them in the eye, and feel good about winning over helpless, powerless, ordinary people whose lives you had ruined.

An image formed in his mind: a line, drawn in the sand. He had to decide. Now, right here. Choose or be lost to himself and to all that was good in him forever. And he knew without a doubt whose side he wanted to be on.

★ ★ ★

Drew Laporte watched as a strange transformation took place on the face of Orris Craven. From their first meeting, Thelma had been convinced that the rat had a heart, that he needed prayer, that God could change him. Drew had humored her but hadn't been persuaded. Men like Orris Craven had bartered their souls to the corrupting influences of greed and success and power. They were beyond hope, past all redemption.

Now Drew wasn't so sure, and he found himself fighting against the temptation to give Craven the benefit of the doubt. As Bennett had talked about why they had spent so much time and effort on this case, Craven's expression had altered. When Bennett was finished, Craven sat silent for a moment or two, and then began to speak.

"When I was in law school," he said with a wistful sigh, "my mother gave up everything to support me. We didn't have much, but she worked hard to help me with tuition, and she was always there, standing behind me, encouraging me. She . . . she believed in me. Believed I would do something good and noble with my life. You know, help other people."

"Help yourself to their money, you mean."

Bennett poked Drew in the ribs to silence him, but Craven didn't seem offended.

"That's exactly what I did, Mr. Drew." The rat lifted his shoulders in resignation. "I let other people dictate what I would do, what kind of lawyer I would become. I went to work for unscrupulous men and became like them. The money has been pretty good, but lately I've begun to realize that money isn't enough."

"You met us, found out how wonderful we are, and wanted to be just like us," Drew muttered sarcastically. "Yeah. Right."

"Give him a chance," Thelma said.

"It's all right. I don't blame you for not trusting me." Craven's eyes met Drew's. "But please, hear me out."

Drew waved a hand for Craven to continue.

"You were right when you said I probably wouldn't understand what you've done here," he went on. "And I might not have, except that . . . well, other things have been happening to me."

Thelma squeezed Bennett's hand and leaned forward. "What kinds of things?"

"For one thing, memories of my mother kept surfacing in my mind. How she always believed in me. And for the first time in years, I felt ashamed of what I was doing. Then I met a woman—my employer's wife, in fact. She wasn't what I expected . . . not like him at all. She reminded me a little of my mother, and she kept telling me about her son. She was so proud of him, of his integrity and his honor." He sighed. "I was a little jealous, I'm afraid. I didn't know her well, but I felt a little like the black-sheep son, and I couldn't help thinking what I'd give to be like her Andrew."

All the blood drained from Drew's head, and the room started to spin. He reached across the table and grabbed Craven by the lapels of his coat. *"Andrew?"*

"Y-yes," Craven stammered. "That was her son's name, you see. Hearing about him stirred something in me, some long-buried desire to—"

"What was your employer's name?" Drew demanded, shaking him like a rag doll.

Craven went pale. "I-I'd rather not say, sir. You have enough information to put a stop to his activities, and I couldn't betray—"

Drew heard Bennett's voice from a great distance and felt strong fingers prying at his hands. "Drew! Let go of him!"

"His name!" Drew repeated.

"La-Laporte," Craven stammered helplessly. "Colonel Beauregard T. —"

Drew let go and sank into his chair. He should have known, should have put it all together, but even now his mind would not let him believe it. "You're lying," he said in a monotone.

"No, sir, I'm not. Why—?"

"My father," Drew whispered to himself. "My own father."

Orris's heart was pounding in his ears when the young lawyer dropped him back into his chair, and for a minute he thought he had heard wrong.

"Your *what?*"

"My father," Mr. Drew repeated listlessly. "Beau Laporte is my father."

"You're Andrew Laporte?" Orris took a closer look, and now that he thought about it, there was a resemblance. Put another twenty-five pounds on him, a white suit and gray hair, and yes, he could believe it. Andrew Laporte, the golden son, the icon of integrity, had nearly taken his head from his shoulders.

"Forgive me," Laporte murmured softly. "I shouldn't have lost control like that. Did I hurt you?"

"No, Mr. Drew—" Orris stopped suddenly. *Mr. Drew.* Of course. When they had met at the Jefferson House, Drew had introduced himself with his first name, and Orris had mistakenly assumed it was his surname.

He watched as the young lawyer put his hands over his face and sighed miserably. Orris felt sorry for him—sorry that Drew Laporte had a father like the Colonel, sorry that he had been the one to break the news. But more than that he felt shame at having been right in the middle of it all, lying and cheating and stealing with the worst of them—and making it his business to cover all the bases and make everything look clean and legal.

"Drew," Mr. Winsom said softly, "what do you want to do?"

Drew looked up at him with a lost expression. "I don't know. He is my father, and I love him. But I can't let him continue ruining other people's lives." He shook his head. "I don't understand it. We've never needed the money."

"It's not about money," Orris corrected. "It's about power."

Drew nodded. "I don't want to hurt him—or Mother. But I know too much to let it go on. I have to stop him."

"Drew," Bennett Winsom interrupted, "you don't have to be involved in this. We can—"

"No, you can't," he countered. "It has to be me. It has to be personal. You could shut his operation down, but what good would that do? It won't change his heart, his motives. He'll just be back at it again. I'm the only one who has even a chance of getting to him."

"Let me help," Orris said quietly.

Drew stared at him. *"You?"*

"I want to do something right for once. Something good." Orris swallowed hard and forced a smile. "I have to start somewhere, and I sure don't have a job to go back to."

Here in this dismal little cafe, Orris had made his decision. He couldn't just turn over a new leaf and start again. It wasn't that easy. The filth still clung to him, and the only way to wash his own hands was to begin cleaning up the mess he had helped to make.

Bennett put a hand on his arm. "You're serious about this, aren't you?"

"Dead serious." Orris lowered his eyes. "Or maybe that's the wrong way to say it. The truth is, I haven't felt this alive in years."

29

Forgetting What Lies
Behind . . .

September 15, 1945
New Ulm, Minnesota

Owen Slaughter awoke to bright autumn sunlight streaming in his window. Nothing in his experience had prepared him for fall in Minnesota—the bright blue skies, the riot of changing color against the hillsides, the scent of burning leaves, the snap of chill in the air that awakened the spirit and roused a bittersweet longing in the soul.

He propped his hands under his head and smiled. An autumn like this surely would have the power to stir memories of a fellow's boyhood, of romping in the fallen leaves, playing football in a vacant field, coming in with wind-whipped cheeks to the warmth of a fire and the comfort of a mug of hot chocolate. He had no such memories, but even so, he enjoyed a sense of well-being, a contentment with life and with himself. As Nature cloaked herself in the many hues of change, Owen Slaughter felt his own heart settling into contentment.

He had been with Fritz's brother and sister-in-law for nearly two weeks now, and their initial hospitality had deepened into a firmly rooted friendship. Little Steffie had taken to calling him "Unca Owen," and Kurt and Leah regarded him as a brother, a member of the family. Even Vallie had found her place in the household, sleeping every night on the rug in front of Steffie's door, guarding the child with a fierce and adoring determination.

Owen loved these people, loved the sense of belonging he felt in their presence. And yet somehow it wasn't enough.

There was some piece missing, some important piece, that nagged at his mind and made him feel incomplete.

A rustling sound at his door arrested Owen's attention, and he sat up. The door opened just a crack, and Vallie's long narrow nose pushed through. "Come on, girl," he said.

It was all the invitation the collie needed. She bounded onto the bed, followed by pudgy, round-faced Steffie in pink footed pajamas.

"Unca Owen!" The child bounced up and down, curls flying, her wide brown eyes sparkling with mirth. "Get up, Unca Owen!"

"Steffie!" Leah's stern mother-voice came from the doorway. "Do not bother your Uncle Owen."

"She's fine." Owen laughed as Steffie reached her little hands to tug at his beard. "I was already awake."

"Breakfast will be ready in ten minutes."

"And I'll be ready for it." Owen hugged Steffie and kissed her on the top of the head, then set her down on the floor and gave her a gentle swat on her well-padded bottom. "Go on with Mommy," he said gently. "I'll be down in a couple of minutes."

As he watched her toddle out of the room with Vallie on her heels, Owen found himself battling against a surge of longing that almost overwhelmed him. This was what he wanted—a home, a family, children. Stability. Being here with the Sonntags had brought a measure of healing to his soul, and for that he was grateful. But soon he would have to move on . . . to what? He couldn't go back to live in North Fork, even though Gert and Earl had invited him to move back in permanently. It would be too awkward, being in close proximity to JoLynn—and much too painful to see Buddy. Besides, there was no future for him there, only an attic full of memorabilia from the past.

Owen pulled on his clothes, went to the bathroom to brush his teeth, and made his way down the stairs to the kitchen. He sat down at the kitchen table and played peekaboo with Steffie in her high chair while Leah served their plates.

"Kurt had to go in early this morning," she explained as she set his breakfast in front of him and turned back to get the coffeepot. "Steffie, eat your cereal."

Steffie peered down into her bowl of oatmeal, then grabbed at a slice of toast on the side of Owen's plate. "Egg!" she demanded.

"No, you cannot have egg," her mother said firmly. "You had egg yesterday."

"Egg!" the child repeated, waving Owen's toast in her chubby little fist.

Owen laughed and pried the toast out of her grasp. "Look, Steffie," he said, picking up her spoon. "Yum, yum!" He pretended to eat her oatmeal, then fed her a spoonful. She took it willingly, giggling and mimicking him, then suddenly put her fingers into the bowl and smeared a handful of the goop into his beard.

"Oh, Owen, I am so sorry," Leah said, handing him a napkin. "Steffie, *nein!*"

Steffie puckered up and began to cry.

"Don't worry about it." Owen removed the tray from the high chair and settled Steffie in his lap. "Uncle Owen has everything under control." He scraped the oatmeal out of his beard and bounced Steffie on his knee. As her tears dried up, she snuggled into the crook of his arm, a warm little bundle against the side of his chest.

"You will make a wonderful father," Leah said as she sat down across from him.

He tried to hide the pain that slashed through him, but she saw.

"You are troubled?"

"I . . . I don't want to bother you with my concerns," he said hesitantly.

Leah raised one eyebrow. "We are not your friends? You do not feel a part of this family?"

"Yes, of course, but—"

"But you think I would not understand, that your troubles are beyond my comprehension. Or perhaps that in comparison with what I have experienced, your own concerns would seem petty and unimportant. You do not want to—what is the word—whine?"

Owen shook his head in amazement. "Yes, that's it exactly. I don't want to whine." He paused for a moment. "You have been through so much, Leah. You've lost your family, your home, everything. I've only lost my memory. I should be able to get over it and go on with my life."

She seemed to think about this for a minute, then said, "Indeed, my pain has been great. Except for Kurt and Steffie, I have, as you say, lost everything. But my family is still with me—in my mind, in my heart. They will never leave me." She gave him a penetrating look. "Perhaps yours is the greater pain. I remember the terror, but I also remember the love."

A warmth stung his eyes. These people had been so good to him, so loving and understanding. Only by sheer force of will could he say what had to be said. "It's time for me to leave here, Leah."

She nodded. "I know. We will send you off with a blessing, but we will miss you."

Owen hugged Steffie tighter and blinked back tears.

"Where will you go?"

He swallowed hard and shook his head. "I have no idea. That's the problem. I came seeking my past, and in some ways I've found what I was looking for. Although I still don't feel the connection, at least I know who I am and where I came from. But I still don't have any memories. Besides, now that I've found my past, how do I find my future? Where do I go?"

"I think you already know," Leah said softly.

"If I knew, wouldn't I be doing something about it?"

"Perhaps. Perhaps not." She smiled gently at him. "Perhaps you are afraid."

"Afraid of what?" he countered.

"Afraid of listening to your own heart. Afraid of taking a risk and being hurt."

The truth hit its mark, and Owen reeled. She was right, but he wasn't sure he could admit it to her, and he resisted admitting it even to himself. Only one option presented itself to him, but he rejected it. He had been away too long.

As if she had read his mind, Leah whispered, "Is Eden calling to you, Owen?"

Images of Willie Coltrain filled Owen's mind, and he struggled to get his breath. It had been more than three months since he had left, and he had never gotten through a day without thinking about her. She had probably forgotten all about him by now. Or if she remembered, she would never want to see him again. How could he go back now, to—?

"Let me tell you something I have learned," Leah said quietly. "The past is important for one reason only—because it makes us the people we are today. But we cannot live there. No one can, even those of us who have all our memories intact. Wherever you go from here, you are not going *back;* you are going *forward.*"

She paused and looked into his eyes. "There are two ways to approach the future, Owen—with anxiety or with anticipation. The future is always hidden to us. We cannot know it or control it—that is God's domain—but we can decide how we will *perceive* it. Whether we will take risks and reach out, or whether we will give in to fear and never know the possibilities."

Owen thought about this for a moment and wondered how Leah had become so wise. "So if I want to be a person who faces the future with anticipation rather than fear, how do I do that?"

She shrugged. "You *decide.* For some it comes naturally, but others have to work harder at it. I think it depends in part upon how a person was raised, taught to perceive. But it is also a matter of faith."

"Faith?"

Leah nodded. "In the book of the prophet Isaiah, the Almighty says: 'Do not remember the past or dwell upon what has gone before. See? I am doing a new thing. Even now I am causing rivers to spring up in the desert and waters in the wilderness, so that my people may drink and be refreshed.'" She gave him a crooked smile. "You are one step ahead of the rest of us, Owen—you have already forgotten the past."

"Very funny."

"The point is," she went on, "that we are more than one step ahead if we face the future believing in a Messiah who loves us and wants the best for us. When we stand at a crossroads and do not know which way to go, we can ask for guidance and trust that Almighty God will lead us in the right way."

"Charlie believed that," Owen mused. "And so did Fritz."

"And you?"

"I don't know," he said honestly. "I want to, but—"

"Wanting to is enough," Leah assured him. "God sees the heart and knows what even we ourselves cannot understand. Ask."

"Ask what?"

"Ask for what you need," she responded simply. "And open your heart for the answer."

★ ★ ★

All day, as he played with Steffie and Vallie, counted out his gas ration coupons, and packed his bags, Owen thought about what Leah had said to him. He felt a bit like Father Abraham in the story she had told him, preparing to go out without knowing where he was going. And yet a sense of anticipation began to rise in his heart. What if it were true? What if God did indeed care enough about him to answer his prayer and give him direction for the future?

Owen wasn't at all sure exactly what *kind* of direction he was expecting, but he was willing to try. He just hoped that, if and when it came, it would be clear enough that he would get it.

As the quietness of night enveloped the house and settled over him, he got into bed and lay staring at the ceiling. "I'm not quite sure how to do this, God," he began, startled at the sound of his own voice in the silence of the room, "but I'm going to give it a shot. Leah says I should just ask for what I need. Well, what I need most right now is some kind of assurance as to what I ought to do next. I know you won't tell me what the future holds, and I probably don't want to know anyway. But at least the next step or two would be helpful. I'm leaving tomorrow, God, and I don't have the foggiest idea where I'm going. So please show me, and give me enough faith—and enough sense—to see what your answer is." Owen paused for a moment and then added, "Amen. Oh, and one more thing." His eyes blurred and his throat grew tight. "Tell Charlie I love him, would you? And thank him for being such a good friend to me."

After a while Owen drifted into sleep. And, as they had for months, the dreams came again. Obscure, shifting images of a train platform and a crowded station, of himself coming through the crowd looking, looking . . .

Where had he come from? Where was he going? Who was he looking for?

Then he saw her, standing off to one side in the shadows. A woman in a dark blue suit.

Even in his sleep, Owen was vaguely aware that this was where he always woke up, at the last moment as she moved into the light. The woman turned and took a step in his direction, apprehensively raising one hand in greeting.

He waved back, peering through the darkness. Just then the train let off a burst of steam, and she disappeared in the haze. *No!* his mind shouted. *No!*

Gradually the smoke cleared. He could see her feet, still moving toward him with hesitant steps. Then her blue suit, with one hand clutching a navy bag. She was coming closer. She was tall—taller than he was by a head. The last of the steam vanished, and he looked up into a halo of strawberry blonde curls and a shadowed countenance. One more step, and—

"Hello, Curly," the deep, rich voice murmured. "It's about time you got here. I was afraid you had forgotten me."

Owen looked into the dusky gray eyes, and his heart pounded. It was . . .

Willie Coltrain!

His pulse beating wildly, Owen sat straight up in bed and gasped for air.

Willie! It had been Willie all the time!

His mind raced. What had she said? *"It's about time you got here. I was afraid you had forgotten me."* What did that mean? He had never forgotten her, not for a single moment. He had fought against his feelings for her, tried to deny them, even when he was planning to do his duty and marry JoLynn Ferber. He had mistakenly believed—maybe because he was so desperate to find a place to belong—that JoLynn was the one who had been waiting for him.

But it was Willie! His Willie, standing on the platform, coming to him, speaking to him in that deep smoky voice that never failed to make his heart turn over.

Slow down, a voice inside him warned. *It was a dream. Only a dream.*

Yes, but it was *his* dream, the one that had haunted him in various forms for months. And now, finally, he had seen the face in the shadows. Was it possible, even remotely conceivable, that Willie felt something for him and was indeed waiting and hoping that he would come back? Even more incredible, had God heard his prayer and answered him through the dream? Or was it just coincidence?

Owen turned the lamp on and peered at the bedside clock. Five-thirty.

Coincidence or not, it had happened—and it had given him the courage to follow Leah's advice. To step out, take a risk, listen to his heart.

It was about time for Owen Slaughter to go home.

30

Homeward Bound

North Fork, Iowa
September 16, 1945

A little after noon, Owen pulled into the driveway of the old family farm-stead. Ever since they had crossed the river and begun the last stretch of the drive home, Vallie had grown increasingly agitated. Now, when he slowed to cross the cattle gap at the base of the driveway, she leaped from the car and ran barking up the road toward the house. By the time Owen pulled to a stop, both Aunt Gert and Uncle Earl stood in the yard staring at him.

"Welcome home, boy," Earl said, reaching out to give him an awkward one-armed hug. "We didn't expect to see you back here so soon."

"I didn't expect to be here so soon either." Owen leaned down and gave Aunt Gert a kiss on the cheek.

"We just got home from church and were sitting down to eat," Gert said, patting him on the cheek. "Come on in."

During the enormous Sunday dinner—baked chicken and stuffing, home-canned sweet corn, green beans, and Aunt Gert's fabulous rolls—Owen filled them in on the events of the past two weeks. He told them all about Kurt and Leah and little Steffie, how he felt that he had found a brother and sister, and how difficult it was to leave them after so short a time. When he had finished his third helping of chicken and was starting on his second piece of cake, Aunt Gert leaned over and fixed him with an intense gaze.

"That doesn't explain why you're here," she said in her typical no-non-sense manner. "We're happy to have you, of course, and mind you, you're always welcome under our roof, but I for one would like to hear the rest of the story."

Owen laughed. "I could never fool you, Aunt Gert. Of course there's more. But it . . . well, it's a little hard to explain."

"Try."

He took a deep breath. "Well, after the—the thing—with JoLynn, I was really confused. I had come here, as you know, to try to find some links to my past, maybe even to stir up the memory I'd lost in the war. But it didn't work. I got plenty of information, of course, and I did find family I didn't know I had." He patted Gert's hand and smiled. "When I left to go to New Ulm, I was looking for something, but I didn't have the faintest idea what it was."

"Maybe it was yourself," Gert offered. "Not your past, but your present and your future."

Owen gazed at her in wonder. Was there anything this woman didn't understand? He nodded and went on. "Leah Sonntag helped me see exactly that. She lost her home and all her family—everything—in the war. But she doesn't live in the past, and she doesn't fear the future. She helped me understand that although the past is vital for what it can teach us, what's really important is what we do with the people we are right now. The choices we make for the future, with—" He paused for a moment, a little embarrassed, but summoned his courage and finished, "with God's direc-tion."

Aunt Gert lifted her eyebrows and quirked a smile at him. "God's direc-tion?"

Owen nodded, feeling a bit sheepish. "When we were in the prison camp, I spent months listening to Charlie Coltrain talk about God's guidance. But I never experienced it for myself, not until now."

"What made the difference?"

Owen shrugged. "Leah told me to ask."

Gert chuckled and cast a glance at Earl. "Sounds like good advice."

"Leah's a very wise woman," Owen mused. "I wonder where that depth came from."

"From her pain, probably," Aunt Gert answered firmly. "Suffering changes people—either makes them softer and more sensitive, or hard and calloused. Either deepens people's faith or drives them away from God. Sounds like Leah has let her struggles work for the good." She paused and smiled at Owen. "She advised you to ask. And you did, I assume."

"Yeah, I did." Owen scratched at his beard. "It all seems so simple now, but then it felt like a major step—and a difficult one."

"The first steps are usually the hardest," Gert agreed.

"I felt awkward doing it—praying, I mean. But then something happened. I just asked for God's direction, and, well, it came." Owen didn't say *how* it came, didn't go into the details of the dream in which he had finally seen Willie's face in the shadows. "The next morning I knew what I had to do."

Aunt Gert took the plates from the table, refilled their coffee cups, and sat down again. "And just what is it that you have to do, Owen?"

"I'm going back to Eden," he answered resolutely. "I've been trying to fight my feelings for Willie Coltrain, but I love her. Not as a sister or as a part of my best friend's family, but for herself, as a woman. If she'll have me, I want to marry her."

Owen felt a strange wave of liberty rising in his soul as he said the words *I love her.* The more often he said it, out loud or to himself, the more certain he was that it was true. And with every fresh burst of certainty, his hope surged. This was the right thing to do. He knew it.

"I need to go right away," he went on. "Before I lose my nerve. I only came back to say good-bye and return Thomas's car. And to tell the two of you how much I appreciate all you've done for me." A lump formed in Owen's throat, and he swallowed hard. "I'm taking the bus out this afternoon, but I'll be back to visit, you can count on that. And I'll let you know what's happening—"

"Son," Earl interrupted, putting a hand on Owen's shoulder, "that car is yours. I've already changed over the title. We want you to have it, to keep it." He glanced at Gert, who nodded. "Besides, you'll make a lot better time getting back to that gal of yours. Bus doesn't run on Sunday evening, and I'm not sure they'd allow Vallie to have a seat of her own, anyway."

Owen stared at his uncle and couldn't speak. He hadn't even considered the fact that Vallie wouldn't be able to go with him if he took the bus. And he couldn't imagine leaving her behind.

"I assume that girl Willie likes dogs?"

"Yes, but—"

"Well, it's a good thing. We couldn't possibly approve of any woman who wouldn't accept Vallie as part of the package." Earl chuckled and patted him on the back. "You take the car. And the dog. She needs you, and you sure need her."

An image flashed through Owen's mind of himself driving up to the Coltrain farm in the blue convertible, with Vallie in the seat beside him. As much as Willie loved her little spaniel pup, Curly, she was bound to be enchanted by the beautiful, well-mannered collie. Vallie's presence just might break the ice a little and help his cause with Willie. Then a discouraging thought struck him.

"There's no way I have enough gas rations to get to Mississippi," Owen said miserably. "It's such a long trip. I'd better just take the bus."

Gert frowned at her husband. "Earl, do we have any ration coupons we can spare?"

"A few," he answered. "But not enough."

"We'll check around and see what we can round up," Gert told Owen. "Stay over until tomorrow. One more day won't hurt."

Owen didn't want to delay another minute, but he didn't seem to have much choice. He'd probably end up taking the bus anyway, leaving both Vallie and the convertible behind. It would be nothing short of a miracle if they could scrape together enough coupons to get him halfway across the country.

Still, when he went to bed that night, he would ask for the miracle. It couldn't hurt.

★ ★ ★

Aunt Gert and Uncle Earl always listened to *The Great Gildersleeve, The Whistler,* and *The Fred Allen Show* on Sunday nights. Owen sat in the parlor with them, half-listening and staring into the small fire as he thought about Willie. What was she doing, right now, this very minute? Was she thinking about him, did she miss him? Or had she written him off as some insensitive lout who didn't have the courtesy to tell her good-bye in person?

He had to stop this. His imagination was running away with him, and if he didn't get a rein on his thoughts, he'd lose his nerve altogether. He had decided to take the risk and go to Eden to face her, and he believed that God somehow had played a part in that decision. Now he had to follow through, or what good was any faith at all?

Aunt Gert had made a few calls and talked a few of her friends into giving up some of their precious gas ration coupons for the cause. But it wasn't enough, not nearly. Uncle Earl promised to go to the grain elevator first thing tomorrow morning and see what he could do. But in all likelihood, Owen would end up on the bus, alone, sometime tomorrow afternoon. If he didn't chicken out, that is.

He looked over at his aunt and watched her for a minute as she frowned at her knitting and then continued. The soft clicking of the needles beat a gentle counterpoint to the snapping of the logs in the fire and the rustling of pages as his uncle flipped through the *Farmer's Almanac.* What a peaceful, untroubled world they shared! Anyone looking in from the outside would see a middle-aged couple, comfortable and content with their life together. No one would ever know the pain they had endured at losing a son, at facing the sudden, violent death of their closest relatives.

Owen sighed and returned his gaze to the fire. He wanted this kind of life for himself and Willie. The unspoken communication of real love. A chance to grow old together, to create memories that would replace the ones he had lost. Surely God wouldn't begrudge him a little happiness in life. He had asked, and he had received his answer—or at least he thought it was his answer. Still, this delay was maddening, and the exhilaration he had experienced earlier this morning was rapidly being replaced by frustration and doubt.

He wished he had some sort of sign, some confirmation that he was making the right decision.

Just as the theme song to *The Whistler* came over the radio, the telephone began to ring in the hallway. Gert started to get up, but Owen stopped her. "You like this program, Aunt Gert. Stay put—I'll get it."

"I am the Whistler, and I know many things, for I walk by night," Bill Forman, the star of the program, intoned. Owen could hear the introduction to the show as he went into the hall and lifted the receiver. "Slaughter residence," he answered formally. "May I help you?"

"Is this Mr. Slaughter?" a female voice inquired.

"No, this is Owen Slaughter, his nephew. Just a minute—"

"Wait!" the voice interrupted. "Owen, is that you? This is Ardyce Hanson, from Frost."

"Yes, it's me," Owen said. What on earth would she be calling him for?

"I didn't expect to find you there," she said. "I'd heard you left town."

"News travels fast," he quipped. "I went to visit some friends in New Ulm. Now I'm back, but I won't be here for long."

"Then I'm glad I caught you. I was going to leave a message with your aunt and uncle."

"Is something wrong? You sound . . . I don't know, tense."

"It's Mabel Rae Coltrain—I mean, Rae Laporte. Willie's sister."

"I know who she is, Ardyce. What's going on?"

"You know she's expecting?"

"Yes. Ardyce, get to the point." Owen didn't intend to snap at her, but he was beginning to worry.

"She's not due until the third week of November, but she's apparently having some problems with the baby."

"What kind of problems?"

"I'm not sure. I got a letter from her today, but the details were pretty vague. She's scared, though—I can tell that much."

"And you want me to—?" Owen faltered, uncertain what his response should be.

"I'm not sure why I called, Owen. I just felt like I should—I thought you'd want to know. I can arrange some time off, and I'd go down there myself and be with her, but my car is having transmission problems, and I couldn't make it that far. I guess I figured that if you had any contact with them, you could—I don't know, call them, encourage them . . . something."

A light went on in Owen's mind, and for a minute he couldn't speak. This might be his answer, and he hadn't even gotten around to praying. Or had he? Had God read his thoughts and understood his need before he had even asked?

"Owen? Are you there?"

"I'm here, Ardyce. Look, will your car get you down here to North Fork?"

"Sure. I'm just not comfortable with taking it long distances."

"How's your gas situation?"

"I've got plenty of ration coupons, if that's what you mean. The nursing job keeps me supplied in case of emergencies, but I don't drive all that much."

Owen laughed out loud. "All right. Meet me here in the morning, packed and ready to go. Can you leave by seven-thirty?"

"Leave for where? Owen, what are you talking about?"

"We're going to Mississippi, Ardyce. You and me and Vallie."

"Are you serious?"

"Absolutely. I'll tell you all about it tomorrow. You'll be here?"

"Bright and early."

"Don't forget your ration coupons."

"Don't worry. And, Owen?"

"Yes?"

"I don't think it's a coincidence that you were there tonight."

"Neither do I, Ardyce. See you tomorrow."

Owen hung up the telephone and stood gripping the wall for a minute. He couldn't believe it. Five minutes ago he was considering scrapping the whole idea of going to Mississippi. Now he had a car, enough ration coupons, and company for the journey. And apparently his dreams and hopes had somehow dovetailed with Rae Laporte's need for a friend. His mind reeled. This faith thing really worked. If God could do this—answer his prayer and someone else's in a single blow—then anything was possible. Even having Willie Coltrain love him back.

Obviously, Leah Sonntag had been right. You were a step ahead if you faced the future believing in a God who loved you and wanted the best for you. He breathed a fervent thank you and went back into the living room.

Aunt Gert looked up expectantly. "Who called, dear?"

Owen grinned. "God."

"God was on the telephone?" His aunt slanted a look at him. "That's odd. Usually the Lord's communication is a bit more direct."

"Well, it wasn't God personally, but it was pretty close."

Gert laid her knitting needles in her lap and peered into his face. "Are you all right, Owen?"

He leaned over and kissed her on the cheek. "I'm wonderful. And now, if you'll excuse me, I'll go put my bags back in the car. I'll be leaving right after breakfast."

31

The Zaccheus Factor

Eden, Mississippi
September 17, 1945

Willie came upstairs with a basket of laundry and found Rae standing in the bedroom, staring forlornly at the blank wall where the door to the baby's room was supposed to go. Rae didn't hear her come in, and Willie stood there for a moment, watching. Her sister had one hand on her swelling abdomen and the other on her back. A single tear rolled down her cheek, and she gave out a sigh.

"It'll get done, Sister. Don't worry."

Rae turned, startled. "Willie, don't sneak up on me like that."

"I wasn't sneaking." Willie inclined her head toward the basket of clean laundry. "I was just coming up to put these away."

Rae waddled over to the bed and sank down on the mattress. "Sorry. I didn't mean to be snappy. I just wish—" She shrugged.

"You wish Drew would do some work around here," Willie finished for her. "I promise, I'm about ready to take a sledgehammer to that wall myself."

"After you work him over with it, you mean?" Rae smiled wanly.

"The idea had occurred to me." Willie set the basket on the floor and began removing folded clothes. "Where do these go?"

"You shouldn't be doing our laundry, Willie. It's not your job."

"Nonsense. You're on your feet enough, and I know your back hurts. It's just as easy to do it all at once."

Rae swung her feet up onto the bed and leaned back against the head-board. "I'm so tired all the time, Willie. I don't know what's wrong with me."

"You're pregnant, silly. You're supposed to be tired."

"Maybe. But I've still got more than two months to go. What's it going to be like then?"

"Worse," Willie said with a grin. "Much worse."

"You're so encouraging," Rae responded sarcastically, but she did smile a little. "What would I do without you?"

"You'd be doing your own laundry, that's what."

Rae leaned forward and peered into Willie's face. "How are *you* doing, Sister?"

"Well, I'm not expecting, if that's what you mean. Not expecting anything at all."

"You still miss him, don't you?"

Willie sat down on the edge of the bed. "I suppose I do. Maybe I always will. But there's nothing I can do about it. He's gone, and that's the end of it."

"Do you think he'll ever come back?"

Willie sighed. "I'm not counting on it. I said I was going to trust God in all of this, and that's what I'm trying to do. I can't spend the rest of my days mooning over Owen Slaughter and carrying a torch for him. I've got to get on with my life."

"And just what does that mean, exactly—getting on with your life?"

"It means," Willie said with determination, "that whatever is going to happen will happen. I can't change it or make things different by moping around like a lovesick schoolgirl."

"Do you pray about it?"

"Sure I do. But I don't pray for Owen's miraculous return anymore. I pray . . . I don't know. I guess I pray that God's will is done, in my life and in Owen's." She paused and looked at Rae, feeling the old longing welling up in her again. "All right, I'll be honest. I still love him. And yes, I would welcome him back if he came. But I want what's best for him and for me. I don't want him coming back out of some kind of distorted sense of duty."

"Do you think he loved you?"

"I don't know. I was beginning to think so, right before he left. He looked at me in an odd way, as if—"

"As if he were getting some of his memories back?"

"Not exactly. More like he was feeling something he didn't understand, something that scared him."

"Well, love can be pretty scary sometimes," Rae mused. "Look at me. I love Drew, and I know he loves me, but things haven't exactly turned out the way I planned."

"I know." Willie patted her sister's hand. "He'll come around. Give it time."

Rae shook her head. "I'll be so glad when this case of Ivory's is settled once and for all. Maybe then I'll get my husband back."

"I hope that happens soon," Willie agreed. "Or I *will* take a sledgehammer to this wall."

★ ★ ★

When her sister had gone back downstairs, Rae leaned against the headboard and wept. Willie was doing her best, and Rae was grateful, but it didn't change the situation. Drew was still absent, emotionally if not physically, and she was still lonely and afraid.

She hadn't told Willie what the doctor had said last week—that there was a chance this baby could come earlier than expected, that she needed to stay off her feet, get plenty of rest, let others do for her. Willie was already doing more than her share, and if she knew the truth, she would put Rae to bed and not let her lift a finger. Besides, Willie had enough on her mind without worrying about this baby.

She hadn't told her husband either. Not that it would make any difference. He hadn't listened when she had confided her fears for their child— he had simply told her she was letting her imagination run away with her. Drew couldn't see anything right now except his obsession for catching the crooks who had tried to swindle Ivory out of his land. And although she told Willie the situation would get better once the case was settled, she wasn't sure she really believed it. At the back of her mind, a nagging voice told her to get used to it, that there would always be another case occupying his attention, and then another, and another. . . .

Rae wondered if this was the way of all marriages—that once the honeymoon was over and real life began, people went their separate ways, living under the same roof but without the depth of connection and communication they had enjoyed when they were courting. No one had ever told her how lonely married life could be. She had always assumed that love was enough, that the relationship would always be the main priority. How long had it been since Drew had told her that she was beautiful, that he adored her? How long had it been since he had really *looked* at her?

She got up and went to the dresser, peering at her reflection in the mirror. Maybe she didn't want him to look at her. People always said that pregnant women were radiant and glowing and lovely. But it wasn't true. She was fat and ugly and felt like a watermelon on duck feet. She waddled when she walked, and her stomach entered a room ten minutes before the rest of her. No wonder Drew was throwing himself into his work.

But ugly or not, she needed him. Needed his attention, his love. Needed for him to take seriously the fears she had about their baby. A chasm was opening up between them, and every day he seemed more distant, more unreachable. Could the separation be bridged after the baby was born, or would it just get worse?

Maybe she should tell him what the doctor had said. Maybe she should try one more time. But she was afraid—afraid that if he didn't listen, the gulf between them would widen and the resentment within her deepen. Her nerves were already frazzled and on edge. She wasn't sure how much more of this she could take.

Rae had divulged the information about her physical condition to only one person—and ironically, it was someone she had never even met face-to-face. Ardyce Hanson. Ardyce was a nurse and could appreciate the medical aspects of pregnancy complications. But it was more than that. When Rae had rekindled her friendship with Ardyce through letters, she had found a friendship that gave her hope and encouragement. Ardyce wasn't family, she didn't *have* to love and accept Rae the way Willie did. But Ardyce seemed to understand—in a way that Willie could not and Drew would not—how Rae felt, what was going on in her heart.

Rae's correspondence with Ardyce had become a kind of catharsis for her, an opportunity to pour out her feelings and work through her anxieties on paper. When she wrote to her, Rae felt that someone, at last, was listening, someone who wouldn't minimize her emotions or belittle her fears. It was rather like praying, or writing in her journal—it put things in perspective and helped Rae understand what was really going on in her own soul.

In return, Ardyce's letters had become a source of strength for Rae, and her empathy had made Rae feel less alone. She had a direct, no-nonsense way about her that made Rae feel like an equal, like she wasn't being coddled or patronized. And Ardyce took her fears seriously, helping her think through her options. If something was indeed wrong with the baby, if there were going to be complications with this pregnancy, Rae wanted Ardyce to be here to help.

But she couldn't ask her to come. You didn't just expect someone you had never met to set aside her job and her life to travel halfway across the country on a whim. It wasn't rational.

No, the letters would have to be enough. God had answered some of her prayers, at least, through this long-distance friendship. She wouldn't try the Almighty's patience by asking for anything more.

★ ★ ★

"More coffee?" Thelma smiled down at Orris Craven and poured his cup full without waiting for him to answer. The thin, pale lawyer sat in a back booth with Bennett, Drew, and Ivory, their heads bent over a sheaf of legal papers, making plans for the undoing of one Beauregard T. Laporte.

Nothing short of a miracle, this change in Orris, Thelma mused. He had arrived in Eden exactly one week ago and had been staying at Judith Larkins's boardinghouse while they worked out the details of their plan. He was still pale, but his eyes had lost that vacant look, and he seemed more comfortable, more at home with himself. Amazing, what a little dose of conscience and a sprinkling of contrition could do for a man. He had even attended church with them on Sunday.

To demonstrate his sincerity in wanting to help them nail Laporte, Orris had given over everything—names, dates, property titles, and the lot—to Bennett and Drew. They had spent the last week going over all the papers, and Bennett had told Thelma that Craven was a crack lawyer, despite appearances to the contrary. What he knew about the inner workings of Laporte's corporations would give them the edge they needed to put him out of the foreclosure business once and for all.

But while Orris looked to be coming back to life after a long and deadly sleep, Drew Laporte seemed to slide in the opposite direction. His enthusiasm had waned, his appetite vanished, and his eyes took on the expression of an animal caught in a trap. Bennett repeatedly asked Drew if he wanted to give it up, to let it go, but he refused. Still driven, but without passion or joy, he mechanically went about the business of ruining his own father.

"Drew?" Thelma repeated for the third time before he looked up.

"What?"

"I asked if you wanted more coffee."

"Yeah, I guess so." He turned away from her searching gaze. "Thanks."

"Are you finished?" She pointed to his untouched plate, where the fried chicken had grown cold and the mashed potatoes had congealed in green-bean juice—an unappetizing combination. "You haven't eaten your lunch. Do you want something else?"

"No thanks, Thelma," he said dully. "I'm not hungry."

Bennett cast a glance in her direction and shook his head. Thelma pulled up a chair and sat down beside Drew. "How is Rae doing? I haven't seen much of her lately."

"Rae?" he repeated as if he hadn't the faintest idea who she was talking about. "Oh, Rae. She's all right."

"I'll bet you can't wait for that baby of yours to get here," she prodded. "It won't be long now."

"Coupla months," he muttered.

"Are the renovations coming along? I'm eager to see the changes you're making out at the farm. Rae and Willie came in a while back and showed me some wallpaper samples—"

He turned and fixed her with a scathing look. "I haven't had time to get to it," he said pointedly. "I've been busy."

Thelma couldn't have recoiled faster if he had slapped her across the face. And Drew noticed, too, because the hostile expression vanished and weariness washed over his countenance. The deep blue eyes, usually so full of excitement and vitality, had gone dull and lifeless. His dimples had disappeared, and the flesh on his cheeks sagged. He looked . . . old. Old and worn.

"Sorry, Thelma," he apologized listlessly. "I don't mean to be rude, but we've got work to do here, so if you'll excuse us—"

"Drew!" Bennett snapped, his eyes flashing. "I'd appreciate it if—"

"It's all right," Thelma sighed, patting Bennett's hand. She rose and cleared the rest of the dishes from the table, then went back to the kitchen.

Those two young people were in deep trouble. She recalled the look on Mabel Rae's face the last time she had seen the pair together. And she saw the pain in Drew's eyes as clearly as if he had been wearing a sign on his chest. What that boy needed most was prayer, Thelma thought as she scraped the plates and slid them into a sink full of soapy water. Prayer and peace of mind.

But even prayer did little to lift the heaviness from Thelma Breckinridge's spirit.

★ ★ ★

Orris Craven had never felt better in his life. At last he was doing what he knew he was meant to do—using his knowledge and his expertise on the right side of the law. He had no idea where he would go after this was all over, but that didn't matter at the moment. For the first time in years he was free from the burden of guilt and shame.

He didn't know quite yet what he thought about the faith these people seemed to operate by, but it was certainly something he wanted to explore. He had actually gone to church yesterday, sang the old hymns his mother had taught him when he was a child, and listened to a sermon about

Zaccheus, the crooked tax collector who made restitution to the people he had cheated. Orris had come away feeling as if he had taken a long walk in the spring rain. And although he didn't understand all this talk about being in right relationship with God, he had gotten back into right relationship with himself, and that was enough for now.

He felt . . . renewed, somehow. Cleansed. Honorable.

And just a little embarrassed at feeling so good when Andrew Laporte obviously felt so miserable.

Orris could understand Drew's misery. Heaven knows, he had spent enough years of his life betraying people who trusted him. But that was different. He had betrayed people for all the wrong reasons. Greed. Pride. Ambition. The compulsion to succeed. Drew had purer motives: the desire to do the right thing, to help Harlan Brownlee and others like him. And if they succeeded in flushing Beau Laporte out and confronting him with his illicit dealings—and they would, Orris was certain of it—they might even be doing Laporte himself a great service. People, especially power-hungry people like Beauregard T. Laporte, tended to rationalize what they were doing until some unanticipated turn of events brought them to their knees. The Colonel's demise could well be a blessing disguised as a curse.

To his everlasting credit, Drew wasn't backing down. He knew what he had to do. But clearly, it was tearing the man apart.

When Bennett Winsom and Harlan Brownlee left the table to go talk to Thelma, Orris turned to Drew. "I know how difficult this is for you."

"Sure you do. Let me guess—this happened to you once. You set your own father up and had to stand by and watch while he completely destroyed himself."

"No." Orris hedged. "That's not quite what I meant."

"What did you mean, then?"

"Just that . . . well, I've spent most of my adult life trying to convince myself that what I was doing was morally acceptable. My conscience, such as it was, told me differently, but I didn't listen. And gradually that voice grew fainter and fainter until it wasn't difficult at all to ignore it." He paused and shut his eyes, trying to find the right words. "I let my mind, that part of me that could rationalize my actions, tell me that betraying others was just part of the job description, even though my conscience was telling me otherwise."

"So?"

"So your present situation is the opposite: Your conscience is telling you that what you're doing is right, but your mind is resisting."

"I just can't figure out where family loyalty lies in all of this," Drew sighed.

"If it were anyone else, I wouldn't hesitate for a minute. But this is my *father* we're talking about. Don't I have some responsibility to protect him?"

"To protect him from what—the consequences of his own actions?"

"When you put it like that, I see your point. But what about my mother? This will devastate her."

Orris leaned forward, and his eyes met Drew's. "When I met your mother and heard her talk about you, how proud she was of you, I thought, *That's the kind of man I'd like to be.* More than anything else, Drew, your mother values your integrity. Your honor. She wouldn't expect you to turn a blind eye to this."

"I suppose not."

"If you did, you would not be the kind of person she thinks you are," Orris went on. "I know that doesn't make it any easier, but there's something else you might want to consider."

"What's that?"

"You were in church yesterday. Did you listen to the sermon?"

"I guess so. What are you driving at?"

"Zaccheus—the crooked tax collector who cheated all the powerless little people. What happened to him?"

"He . . . well, he changed."

"Why did he change?"

Drew frowned. "Because he met Jesus?"

"Partly," Orris chuckled. "But I'm not talking about the spiritual message. I'm talking about practicalities. Jesus was the catalyst for Zaccheus's transformed life, certainly, but I think it was because Jesus helped him to face the truth about himself—that he was a liar and a cheat and a dishonorable scoundrel."

"Those are pretty strong words."

"And Zaccheus was a pretty rotten fellow," Orris countered. "Do you think he would have reversed his position so radically if Jesus had said to him, 'It's all right, Zack; you're not such a bad guy after all'?"

A glimmer of a smile touched Drew's lips. "I suppose not."

"Then think about this: Your willingness to confront your father with what he has done just might be the catalyst for a whole new perspective for him, just as your mother was a catalyst for me. We can't change, Drew, until we see the truth about ourselves. Once Zaccheus saw it, he demonstrated his conversion by repaying the people he had cheated."

"And this is what you expect from my father?" Drew let out a hollow laugh.

"It's possible, isn't it?"

Drew shook his head. "Never in a million years. I believe in miracles, but no, not one that big. Not if the archangel Michael came down with a flaming sword."

"Don't be too sure." Orris raised one eyebrow and smiled. "It's happened before. And fairly recently, if memory serves."

32

Unexpected Answers

Eden, Mississippi
September 18, 1945

Rae Laporte sat on the bed and watched her husband's reflection in the mirror as he knotted his tie and brushed at the cuffs of his pants. "Dog hair," he grumbled. "You'd think Willie would keep that beast outside."

"Curly is not a beast," she countered, trying to keep her voice light. "She's a wonderful little dog and a good companion for Willie."

"And the only companion your dear sister will ever have if she doesn't stop moping around about Owen Slaughter." Drew turned to look at Rae, his dark blue eyes frigid. "What's wrong with that woman, anyway? Doesn't she realize he's never coming back? She needs to give it up and get on with her life."

"She *has* given it up," Rae answered pointedly, "to God. What would you have her do, Drew? Go down to the depot in Tillatoba and stand around waiting to snatch some returning soldier off the train? These things take time."

"She's had time," he muttered. "Plenty of time. Other people have problems too, you know. The world doesn't revolve around her."

Yes, Rae thought. *Other people have problems, too.* And she wondered, as she had for a week now, just what *Drew's* problem was. It was more than just preoccupation with Ivory's case. Something else had happened, something that had changed her husband at the core. He had grown increasingly distant and cold, even hostile. He ate little and slept with his back to her,

224

putting as much space between them as the double bed would allow. Sometimes she awoke in the middle of the night to find his side of the bed empty, and once she had gone to find him and discovered him on the front porch, leaning on a post and staring vacantly into the dark fields.

Still, no matter how much she pleaded, he wouldn't tell her what was wrong. She could see it on his face, in the sagging circles under his eyes and the dejected stoop of his broad shoulders. But when she begged him to confide in her, he would brush her off. "It's not your concern," he had said more than once. "Just something I have to deal with. And I will. Believe me, I will."

He gave her a perfunctory kiss on the cheek and managed a halfhearted smile. "Don't wait dinner—I'll be late," he said. Then he was gone.

Rae watched him disappear through the doorway, and an unutterable loneliness rose up in her soul. She was losing him.

Oh, she didn't expect him to ask for a divorce or abandon her and the baby. Andrew Laporte wasn't that kind of man. And Rae clung firmly to the belief, even amid all the evidence to the contrary, that he still loved her and cared about her. But she was losing him all the same.

She had dreamed last night, a disturbing dream in which she found herself in a bleak desert, poised on the precipice of a vast canyon, holding the hand of a small, dark-haired child. On the other side of the chasm stood Drew, tiny and almost invisible—but she knew instinctively it was him. She called to him and waved, pointing frantically to a narrow swinging bridge that spanned the gulf. But her voice was not strong enough to reach him; it simply echoed back to her in a plaintive cry. And all the while he stood there staring in her direction, not responding,

There was nothing more she could do. She had tried to talk to him, she had prayed, she had asked God for some kind of miracle, the nature of which she couldn't even fathom. Now all that was left to her was to take care of herself. To eat healthy meals even when she wasn't hungry. To force herself to rest. To try not to worry. To give Drew into God's hands.

For her sake and the baby's, she would do nothing to jeopardize the life she carried.

Willie sat on the porch swing and watched as Curly came bounding across the yard with a rubber ball in her mouth. The dog lunged onto the porch and laid the treasure at Willie's feet, and in spite of herself, Willie smiled. "Good girl!"

Curly sat down and pounded her tail against the porch boards, and when Willie reached down to pick up the ball, nudged her hand.

"You want to play? All right." Willie got up, went to the edge of the steps, and flung the ball into the front yard. Curly dashed after it, turning head over tail as she tried to grab the ball on a bounce. At last she had it and came running back, her ears flying.

Willie sat down on the porch steps, and Curly threw herself into her lap, wriggling all over and licking Willie's face. Willie began to tickle the dog, and before she knew it they were wrestling on the porch, with Willie down on all fours and Curly making mock attacks from every angle. Breathless, Willie collapsed in a heap laughing and lay there holding her aching sides.

When she opened her eyes, she saw an upside-down, ant's-eye view of her sister standing over her with her hands on her hips. Rae's protruding belly obscured her chin and mouth, but above the arched curve of the baby, Willie could see Rae's face rising round and pale like the moon over the hill. The dark eyes flashed, and a frown furrowed her brow.

"Willie, what on earth are you doing?"

Willie scrambled to her feet and grinned. "Playing with the dog. And laughing."

"I can see that. Why?"

Willie thought for a minute. "Because it was fun. Sister, it feels so good to *laugh.*" She brushed off the seat of her jeans and ran a hand through her wild curls. "It's about time I started having fun again. I've been moping around like the world has come to an end, when the only thing that's come to an end is a relationship that never got off the ground in the first place." She shook her head. "I haven't felt like a whole person in a long time. But mourning for Owen isn't going to help. If there's going to be a miracle here—and I don't expect one—it won't happen because I've wished it into existence."

Even as she said the words, Willie felt something open up inside her—a freedom, a liberty she had almost forgotten. It was true. She had prayed, committed herself and Owen to God, and done her best to trust. The rest was up to the Lord, and for once she didn't have any preconceived ideas of how God's will should be worked out in her life. Her responsibility was to live her own life, not try to control how everyone else lived theirs. It was a heady feeling, this sense of emancipation. Like the warmth of Indian summer after the first frost.

She motioned for Rae to join her in the swing. "Come sit. You ought to be off your feet."

"I'm all right." Rae waddled over to the swing and plopped down heavily.

"One more month, and your swing will be scraping the ground," Willie quipped.

"Thanks for the encouragement. It's not as if I don't feel fat and ugly enough as it is."

"Ah, Mabel Rae, I didn't mean it like that." Willie twisted sideways and peered into her sister's eyes. "I saw Drew tear out of here a little while ago. Is he still . . . well, being like he's being?"

Rae nodded, and Willie saw a flash of pain shoot across her countenance. "What is his problem, anyway?"

"I don't know. I can't get him to talk about it. He just keeps getting more and more distant."

"And what about you? Are you feeling OK?"

A strange look passed over Rae's face, as if there were something she wanted to say to Willie. Then she shut her mouth and shifted her gaze out toward the fields.

"What is it, Rae?"

Rae shook her head. "Nothing."

"Come on. I know you too well. You're my sister, remember?"

A full two minutes went by while Willie waited for an answer. When Rae turned back, her eyes were filled with tears, and she was obviously fighting to maintain her composure. Willie took her hand and stroked it gently. "It's all right, Rae. You can tell me."

Rae gulped hard. "Remember how I told you I was scared about this baby—like something might be wrong?"

"Yes. But the doctor said everything was progressing normally, didn't he?"

Rae nodded. "Until last week. Then—" She choked up and couldn't go on.

"Then what, Mabel Rae?" Willie squeezed her hand. "What happened?"

"He said there were indications I could deliver early, and I had to be very careful. Get plenty of rest, not exert myself, call him at the first sign of anything wrong. That sort of thing. Otherwise—"

"Otherwise what?"

"Well, he didn't say I could lose the baby—he didn't say much of anything, actually. You know how doctors are. But he had a funny look on his face, like he was keeping something from me."

"Have you told Drew?" Willie watched Rae's eyes carefully. "Of course you haven't."

"Drew's too wrapped up in himself to care," Rae snapped, then her tone softened. "That sounded pretty nasty, didn't it? I know he's got problems of his own, and—"

"He's your *husband,* Rae!" Willie interrupted. "Don't you think he has a right to know? And don't you have a right to have some support from the father of your child? I ought to—"

"You'll do nothing, Willie Coltrain," Rae said firmly. "You'll stay out of it."

"Stay out of it? He ought to be horsewhipped, the way he's been treating you—or, I should say, ignoring you."

"Your concern for me is very touching, Willie." Rae smiled wanly. "But it's a little late to be trying to protect me, don't you think?"

"So what are you going to do?"

"I'm going to do the only thing I can do. Take care of myself and the baby. And pray."

"All right, I won't confront Drew," Willie agreed. "At least not right now. But we'll both pray. As Thelma would say, God's got ways of bringing answers when we least expect it."

"I sure hope so," Rae said. "Because I'm fresh out of expectations."

★ ★ ★

The closer they got to the turnoff to Eden, the more wildly Owen's stomach churned. Whoever had first come up with the image of "butterflies" had never done what he was doing now. This wasn't butterflies—it was more like a swarming hive of angry bees.

As if she had read his mind, Ardyce Hanson reached across the seat and patted his arm. "It'll be fine, Owen, you'll see." She smiled at him and adjusted the scarf around her head. "It's a glorious day—what could possibly go wrong?"

Owen looked around and nodded. They had the convertible top down, and the autumn sun shone warmly on his face. In the backseat, Vallie gazed contentedly at the countryside, her tongue lolling to one side.

This woman, Ardyce Hanson, had surprised him at every step of the way. She had that blunt, no-nonsense manner that he assumed came with the nurse's cap but tempered with a wildly quirky sense of humor, a profound compassion for others, and a sensitivity so incisive that it gave him chills. He hoped Rae Laporte knew what a good friend she had—even if the two of them had never met face-to-face.

Owen tried to get his mind off the dire possibilities of this meeting, to quit asking himself, *What if Willie doesn't want to see me?* He had spent the past two days on the road brooding about his decision, wondering if he should turn back and forget the whole thing. But every time he was about to abandon ship, the image from his dream came into his mind—Willie standing on the platform, saying to him in that velvet voice, *"It's about time you got here. I was afraid you had forgotten me."* The memory caused his heart to race and his palms to sweat.

He had filled Ardyce in on the whole story, of course. For thirty-two hours they had alternated driving and sleeping, stopping only for gas and food and bathroom breaks. Long-distance travel tended to break down barriers between people, even relative strangers. Between Watermelon, Iowa, and the Missouri state line, he had told Ardyce about his time in the German stalag, about Charlie, the escape, and Fritz Sonntag. Somewhere east of Chillicothe he had confessed his love for Willie, and by the time they reached St. Louis and headed south toward Memphis, she was helping him plan how to handle the situation.

Both of them agreed that rushing in and declaring his undying love for Willie was probably not the best approach, but Owen couldn't figure out how to explain his return without divulging his feelings. Ardyce, with her typically logical approach to problems, finally suggested a workable solution: They would tell the Coltrain sisters that when he had found out that Ardyce wanted to come see Rae, he had volunteered to drive down with her and take the opportunity to visit his friends again. Owen would apologize for leaving on such short notice and volunteer to help out around the farm for a while. Given what Rae had confided to Ardyce about Drew Laporte's present state of mind—as well as the lack of progress on the house renovations—Owen's presence would no doubt be welcome for that reason alone. And it would give him a chance to survey the romantic landscape and find out if Willie had any feelings for him.

At four o'clock on Tuesday afternoon, they pulled to a stop in front of a small cafe on the square in Grenada. After a sponge bath and a change of clothes in the tiny cramped washroom, Owen felt slightly more presentable and a little closer to human. They downed a hurried lunch, took Vallie to an empty field just outside of town to run a bit and do her doggy business, then headed into the last leg of the journey.

One more hour until the moment of truth.

Willie stood on the porch and shaded her eyes as she looked into the setting sun. The days were growing shorter, and an autumn nip permeated the late-afternoon breeze. She should go wake Rae from her nap and get supper on the table, but a reluctance to disturb the peacefulness of the early evening restrained her. For the first time in weeks, Willie felt a sense of anticipation, an expectancy that came upon her entirely by surprise. Despite the turns her life had taken, something good lay ahead of her. She didn't understand it and had no idea what it was, but it was there. Hope. Hope for letting the past go and embracing the future.

The promise came not as a product of her own effort but as a gift, and she breathed a prayer of thankfulness into the deepening sky.

Then a sound came to her ears, echoing across the fields. A car, coming this way.

She went to the steps and peered out across the yard to where the road curved just beyond the creek. A dark blue convertible headed toward the farm, slowed at the driveway, and pulled in.

A bearded man at the wheel. A woman next to him in the passenger's seat. And in the back, a large sable-and-white collie. Her heart thudded against her rib cage. It couldn't be . . .

But it was.

Owen Slaughter, with a woman at his side.

A riot of conflicting emotions battered at Willie's heart. Owen had come home! But who was the woman with him? A wife? A fiancée? Had he come in person to break the news that he was marrying—or had already married—someone else?

And why shouldn't he? She had given him no encouragement. She had kept her feelings to herself, afraid to hurt him further by jogging his memories too quickly. She had been . . . a friend. And now here he was, opening the door for some other woman, helping her out of the car.

He took the woman's arm and stepped forward. "Hello, Willie," he said hesitantly. Even in the waning light she could see the spark in his eyes. Such blue eyes . . .

Obviously he was uncomfortable, ill at ease. He raked his free hand through his hair and pushed at the ground with the toe of his shoe. "I know you weren't expecting to see me, but I—"

Willie straightened her shoulders and took a deep breath. She would be civil, welcome Owen's lady with all that famous southern grace and hospitality. Surely anyone Owen loved would be a fine person. She couldn't be angry at him. She had just missed her chance, that was all.

She stepped forward and gave him a brief, sisterly hug. "Hello, Owen. We've missed you." Then she retreated a couple of paces and waited for him to make the appropriate introductions. But he didn't speak, didn't move. He just stood there with a dumbfounded look and an absurd grin on his face.

The woman approached and shook her hand. "Owen has obviously lost track of his manners—or his mind," she said in a forthright manner. "Allow me to introduce myself. I'm Ardyce Hanson."

"Happy to meet you," Willie answered absently, still watching Owen out of the corner of her eye. "Any . . . ah, friend . . . of Owen's is a friend of ours." Her gaze shifted to the woman—tall and willowy, with a narrow face and eyes that flashed with mirth. Oddly, Willie found herself drawn into the compelling gaze. Owen had good taste, she had to give him that much. She found the woman's frank, open manner refreshing. Under other circumstances, she could imagine them being friends. . . .

"I'm sorry," Willie said, coming to herself. "I didn't catch your name."

"Hanson," the woman repeated. "Ardyce Hanson."

Suddenly the truth hit Willie like a physical blow. "Did you say *Ardyce Hanson?*"

"Yes." The woman lifted one eyebrow. "Rae's friend . . . from Minnesota."

Willie closed her eyes and shook her head. "Then you're not—" She pointed to Owen, then back to Ardyce. "You're not—?"

"No, Willie, I'm not." Ardyce gave her a perceptive smile. "Rae wrote to me about her condition. I had some time off, and I wanted to come down and see if I could be of any help, but my car wouldn't get me here. Owen volunteered to drive me."

Willie tried to restrain the grin she felt spreading across her face, but to no avail. And Ardyce obviously saw it because she smiled back and winked at her. "We're welcome, then?"

"Welcome? Of course you're welcome. Supper's just about ready."

"If it's too much trouble, we could stay at a boardinghouse in town."

"Nonsense. We wouldn't dream of it. Owen can have his old room in the attic—Charlie's room, that is. And there's a guest room next to mine. You'll be close to Rae, and—"

Willie broke off suddenly as she caught sight of Owen. He was still rooted in place, his eyes wide, gazing at Willie. "Owen? Are you all right?"

He jerked his head abruptly as if coming out of a dream. "Oh, sure. I'm fine. Ardyce wanted to come down to visit Rae, you see, and so I volunteered to drive her. Gave me a chance to come back and see if . . . ah, to see you. All of you," he added abruptly.

"Ardyce already told me, Owen."

"Oh. Yeah." He grinned inanely. "There's one other thing, Willie."

"What's that?"

Owen whistled, and the collie, who had been sitting patiently in the backseat of the convertible all this time, leaped over the side of the car and came to sit next to Owen's knee. "This is my dog, Valentine. Vallie, say hello to Willie."

The dog barked softly and lifted a paw. Charmed, Willie leaned down and shook it, then scratched the collie between the ears. Suddenly Curly appeared, her hackles up and her lip lifted in defiance. "She's jealous," Willie chuckled. "Look, Curly, it's all right." Willie rubbed the spaniel's ears, then patted the collie's head. "We're all friends."

Curly moved cautiously toward Valentine and moved around her sniffing, while the collie stood waiting. At last the spaniel came full circle and touched Vallie's nose with her own. Within a minute or two they were running around the front yard, chasing each other playfully.

"She's beautiful, Owen. Where did you get her?"

"It's a long story," he said over his shoulder as he went to get their bags out of the trunk. "I'll tell you all about it later."

"I see you've changed in at least one way," Willie quipped. "You've got a suitcase instead of a burlap bag."

"I guess I'm coming up in the world. That's another long story."

Willie waited while Owen put up the top on the convertible and rolled up the windows, then followed him onto the porch.

"We've got a lot to talk about, Willie," he said as he held the door open for her.

She looked into his eyes and nodded solemnly. "A lot of *long stories?*"

"I'm afraid so."

A look of apprehension flitted across his face, and she patted his shoulder lightly. "I've got all the time in the world, Owen," she said. "That's what friends are for."

33

Righteous Judas

New Orleans, Louisiana
October 3, 1945

Orris Craven stood outside the door of Beauregard Laporte's study, shut his eyes, and breathed a prayer for support and direction. He had been in Eden for three weeks and in that time had discovered, or perhaps rediscovered, a life free from the burden of guilt, shame, and duplicity. Now, coming back to New Orleans—particularly to the Colonel's oppressive presence—he felt as if he were entering a dungeon devoid of light or air.

But this time it would be different. This time *he* was different.

He wasn't exactly sure what he would say to Laporte, but Thelma, bless her heart, had assured him that the Spirit would provide him the words he needed. Orris wasn't very familiar with this Spirit she talked about, but he was willing to give it a try.

He straightened his shoulders and knocked on the door.

"Who is it?" Laporte bellowed.

Orris opened the door. "It's me, sir. Orris Craven."

"Well, don't just stand there like a gawking idiot, Craven. Get in here!"

Orris entered the room and shut the door behind him. For the first time since he had begun working for the Colonel, he found himself unintimidated by the impressive office and the even more imposing aura of Beauregard T. Laporte. Orris's legs were steady, and his pulse, though beating a little faster than normal, seemed constant. He could do this.

"Where the blazes have you been, Craven?" Laporte demanded. "I expected to hear from you a week ago."

"I was detained, sir, by some unanticipated developments." Much to his own surprise, Orris's voice came out low and unwavering, not high and squeaky as it usually did when he was nervous.

Laporte leaned forward and peered at him through a cloud of smoke. "Are you all right, Craven?"

"I'm fine, sir."

Laporte waved his cigar. "Well, then, get on with it. I trust you have good news, or you wouldn't be here." He cast a threatening glare in Orris's direction.

Good news. Orris suppressed a smile. Yes, he had good news—for himself, anyway. "My appointment with the Breckinridge people was for the fifteenth," he said evenly. "But I decided to go a few days early, to seek out the owner of the property, one Harlan Brownlee. I believed that since he had been cheated out of his land, he might know something about the Breckinridge Foundation, be willing to help us get the upper hand."

"Good thinking," Laporte muttered. "And?"

"I found him, all right," Orris continued. "But I discovered something very interesting in the process." He paused. Always before, he had used deception to attain his desired ends, and it had worked. It had lined his pockets, at least, but it had emptied his soul.

This time Orris was determined not to lie. But it was a new approach for him, unfamiliar ground. If he told Laporte the truth—even part of the truth—it might backfire on him. Still, he had to take the chance.

"Craven!" Laporte's voice drew him back to the present.

"Sir?"

"I'm waiting, Craven—and not very patiently, I might add. Now what did you find out?"

Orris took a deep breath and looked into Beauregard Laporte's blazing eyes. "There is no Breckinridge Foundation, sir."

"What the—?"

"That's right." Orris nodded. "It was a setup. A crafty lawyer determined to put an end to our land scam."

At the word *scam,* Laporte cringed visibly. Maybe the man did have a conscience after all. Maybe there was a weak spot in that armor, a place for the truth to get through. Then, as Orris watched, the vulnerable expression closed like a door slamming shut.

"Are you telling me that some—some *amateur*—is beating us at our own game?" Laporte's normally florid face grew redder by the moment.

"Exactly. They know everything, Colonel. They have copies of contracts, reports on our mineral-rights studies, all the names of our various corporations. They know about Clinton Marston and the Memphis firm—"

"Wait a minute!" Laporte shouted. "None of this is illegal. You've made sure of that." He narrowed his eyes at Orris. "You *have* made sure, haven't you?"

"Yes, sir. It is legal, all right. But it is not ethical. And this attorney Winsom is a stickler for ethics. Once this information becomes public—" Orris felt a power surge through his veins. Thelma had told him that the truth would set him free, but she had failed to mention that it would give him such inner strength. He looked directly at the Colonel and played his trump card. "I gather Winsom has . . . ah, friends in high places."

Laporte sank into his chair, and all the color drained from his face. "They could ruin me. They *will* ruin me." He gazed bleakly into the distance and stubbed out his cigar. "Craven—"

"Yes, sir?"

"You're fired."

Orris felt no disappointment, no anger. Just relief. He kept his eyes fixed on Beauregard Laporte's face and smiled. "Yes, sir."

"You're not surprised?"

"My car is already packed. Here are the keys to my office." He held out the key ring. "But you do have one option, sir."

Laporte straightened in his chair. "Maybe you're not fired. Give it to me."

"Mr. Winsom has agreed not to go to the authorities right away with this information—on one condition."

"Condition?"

"That you meet with them personally. Within the month. He has promised to hold off on any action until he has your answer."

"Do you trust him to keep that promise?"

Orris smiled to himself. "Yes, sir. I trust him."

Muttering curses under his breath, Beauregard Laporte reached into his desk drawer and pulled out his appointment calendar. He slapped it down on the desk with a resounding *thwack* and flipped through the pages. "How much is it going to cost me to make this go away?"

"Sir?"

"How much money does he want, Craven?"

"I don't know, sir. I don't think Mr. Winsom is the kind of man who will respond to a bribe—"

Laporte's head snapped up. "Every man has a price, Craven. I intend to find out exactly where this Winsom draws the line between ethics and money." He stared at the pages of the appointment book. "Get back to Mississippi. Set up an appointment for Thursday the twenty-fifth." He frowned. "Where should we meet?"

"I recommend the Jefferson House in Grenada. Nice old hotel, very classy."

"All right. Make a reservation for me and Mrs. Laporte for a week, the—ah, the twenty-fourth through the thirty-first."

"Mrs. Laporte?" Orris didn't want to see that nice lady dragged into this. "Do you think that's wise, sir?"

Laporte glared at him. "Where's your common sense, boy? I want this high-and-mighty Mr. Winsom to see me as a stable family man, not some kind of money-hungry monster. Besides, my wife has been nagging me for months to take her to see our son and daughter-in-law. They're living on some broken-down dirt farm up there somewhere. Eden, I think. That's fairly close to Grenada, isn't it?"

"I believe so, sir."

"Then do it. And stop second-guessing me. You've fouled this deal up enough as it is."

Orris opened his briefcase and jotted notes on a pad. "There's just one thing, sir."

"What?" Laporte growled.

"You've already fired me."

The Colonel shook his head. "Never mind about that. Just do it. And in the meantime, try to do some damage control up there, will you? Soften them up a little."

Orris nodded and snapped his briefcase shut. He turned his back on Laporte and walked out of the study without looking back.

The old buzzard had bought it, hook, line, and sinker. And all Orris had needed to do was tell the truth.

★ ★ ★

When the little weasel was gone, Beau Laporte wheeled his chair around and stared out the window. Blast! He couldn't believe he had been taken for such a ride by some amateur. He was so sure he had covered all his tracks. Now everything was about to blow to kingdom come, and the only thing that stood between him and utter ruin was a pasty-faced wimp of a lawyer who didn't know a legal brief from his boxer shorts.

On the other hand, maybe he did. Maybe this wasn't Craven's fault at all. Was it possible that Beau had, as his wife had warned him time and again, gotten too greedy, wanted too much too fast? She was right—they didn't need the money. But his pride was at stake, and his control. He couldn't let every country bumpkin who passed the bar and hung out a shingle get the best of him. He was Beauregard T. Laporte, for pity's sake. Just the mention of his name was enough to strike fear in the hearts of most of the lawyers and land dealers east of the Mississippi.

Why then did he get the feeling that this pathetic little Orris Craven was laughing up his sleeve? If the idiot had any sense, he would be trembling in fear. Beauregard's anger was not to be trifled with.

Then a thought struck him, an idea so ludicrous that he dismissed it almost immediately. Once, just once, he had caught the faintest hint of a smug expression on Craven's face . . . as if he knew something he wasn't telling. But it was unthinkable. A worm like Craven didn't have sense enough or guts enough to play both sides of the fence for his own benefit.

No, the fool was simply incompetent. He had evidently left a paper trail that led straight back to himself—and to Clinton Marston. It was only a matter of time before these Breckinridge people followed it to Beau's own doorstep. Better to nip this in the bud before it got out of hand.

Oh, Beau would meet with this attorney, Winsom, all right. But he wouldn't try to bribe him, and he wouldn't bully him. He would use a weapon even more lethal than money or force: charm. By the time he got finished, Winsom would believe Beauregard T. Laporte was the most maligned, well-meaning, misunderstood entrepreneur in the South. Beau knew how to handle people like this. A little oil in the right places, and he would slip right through Winsom's fingers and leave him thinking he had won a glorious victory.

Clinton Marston would take the fall for this—Marston and his little trained ferret, Craven. If somebody was going to be ruined by this fiasco, it wasn't going to be Beauregard T. Laporte.

34

Renovations

The Coltrain Farm
October 9, 1945

Willie stood in the doorway and watched as Owen Slaughter took a sledge-hammer to the wall between Mabel Rae's old bedroom and the smaller room next door. The plan was to frame a doorway between the two rooms and use the second one as a nursery for the baby. Willie's whole frame shuddered with every blow of the hammer. In a way she couldn't quite understand, she identified with the wall—as if in the past year or so her very soul had been chipped away like the shattered plaster that lay strewn across the floor.

She was glad to have Owen back, of course. And this time it looked as if he meant to stay. But still, her heart had been pulled this way and that for so long that she dared not let herself hope.

That first day he arrived, he said he had a lot to tell her. And yet most of their conversation had centered around Mabel Rae and the baby, Ivory Brownlee's situation, Drew's preoccupations. He had told her about meeting his Uncle Earl and Aunt Gert, the memorabilia his mother had saved that helped him understand—at least intellectually—what kind of family he had come from, what kind of person he had been. But there were other things, deeper things, that he wasn't saying. It was as if they were dancing around the real issues they needed to discuss, keeping their interaction light and uncomplicated—at least for the moment.

It was maddening. Willie wanted to shake him, to demand that he tell her what had happened to him. For something obviously *had* happened. Something more than a few uneventful weeks in his childhood home.

Curly and Valentine appeared at the doorway. Vallie, ever polite, sat down in the hall outside the door and waited. Curly barged right in, scattering plaster dust in her wake, and began pulling on the bottom of Willie's jeans. Willie reached down and scooped the dog up, accepting a sloppy kiss on the cheek. The dogs were so much like their masters, Willie mused—Vallie hesitant and careful, Curly impetuous and demanding.

"Something wrong, Willie?"

The voice startled her, and she turned. Owen stood leaning on the handle of the sledgehammer, sweat running down his face.

"No . . . nothing's wrong." Curly squirmed out of her arms and jumped to the floor, plowing through plaster and debris to get to Owen. He grinned and leaned down to pet her.

"She's settled right in, hasn't she?" He kept his eyes fixed on the dog as he spoke.

"Just part of the family," Willie answered, trying to keep her voice light.

At the word *family,* Owen stiffened visibly and stood back up. His right hand gripped around the handle of the sledgehammer until his knuckles turned white, and he cleared his throat. "Willie, I need to tell you something."

Willie's heart constricted. *Here it comes,* she thought. He had been very careful, since his return, to keep their relationship noncommittal, a friendship. Obviously, the very idea of a home and family scared him to death.

"It's about what I found out when I was . . . away. And why I left."

"All right," she murmured. "Does this have anything to do with your memories?" She held her breath. If he had remembered something, what had he remembered?

"Sort of. Well, maybe."

"That's perfectly clear to me."

He grinned and ran a hand through his plaster-covered hair. "Sorry. I'll try to be more specific."

"That would be helpful."

He led her over to the settee by the window, and they sat down. "Something was nagging at me, some fragment of a memory that seemed like it was trying to push through."

"You mean when you left?"

"Yes." He nodded. "I was getting this feeling, Willie, that even if I didn't have family out there according to the army's records, there might be somebody, somewhere, who cared about me and was waiting for me." He shook his head. "Does that make sense?"

Oh, yeah, Willie thought, *it makes perfect sense. If only I could tell you what it means.*

★ ★ ★

Owen watched Willie out of the corner of his eye. He wasn't sure how she would react to what he was about to say, and her face wasn't giving anything away. She just sat there, watching him, waiting.

When he had gone to Iowa and then to Minnesota, he had thought that if he just put some distance between them, things would get easier, and he wouldn't have to battle with his feelings all the time. But the distance didn't help. Even when he was making wedding plans with JoLynn Ferber, his love for Willie had always been in his mind, haunting him, tugging at him. And he hadn't realized it until that night in New Ulm, when her face had finally appeared in his dreams.

"I don't quite know how to say this," he began hesitantly. "I don't want to upset you."

Suddenly her expression changed to one of dismay, and she got up and stood with her back to him. "You met someone, didn't you?" she said in a low, controlled voice. "While you were away?"

"No!" He jumped to his feet and came to her side in an instant. "I mean, yes. Well, sort of."

She crossed her arms in front of her and went to sit down on the dusty cedar chest at the foot of the bed, and he followed. "Sorry," he muttered as he swiped a hand at the plaster dust that covered the wood. "I should have put down a drop cloth."

"It's OK," she managed. "It'll clean up just fine."

Owen sat down beside her. If only he could clean up the mess he was making of this conversation as easily. Well, there was only one way to do that—he had to start being candid with her, even if it drove her away. "Willie," he said softly, cringing as she jerked her arm away from his hand, "can I talk to you . . . honestly?"

She kept her head averted but slanted her eyes back toward him. "I wish you would."

The rebuke stung, and he winced. "I guess I deserved that. I haven't . . . well, I haven't been myself lately. Not for a long time."

"And just who have you been?" Her head swiveled in his direction, and a ghost of a smile flitted across her lips.

Owen chuckled. "I have no idea. But then, I have no idea about a lot of things."

At last she turned and looked at him, her eyes filled with pain and confusion. "All right, let's talk."

He rubbed at his forehead and frowned, trying to figure out where to begin. At last his gaze settled on the gaping hole in the wall between the two bedrooms, its ragged plaster like an open wound. Beyond the hole, from the windows in the nursery, morning light streamed through to the bedroom where they sat.

"I've felt like—like that." He pointed to the hole in the wall. "Since I lost my memory, I've been walled off, separated from myself, not knowing who I am or where I've come from."

"According to the army, you came from North Fork, Iowa."

He grinned at her attempt at levity. "That's not what I mean, and you know it. For a long time—even before Charlie's death, but more so since I came to Eden—I had this feeling that if I could just get to what was on the other side of the wall, everything would fall into place."

"You'd remember, you mean?"

"Not so much remember as *understand,*" Owen corrected. "Understand who I was, and why I was here." He got up and went to the demolished wall, running his hand over the jagged opening. "These two rooms will be really nice when we're done," he mused. "The doorway will let light into this room and give a feeling of openness. But right now it's a mess, and it doesn't seem like it will be anything but a mess." He paused and inhaled deeply. "That's the way I felt, Willie—as if I was in the demolition stage, as if a deconstruction had to take place before the reconstruction could begin."

"And the reconstruction is—?"

He shrugged. "Myself. My life. My soul, I guess." He returned to the cedar chest and sat down beside her. "I'm going to take a big risk here, Willie. I may find that I'm taking out a load-bearing wall, and it may all come crashing down on my head. But if I don't, well, I'll never forgive myself."

A strange look passed over her face. "Go on."

"I went to Iowa to find out who I was and where I had come from. But I discovered more than I bargained for."

"What did you discover?" Her mouth formed the words, but her eyes begged him not to answer.

"There was a woman in North Fork," he began hesitantly, "with a six-year-old son. . . ."

★ ★ ★

Willie felt the room spin. *He had a wife and child?* All this time, when she thought she knew him, thought he was the man she had always dreamed of, he had been hiding this from her? He wouldn't have remembered it, of course, not when he came back from the war. But what about *before,* when she and Owen first met? How could he have been such a dog, to declare his love for her when he . . . he . . . ?

And what about *now?* How could he just blithely abandon a family a thousand miles away and trip across the country? Did he have no heart, no morals? He had been here almost three weeks, for heaven's sake! Three weeks without saying a word about any of this!

No, he wasn't a dog. Dogs were loyal and loving. This was simply beyond belief. He was a cad, a scoundrel, a two-timing—

"Willie?"

"What?" she snarled. The pain was turning to anger, and she wheeled around to glare at him. Then she pulled back. She wouldn't give him the satisfaction of knowing he had hurt her.

"Did you hear what I said?"

"You said you had a wife and child in North Fork." She kept her voice emotionless.

He gave her a baffled look. "Is that what I said?"

"Look, Owen, I don't see any point in talking about this. You said you didn't want to upset me. Well, I think you should just go. You don't owe us anything because of our friendship." She looked toward the jagged hole in the wall, and a knot formed in her throat. Yes, he had done quite enough damage. "I'm sure your family in Iowa is anxious for you to return."

He grabbed her arms and turned her toward him. "Willie, what are you talking about?"

"I'm talking about your wife and son," she said flatly.

"I don't have a wife and son."

"But you just said—"

"You weren't listening. Look, I know this is confusing—it was pretty confusing for me, too, but just hear me out."

Willie sighed. "All right. Go ahead." She extricated herself from his grasp and turned her eyes away.

"Her name was JoLynn Ferber. Shortly after I arrived in North Fork, I got a call from her asking me to come see her. When I went, she—well—she was very, ah, affectionate toward me. I didn't have the slightest idea who she was. And then she introduced me to Buddy—"

"Your son."

"Her son," he corrected. "I mean, I thought he was my son. She told me he was. And he was a wonderful little boy. I almost wished he was mine."

"So why didn't you just stay there and marry her?" Willie knew the tone of her voice gave too much away, but she couldn't help herself. She was hurt and angry, and she didn't care.

"I almost did," he said softly.

Willie fought against the tears that rose to her eyes and swallowed down the knot in her throat. "What changed your mind?"

"He had brown eyes."

Willie's mind reeled, and she struggled to follow his logic. But the patent absurdity of the statement helped to clear her head. She uttered a short, cynical laugh. "You have something against brown-eyed children?"

"Of course not. But my eyes are blue, and so are JoLynn's."

"Owen, none of this is making any sense."

He exhaled heavily. "I'm sorry. I'm not doing this very well. It was all because of Ardyce, you see, and her genetics class—"

Willie had just about heard enough. "Do you think you could just finish the story and put both of us out of our misery?"

"I will if you'll be quiet and let me finish. I'm having a hard time getting this straight. And why are you so angry with me?"

"I'm not angry. Just go on."

"All right. But don't interrupt. This is important, and—"

"I don't interrupt!"

"Yes, you do. You just did. Now please just sit there and listen."

Willie folded her arms and waited.

★　★　★

Owen's stomach was in knots, and his pulse pounded. This wasn't going well, but he had to do it. He had to explain to her why he had come back and tell her how he felt. Right now he was pretty sure he knew how *she* felt, but he didn't know why. And so he had no choice but to plow on through to the end and hope for the best.

"When JoLynn told me that Buddy was my son, I believed it. I *wanted* to believe it because I needed to have a place to belong. Then Ardyce got involved because she worked at the clinic where JoLynn was a patient. When she found out that JoLynn was pregnant again, and JoLynn gave her my name as the father, Ardyce knew who I was because of Rae's letters. She put two and two together and came to North Fork to see me. I told her that

JoLynn and I had never . . . well, you know . . . and she began asking me questions about Buddy. Turns out that two blue-eyed parents, like me and JoLynn, can't possibly have a brown-eyed child like Buddy. I wasn't the father. JoLynn had heard about me, about my amnesia, and since we had known each other and dated briefly in high school, she saw her chance to get a stable, live-in father for both of her children and a better life for herself. She didn't mean to hurt me, I don't think. She just figured no one would ever be the wiser. But—"

Owen looked up into Willie's face and saw an amazing transformation take place. All the anger had vanished, and in its place was an expression of compassion and empathy. "Oh, Owen, I'm so sorry," she murmured. "It must have been very hard for you."

"It was. If it hadn't been for Ardyce, I would have married her. I would have done my duty. And I'll have to admit that I adored Buddy. But I wouldn't have been happy."

"Why not?" she whispered, her eyes searching his.

Owen's heart latched onto a tiny shred of hope. She was hearing him now, and maybe, just maybe, she wouldn't think he was crazy when he told her the rest of the story. "Do you want me to go on?"

Willie nodded, and he briefly related his trip to New Ulm and his time with Kurt and Leah Sonntag. "Leah told me to have faith, to ask for what I needed," he finished. "And so I did."

"Then what happened?"

"For months I had been having this recurring dream of myself on a train platform, with mist and shadows all around. Someone was there waiting for me, but I could never see who it was. I did as Leah had suggested—although it felt a little awkward—and prayed for direction and guidance. That night I had the dream again, and this time I saw the face of the person who was waiting for me."

He paused and took a shaky breath. "Willie, in my dream, the person on platform was . . . it was you."

"Me?" A panic-stricken look crossed her face, and he hastened to finish before he lost his nerve.

"Willie, all this time I've tried to be a brother to you, to do right by Charlie's memory, but I wasn't succeeding very well. That's one of the reasons I left so abruptly. I didn't know how to handle what . . . well, what was happening. When I saw your face in my dream, I finally understood why. I think I might be falling in love with you."

The words all came out in a rush, and when he was done, Owen ventured a glance at Willie. All the blood had drained from her face, and she was looking at him as if she had just received an electrical jolt.

"I'm sorry, Willie, I didn't mean to shock you," he said quickly. "I mean, I don't have any reason to think you'd feel the same way about me, and I know this could make you uncomfortable, with me being here all the time, so if you want me to leave, just say so, and I'll pack my bags and be out of your life forever. But I just felt like I needed to be honest with you and with myself, so I came back, but if—"

She laid a finger over his lips and smiled into his eyes. "Owen," she said in that husky voice that from the first moment he had heard it, never failed to warm his heart, "I think you've said quite enough."

She shifted and moved toward him, and he could feel the warmth of her arm against his shoulder. Without thinking, he reached a hand around her waist and drew her closer. She smiled again and leaned down toward him. "Does this mean . . . ?" he began, but before he could finish his sentence, their lips touched.

The kiss, brief and sweet, touched him to the core, and he closed his eyes.

Then he felt more warm kisses caressing his cheeks, his chin, his neck, and he heard a deep laugh close to his ear. His eyes snapped open. Curly, the little brown spaniel, was in his face, covering him with slobbery dog-kisses, and Willie was laughing as he had never seen her laugh before.

★ ★ ★

When the kiss she had dreamed of finally came, Willie never wanted it to end. But Curly's insistence upon getting in on the affection called an abrupt halt to their romantic moment.

"She sure knows how to spoil a mood," Owen said, wiping his beard with one hand. Vallie had slipped in from the doorway and sat beside Owen's knee waiting to be noticed. "And this one has to get her share of attention as well."

Willie linked her fingers in his and smiled down at him. "That's the price of having children," she quipped. "Never a moment's privacy." As soon as the words were out, she could have bitten her tongue.

But he didn't seem to mind. He scratched Vallie behind her ears and grinned at Willie. "I gather from your response that you're not . . . ah, opposed to the idea."

"The idea of kissing you?" she teased. "Certainly not."

"The idea of you and me . . . well, us . . . as more than just friends." His ears reddened, and he pulled at his beard nervously. "I mean, will it be awkward for you, having me here? Usually two people who are . . . you know, getting to know each other . . . aren't living under the same roof."

Willie reached over and tousled Curly's head. "With two dogs in the house, and Rae and Drew and Ardyce, and the baby on the way, I'd say we'll have plenty of chaperons."

He gave her a serious look. "I promise I won't try to take advantage of the situation."

A laugh welled up in Willie from deep within her soul. "I know you won't, Owen. We'll take things slowly, get to know each other, as you say. And, well, see what develops."

"I meant what I said, Willie. I love you, and I'll do everything in my power not to hurt you." A frown creased his brow. "But I still feel like there are a lot of things I need to find out about myself. I hope you'll be patient with me."

She squeezed his hand. "I can do that, Owen."

Willie gazed through the hole in the wall into the room that would become a nursery for her first nephew—or niece. Dust motes danced in the beams of sunlight, and Willie's heart danced with them. It was true, what Owen said about the wall. Sometimes deconstruction had to take place before reconstruction could begin. In the meantime, it was a mess, but it would be worth the effort in the long run.

And if Owen's kiss was any indication of the future, well worth the effort.

35

Ardyce's Calling

Eden, Mississippi
October 12, 1945

Ardyce Hanson paused at the bottom of the stairs and shifted the glass of orange juice on Rae's breakfast tray away from the edge. When she and Owen had arrived three weeks ago, she had a plan worked out in her mind—she would stay a few days, give Rae some support and encouragement, and take the bus back to Frost.

Now her plans had changed—or, she ought to say, God had changed her plans.

Where Ardyce came from, where almost everyone was both Scandinavian and Lutheran, people didn't talk about faith much. They considered a person's religion a private matter and not an issue for public discussion. And although Ardyce was reticent, in her Norwegian way, to make an issue of it, her belief in God ran strong and deep, and an awareness of God's direction permeated her consciousness.

Most of the time the Lord's guidance came naturally, through common sense and instinct and perception. But on occasion, it ran directly counter to her natural tendencies—like when she went to North Fork to confront Owen Slaughter about JoLynn Ferber. And now, when she knew she wouldn't be going home right away. At least not until the baby was born.

She had known it as soon as she laid eyes on Rae Laporte.

The woman showed all the signs of deep depression. She had to force herself to eat for the baby's sake. She wasn't sleeping well, and even when she did sleep, she woke up exhausted and lived with constant fatigue—much more than could be accounted for by pregnancy, uncertainty, and emotional stress.

Mabel Rae had rallied a bit the first week after Ardyce came. They had talked for hours, filling in the missing pieces of the lives they had shared through letters. But when Rae began to talk about the baby, something happened. It was more than just new-mother jitters, more than the normal fears women often have for their unborn children.

Something was wrong.

Ardyce knew it instinctively, almost like a revelation, like second sight. For some reason Ardyce did not yet understand, Rae seemed justified in her concern for the baby. And Ardyce had no intention of going anywhere until that child was born and Rae was back on her feet.

Ardyce mounted the stairs and stood at the doorway of Willie's bedroom, now occupied by Rae and Drew until the renovations on their bedroom and the nursery were completed. Willie had readily given up her room and moved downstairs to the daybed in the tiny alcove off the parlor. She didn't mind, she insisted. Ardyce suspected she was so preoccupied with Owen that she would have slept on the kitchen table without a word of complaint. Love did strange things to a person's need for creature comforts.

Love. That was another problematic issue for Rae. She loved her husband and was convinced that he loved her. But it was patently obvious to Ardyce that the handsome Drew Laporte carried an unspoken burden of his own—some deep grief that he had not communicated to his wife. He hadn't communicated much of anything to his wife, in fact. According to Rae, their relationship had been growing increasingly strained for months now, and although she had tried to talk to him, he wasn't listening.

One more reason Ardyce needed to be here.

She propped the breakfast tray on her hip and knocked softly on the bedroom door.

"Come in."

Ardyce opened the door. Rae sat upright against the headboard with a pillow under the small of her back. She smiled when Ardyce entered, but the expression quickly faded.

"Good morning." Ardyce set the tray on the edge of the bed. "Biscuits and grits and scrambled eggs. Are you hungry?"

"No, but I guess I'll eat anyway."

"The doctor says you've been losing weight, and that's not a good sign."

"Says who?" Rae countered. "I've been trying to lose weight all my life."

"Now is not the time," Ardyce answered in her professional-nurse voice, then gave a brief laugh. "But I must admit, I could never figure out the attraction of grits."

"It's a southern thang," Rae drew out the word *thang* in an exaggerated drawl. "You're a Yankee, and Yankees don't understand southerners."

"I understand enough to be thankful you didn't use the adjective that usually precedes *Yankee.*" Ardyce handed Rae a napkin and pointed to the tray. "Eat."

"Yes, ma'am." Rae took a forkful of eggs while Ardyce buttered the biscuit. "I'm really glad you're here, Ardyce. I know I'm being a baby, and you don't need this kind of burden, but—"

Ardyce caught the plaintive tone in Rae's voice and looked up. "Nonsense."

"It's not nonsense. You've got a job, a life—"

"And I've also got a friend who needs me. Now, eat your breakfast."

"But what about your work at the clinic?"

"My work at the clinic will wait. I had some time off coming anyway. It's all taken care of. And get used to having me around. I'm not leaving until this baby makes his—or her—appearance and you're back to normal."

Rae laid down her fork and stared at Ardyce. "I'm not due for six weeks."

"And you don't think you can stand my company that long?"

"You know that's not what I meant. It just seems like . . . well, a lot to ask."

"You didn't ask. I offered."

"You're a good friend, Ardyce. The best."

Ardyce grinned. "Yes, I am. And it's about time you appreciated it."

Rae smiled wanly in return. "I've appreciated it. Everybody has. Willie can't believe you'd just come down here on a moment's notice—although she is thankful, I can tell you."

Ardyce raised one eyebrow. "Willie," she said deliberately, "can't see anything except Owen Slaughter's cute little face. I feel like a matchmaker."

"The match was made a long time ago. But it's nice to see her so happy. And you did play a big part in that."

"I just nudged a little."

"Don't be so modest," Rae protested. "If it wasn't for you, Owen would be married to that floozy in Iowa and playing daddy to two children who weren't even his."

"JoLynn wasn't a floozy, exactly. Just a misguided girl who made some mistakes and thought she had found the perfect way out."

Rae leaned back against the pillows and sighed. "There is no perfect way out. I wish there was."

Ardyce caught Rae's gaze and held it. "Do you want out?"

"Out of this pregnancy? It's a little late for that, don't you think? And no, I don't want out of my marriage either. What I want is—" she shut her eyes and sighed—"for my life to get back to normal."

Ardyce moved the breakfast tray aside and sat down on the edge of the bed. "Tell me about normal."

Tears seeped out of the corners of Rae's closed eyelids. "I was already in love with Drew before we ever met," she whispered. "I knew his heart and soul through his letters, even though I had never seen his face. Or I thought I did. Now I'm not so sure."

"What's changed?" Ardyce prodded gently.

"Everything," Rae choked out. "Drew always told me he never wanted to become like his father—distant, preoccupied, always obsessed with work and money." She heaved a ragged sigh. "With Drew, it's not money but principle, and I guess that's better. Still—"

"Still what?"

"The effect is the same. I'm worried about the baby, Ardyce, but he doesn't care. He doesn't listen. He brushes me off with a superficial kiss and a pat on the head, like I'm some kind of house pet. That is, he has until lately. Now I don't even get the kiss or the pat." She sat up and opened her eyes, and Ardyce saw a look of despair there that made her heart break. "Is it supposed to be this way, Ardyce?"

"I don't know." Ardyce hated being this helpless in the face of her friend's pain. "I don't think so, but then, I'm not in your situation."

"Count your blessings."

Then Ardyce felt it—a quiet nudging in her spirit. Perhaps she should talk to Drew, try to make him see how troubled his wife was, and how much she needed him. *No,* her mind responded. *I am not going to meddle in this.* Pray, yes. Try to support Rae, certainly. But not meddle.

Just as she formed the thought, Rae reached out and took her hand. "Do you think maybe . . . could you . . . I mean, would you . . . talk to him?"

"Me?" Ardyce flinched. "Why me?"

"Because you're a nurse. Maybe he would listen to you."

"You want me to wear my little white hat?"

This suggestion, ridiculous as it was, got a laugh out of Rae, the first glimmer of mirth Ardyce had seen in several days. "No, of course not. Just—well, talk to him. See if you can make him understand."

Ardyce sighed. Inwardly she thought, *This isn't going to work. It will probably only make things worse.* But to Rae she said, "All right. I'll try."

★ ★ ★

At ten after two, Ardyce found herself in Owen Slaughter's car, driving the country road that led from the Coltrain farm into Eden. All the way into town, she argued with herself and God about the wisdom of doing this. She had barely spoken to Drew Laporte in the time she had been living under their roof, and even then he had given one-word answers to her attempts to coerce him into conversation. But she had promised Rae she would try, and despite her better judgment, she would keep that promise.

Ardyce parked the convertible on Main Street in front of the hardware store and went to the glass door of the office next door that bore the names *Winsom and Laporte, Attorneys-at-Law.* She peered in the window and saw Drew at his desk, a stack of papers in front of him and his head down on his hands.

Apparently he was alone, and she breathed a sigh of relief. She didn't want to take the chance of anyone else overhearing their conversation— both Rae's confidence and his needed to be guarded carefully. Just before she pulled open the door, she sent up a quick prayer for help: *All right, you got me into this, so I'll need all the wisdom I can get.*

Drew didn't hear her come in. She stood in the doorway of his office for a full minute, watching. At first she thought he might be asleep, but then she saw his shoulders shaking and heard a deep shuddering sigh. Clearly, this man carried some heavy burden—something that his wife knew nothing about.

"Drew?" she said softly.

He turned, and she could see that his eyes were rimmed with red, his face pallid and haggard. He quickly straightened up, adjusted his tie, and ran a hand over his eyes. "Oh, hello, Ardyce." His expression betrayed his momentary confusion—a what-on-earth-are-you-doing-here look. Then it changed to panic. "Is everything all right?" he demanded, getting unsteadily to his feet. "Is something wrong with Rae?"

He loves her, Ardyce thought instinctively. *This is not the reaction of a man who doesn't care.* "Everything's fine, Drew. Do you have a few minutes?"

"Uh . . . sure." He dropped back into his seat and motioned to the chair on the other side of the desk. "Come on in."

Ardyce faced him and made a quick diagnosis: exhaustion, probably, coupled with a debilitating worry. Bags under his bloodshot eyes. Pasty-looking skin. A permanent frown furrowed between his thick eyebrows.

"Have you been getting enough sleep, Drew? You look terrible." She blurted the words out before she could stop them, and his frown deepened. Clearly she had struck a nerve.

"Did I ask for a medical opinion?" he snapped.

"No." She sat back in the chair. "It's just that—well, your wife is worried about you."

"My wife," he said with a snort of derision, "is worried about everything."

"So you *have* been listening."

"What's that supposed to mean?" Drew shuffled the papers in front of him and avoided her gaze. "Ardyce, I don't want to be rude, but I'm very busy, and—"

She held up a hand. "I won't take up much of your *valuable* time, then. I'll get right to the point."

Drew missed the sarcasm completely. "Please do." He folded his arms and waited.

Ardyce's mind scrambled for the right words, words that could pierce this protective armor and get to his heart, to his love for Rae. "I know you care about Rae," she began.

"Of course I do."

"And she cares about you. She loves you a great deal."

"I'm aware of that."

"But she's having a difficult time right now," she went on. "She feels that—well, that you've been so caught up in your work and in other concerns that you haven't had time for her."

"And she told you all this?"

"Yes."

"Why should she tell you, a complete stranger? Why didn't she tell me?"

"I'm not exactly a *stranger* to Rae," Ardyce said. "We met through letters, just as you did, and we've gotten to know each other pretty well. Besides, I gather she *has* tried to tell you, on any number of occasions."

"I know, I know," he said impatiently. "She's worried about the baby. She's got some crazy idea that something is wrong with our child, that it's going to be born with some kind of defect. How am I supposed to respond to that?"

"With understanding, perhaps," Ardyce answered carefully. "With compassion."

"But it's all in her mind," he protested. "She's imagining it. Isn't she?"

Ardyce closed her eyes. "No. I don't think so."

"What are you, some kind of psychic? You're just a nurse. The *doctor* said—"

Ardyce's temper flared, and she struggled to keep her voice controlled.

"How long has it been since you've been to the doctor with her, Drew? How long since you heard for yourself what the doctor has to say?"

He shrugged. "A couple of weeks, I guess."

"Three *months*," she corrected, fixing him with a glare. "The doctor thinks there is a good chance she could deliver early. He's avoiding her questions about the health of the baby, and Rae suspects he's not telling her everything."

"That's ridiculous. There's nothing wrong with the baby."

"Why are you so sure, Drew? Because it's not possible for you to produce anything but a perfect child? Because everything you do has to be perfect?"

She saw him wince, saw the pain that flashed through his eyes.

"Look, Ardyce, I know you mean well. I know you're Rae's friend, and you care about her. But I've got a lot on my mind right now, and I don't need this—"

His superior attitude galled Ardyce, and her concern for Rae rose up in a wave. "What exactly is on your mind, Drew?" she asked through clenched teeth. "What is so important that it comes before the welfare of your wife and child?"

His face went white. "That's none of your business."

"And none of Rae's business either?"

"That's right. Some problems I just have to handle myself. And until I can get things straightened out, she'll just have to trust me."

"You're making it hard for her to do that right now, Drew."

"I'm sorry. It can't be helped."

"I don't expect you to confide in me," Ardyce said, forcing a note of conciliation into her voice. "But can't you confide in her?"

"No. Not now. Not about this."

Ardyce sighed. Whatever his problem was, he was determined to keep it to himself. And as long as he did, he wouldn't be able to see beyond it to Rae or anyone else.

"So what else did Rae tell you about me?" he challenged.

She stood up. "Not much. Only that you were in danger of becoming just like your father."

As soon as she had said it, she knew it was a mistake. Something in him snapped. His face flushed, his breathing grew shallow, and his eyes shot fire. "Like . . . like my *father?*"

"I gathered it wasn't a compliment." She laid a hand on his trembling arm. "I'm sorry if I said anything that hurt you, Drew. That wasn't my intention. I was just concerned about Rae, and I hoped that—"

He jerked his arm away and turned his back on her. "I think you'd better go now."

"Yes, I think I'd better." She closed the door behind her and stood for a moment leaning on the doorjamb. The look in his eyes had shaken her to the core. It was an expression of . . .

Fear. Abject terror, like an animal caught in a leg trap.

She went outside, got into the car, and sat there for a long time, unable to move. She had made some mistakes in her time, thinking she was being led to do something and finding out later that it was her own bullheadedness rather than God's direction. But this one would go down in the record books as the biggest blunder of her entire life. She only hoped it wouldn't make the situation worse for Rae in the long run.

I told you this wouldn't work, she thought with a glance toward heaven as she started the car and backed out into the street. *If you ever again ask me to get involved in something like this, you'd better send the archangel Gabriel with a flaming sword. Otherwise, my meddling days are over. Forever.*

36

Beauregard's Last Stand

Eden, Mississippi
October 28, 1945

Beauregard T. Laporte gripped the steering wheel of his sleek black Cadillac and sped down the highway with the accelerator to the floorboard and one eye on the rearview mirror. It would be just his luck, after this disaster of a trip, to end up in a one-room jail on a speeding violation from some yokel sheriff. He had already wasted half the morning taking Bea out to that rundown dirt farm his son now called home. And he'd have to come back again this evening to pick her up.

Beau shuddered at the thought. He had already enjoyed about as much of this family togetherness as he could stand. Willie Coltrain and that Hanson woman, the nurse, hovered around his daughter-in-law and catered to her every whim, and now Bea had joined the circle. Rae wasn't an invalid, for heaven's sake, she was *pregnant*. A perfectly natural occurrence, and not one which should be the cause of such a ruckus.

But it was his grandchild, of course, that they were making all the fuss over, and he couldn't much blame them for that. Beau smiled to himself. His *grandson*. Someone to carry on the Laporte name, to take into the family business. His heart warmed at the thought. Maybe they would name him Beauregard, after his granddaddy. Surely Andrew would think of that—or if he didn't, a few well-placed hints might do the trick.

Andrew. Beau felt his smile turn to a frown, and he urged the Caddy on a little faster. What was that boy's problem, anyway? He had barely given Beau the time of day since they arrived, and he seemed so withdrawn, distant. He hardly spoke, and when Beatrice tried to talk to him once about the baby, he had mumbled a few words about how excited he was to be a father and then changed the subject.

He didn't seem excited, that was for sure. He looked haggard and tired, and he seemed preoccupied, worried about something. Maybe it was money. He wouldn't talk about his practice or his new law partner or any of the cases he was involved in, wouldn't even take Beau to see his new office. And he couldn't be making any kind of a living out here in the sticks. Maybe Beau should work on him, try to convince him to come home and take over where that idiot Orris Craven had messed up. Surely by now he would have faced the practical realities of life and found out that you can't live on love—or on a good name.

The problem was, there might not be a family business for Andrew to come back to if Beau didn't get this mess with the Breckinridge people straightened out. He had spent most of this week with Craven, trying to extricate himself from the noose tightening around his neck. These Breckinridge folks were sharp, he would give them that much. But there had to be some dirt on them somewhere—if only he could find out what it was.

Beau had met with Winsom and Mrs. Breckinridge only once and very briefly. He had made an error during that meeting—a big one, maybe a fatal one. His respectable family-man facade hadn't worked, and in the end he had tried to buy them off. Craven had warned him that it was a mistake, and wouldn't you know it, the one time the weasel had been right, Beau hadn't listened. But the blustery, bullying act that usually worked so well had failed him this time. They didn't cower to his threats, and they didn't seem in the least tempted by his money. The only card Beau had left to play, other than giving in to their demands for all his records and a ridiculously lopsided partnership, was to get to Harlan Brownlee.

That's why he was headed now to the Brownlee place. If Beau could corner this Harlan Brownlee and buy him off without that lawyer Winsom around, he might have a chance at getting out of this. Surely Brownlee would cooperate . . . for the right price.

He glanced at the map Craven had drawn for him. Shouldn't be hard to find the place. About five miles farther, he figured. He gave the Cadillac more gas and slid around a curve in the road. Everything he had worked for all his life was on the line. There was no time to waste.

★ ★ ★

Thelma Breckinridge took a step up onto the front porch of the Brownlee house and stood for a moment, gazing up at the vast columns. The flowers were gone now, and only the last few leaves of autumn clung to the boughs of the old maple tree that shaded the porch in summer. Its bare branches stirred a nostalgia in her, rather like the feeling the house itself evoked. A sense of grandeur long past . . . but without the hope of a spring to come.

With Ivory's permission and Bennett's reluctant agreement, Thelma had come out here to the ruined plantation to pray. For one thing, she needed the solitude. And despite her best intentions, the house continued to draw her, to call to her as if it needed her prayers as much as she needed its peace.

Two days ago she and Bennett had met with Drew's father, and the confrontation hadn't gone well at all. Bennett had hoped, for Drew's sake, that they might be able to reason with the man. But evidently it would take more than reason to break through the shell Beauregard Laporte had built around himself. He hadn't let them get a word in edgewise, but instead tried to bully and bribe them into giving in. The meeting had ended without any satisfactory resolution, and it appeared that Drew would have to get involved after all. It was their last hope, short of reporting Laporte to the authorities. If Drew revealed his involvement in this and his knowledge of his father's activities, maybe the man might be shamed into seeing the error of his ways.

It would be hard on Drew either way, Thelma knew. And everything was hard on that poor boy these days. As obsessed as he had been before he had discovered the identity of the man they were after, he was doubly so now. He couldn't think of anything except how his own father had connived and manipulated the law for his own purposes. Drew had withdrawn even further from Rae and abdicated any responsibility for her care to Ardyce Hanson, Rae's nurse friend from Minnesota. Thelma was glad Rae had Ardyce, of course, but she was no substitute for the presence and understanding of Rae's husband.

Thelma could see the pain in Drew's eyes every time he came into the cafe, and from what Willie had told her, Rae wasn't in much better shape. But nobody could figure out what to do, and it seemed to get worse by the day.

The sudden and unexpected appearance of Drew's parents had just made things that much more difficult. According to Willie, Drew's mother seemed completely bewildered by the changes in her son and daughter-in-law. And having to pretend to be ignorant of his father's business dealings just put more pressure on Drew. If this situation didn't improve soon, that boy was going to break.

Thelma felt the burden in her own body, a numbness in her limbs and a heaviness in her heart. And so she had come to pray, to bring those problems to the only One who knew what the future held. Perhaps here in the quietness of this empty old house she could concentrate on prayer and find peace in the midst of the turmoil.

With a deep sigh, she opened the front door, went inside, and climbed the stairs to the third floor.

★ ★ ★

Halfway up the rutted driveway, Beau cut the engine of the Cadillac and stared through the windshield. He could make out movement on the porch—someone was here. And it was not Harlan Brownlee.

It was a woman.

A large middle-aged woman, from what he could see, with red hair exactly like . . . that Aurelia Breckinridge, who headed up the phony foundation. But it couldn't be. This was no aristocrat. The woman wore a frumpy-looking cloth coat and drab black lace-up shoes. Still, the resemblance was remarkable.

Apparently she hadn't seen him, for after pausing on the porch for a minute or two, she went on inside.

Beau left the car where it was and got out. Whatever she was up to, he intended to find out. Harlan Brownlee could wait a few minutes. He eased up onto the porch, grimacing as the boards creaked under his step, and gently opened the front door.

No one was in sight. He glanced to his left, where big double pocket doors stood open to reveal a parlor with an ornate piano. Empty. The parlor on the right was vacant, too. Then he heard a noise above him, up the stairs. He followed the sound, pausing at the landing for a moment, then moving up past a huge ballroom that took up most of the second floor.

Whoever the woman was, she was making no effort to keep quiet. Her heavy shoes echoed over his head, and he heard a voice speaking aloud as she paced.

Beau ascended the second flight of stairs, hesitated, and listened.

★ ★ ★

For a few minutes Thelma paced up and down the long hall on the third floor of the old house, praying aloud and growing more restless by the minute. For a brief moment she considered returning to the bedroom where the secret door led into the attic shrine, but she shrugged the idea away. She wasn't here to explore; she was here to talk to God, to find some peace for herself and, she hoped, some insights for the people she loved.

"This just doesn't make sense, God, and to be perfectly honest, it doesn't seem fair," she said. "OK, yes, you provided a way for Ivory to pay his taxes and keep this place, and it seems that you've brought Owen home where he belongs. But what about the rest of it? What about that poor boy who is worrying his life away and ruining his marriage in the process? What about that sweet girl who is having all her dreams dashed—and her concerns about her baby? What about *them?*"

She slammed an open hand against the wall of the hallway and stalked down toward the far end of the corridor. "I know you can intervene in these situations, Lord. I know that you love them—all of us—and want only our best. And I know that you have your own timetable and plans for circumstances like this. Theoretically, that is. But to be perfectly honest, theories aren't helping very much right now."

Thelma leaned heavily against the far wall of the corridor and stared back toward the other end of the hall, where a door led to the high balcony on the front side of the house. Her mind flashed to the first time she had ever been in this grand old mansion, when she had insisted to Bennett that there should have been a matching balcony here, where she stood. But there was only this blank wall, like the wall she faced now in her faith. No exit. No way out. Only a dead end.

She waited, but no answer came. No peace in her spirit. No light in the tunnel. She sighed and slid to a sitting position on the dusty hardwood floor.

Then she heard a click and felt a slight pressure against her spine.

Thelma jumped up and turned, not daring to believe what she was seeing. In the back wall of the hallway was a hidden door, expertly concealed by a small flap of wallpaper that overlapped the opening. She must have tripped the latch when she slid down the wall!

Her heart pounding, Thelma swung open the doorway and peered in. It was dark, but she could make out a narrow alcove, barely three feet wide, going down the three floors on the back side of the house—what Bennett had taken for an old closed-up chimney. It was like a square tunnel, with a heavy wooden ladder affixed to the wall. On the right side of the alcove, Thelma could see a sliver of light—a crack, like a doorway. She did some quick mental calculations. It probably opened directly into the hidden attic room where she had discovered the Mathew Brady photograph of Lincoln.

She ran her hand down the edge of the doorway and found the latch, which looked, when the door was closed, like a small nail protruding from the wall. Someone had gone to a lot of trouble to build this tunnel and conceal it so well. A person with something to hide. Or *someone* to hide. Was it possible that old Seth Brownlee, Ivory's ancestor, had been more than just a Union sympathizer—that he had been actively involved with aiding and abetting Union forces? Lincoln's inscription had, after all, mentioned his work in *furthering the cause*. And this was a perfect setup for hiding or smuggling Union troops—or runaway slaves. . . .

Thelma's mind raced. There must be an exit downstairs, perhaps underground, that led from the back of the house into the woods. She could just imagine a midnight rendezvous, where frightened slaves were hurried down this ladder and out into the darkness to meet an escort who would take them North to freedom. Or a wagon load of supplies and medicine for the Yankee troops shuttled up into the secret attic.

Thelma peered down into the dark passageway and smiled. A hidden door. A secret way out. Maybe it was an object lesson for her. Maybe God was telling her that there *was* a way through this present darkness—a way known only to the Lord and not yet revealed to the parties involved.

An overwhelming curiosity washed over her. She had to find out where the secret passage led, what was down there. She didn't have a flashlight, but there were probably candles somewhere in the house, and matches. She would—

Suddenly a rough hand yanked at her elbow and jerked her away from the door. Her heart leaped into her throat, and she wheeled around to find herself face-to-face with . . .

Beauregard T. Laporte.

★ ★ ★

Beau grasped the woman's arm in a vise-like grip and peered into the her face. It looked like Aurelia Breckinridge, all right. Same henna-dyed red hair. Same brown eyes, same features. But the printed housedress didn't fit the image. Where were the makeup, the mink stole, the white gloves? His gaze shifted to her hand, raised in a defensive posture. Cracked, reddened—the hands of a working woman, not a society lady.

"What are you doing here?" he demanded, giving her arm a shake.

An expression of shock glazed her eyes, and she croaked out, "Mr. Laporte!"

In that one word, reality came home to Beau in a blinding flash. It *was* the same woman, and she was not what she had pretended to be. He had been taken. Deceived. Betrayed.

"Who are you?" he wrenched her arm behind her. "The truth!"

"Breckinridge," she gasped.

Beau's anger flared. "I said, the truth!"

"My name *is* Breckinridge," she protested. "Thelma Aurelia Breckinridge."

"But you're not a wealthy widow, I take it?" He tightened his hold.

"No. I own the Paradise Garden Cafe in Eden."

Beau felt himself losing control, but he couldn't seem to help it. He had been duped, and it was going to cost him everything. He had lost it all. His land deals. His reputation. His financial independence.

He pushed the woman up against the wall and held her there. "So what's your part in all this?"

"I'm a friend of Ivory . . . ah, Harlan Brownlee," she answered evenly. "We were determined not to let you take his land. It's all he's got."

"And you succeeded," he sneered. "So why all this charade?"

She swallowed with some difficulty as he pressed his hand against her throat. "You're hurting me."

"You haven't begun to hurt, lady," he said. "Now, talk."

"We—that is, Bennett—"

"Winsom? That lawyer?"

The woman nodded. "Didn't want you to get away with hurting other poor people like Ivory," she gasped. "Had to stop you."

"And what did you get out of it?" He shook her violently and increased the pressure of his fingers around her neck.

"No—nothing. Just—" she struggled for air—"just did what was right."

Another do-gooder, Beau thought. *Just like—*

Suddenly the face of his son flashed into his mind. The way Andrew had avoided looking at him, talking to him. The distance between them. The icy stares. The vague answers. No, it couldn't be—

"Who else?" he demanded through clenched teeth. "Who else was involved?" The woman shook her head and tried to look away. *"Who else?"*

She fixed her eyes on him, and all at once he realized that she wasn't afraid. Her expression was not one of fear, but of . . . pity. "Your son, Drew," she whispered hoarsely. "He's been part of this from the very beginning. He knows everything. And it's killing him."

★ ★ ★

At the mention of his son's name, something snapped inside Beauregard Laporte. Thelma saw it coming, but there was nothing she could do to stop it. Blood rage filled his eyes, and he brought the back of his hand across her face in a powerful blow.

As if in slow motion, she watched the meaty hand coming down toward her cheek, caught a glimpse of the huge signet ring on his finger, felt herself go down. For a moment there was nothing, just numbness, and then the pain sent her reeling. She shook her head and tried to rise, but his heavy boot caught her square in the stomach.

"No!" he screamed over and over again. "No, no, *no!*" With each word he pummeled Thelma again, jerking her upright and forcing her to the wall. "You think you'll get away with this, but nobody double-crosses Beauregard T. Laporte. Nobody!"

He grabbed her by the arm and flung her toward the end of the hallway, where the hidden door to the tunnel still stood ajar. She hit hard and collapsed into the passageway, clutching at the rungs of the ladder as she fell. A flame shot through her shoulder, her head cracked against something hard, and she struck bottom.

Through a haze of pain, Thelma looked up. She could make out daylight above her, as if from the deep recesses of a well. Then abruptly the light narrowed to a crack and disappeared. She heard a distinct click, and everything went black.

FOUR

Till the
End of Time

WINTER 1945

37

A Door in the Wall

Tullahoma County Hospital
November 1, 1945

Thelma opened her eyes and squinted against the light. Had she died? Was she in heaven? The room was white and brightly lit, and someone was standing over her, peering down at her, murmuring something.

"She's coming around."

The first figure stepped back and a second, dressed all in white with some kind of funny halo, moved in. "We're here, Miss Breckinridge. You've had a nasty accident, but you're going to be all right."

Her vision cleared, and Thelma found herself staring up into the smiling face of a young woman in a nurse's uniform. "I'll get the doctor. You'll be fine now."

"Easy for you to say," Thelma muttered to the woman's retreating back. "Get inside my skull and see how you feel." A hand reached out to grasp hers, and she turned her head to look. "Ow!"

"Take it easy, Thelma." Bennett stood over her, stroking his fingers under a painful wound on her right cheekbone. "Don't try to move around too much."

Tears stained his face, and she tried to reach up to wipe them away, but she couldn't move her arm. "Where am I?"

"You're in the hospital." He closed his eyes and sighed. "I thought I had lost you."

"Well, you found me, it seems." She chuckled a little, but her chest hurt and the movement brought a spasm of pain.

"You have a concussion," Bennett explained. "And a broken arm and a separated shoulder." He shook his head. "I never should have let you go out to that old place by yourself. Something was bound to happen."

"What exactly did happen?"

"When you didn't come back, we went looking for you. Found some blood—not much, but a little—in the upstairs hallway. But we couldn't locate you. Everybody came to help, but it was Owen's dog, Vallie, who finally sniffed you out. In the cellar, in an alcove back behind some shelves." He squeezed her hand. "There's a passageway that runs up through the house."

"No kidding." Thelma closed her eyes.

"Well, yes, I guess you'd know that. But how did you get in there?"

"From the third floor. Remember that hallway, where I said there should be another balcony on the back side?"

Bennett nodded. "I remember. It looked like a closed-up chimney."

"It's a tunnel. Runs from the secret attic room all the way down. There's a hidden door at the end of that hallway."

"But why did you try to climb down there? Why didn't you come get one of us to explore it?"

Thelma fought against the pain that raged through her head. She wasn't thinking straight, she knew, but she hadn't gone into that passageway of her own accord. Of that much she was certain. "I didn't exactly fall," she said. "I—"

"Well, well, I see our patient is finally awake." A middle-aged man with thinning hair came into the room and bent over her. *Dr. Willis*, his name tag said.

A thought struck Thelma, and she frowned. "How long have I been asleep?"

"Three days," the doctor replied. "You've got a nasty concussion there."

Three days? Thelma struggled to put all the pieces into place. "I went to the house," she began hesitantly, "and was upstairs in the hallway. And then—"

Dr. Willis patted her shoulder. "Don't try to talk, ma'am. We can sort all of this out later. You're lucky to be alive, after the fall you took."

Thelma started to protest that luck had nothing to do with any of it, but the pain in her head got in the way of her words.

"Just rest," the doctor repeated. "I'm going to give you something for the pain."

Bennett leaned down and kissed her on the forehead. "You're going to be all right, honey. Don't exert yourself."

Thelma nodded and smiled up at him. There would be plenty of time for explanations later. Plenty of time . . .

★ ★ ★

"I don't understand it," Drew raged, pacing back and forth. He stopped and glared at his mother, who sat on the sofa in the Coltrains' front parlor with her hands folded in her lap. "He said *what?*"

"He called from—well, I don't know where he was exactly—and said that he needed some time to himself and not to worry about him. That I should stay here, and he'd come back for me in a few days."

The calm tone of her voice infuriated Drew, and he fought to keep his temper under control. His father had been gone for three days, and his mother had been reduced to borrowing Bess Coltrain's old housedresses, three sizes too big and worn nearly to threads. "And you have no idea where he is?"

"No. I called the hotel in Grenada, but they told me he had checked out."

"How could he do this to you? Just dump you like this?"

"I'm not exactly 'dumped,' Andrew. I am with my children, after all."

"That's no excuse, Mother, and you know it!" He turned on her. "He's done this before, hasn't he?"

She shrugged. "A few times. Now and then he just seems to have to get off by himself. He always comes back."

"And you accept this? I can't believe it! What kind of man would just abandon his wife without a word of explanation? What kind of man—?"

"Andrew," she interrupted. "Stop pacing and sit down."

He complied, shifting restlessly in the chair across from her. "All right, I'm sitting. What?"

"Your father is—well, a complex man. He has his problems, things he tells me nothing about. But a woman discovers sooner or later that she can't change a man. She simply finds ways to adjust, to accommodate. Or she leaves. I have learned over the years to live with his eccentricities, with his—"

"Mother, stop it!" Drew broke in. "Stop making excuses for him. There is no excuse for this—none!"

"Isn't there?" she asked quietly.

"No man with a single grain of honor would do such a thing," he continued, his voice rising as his anger gathered force. "Whatever problems he has, he should be confiding them to you, not going off on his own. You're his wife, for heaven's sake! You're supposed to be his first priority. Not his job or his deals or his moneymaking schemes or whatever hot water he's gotten himself into because of them. He has no right—no right at all—to expect you to sit meekly by and wait for him until he decides he's ready to come back. What about you? Does he think you're some kind of possession, like a favorite cigar he can ignore or enjoy, depending upon his mood? It's outrageous, I tell you. I would never do such a thing—never! Just let me get my hands on him and I'll—"

Suddenly Drew stopped in mid-sentence, caught by the look of anguish and concern on his mother's face. Concern not for his father but for . . .

For him.

Unbidden, an image rose to his mind, of Rae's friend Ardyce Hanson standing in his office on Main Street. *You're in danger of becoming just like your father,* she had said. The metallic bitterness of fear and disgust filled his mouth. Still, the nerve had been struck, and despite the pain, he had to face the truth. He *had* become like his father. He had done exactly the same thing to Rae—only he had justified it because of his noble motivations and because he hadn't physically left her alone. But it was the same thing, wasn't it?

Rae had tried to tell him, not once but many times, that he was becoming obsessed with his work, with the challenge of ferreting out the scoundrel who was stealing valuable property from defenseless people like Ivory Brownlee. Well, he had won, but the victory left a vile taste on his tongue and a hollow emptiness in his chest. No cause was worth losing the woman he loved. And until he saw his mother sitting here alone in a borrowed dress, he hadn't realized—hadn't let himself realize—what he was doing.

Now he saw it so clearly. At the beginning Rae had practically begged him to pay attention, not to let their relationship slip away. But after a while, after he brushed her off and minimized her concerns long enough, she quit asking for anything. Now her support came not from him, as her husband, but from her sister, Willie, and her friend Ardyce.

He looked at his mother. "I've become just like him, haven't I?" It was not a question but a statement of hard fact, and misery rose up in him like a tide.

She didn't contradict him. Instead she smiled faintly and said, "It's not too late."

Drew grasped onto this straw of hope, the first he had felt in weeks. "Maybe you're right. Maybe it's not too late. But what do I do to make it up to her?"

"It seems to me you've already begun, simply by admitting the truth." She fixed him with a meaningful look. "But I don't think I'm the one you should be admitting it to."

Drew went to the sofa and sat down next to his mother. He put his arms gently around her narrow shoulders and hugged her close. "Thank you, Mother," he said.

"You're welcome, Son. Now, go." She pushed him to his feet.

"What do I say?"

She shook her head. "You'll think of something."

Drew squared his shoulders and started for the stairs, nearly colliding with Ardyce Hanson as she raced into the room. "Ardyce! Is anything wrong?"

"Get the car," she commanded, her words clipped. "Rae's water just broke, and she's starting into labor."

"That's impossible!" Drew protested. "She's got nearly a month to go."

"Not according to this baby, she hasn't. You're about to become a father. Now, move!"

Drew sprinted for the front door, his heart pounding. Where were his car keys? Did he have enough gas to get to the hospital? Why was it happening so soon? Had Rae been right all along—was something wrong with the baby?

Concern for his wife and child obliterated any other thought. Everything else would have to wait—even making amends with Rae. There would be time enough for that later, if . . .

Dear God, he prayed as he raced for the car. *Let her be all right.*

★ ★ ★

Beau Laporte sat in his opulent suite at the Jefferson House in Grenada, barely aware of his surroundings. The bed was unmade, for all the good it had done him. He hadn't slept more than an hour or two for the past three nights, and most of the food that had been brought to him by the bellboy had gone uneaten. A half-empty bottle of port stood on the night table next to the bed.

He got up, stumbled to the bathroom, and looked in the mirror. Three days' growth of beard. Sagging circles under bloodshot eyes. When had he become a tired, decrepit old man?

He knew exactly when, the day and the hour. The very moment, even. It was the split second when he had drawn back his hand and smacked that Breckinridge woman across the face. He would never forget it as long as he lived—the gash his ring left across her cheek, her blood dripping onto the hardwood hallway on the third floor of the Brownlee mansion.

Beau Laporte had done a lot of disreputable things in his fifty-two years, but he had never struck a woman. And he had struck her more than once, although from that point on, his recollection of events became rather vague. He remembered kicking her, he thought, and trying to choke her, then throwing her down some kind of pit and leaving her.

How had he sunk so low? He could have killed her. Even now she might be dead, for all he knew. He had only been aware of his rage—blind, irrational anger that drove him to protect his financial interests at any cost.

Beau closed his eyes to rid himself of the sight of the man he had become, then turned and wandered back to the bed. He flopped down and flung one arm over his eyes.

He could shut out the light, but he couldn't hide from the images that rose in his mind—his wife, Beatrice, that frail, birdlike woman who had stuck by him all these years, who kept trying to tell him that they didn't need the money from his deals. His son, Andrew, who had left his own father's house to try to preserve his integrity. Andrew's wife, round little Rae, who carried in her body his son's first child.

By now they all knew. He was certain of it. In desperately trying to preserve what didn't matter at all, he had lost everything that did matter. He was utterly alone.

A knock on the door startled him, and he sat up. He waited, not sure what to do, and the knock came again.

"Go away."

"Colonel? Are you in there?"

Beau's mind scrambled to place the voice. Familiar, and yet not his son's. Someone who would call him "Colonel," not "Mister." Then it hit him: Orris Craven.

"I said, go away."

"I'm sorry, Colonel, I can't do that." Beau heard a key turning in the lock, and the door swung open to reveal the little weasel in his tan suit, holding up a hotel passkey.

"Get out of here."

The weasel came in and shut the door behind him. "Colonel, we need to talk."

Beau looked up and blinked. "I have nothing to talk about."

"Then just listen." Craven crossed the room and sat down in the chair opposite the bed.

"How did you know where to find me?"

"I made the reservations, remember?" He raised his eyebrows. "No one figured you'd come back here, and apparently your money is sufficient to keep the clerks silent. But where else would a man like you hide out?" He waved his hand at the luxurious suite. "All the comforts of home."

Beau peered at Craven. Something about the man had changed, something Beau couldn't quite put his finger on. "What's with you, Craven? You look . . . I don't know, different."

A glimmer of a smile flitted across the pale little man's face. "And you look terrible."

"I feel terrible. And now, since we've had our little chat, would you just leave?"

Craven shook his head. "Not so fast. But since you mentioned it, I have changed."

"What are you talking about?"

The younger man leaned forward intently, his fingers intertwined over his knee. "You went out there, didn't you?"

"Went where?" Beau's heart leaped into his throat, and his pulse accelerated.

"To the Brownlee place. You were there—I can see it in your eyes. Probably surprised Thelma Breckinridge, recognized her, and put two and two together. You're responsible for her so-called accident."

Beau felt all the blood drain from his face. "She's dead, isn't she?"

Craven sat back in the chair. "Dead? No, she's not dead. A concussion, a broken bone or two—and a nasty gash across her face." He let his eyes linger on the signet ring on Beau's right hand.

"So I guess everyone is looking for me."

"Not yet. But they will, as soon as Thelma regains consciousness. I'd watch out for Bennett Winsom if I were you. He's pretty protective about the woman he loves."

Beau frowned, trying to make sense of Craven's babbling. "That lawyer . . . and that Breckinridge woman? You've got to be kidding."

"I'm perfectly serious. They're engaged to be married—or will be soon." He ran a finger over his blond mustache. "But I didn't come here to fill you in on the latest developments in a radio soap opera."

Beau's head was throbbing, and he was growing impatient. "Exactly why *did* you come here, Craven?"

Craven paused for a moment, and when he spoke, his voice was low and subdued. "I thought you might need a friend."

Beau almost laughed out loud. "A friend? You?"

"You could do worse." His eyes pierced through Beau's defenses. "From the looks of you, you've already done worse."

The wall began to crumble, but Beau wasn't quite ready to capitulate. "Why should I believe you? And why should you bother?"

Craven smiled. "Because recently, when I was at a turning point in my own life, someone believed in me. Gave me a chance to redeem myself. Or rather, to accept myself as redeemed."

Beauregard Laporte sat there for a few minutes, battling with the old self-sufficient Beau, the man who didn't need anyone except as pawns in his strategy for more money and more power. But he had seen too much. He knew now what was at the heart of that old Beau, and he didn't like it one bit. Thank God, the woman wasn't dead. But that didn't change what he had done, what he had become.

"I'm listening," he said at last.

38

Day of Atonement

It was nearly dark by the time Beau Laporte and Orris Craven got to the Tullahoma County Hospital. Laporte sat in the car for a long time, still as a statue, obviously trying to summon up his courage to go inside.

At last Orris touched his arm. "It's time."

"Do I really have to do this?"

"What do you think?"

"I know. But I'm just no good at this kind of thing. I don't have any experience at it."

Orris suppressed a laugh. "If by 'this kind of thing' you mean humbling yourself and taking responsibility for your actions," he said frankly, "then no, you don't have any experience. But you have to start somewhere, and this is the only place to begin."

Beau looked over at him, and in the waning light Orris could see an expression of panic on his face, like the look of a little boy who has just broken the neighbor's window with his baseball. Once the Colonel let his defenses down, it was clear that he was ready—ready to hear what Orris had to say, and ready to make some changes in his own life. This was only the beginning, but if he could go through with it, it would be a very good start.

"It's your decision," Orris prompted. "Nobody else can do it for you."

Beau grabbed him by the sleeve and held on. "There's just one thing. I want you to know that I'm not doing this to put on some kind of show or try to get out of my responsibilities here. If they press charges, I'll go to jail—I know I will. And I deserve it." He heaved a ragged sigh. "In fact, I think I'd feel better if I did end up serving time."

"So you could pay for your own debt?" Orris asked.

"I guess that's not the way it works, is it?"

Orris shook his head. "You can't control what they do, Colonel. You can only decide what's right for you to do. But even serving time in jail won't pay for your sin—not in God's sight."

"It's that grace thing, right?" Beau sighed. "I'm going to have a hard time getting used to that one."

"God help us all if we got what we deserved," Orris murmured.

"It's just that, well, I'm used to paying my own way in the world."

"And making other people pay as well," Orris chuckled. "As I recall, trying to pay your own way in the world is what got you into this mess to begin with. The wrong kind of independence can be deadly to the soul."

Beau stared at him. "You *have* changed, Craven. Nobody's ever confronted me this bluntly—nobody. I think I liked you better as a groveling weasel."

"No you didn't," Orris countered. "You hated my guts. Besides, you've needed someone to talk candidly to you for a long, long time."

"And you're just the man for the job, is that it?"

"Something like that." Orris turned and clamped a hand onto Laporte's shoulder. "You can do this, Beau. And it just may be the finest thing you've ever done in your life."

Beau nodded. "You may be right. And . . . well, thank you."

"For what?"

"For everything. For calling me 'Beau' instead of 'Colonel.'"

Until he said it, Orris didn't realize he had used Laporte's given name, but now that he thought about it, it seemed fitting. "You're welcome to call me Orris, if you like."

"I think I'll stick with Weasel." Beau gave a low laugh and slapped him on the back. "Well, let's get in there. This job won't get done out here in the parking lot."

★ ★ ★

Beau paused in the doorway of Thelma Breckinridge's hospital room. The room was dim, lit by a single lamp on the bedside table. Bennett Winsom stood next to the bed with his back to the door, leaning over her and murmuring in low tones.

Taking a deep breath, Beau stepped closer and cleared his throat.

Winsom turned, and when he recognized Beau, the look on his face said that he knew everything. Beau half expected the lawyer to flatten him, and he would have deserved it, perhaps even welcomed it. Instead, Winsom approached him and planted himself between Beau and the bed.

"I think you've done quite enough damage here, Mr. Laporte." he said in a low, threatening tone. "Obviously you've gotten your directions confused. Obstetrics is on the fourth floor." He paused and narrowed his eyes. "I think you should leave—now."

Beau opened his mouth to respond; then the full impact of Winsom's words hit him. "Obstetrics?"

"Didn't you know?" Winsom peered at him. "Of course you wouldn't. You've been—ah, shall we say, indisposed?"

"What are you talking about?"

"I'm talking about your grandchild, Mr. Laporte. Rae has been in labor since early afternoon." He pulled out his pocket watch. "You may have a long wait ahead of you, but I'm sure your family will be grateful for your support." He turned his back on Beau and returned to the bed.

Beau's mind reeled. Rae, in labor? His grandson was on the way! He had to get up there, to—

But, no. This had to come first. He would not, could not face his grandchild with this stain on his soul. "Mr. Winsom," he insisted, "I must speak to Mrs. Breckinridge. Please!"

"When it's Mrs., it will be Mrs. Winsom," the lawyer corrected sharply. "And Miss Breckinridge has nothing to say to you."

Beau felt a calming hand on his shoulder, and Orris Craven stepped into the light. "Bennett," he said softly, "I think you should hear him out. Is Thelma awake?"

"I'm awake," came a muted voice from the bed. "How could a body sleep with all this racket going on? And stop talking about me like I'm not here."

Craven smiled and went to the bedside. "Thelma," Beau heard him say, "Beau Laporte has come to see you. Are you up to talking with him?"

Beau moved forward toward the foot of the bed. His heart wrenched at the sight of her lying there with a plaster cast encasing one arm and a needle running into the soft flesh on the inside of her other elbow. She had dark circles under her eyes, a violent purple bruise on her forehead, and a deep gash across one cheek.

He shut his eyes for a moment. What kind of madman could have done such a thing?

He twisted the gold signet ring off his finger and dropped it into the trash can.

★ ★ ★

Thelma watched Beauregard Laporte's face with interest. Bennett was shaking his head no, but something about this whole scenario intrigued her. She felt no fear of the man, only pity for him . . . and compassion. When she looked into Orris Craven's eyes and saw his brief nod, she knew that something had happened. Curiosity might have killed the cat, but it woke Thelma up. Whatever Beauregard T. Laporte had to say, she wanted to hear it.

"I have a confession to make," Laporte began in a wavering voice he couldn't seem to control. "But if you don't mind, I'd like to make it all at once."

He drew Orris Craven aside and whispered something into his ear, and the little lawyer slipped out the door. In a few minutes he returned, followed by Drew Laporte and his mother.

The diminutive Beatrice went to her husband immediately, but Drew hung back, a look of suspicion and anger on his handsome countenance. Laporte motioned him closer, and he came reluctantly into the circle.

"I suppose you're wondering why I've called you all here," Laporte said with a forced laugh, but the lame joke fell on unresponsive ears.

"Get on with it," Bennett snapped.

The man drew a ragged breath. "All right. You all know by now what happened out at the Brownlee place three days ago." He turned and looked directly at Thelma. "I am responsible for your injuries, and I—well, I want to apologize."

"Apologize!" Bennett sputtered, but Orris Craven laid a hand on his arm to stop him.

"I know that no apology in the world can make up for what I've done," Laporte went on in a rush, "but I am sorry. I-I wasn't myself." He stopped and shook his head. "Let me correct that. I *was* myself. My worst self. I let my greed and my anger take over, and this was the result."

He swallowed hard and ran a hand through his silver hair. "I have never in my life struck a woman," he said, dropping heavily into a chair at the side of Thelma's bed. "I've spent the past three days alone with myself, thinking about what I did—and what I've become. And—" The words caught in his throat, and he couldn't continue for a moment.

"It's all right," Orris Craven said, patting his boss's shoulder. "You're doing fine."

"I've been so wrong about so many things," Laporte went on when he had recovered his composure, "and what I did to you, Miss Breckinridge, brought me to my senses. There's no way I can ever make up for it, but I'm going to try."

Thelma looked up at Bennett and squeezed his hand, but his skeptical expression remained firmly in place. "What exactly does that mean?"

"Orris found me and forced me to talk about it," Laporte said. "About everything. And he told me what had happened to him, how he came to see the light about himself." He turned toward Drew and held out a hand. "You've been right about everything, Son. And I've been wrong. I want you to know that, and know how proud I am of you, and how much I've come to respect your honor, your integrity. It's an example I'd do well to follow."

Drew stood rooted to his spot next to his mother and did not respond.

"I've already asked God's forgiveness," Laporte continued with some difficulty. "Now I want to ask for yours, Miss Breckinridge. And yours, Andrew and Bea. I know it will take a long time for any of you to trust me again, and I realize the changes are likely to come slowly. I'm an old dog, and new tricks aren't easy to learn at my age. But I've made the first step, and I hope someday to be the kind of man who can deserve your love and respect." He gestured helplessly toward Drew and Bennett.

Thelma lay back against her pillow and watched Beauregard Laporte's face with a rising sense of wonder. She believed him, every word of it. How odd, the ways God had of using the worst situations to bring people to their knees! Grace was free, but it certainly didn't come cheap, and if her physical wounds were the motivation behind Beau Laporte's salvation, she would cherish the scars.

"Craven and I have devised a plan," Laporte was saying, "to liquidate the holdings of the Southern Historical Preservation Society and all the other corporations. All the property will be signed back to the rightful owners, and the profits I've made so far will be set aside to help those people take advantage of their mineral rights and other options." He smiled and swiped the tears from his ruddy cheeks. "There are two old ladies in Tennessee who stand to become millionaires once the first oil well is drilled on their back pasture. And countless others who will never have to worry about money again. They just need the right information and a little direction to make the most of what they have."

"And we have the information to give them," Orris put in.

Laporte fixed his gaze on Bennett. "If you wish to press charges, either for the assault or for my shady business dealings, I'll plead guilty. I'm prepared to accept the consequences of my actions. Craven here has agreed to return to New Orleans and manage my affairs while I serve my time." He slanted a glance at Bea. "And once I get out, things will be different, I promise you that. If you'll still have me."

His wife came to his side and put a thin arm around his shoulders. "Thank you," she whispered, and her gaze was directed not at her husband, but heavenward.

After a moment or two of awkward silence, Thelma looked at Bennett and saw his expression beginning to soften. "I don't think there will be any charges pressed," she said quietly. "I certainly wouldn't want to get in the way of what God is doing here."

Laporte stood up and went over to the other side of the bed to face Bennett directly. "If you're willing to do it, I would like to be accountable to you—and to Andrew—for my actions. I'll send you monthly reports of my activities and copies of my accounts. Perhaps, in time, we could set up a trust to help people like Mr. Brownlee who are in danger of being taken advantage of." He smiled sheepishly. "The *real* Breckinridge Foundation."

All this time, Drew had been standing in the shadows, watching, saying nothing. Now he stepped forward and put a hand on his father's shoulder. "Someone told me recently that I was in danger of becoming like you," he said in a husky voice. "It was true, and it brought me to my senses. I haven't been the person you think I am, Father. But maybe, with God's help and each other's support, we can both change."

Laporte turned, and Drew fell into his arms. They stood there for a long time in a silent, tearful embrace until the door flew open to reveal a flush-faced, panting Owen Slaughter.

"The baby!" he shouted. "It's time!"

Drew pulled back and looked into his father's eyes. "Are you coming?"

"Coming? Of course I'm coming. This is my first grandbaby you're talking about. I wouldn't miss this for the world!"

39

Angelique

At 9:01 P.M. on November 1, Angelique Beatrice Laporte made her entrance into the world—a noisy, bloody, screaming, barbaric miracle. Five pounds, seven ounces. Three weeks early, but apparently with all parts in place.

When the news came, Drew was pacing back and forth in the smoke-filled waiting room. He cast a glance at his parents seated on the sofa, holding hands and conversing in muted tones. At this moment he almost envied his father, for he himself had not had a chance to make peace with his wife, and if he lived to be a hundred, he would never forget this season of deep regret. She had gone into delivery without knowing how much he loved her, how desperately he wanted to make things right between them.

It was a difficult labor, but fortunately, Rae had survived the ordeal with the same hope and courage as millions of other women before her. In the joy of birth, the pain would be forgotten. Drew only hoped that the wounds he had inflicted upon the woman he loved could be healed as readily.

"Can I see her?" he asked when Ardyce Hanson brought him the news.

Ardyce gave him a quick hug. "Which her?"

"Ah, both of them," he stammered. "But I meant Rae."

"Rae's exhausted and needs rest," Ardyce hedged. "I'll take you to the nursery in a few minutes."

Drew's mother came up beside him and stood on tiptoe to kiss him on the cheek. "Angelique Beatrice," she murmured, tears glistening in her pale blue eyes. "I don't know how to thank you, Andrew. This means so much."

He grinned down at her. "It was Rae's idea," he admitted. "She wanted the baby to have her grandmother's name."

"Congratulations, Son!" His father pumped Drew's hand and clapped him on the back, but the usual booming bravado was gone, and in its place was a quietness that Drew had never seen. His mind held onto a thousand questions, but his heart told him that the changes in his father were real. Only time would tell, but for now Drew would give him the benefit of the doubt.

"A little girl," Drew breathed in awe. "I have a daughter."

★ ★ ★

At six the next morning, Drew stood at Rae's bedside and watched in wonder as the tiny form of his firstborn snuggled sleepily against her mother's breast. He extended a finger to touch the baby's hand, and the little fist curled around it and hung on.

"Oh! Look, she's holding my hand!" His eyes swam with tears as he examined the miniature pink fingers with their perfectly formed fingernails. "She's incredible. Beautiful."

Rae laughed—the first laugh Drew had heard from her in weeks. "Beautiful? She's red and wrinkled, Drew. She had a rough time getting here. But she will be beautiful, I'm sure of it. She's going to look just like you."

"She does look kind of . . . funny, now that you mention it."

Rae shook her head. "She's a baby, for heaven's sake. All newborns look like that."

He sank down into the chair at the side of the bed and stroked Rae's hair. "If you're up to it, sweetheart, I need to talk to you about something."

Rae shifted the baby and sat up a little. "All right."

"It's about—well, about me. And you. Us."

"Drew, you're babbling."

"I know. Sorry. I'm just not quite sure how to say this." He closed his eyes and tried to order his thoughts, and when he opened them again, she was gazing at him expectantly.

"Do you remember the day Ardyce came downtown to the office to talk to me?"

A cloud passed over her face. "Yes. It wasn't, as I gathered, a very . . . fruitful conversation."

"That's where you're wrong. Ardyce told me I was becoming just like my father, and I didn't want to hear it. But it got through—eventually." He lifted his shoulders. "I'm a slow learner, I guess."

Rae raised her eyebrows but said nothing.

"Anyway, I wanted to tell you this yesterday, but before I had a chance, you went into labor and, well, everything got pretty hectic from there."

"It probably wasn't the best time for a serious conversation," she agreed.

"It's just this, Rae—I've been a fool. An absolute idiot. And I'm sorry."

"Could you be a little more specific?"

"For months now, you've been trying to tell me that I haven't been paying attention. I was so caught up with Ivory's case, with my duty to him and to my obligations as an attorney, that I completely lost sight of my duty to you—"

"Our marriage feels like a duty?"

"No, no, that's not what I meant. I mean my responsibilities. As a husband. As a lover and a friend. And now as a father." He took a deep breath and tried to still his pounding heart. "I love you, Rae. I always have, and I always will. I just haven't been doing a very good job at showing you. But I do love you. I do."

"So you're saying—?"

Drew's mind flashed to his father's confession, the simplicity and directness of it, the sincerity. "I was wrong," he heard himself saying, "and you were right. I want to ask your forgiveness. And I promise I'll do everything in my power not to treat you that way again. Ever."

She reached out a hand to him. "Thank you."

"From now on, you'll see, things are going to change. I'm going to spend more time at home. Talk to you about what's going on—and believe me, there's a lot to tell. Let you share my problems, and be there to share yours. And I'll be the best father you ever saw, honey. I'll learn to change diapers and make formula, get up for 2 A.M. feedings—"

"Hold it!" she interrupted. "Don't go making any promises you can't keep."

"I've already made promises I haven't kept," he said quietly. "I promised to love and honor and cherish you, and I haven't done that." He felt his throat tightening up, and he swallowed hard. "I don't want to lose you, Rae. You're the best thing that ever happened to me."

She stroked the hair at his temple. "You haven't lost me, Drew. I think you just lost yourself for a while there." She sighed. "I never thought about leaving, not for a minute. I just wanted to have my husband back—the man I fell in love with, the man I married."

He captured her hand and kissed it. "Can you forgive me?"

Rae looked into his eyes. "Yes. I forgive you. And I love you."

"You are the most wonderful woman in the world," he whispered as their lips met. "And the most beautiful."

"Drew, you *are* an idiot. Look at me. I'm all bloated, and my hair hasn't been washed, and—"

"You're beautiful," he repeated. "Now stop complaining and kiss me."

★ ★ ★

Ardyce Hanson moved slowly and silently along the hospital corridor. Her mind resisted, told her to turn back, but her feet kept plodding inexorably forward. She didn't want to do this, and yet . . .

It would be easier coming from her than from the doctor.

Easier on whom? Ardyce wondered. Not herself, certainly. Not Rae and Drew, or his parents, or even Willie and Owen. Nothing could make news like this easier to digest. Nothing.

When she got to the door of Rae's room, she paused and sent up a silent prayer for help. But what kind of help did she expect? Nothing short of a miracle would make this any better.

She opened the door and slipped inside. Rae was in bed, surrounded by Drew, her in-laws, Willie and Owen, Madge Simpson, Bennett Winsom, and Thelma Breckinridge in a wheelchair, with one arm in a plaster cast.

"Thelma, you've had her long enough," Owen was saying. "I think it's my turn."

He reached down and took the baby from Thelma, holding her up and cooing to her. "Ooh, little Angelique," he murmured, "what a beautiful little girl you are." He looked over at Willie. "Wouldn't you like to have one just like her?"

All conversation in the room halted abruptly, and every eye turned toward Willie. Her face flushed, and she looked desperately around the room for someplace to hide. "Owen!"

He grinned at her. "What?"

"How could you say such a thing in—in *public?*"

"This isn't exactly public, Willie. These are our friends. Besides, I didn't mean right now, this very minute. I meant—well, someday." He gave a broad wink, and everybody laughed.

Ardyce went up to him and took the baby from his arms. "Don't you have work to do, Owen?"

He blinked at her. "I'm going to finish the upstairs bathroom this afternoon, if that's what you mean. Everything in the nursery is done except the wallpaper, and I'll get to that tonight."

"Well, I'm sorry to break up the celebration, but this is a hospital. This child is barely two days old. And Rae needs some rest."

Drew leaned down and kissed his wife. "I'll be back later this afternoon, honey. I'm going to go home for a while and help Owen lay the tile in the new bathroom."

Ardyce went over and touched him on the arm. "Can you stick around for a little bit, Drew? There are some things we need to talk about before you take Rae and the baby home."

"Sure." He frowned slightly.

She turned to the group of friends gathered in the room. "OK, everybody. Party's over."

Amid good-natured grumbling, they all began to file out of the room. Bennett, pushing Thelma's wheelchair, paused next to the bed. "Thelma is being released this afternoon," he said. "We'll stop by for a few minutes on our way out."

Rae looked at Thelma. "You're doing better, I take it."

"I'm just fine, hon." Thelma nodded at the cast on her arm. "I'll be sporting this for a few more weeks, and I've still got a bit of a headache, but otherwise I'm healing faster than the law allows."

"Funny, isn't it," Rae mused, "how something so awful—Beau attacking you like that—could turn out for so much good. I mean, look at the changes in him. And in Drew." She smiled. "I feel like I've got a whole new family."

Thelma leaned forward and patted Rae's hand. "Just the way God works sometimes. With some folks, it takes hitting bottom to find out what they're really made of, good or bad."

"And even seeing the bad can end up being good—like with Beau."

"He's a different man, that's for sure." Thelma nodded. "Looks like you've got yourself a real granddaddy for that little one. In addition to Bennett, of course."

"And *two* grandmothers. I want all of you to be Angelique's godparents."

Thelma smiled and squeezed her hand. "I'd be honored. That's a baptism I won't miss even if I have to get to it in this contraption."

When Ardyce finally got them out of the room, she shut the door and leaned against it, summoning courage for the task ahead. After a moment or two, she went to Rae, laid the baby in her arms, and pulled two chairs next to the bed.

"Sit down, Drew."

He sat. "What's up?"

Ardyce took a moment to collect herself. She had always believed in a no-nonsense, direct-and-to-the-point approach to problems, and she supposed this situation was no exception. But usually her own emotions weren't so involved. This was her friend Rae, and the baby she had helped to deliver with her own hands. This time she would have to make a deliberate effort to stay objective. Rae and Drew would need for her to be rational and levelheaded, and she didn't intend to let them down.

She drew a deep breath and began. "Rae, do you remember writing to me about your fears for this baby, how you couldn't help thinking that something was wrong?"

Rae nodded. "Stupid of me, I guess. Just overreacting, like Drew said."

"I should have listened better, honey," Drew interjected, "but I'm glad I was right on this count."

"Yes, just look at her." Rae pulled back the blanket and gazed lovingly down at the child. "Our little Angelique. A perfect angel."

"She is beautiful," Ardyce agreed. "And in general, she's healthy."

"In general?" Drew repeated. "What do you mean, *in general?*"

Rae clutched the baby to her breast and stared at Ardyce. "Nothing is wrong with my baby. She just came a little early, that's all. She's small, but everything is in working order. Ten fingers, ten toes. A little jaundiced, the doctor said, but—"

Ardyce closed her eyes. This wasn't going to be easy, no matter how she did it.

"It's more than jaundice. Haven't you noticed anything . . . unusual . . . about her?"

"I don't know much about babies," Drew said. "I've never seen one quite this young before—especially not one who was premature." He narrowed his eyes at Ardyce. "What are you getting at?"

"The large head," Ardyce said, pointing, "the flattened nose and heavy eyelids—"

"There's some Cherokee in my background," Rae said, that familiar sense of dread growing again.

"And probably some Creole in mine," Drew added. "Could that account for it?"

Ardyce shook her head. "No. I'm sorry, but I've had a long talk with the doctor. We're pretty sure Angelique is—" She paused and worked to keep an unemotional expression. "The term most often used is *Mongoloid.*"

Rae took a deep breath. "What does that mean?"

Ardyce sighed. "The physical characteristics will become more pronounced as she grows older—enlarged temporal lobe, slanted eyes. She will be . . . slow."

"Retarded?" Drew choked out.

"I'm afraid so. The good news is, she is otherwise quite healthy. Many babies like this have serious heart problems and don't live to be more than six or seven. Angelique shows no signs of heart trouble at all. She should live into her twenties at least."

Rae's breath came in short, shallow gasps. "Why?" she whispered, her voice a tortured croak. "Dear God in heaven, *why?*"

"There's no answer to that question," Ardyce said quietly. "We don't know why these things happen—"

"Yes, we do. This is all my fault," Drew moaned. "If only I had listened—"

"If you had listened, you would have given your wife more support," Ardyce said sharply. "It wouldn't have changed the outcome." Ardyce looked up at Rae and saw huge tears pooling in her eyes.

"My baby is retarded?" she whispered.

"A Mongoloid child can have an IQ as high as sixty," Ardyce said. "They can learn and grow and live practically normal lives."

"Practically normal," Drew repeated dully.

"You have a number of options," Ardyce went on doggedly. "Some parents opt for putting a child in an institution for protection from the prying eyes and cruel comments of others—"

"No!" Rae blurted out, suddenly coming to life. Her eyes blazed with conviction. "This is my baby. I will not put her away."

"Drew?" Ardyce prodded.

He stared at the floor for a full minute, and when he raised his head, she saw the same determined look in his eye. "Absolutely not. We will raise this child and do whatever we have to do to give her a good life."

Good, Ardyce thought. *They're going to fight rather than capitulate.*

"I've had some experience with children afflicted with mongolism," she said quietly. "Are you ready to hear what you're up against?"

Drew squared his shoulders and reached out a hand to touch his wife and daughter. "Yes." Rae nodded through her tears.

"All right. You've heard the worst of it: Your baby will never develop normal mental capabilities. She may be the object of ridicule from other children, and even adults may not know how to relate to her. But you've got a lot going for you. You have a loving family and a circle of friends who care about you and her. Take advantage of their love. You'll need the support, and their involvement can do nothing but help Angelique develop to her fullest potential."

"What will she be like?"

Ardyce smiled. "You'll be amazed. These kids have an unusual capacity for affection. They are sweet-tempered, adorable, delightful children—even as adults. And, depending upon how her mind develops, Angelique can be taught to be a fairly independent person. She just won't have the intellectual abilities of a normal child."

Ardyce watched them for a minute as they examined their newborn baby. Then she said gently, "One other thing you should know. This condition is not hereditary. If, later on, you have other children, the chances are good that they would be perfectly normal."

Drew leaned over and kissed Rae on the forehead. "Are we ready for this, sweetheart?"

"Probably not," Rae sighed. "But Angelique is here, isn't she? God gave her to us as a gift, a product of our love for one another. Now it's time to give some of that love back."

40

The Treasure

"I think," the doctor said, shining his light first into one eye, then the other, "that if you take it easy for a while, you should be just fine. Come back in a couple of weeks and I'll check your arm and shoulder. You should be out of that cast by Thanksgiving."

Thelma blinked as the spots in front of her eyes gradually faded. "Thank you, Dr. Willis. Believe me, I'm ready to get out of here."

"So I see." He surveyed her from head to toe, smiling. "All dressed. You were pretty sure of yourself, weren't you? What if I had said you had to stay another night?"

"You would have made your rounds in the morning and found an empty bed," Thelma quipped.

Dr. Willis turned and leveled a gaze at Bennett. "You're going to have your hands full with this one. Are you sure you're up to the challenge?"

"Not in the least," Bennett answered, squeezing Thelma's hand. "But I'm willing to take my chances."

"Just try to keep her from running any footraces, will you?"

Bennett chuckled. "Doctor, I learned a long time ago not to try to keep Thelma Breckinridge from doing anything she has her mind set to do."

"Why does that not surprise me?" The doctor jotted a few notes on her chart and put his penlight back into the pocket of his white coat. "I'll see you in two weeks."

When he was gone, Thelma waved away the wheelchair Bennett was holding. "I don't need that thing. I'm not an invalid." She looked down at the dress she was wearing. "Where did you find this? It's ancient."

"In your closet."

"Well, we need to work on your taste in women's clothes. What happened to the one I was wearing when I came in here?"

"It's probably in the rag bin by now. It had a huge tear in the skirt, and one sleeve was nearly ripped off."

Thelma reached up and rubbed at her shoulder. "Figures. I guess I should count my blessings that my arm didn't stay behind with it."

Bennett went to the narrow closet next to the bed and opened it. "Your coat isn't in much better shape. As soon as you're feeling up to it, we'll go to Memphis and buy you a new one." He pulled out the coat and held it up. "What's this?"

"What's what?"

"This document—it was half stuffed into your coat pocket. I guess when we brought you in, I was so distraught that I didn't notice it." He grimaced. "It's all covered with blood."

Thelma frowned. "I remember. When I fell, I was bleeding pretty badly from the cut on my face." Gingerly she touched the puckering wound that ran under her right cheekbone. "It was dark, but there were papers in the bottom of the passageway where I landed. I must have used one of them to wipe the blood away and then just stuck it in my pocket without thinking about it."

"Thelma—"

The tone in Bennett's voice caused Thelma to look up. His face had gone completely white, and his hand was shaking. "What's wrong, Bennett?"

"Look at this."

Thelma looked. It was a certificate of some kind, but so obscured with blood and dirt as to be almost unreadable. "What is it?"

"It's a bond," he breathed. "Did you say there were more of these in that passageway?"

"I think so. I was in pretty bad shape down there, but I'm almost certain there were more, all over the floor. Why? What kind of bond is it?"

"A Civil War bond. The kind issued to finance the conflict."

"Wonderful," Thelma scoffed. "A bunch of useless Confederate bonds. We'll paper the cafe with them and turn it into a museum."

Bennett shook his head. "No, we won't. This is not a Confederate bond, Thelma. It is issued by the government of the United States of America."

"What?" Thelma grabbed the paper out of his hand and peered at it. "One hundred U.S. Treasury dollars, payable to the bearer at maturity."

"During the War, these were sold to raise money for the cause, much like our current war bonds. You bought them at a reduced rate, and when they matured, they were worth face value."

"And if you held them past maturity—?"

"They accrued interest at the rate of—" He turned the bond over and scrutinized it. "I can't tell."

"Are they worth anything?"

Bennett shook his head in wonder. "Let's not say anything until we're sure, but if there are more where this came from, it's possible Ivory Brownlee has suddenly become a very wealthy man."

Drew sat quietly by the bedside, watching Angelique nurse and marveling over his wife and daughter. The baby rested on Rae's chest, snug and safe and contented, and he sent up a silent prayer that they would always be able to provide such a safe haven for their child.

When Ardyce had first come with the news that Angelique was afflicted with mongolism, Drew thought their world had collapsed. But somehow the nearness of the child that had been created from their love helped put things into perspective for both him and Rae.

He gazed on the flattened-out little face with its hooded eyes and large forehead. Maybe he should have known immediately—maybe they both should have—that this child was different. Still, Drew had no experience with babies, had never even seen a newborn, especially a premature one. He thought they all looked like that.

But it didn't matter. Much to his amazement, he loved this child with the fierce and protective devotion only a father could know. He knew at the deepest level of his soul that whatever the cost, whatever the difficulties, their little Angelique was a gift from God. A treasure. And perhaps God had plans for her that Drew could not even begin to fathom.

As he watched mother and child slip into a peaceful sleep, Drew wondered—did Joseph feel like this as he stood guard over the infant Son of God? That child was different, too—destined to give himself for the life of the world, born to die so that others might awaken to the love of God. How long did it take before Mary realized that the child she had delivered would be her Deliverer? How many trees did Joseph plane before he caught a terrifying vision of the boy at his side spilling his own blood upon those beams?

Jesus, of course, was no ordinary baby. But then, neither was Angelique. Maybe every child who came into the world brought a touch of immortality trailing along behind. Perhaps his child, his sweet retarded baby daughter, would bring new life to her parents. Perhaps she already had.

A soft knock interrupted Drew's musings, and reluctantly he rose and left the bedside. He opened the door to reveal Bennett and Thelma.

Drew held up a hand. "Shh. They're asleep." He pointed to the bed and smiled.

"We won't stay," Bennett whispered. "We just came to say good-bye. When are they going home?"

"Tomorrow, the doctor says. Since we have Ardyce right there in the house to help, we should get along just fine."

"That's wonderful." Bennett's eyes darted from Thelma to Rae, and then back to Drew. "Can you get away?"

Drew looked over at his wife and daughter. "I think Rae will sleep for a while. I'll take Angelique back to the nursery."

"OK. I'm taking Thelma home. Can you meet me at Ivory's place in an hour?"

The urgent tone in Bennett's voice arrested Drew's attention. "What's going on?"

"I'll tell you all about it when we get there. Just hurry."

"All right. But I have something to talk to y'all about as well."

He shut the door behind them and went to Rae's side. Gently he lifted the baby from her arms, and Rae stirred. "Drew?" she murmured sleepily.

"It's all right, honey. I'm taking Angelique back to the nursery. I'm going to be gone for a while, but I'll be back by dinnertime. You get some sleep."

"Mmm-hmmm." She laid her head back on the pillow and sighed, and he leaned down to kiss her. "I love you," she slurred.

"And I love you." Drew's heart swelled with gratitude as he looked at Rae, and the baby stirred in his arms. "You're a very fortunate little girl," he whispered to the child. "And I am a very blessed man." He planted a tender kiss on the baby's broad forehead, and she opened her eyes and gazed at him. Then she smiled.

It was probably a gas bubble, he reminded himself. But his heart told him it was a smile reserved just for Daddy.

★ ★ ★

Bennett stood waiting on the front porch of the Brownlee plantation house, tapping his foot impatiently and looking at his pocket watch every two minutes. He had told Drew to meet him in an hour. That was only forty-five minutes ago, but Bennett couldn't help being agitated.

If they found what he thought they would find . . .

Drew's car pulled up, and he got out and headed for the porch in a dead run. "What's so important," he gasped, "that you had to drag me all the way out here?"

Bennett said nothing, just handed over the bloodstained bond.

Drew examined it carefully, then let out a low whistle. "Where did this come from?"

Bennett pointed toward the house. "The cellar." He handed Drew one of the flashlights he had borrowed when he took Thelma back to the cafe. "Let's go."

Bennett hadn't remembered the steps to the cellar being so steep and rickety. He had been too concerned with finding Thelma to give much attention to his surroundings. Now he moved carefully, shuddering when a cobweb hit him full in the face and wrinkling his nose against the stale, mildewy smell that permeated the air. "Pretty damp down here."

Drew ran his flashlight over shelves full of mason jars. "Some of these date back to the turn of the century," he muttered. "I might think twice about having dinner here."

A mouse scuttled across the floor in front of Bennett, and he jumped. "Here it is." He trained his light on a tall shelf that had been pulled out from the wall. The acrid scent of vinegar filled the corner of the cellar. "Looks like we broke some pickle jars when we were in here the other day."

"Beets," Drew said with a grimace. "I hate beets."

"Well, you don't have to eat them. Just step around them."

"Doesn't even look like the mice have touched them." Drew ran his flashlight beam over a pile of red slices and broken glass. The juice had seeped into the hard-packed cellar floor in a dark puddle. "Smart mice."

Bennett motioned him over to the corner. "Drew, get over here!"

"I'm coming. What is it?"

"You tell me." Bennett gazed in wonder at the sight illuminated by his flashlight. There, in the alcove behind the shelves where Owen's dog, Vallie, had discovered Thelma, lay a shattered wooden box. Around the box and spilling out of it were more certificates like the one from Thelma's coat pocket.

Drew stepped into the oval of light and gathered up a few of them. "All the same," he muttered. "One hundred dollars each in U.S. Treasury bonds."

Bennett circled his flashlight upward into the secret passageway until its beam came to rest on a small recessed hole in the wall about thirty feet up. "Look up there. The box must have been stowed up in the wall, and Thelma knocked it loose when she fell."

"That explains why the bonds are still intact," Drew said. "This box is lined with lead. Probably protected them from the humidity down here."

"Let's round them up and get outside where we can see."

They gathered the papers, stacked them back into the remains of the lead-lined box, and made their way back up the creaking stairs and out to the front porch.

Drew sat down on the steps and began to sort them into stacks while Bennett scrutinized one of the bonds.

"This one's dated to mature in January of 1864," he said. "Do you know what that means?"

"It means you made me lose count," Drew snapped absently. "Now I have to start over."

"Sorry." Bennett waited in silence.

"All right, I'm done," Drew announced.

"OK. Check a couple of those, will you? The date is on the back."

Drew looked. "Yep. January of 1864, at 3 percent."

"How many do you have?"

Drew pointed to his stacks. "One hundred, two hundred, three hundred. And the partial stack is forty-eight."

"All hundreds?"

"Yes. That makes—"

Bennett sank down onto the step next to Drew. "Thirty-four thousand, eight hundred dollars. Plus the hundred in Thelma's pocket. Nearly thirty-five thousand."

"And we thought the Lincoln portrait was a treasure."

Bennett's mind spun. "That's not the half of it. Do you know what this means?"

"I know what thirty-five thousand dollars would mean to me. I can only imagine what it will mean to Ivory."

"No. It's not thirty-five thousand, Drew."

"You mean they're no good? That we went down into that nasty basement for nothing?"

"I mean," Bennett said, his heart pounding, "that it's thirty-five thousand, plus 3 percent interest, compounded over a span of almost eighty-two years."

"What does that come to?"

"I have no idea. We'd have to get a banker to figure it out for us and see if these bonds really will be honored by the government." Bennett's hand shook as he placed one of the bonds back in the stack. "But I'd say we're dealing with a lot of money here."

Drew stared at him. "What time is it?"

Bennett pulled out his watch. "A little after two. Why?"

He scrambled to his feet and extended a hand to Bennett. "I've got three hours or so. I told Rae I'd be back to the hospital by dinnertime. What say we make a quick trip to Grenada?"

★ ★ ★

When he pulled the DeSoto up in front of the Paradise Garden Café at four-thirty, Drew's throat was dry, and he felt as if every nerve in his body were exposed. It had been quite a day.

Bennett parked beside him and motioned to him. "I think we need to break all this news carefully," he said. "Do you want to tell them about Angelique first?"

Drew nodded. "I want everybody to know right up front, so Rae won't have to deal with the questions."

"Don't worry, son. You've got a big loving family here."

"You called Thelma?"

"Yes, and if I know Thelma, she'll have everyone gathered up, just like she promised. Link and Libba won't be here, of course, but everybody else should be."

"Good. I don't want to have to do this more than once."

As soon as they were inside and seated, Madge brought a pot of coffee. *Just what I need,* Drew thought grimly. *Caffeine to make me shakier than I already am.*

His mother and father sat beside him, talking in animated tones to Stork and Madge about the merits of their first grandchild. They, along with Orris Craven, planned to return to New Orleans tomorrow morning. Drew wondered what his news would do to their joy in Angelique's arrival. Society people could be woefully uncompassionate, he knew from hard experience. Would they be ashamed to tell their friends about their newborn granddaughter?

Well, whatever their response—or anyone else's, for that matter—it had to be told. Now, without delay.

Drew cleared his throat. "If everybody could listen for a minute, Bennett and I have some news. I'll give you the bad news first." Solemnly he recounted the information Ardyce had given him and Rae about the condition of their baby daughter. He managed to relate it matter-of-factly and without excessive emotion, hoping that others would receive the news with the same calm with which he related it. But keeping his feelings under control was more difficult than he had counted on, and by the time he was finished, he was exhausted.

He looked over at his mother and father. "Well?"

Mother had tears in her eyes, but she was smiling. His father said quietly, "We knew she was a special baby. We just didn't know how special."

Everyone gathered around Drew to express their sorrow and their support, and Ardyce Hanson stood in the background nodding and giving him the thumbs-up sign. After a few minutes, when the explanations had all been given and the questions answered, Ivory Brownlee shuffled forward.

"Mister Drew," he said solemnly, "you been real good to me, helping me with my case and all. I ain't got much, but I do have 'bout three thousand dollars left from the Lincoln picture. It's yours if you need it—for that little baby girl."

Drew tried to speak, but he couldn't get past the lump in his throat.

Bennett stepped up and put a hand on Ivory's shoulder. "You've got a little more than that, Ivory—that's the good news. You know we told you about that tunnel in the house where Thelma fell?"

"Uh-huh," Ivory said.

"And you remember how we found all that stuff from the war, from the Union side, in the secret attic?"

He nodded.

"Well, we found something else . . . something that confirms the fact that your Grandpa Seth was helping out the Union army."

"You said it was good news," Ivory protested. "Where's the good part?"

"Right here." Bennett held out a check. "You're familiar with war bonds?"

"Like what the movie stars sell? I heard Jane Wyman talking about them on the radio."

"Just like that. Well, we found war bonds in that passageway, Ivory—or rather Thelma found them. Only these were very, very old. United States Treasury bonds. A lot of them."

Owen Slaughter poked his head over Ivory's shoulder. "How many?"

"The face value was nearly thirty-five thousand dollars."

Ivory Brownlee went slack-jawed, and Drew couldn't help smiling. He alone knew what was coming next.

"We didn't think you'd mind, Ivory—we took them to the bank up in Grenada. Turns out they are now worth . . . well, nearly four hundred thousand dollars. This is a cashier's check made out in your name." Bennett handed the check to Ivory, but the man was shaking so badly he couldn't hold on to it. It fluttered to the floor at his feet.

"You're a wealthy man, Ivory," Drew put in. "What do you have to say for yourself?"

"I reckon," Ivory said slowly, pulling in a deep breath, "that my folks never knew traitorin' could pay so good. Otherwise they mighta gone a tad easier on Grandpa Seth."

41

Willie's Hope

The Coltrain Farm
November 4, 1945

"No, a little higher on the right—there! That's straight." Willie stepped back and peered at the strip of wallpaper Owen was hanging in the baby's room. "I hope."

"Well, decide, please. My arms are getting tired."

"I should be on the ladder, and you should be down here," she muttered.

"Are you going to start that discussion about our height again?" Owen turned on the stepladder and gave her a scathing look. "Now is not the time."

"Well, you have to admit—"

"That we make a pretty comical couple, with you being a head taller than I am. Yeah, yeah. How many times do I have to tell you that it doesn't matter to me? Now, is this even or not?"

"It's even."

Owen began smoothing the paper against the wall with a wide brush, and for a moment or two they were both quiet. Willie watched as Owen worked, the muscles in his back flexing under the fabric of his denim shirt. Sometimes she still couldn't believe the way things had worked out. He was home and at peace, and they were cautiously working their way into a relationship. His memories had not returned, but did it really matter? As long as he loved her now, what difference did it make that he couldn't remember loving her before? They were together, and at the moment nothing else seemed important.

"Aren't you supposed to be putting paste on that last strip?"

Willie blinked. "Oh. Sorry. I was just . . . thinking."

Owen came down from the ladder and surveyed his handiwork. "Rae's going to love this room, isn't she?"

Willie let her eyes wander around the nursery. With windows on two sides, it felt bright and open and airy. Owen had painted the woodwork white, and the wallpaper had pastel-colored farm animals and alphabet blocks scattered over a pale blue background. As a surprise for Rae, they had painted the crib and dresser with white enamel, and Richard, the manager of Libba's daddy's hardware store, had managed to find some alphabet block decals. The top drawer of the dresser spelled out Angelique's name in blocks. Once the wallpapering was finished, Willie would hang the white eyelet curtains Madge had helped her make. It was perfectly enchanting, and Rae was going to be thrilled.

"You've done a beautiful job," Willie said. "And just in time. They're coming home this afternoon."

"What time is it?"

"A little after ten."

"Oh, then we've got plenty of time. I'm almost done here, and then we can clean up and get the furniture arranged."

Owen hung the last strip of wallpaper and smoothed it into place, then folded the ladder and leaned it against the wall. "How's that?" He came over to Willie and linked his hand in hers.

"Wonderful." She squeezed his fingers. "But do you know you have wallpaper paste all over your beard?"

He pointed to the wall. "I thought I'd put a couple of those little farm animals in it for Angelique to play with. We do have some extra paper, don't we? Where are the scissors?"

Willie poked him in the ribs. "Let's get this paste and stuff out of here; then we'll take a break for a few minutes. You've worked hard. You deserve a cup of coffee."

"What I *deserve*," he said with a wink, "is a kiss." He leaned forward, but she clamped her lips firmly together and shoved him back to arm's length.

"Oh, sure. And we get our faces stuck together with wallpaper glue. I'd like to see you try to explain *that.*"

While Willie picked up the wallpaper supplies and scraps of paper, Owen began moving the baby furniture back into place. When everything was arranged, she smiled and nodded.

"Go wash up," she said as she headed for the door. "I'll meet you in the kitchen."

"Then do I get my kiss?"

"We'll see."

Owen stood in the bathroom for a long time, scrubbing at his beard and letting his mind wander to everything that had transpired over the past few weeks. He would never understand why people had to take such a roundabout way to get where they were supposed to be, but now at last he had no doubt that God had led him. This was so *right,* being here in Eden with Willie. Memory or no memory, he knew he had come home at last.

But why had it taken him so long to come to peace about it? He hadn't really needed to take that detour to North Fork. He could have just stayed put and avoided the pain he had caused Willie by leaving so abruptly.

Still, if he hadn't gone, he probably wouldn't have the sense of himself that he now enjoyed. Even though he didn't feel emotionally connected to his past, he knew what it was, at least. He had found his roots. Aunt Gert and Uncle Earl. The friendship of Kurt and Leah Sonntag. And . . .

Buddy.

For some reason he couldn't quite fathom, Owen felt a deep connection to the towheaded, brown-eyed little boy. At the oddest times—when he was playing fetch with Vallie and Curly in the front yard, when he was working in the barn, when he was sitting in the front-porch swing looking out over the fields—an image of the child's face would rise to his mind, the memory of those thin little arms around his neck, the tremulous voice saying, *"You'll always be my daddy."*

Owen shook his head. It was no good, dwelling on the past. There was nothing he could do about Buddy, short of keeping in touch with birthday and Christmas cards, and he wasn't even sure that was a good idea. If JoLynn married someone else—and he hoped she would, for her sake as much as Buddy's—his continued presence in their lives might be an unwelcome intrusion.

Owen buried his face in the towel and sighed. If all went well, as he hoped and prayed it would, there would be other children. Another son. Life would go on.

But he wondered if he would ever be able to forget the fatherless little boy whose love had touched him so deeply.

★ ★ ★

"Am I presentable now?"

Willie turned from the sink to see Owen leaning on the doorpost grinning at her. His beard was clean, and he had put on a fresh shirt and combed his hair. Her breath caught in her throat at the sight of him—his ruddy cheeks above the beard line, those sparkling blue eyes. Amazing, how the pain of losing him had so quickly faded to a dim memory. Now, in this moment, she felt like the most blessed woman in the world.

"You'll do," she quipped. "Have a seat. The coffee's ready. Want a slice of coffee cake?"

He pulled out a chair and nodded. "That cinnamon thing you made yesterday? You bet."

Willie pretended to be miffed. "That 'cinnamon thing,' as you call it, is a cherished recipe handed down from my great-grandmother."

"Funny, it didn't taste that old."

Willie laughed and joined him at the table. It felt so good to be with him like this. So comfortable. So right.

"I think I owe you an apology," he said between mouthfuls of cake.

"For what?"

"The other day at the hospital, when I asked you in front of everybody if you wouldn't like to have a baby like Angelique. I think I embarrassed you."

"Nonsense," she huffed. "I wasn't—"

"You *were.*" He captured her hand. "Admit it. You were embarrassed."

"Oh, all right. Maybe just a little."

"I'm sorry for putting you on the spot."

"It's all right, Owen. You didn't put me on the spot. Everyone knew you were just joking." Willie ducked her head and averted her eyes.

But he wouldn't let her look away. He put a hand gently under her chin and forced her to look up at him, into his eyes. "I wasn't kidding," he said softly. "My timing was probably bad, but I was absolutely serious."

Willie's heart lurched. "What are you saying?"

"I'm saying," he said with deliberate slowness, "that I want to have a family. Children. A wife." He grinned sheepishly and shook his head. "Not in that order, and not just any wife, of course. You. I love you, Willie. You know I do. Marry me."

"But-but—"

He laid a finger across her lips. "Let me tell you a story, Willie. During those months in Iowa, I found myself. I discovered some links to the past, of course, found Uncle Earl and Aunt Gert and the old family homestead, but that's not what I mean. It's more than that. I found out who I was inside." He pointed to his heart. "I found out that—well, that I'm a family man at heart."

Willie nodded. "Buddy."

Owen sighed and closed his eyes. "Buddy had a lot to do with it, yes. He's such a wonderful kid, Willie. Sweet and trusting and loving and—"

"And you fell in love with him."

"Yes, I did. If it hadn't been for him, I would never have given a second thought to JoLynn. Part of it was duty, thinking that I had a responsibility to him, but it went far beyond obligation. I loved him. And I believe I would have made a good father for him."

"I don't doubt that," Willie murmured. Owen Slaughter would be the perfect father—loving and compassionate and sensible and funny. Any child in the world would be fortunate to have a dad like him.

"And then when I stood there in the hospital room holding little Angelique," he went on, "all those feelings came flooding back. I looked over at you, and I knew." He gazed intently into her eyes. "What do you think, Willie?"

Willie didn't know how to answer. She loved him, of course—she had loved him for a long, long time, although she couldn't tell him that. In some ways, she was glad he hadn't regained his memories of those early days together. Owen had such a strong awareness of duty, of honor, that he probably would have come back to marry her even if his feelings for her had changed. This way, at least, she knew that his love was genuine, not the product of some distorted sense of obligation. And of course she wanted to marry him, to live with him forever, to have his children and grow old with him. What, then, was holding her back?

An image rose in her mind—her little niece, Angelique, so delicate and helpless, with her flattened baby face and odd, slanted eyes. The news Drew broke to them in the cafe yesterday. The pain of finding out that the first child of their generation of Coltrains had been born . . . different. Retarded.

"Owen," she said in a choked voice, "what would your response be if Angelique *were* our baby?"

He grinned. "I'd be delighted, of course."

"Would you? Wouldn't the prospect of having a retarded child—a child who might not even live to be an adult, or if she did, would be dependent upon us all her life—make you think twice about getting married and raising a family?"

Owen's expression turned sober, and he thought about this for a minute. "I look at it this way," he said at last. "My own experiences lately have taught me that God has strange ways of working in people's lives. Even when we take a roundabout path, we eventually get where we're going. I wondered about this a lot—why, for example, I had to go all the way to Iowa and

Minnesota to find out I belonged right here in Eden." He scratched his beard and gave a faint smile. "I think God put a baby with Angelique's special problems into this family for a reason. Not for punishment, but as a peculiar kind of blessing. And maybe the blessing works both ways. It could be that Rae and Drew—and us, and Thelma and Bennett, and all her extended family—have something to offer this child in terms of acceptance and love and caring. And I suspect she has something to teach us as well."

Owen paused and looked up at Willie. "Everybody prays for a healthy, normal baby," he said, "and so would we. But if we had a baby like Angelique, well, I'd just figure that God had something else in mind for us. Something we were prepared to handle, no matter how unprepared we might feel." He reached over and took her hand, stroking it gently. "Does it really matter that much, as long as we love each other? Isn't love what really counts?"

Willie blinked back tears. "I do love you, Owen," she whispered. "More than you can possibly know. But—"

"But what?" He searched her eyes. "What's wrong, Willie?"

"I think I'm a little bit afraid," she admitted, and the realization surprised her even as she said it. "When you went away so suddenly, I thought I had lost you forever. I made myself accept it, made myself go on. But I'm not sure I could do that again."

"You won't have to, Willie. I'm here to stay."

Various scenes flashed through Willie's mind—those times before Owen had left for Iowa when he became moody and withdrawn, when he would vanish for hours with no word of explanation. When he had finally returned, she had been so certain that it wouldn't happen again. But lately he had been disappearing for long stretches at a time. Working in the barn and giving vague answers as to what was occupying so much of his time. Spending whole evenings alone in his room. He hadn't abandoned his work around the farm, of course—he had finished the bathroom and the nursery and done a beautiful job. He seemed happy and content. And yet he was hiding something. She was sure of it, and she didn't like it one bit.

"Willie," he prodded. "Tell me what's on your mind."

Without stopping to think about how it might sound, Willie blurted out the whole story—how she felt when he would disappear for hours, how insecure it made her feel, how she wasn't sure she could trust him not to vanish from her life forever. And as she talked, a smug, secretive look spread over his face. By the time she was done, he was grinning broadly.

"What?" she demanded, infuriated at his self-satisfied expression.

"Come on." He stood up and pushed his chair back.

"Where?"

"Don't ask questions. Just come." He grabbed her hand and led her out of the kitchen and up the stairs. When they got to the steps leading to Charlie's old room, he turned to her. "Close your eyes."

"Why? Owen, what—?"

"Just shut them, and keep them shut until I tell you otherwise."

Reluctantly, she obeyed, following him up to the attic room, feeling her way along the stair rail with one hand. Finally they got to the top, and he put his hands on her shoulders and turned her.

"Now you can look."

Willie opened her eyes, and she couldn't believe what she was seeing. The entire room, which had once been filled with Charlie's things, had been completely transformed. The high double bed with its tall brass headboard had been moved against the far wall, adorned with a wedding-ring quilt of delicate rose and blue and eggshell white. A matching braided rug covered the hardwood floor. New curtains hung at the windows, and a small bedside table held an embroidered cloth and a delicate white-shaded brass lamp. The old oak rocking chair from Mama's room, refinished, stood in the corner, with an off-white knitted afghan arranged over one arm.

"Oh, Owen," Willie breathed. "What have you done?"

"I got a little help," he admitted, "from Madge Simpson. I figured—well, that if I was going to ask you to marry me, I should be able to offer you a little better than your brother's old attic." He gave her a panicked look. "You don't mind, do you? I mean, all these changes—"

"Mind?" Willie felt tears rising up in her throat. "No, I don't mind. Charlie would approve, I'm sure." She clung to his arm. "But when did you do all this?"

Owen grinned up at her. "All that time I spent in the barn and wouldn't tell you what I was up to. Those nights I went off to my room after dinner." He shrugged. "Rae helped a little, going into labor when she did. Gave me a few hours here alone to bring this stuff in without you seeing it."

"And I was so mad at you for keeping secrets from me," Willie murmured. "I thought you—"

He silenced her with a look. "No. I won't be leaving again. But you'll have to learn to live with secrets now and then. Especially around Christmas-time—and your birthday."

Suddenly Willie's gaze stopped on a piece of furniture she had never seen before—a stout chest, beautifully finished, at the foot of the bed. "What is that?"

"Come look."

He took her hand and led her toward the bed. Willie knelt down and ran her hand over the wood—fine walnut, with a soft satiny finish. She couldn't speak—couldn't even breathe. There, carved into the front of the chest, two interlocking hearts bore the initials *OWS* and *WEC*. On either side of the hearts, two mourning doves held a ribbon in their beaks that swept down under the hearts, framing them with a wide banner.

"That's me—Owen Warren Slaughter. And you—Wilhemena Elizabeth Coltrain."

"I always hated the name Wilhemena," Willie muttered. "You make it sound almost lyrical."

"It *is* lyrical," he answered immediately. "Beautiful, like you." He knelt beside her and put his arm around her. "It's my hope chest. I built it for you, hoping you'd agree to marry me."

Willie leaned against him. "I didn't know you could do this."

"I didn't either," Owen chuckled. "It just sort of happened, as if my hands remembered something my mind didn't." He pointed to the banner below the hearts. "You have to fill in the rest."

Willie stared at the banner. "What do you mean?"

"The date," he said softly. "Our wedding day. I'll carve it in as soon as we get back from our honeymoon."

She turned and melted into his embrace. He kissed her gently, and as her tears of joy fell on his shoulder, she heard him whisper, "This chest is built to last forever, sweetheart—just like our love."

Willie's heart echoed back the long-awaited words: *"Forever . . . our love."* And she knew, finally and for all time, that her dreams had come true.

42

Family Circle

November 18, 1945

Rae looked over at Drew seated next to her in the pew and did her best to force a smile. She was unaccountably nervous, and she didn't know why. It wasn't their wedding, for heaven's sake—it was just a baptism. Their daughter's baptism.

But the sight of him sitting there, his big arms cradling that tiny infant, calmed Rae with a warm rush of love. She looked around at the small Presbyterian church with its bare wood floors and hard narrow pews. The country sanctuary where she and Willie had themselves been baptized, attended Sunday school, sang hymns to the groaning of the ancient organ, fought with their brother Charlie, and ultimately wept together as less than a year ago they buried their parents. She should have been married here, Rae thought, not in the opulent Laporte mansion among people she didn't even know.

But that was all in the past now, and it seemed that life had come full circle. On the other side of Drew sat his parents, holding hands and whispering to each other. Next to Rae were Bennett and Thelma, and behind them, Stork and Madge Simpson with little Mickey and Willie and Owen. On the third row, Ivory Brownlee sat with Orris Craven, Olivia Coltrain, and Ardyce Hanson.

Mickey, eighteen months old now and quite a handful, couldn't hear the music or the words that were being spoken, and his mother was having a time of it trying to keep him quiet. Out of the corner of her eye Rae could see him squirming on Madge's lap, fighting to get a better view of the baby in Drew's arms. From his first glimpse of her, Mickey had been fascinated with little Angelique. "Bee-bee!" he squealed at the top of his lungs. "Bee-bee!"

Then, without warning, he twisted out of Madge's grasp, hurled himself onto the back of the pew, and stuck his head around Drew's shoulder. "Bee-bee!"

Rae reached up and hauled him over into her lap. She took his face in her hands and made him look directly at her, then smiled and put a finger to her lips. He imitated her gesture and repeated softly, "Bee-bee?"

"An-gel-ique," Rae mouthed as he watched her lips intently. "An-gel-ique."

Mickey grinned and turned toward the infant, reaching out to pat her tiny fist with a gentle hand. "Bee-bee," he whispered. "An-gel."

Yes, Drew thought as he watched the little Simpson child gaze in wonder at his newborn daughter. *She is an angel.* He freed one hand and tousled the boy's blond head.

How quickly he had come to love and accept this child, the offspring of his own body, with all her limitations and challenges. She was his—his and Rae's—and it didn't matter whether she was bright or slow, homely or beautiful.

He leaned down and kissed her gently on the top of her head. Angelique, still asleep in the crook of his arm, worked her little mouth and blew out a spit bubble.

Then it was time. Madge retrieved Mickey, and Drew rose and helped Rae to her feet. They came forward with the baby, followed by Drew's parents, Bennett and Thelma, and Willie and Owen.

"Who will serve as godparents to this child?" the pastor asked, his gaze sweeping over the crowd of people jostling into a rough semicircle around the baptismal font.

"We will!" all six sponsors chorused.

"Ah." Flustered, the minister flipped pages in his book, adjusted his bifocals, and cleared his throat. Evidently he was not accustomed to such a show of support. But he managed to get through the charge to the godparents, then motioned for Drew and Rae to approach.

"What name do you give this child?"

"Angelique Beatrice Laporte," Drew answered, his throat clogging. Suddenly it struck him that this was a high and holy moment in their lives and in the life of their daughter. They were committing her, her life and her future, into the hands of Almighty God. There was so much they didn't know about how to raise a child—any child, especially a child like Angelique. So many mistakes they could make, so many opportunities they might miss. Gratefulness rose up in Drew's soul for this moment, that he could place his daughter into the care of an all-knowing, all-wise, all-loving God and trust that he and Rae, as Angelique's parents, would be guided in the way they needed to go.

The minister took the baby from his arms and held her over the baptismal font. "Angelique Beatrice Laporte," he recited, "I baptize thee in the name of—"

When the first splash of water hit her broad forehead, Angelique came to life. Obviously outraged by this invasion into her peace and quiet, she let out a howl that shook the rafters of the tiny country church. Drew glanced at Rae and saw her horrified expression, and he began to snicker. He couldn't help it. Rae jabbed him in the ribs with her elbow, but that just made it worse. By the time the minister got to the part about being sealed in the Holy Spirit and marked as Christ's own, he was practically shouting to be heard over the baby's wails. Muffled laughter had begun to ricochet around the sanctuary.

With a distinctly uncomfortable look on his face, the pastor walked to the altar and lifted Angelique up for prayer. "May this child be drawn to her own faith by the power of your Holy Spirit," he yelled, "and may rivers of living water spring up in her to eternal life."

Evidently God took the request seriously and answered immediately. The prayer was cut short with a quick "Amen," and the clergyman hurried back to the baptismal font and deposited Angelique, soaking diaper and all, into her father's outstretched arms. The pastor grimaced a little as he looked down at the spreading stain on his holy robes, then shook his head and chuckled. "Suffer the little children," he murmured, and turned beet red as everyone laughed.

Only Mickey Simpson understood the truth. As Drew hustled the embarrassed little group back to the pew and fumbled for the diaper bag, Mickey stood up on his mother's lap, pointed to Angelique, and in a loud voice shouted, "Bee-bee, An-gel!"

★ ★ ★

The cafe, normally open at one on Sunday afternoon, was closed for the day. Despite her broken arm, Thelma had, with Madge's help, whipped up a celebration luncheon for the baptismal party, and everyone gathered after church for sandwiches and chicken salad and a layer cake with Angelique's name spelled out across the top in colored candies.

"I wish Link and Libba could have been here," Rae said wistfully as she helped Thelma arrange sandwiches on a platter.

"Libba had to work this afternoon," Thelma said, shifting the plate with her good hand. "But they'll be here for Thanksgiving, and that's only a few days away."

"You really didn't have to go to all this trouble, Thelma. I mean, we are having Thanksgiving dinner here, and even though everyone's bringing something, it will be a lot of work for you."

Thelma smiled and squeezed Rae's arm. "I wouldn't have it any other way, hon. This baby is like a grandchild to me, and I fully intend to enjoy her. So just humor me, all right? It's my job to spoil her, and your job to make sure she doesn't get too rotten."

"That's going to be a full-time occupation, I'm afraid." Rae pointed to the table where Madge Simpson sat with Angelique in her arms and all the others crowded around her. Mickey sat on his daddy's lap grinning and stroking the baby's blanket.

"Mickey has really taken to her, hasn't he?" Thelma asked.

Rae nodded. "He thinks she's his little sister."

"Well, she is, in a way. We're all just one big family."

"Look at Beau and Beatrice, would you? They can't get enough of her. Came all the way back from New Orleans just for the baptism." Rae gave Thelma a meaningful glance. "I never would have believed it if I hadn't seen it with my own eyes."

"Believed what?"

"That Beau could change so much. He's a different person, Thelma. When we found out about Angelique's . . . ah, problems . . . I figured he'd have a hard time accepting it. His first grandchild, you know, being born with her condition. But he adores her."

"And so he should," Thelma said firmly. "God makes all kinds of folks, Rae, and not a one of them is a mistake. The mistake is with us, how we treat people who are different. Seems to me we should celebrate the differences, not ostracize people because of them."

Thelma's mind drifted to this baby, this one who would never live a life that most people would call normal, but who—according to Rae's friend Ardyce—had special gifts of love and affection to offer to those around her. By God's way of reckoning, Thelma didn't think that all the brainpower in the world was more important than a loving, generous spirit. It was too bad society seemed to value intelligence and productivity more than love.

"Did you ever consider," Thelma asked Rae as they finished up the tray of sandwiches, "that in every other area of life, the things that are most different are the most valued? Original artwork is one of a kind, worth a fortune. Diamonds and gold are valuable because they are so rare." She hugged Rae and held her close for a minute. "That child is pure gold," she whispered in Rae's ear. "When life gets difficult, don't forget that." She let go and looked into Rae's dark eyes. "And remember, too, that you've got a lot of help on your side."

"I know." Rae picked up the tray and smiled. "And I appreciate it more than you can imagine. It helps to know we're not alone."

★ ★ ★

Ivory stood up and shifted from one foot to the other. He didn't know how to do this right, and he wanted it to be good. What would Mr. Bennett do? Knowing him, he'd make sure he had ever'body's attention first, and then he'd make a big announcement.

Well, this was a big announcement—the biggest.

He looked around the room at all the people gathered for Baby Angelique's Christmas party. No, not Christmas—that wasn't right. What was the word Mr. Orris had told him? Christ—something—else. *Christening.* Oh, yeah. The baptizing. Ivory figured it must have something to do with giving the baby to Christ. And that sounded like a real good idea to him.

They had told him something was wrong with Angelique—that she wasn't quite right in the head and that she'd probably be slow. Ivory understood slow, all right. And she did look a little funny. But everybody seemed to love her just the same. So giving her to Jesus was probably the best thing that could happen to her. Jesus understood people who were different, and he loved babies. After all, Jesus was the one who came as a baby so people could be saved. Even different people, like Angelique. Like him.

Maybe it wasn't Christmas yet, but *christening* was close enough to *Christmas* to suit him. It would be more than a month before the real Christmas, and for the first time in his life, Ivory had really great gifts to give to his friends. He wasn't about to wait.

He looked over at Mr. Orris and saw him smiling. Mr. Orris liked being in on the secret, and he had helped Ivory a lot. Ivory just hoped Mr. Bennett wouldn't be upset that he had asked another lawyer for help. Lawyers could be funny like that. But when Mr. Bennett found out what the surprise was, he would probably understand.

Ivory ran a finger around the collar of his shirt and straightened his bow tie. "'Scuse me," he began, but nobody was listening. He'd try it again, a little louder. *"Scuse me!"*

People started glancing up at him standing there and nudged each other to be quiet. Finally everybody was looking straight at him, and he grinned.

"I got a 'nouncement to make," he said.

Ivory saw Thelma scrunch up her face in a puzzled look. "What is it, Ivory?"

"Well, you all know about my good fortune—thanks to you, Thelma. And I know it's not Christmas yet, but I got some presents to hand out."

"We don't need any presents, Ivory," Mr. Bennett said. "We're just glad for what's happened to you."

"I know. But y'all have been so good to me—the best friends a fella could ever have." He turned to Willie, who was sitting all close and snuggly with Owen. Owen hadn't got his memories back yet, but he looked pretty happy anyway. And Willie was wearing a nice little diamond ring on her finger.

"You remember last year, Willie, when we had that Thanksgiving dinner out to your place?" Willie nodded and smiled. "And y'all prayed that God would help me find a way to pay my taxes to the gov'ment and keep my land?" He grinned. "Well, I guess God's done made good on that prayer. And all of y'all helped. So I got some presents for ever'body, just to say a little thank you for ever'thing you've done."

It was one of the longest speeches Ivory ever gave, and he felt real good about it. He motioned to Mr. Orris, who opened his briefcase and stood there waiting. "Mr. Orris, he's helped me figure all this out. Willie, you're first."

"Do you want me to come up there, Ivory?"

"That's all right. Mr. Orris will bring it to you."

Willie took the envelope Mr. Orris handed to her, looked inside, and gasped. "Ivory, you can't!"

"Sure I can. It's for you and Owen, so you can do whatever you want to fix up the house."

"What is it, Willie?" Thelma asked.

"It's a check—for twenty thousand dollars." Willie looked like she was going to cry, and for a minute Ivory was afraid he had made a mistake.

"If it ain't enough, Willie, just tell me," he said. "It's like a wedding present for whenever y'all get married."

"It-it's enough," Willie stammered. "But—"

"No, now." Ivory raised a hand to shush her. "We ain't gonna do any *but*s. Stork and Madge—"

Mr. Orris handed them their envelope.

"I figured y'all might need to send Mickey to a special school so he can learn to talk good and read them finger signs. Fifty thousand should cover it."

Ivory looked around the room. Everybody looked shocked, and nobody said a word.

"Drew and Rae, I'm afraid I ain't got a check for you. But Mr. Orris has papers. We set up a—what's that called, Mr. Orris?"

"A trust fund."

"Yeah. A trust fund for the baby. A hundred thousand dollars. You can use it for anything she needs—or anything you need for her. Is that OK?"

Rae just sat there and cried, and Drew looked at him and shook his head. "I don't know what to say, Ivory."

"I know what it's like to be different," Ivory explained. "But you gave her to Jesus, and Jesus will take good care of her. I just thought I might could help a little."

Drew got up and came over, and for a minute Ivory didn't know what he was going to do. Then Drew put his arms around Ivory and hugged, hard. It was a little embarrassing, but Ivory didn't mind. It felt good, real good, to do something to show his friends how much he 'preciated them.

Mr. Orris had called it "sharing the wealth." But Ivory knew that even before he had got all that money, he had been a rich man. Nobody with friends like this could ever be poor.

★ ★ ★

Thelma sat back in wonder, gripping Bennett's hand so hard that she left fingernail marks in his skin. She had never expected anything like this, not in a million years. A long time ago, when they had first prayed about Ivory's tax problem, Ivory had declared that "God's got ways" of dealing with problems like his. They just had no idea how miraculously, how abundantly, the Lord might work in his situation.

She should have known something like this was coming. Ivory had always been a giving soul, a sweet and honorable man. But he was an innocent, too, and suddenly she was afraid he might just give everything away and be left with nothing.

"Ivory," she said gently, so as not to give him the impression that she disapproved, "this is all very generous of you. But are you sure you want to do this? I mean, it is your money, and—"

Orris Craven took over smoothly. "Don't worry, Thelma. We've also set up a trust for Ivory, which I will administer with Bennett's approval. This has all been carefully planned. He'll never want for anything, and he'll be financially independent."

Thelma smiled and nodded. The pale little man, the one Beau Laporte affectionately referred to as "the weasel," had apparently thought of everything. Obviously his weaseling days were over.

"I'll get more coffee," Thelma said, starting to rise. But a gnarled hand on her shoulder stopped her, and she looked up to see Ivory's gap-toothed grin.

"You gotta wait a minute, Thelma. I got a surprise for you and Mr. Bennett, too."

Thelma sat back down with a thud. Her heart turned over and she looked to Bennett for support. He raised his eyebrows as if to say, *I have no idea,* then squeezed her hand and waited.

"Mr. Bennett, you been so good to help me out. I want you to know that even though Mr. Orris here has helped me with this surprise, you're still my lawyer, and always will be. But it 'curred to me that I ain't paid you for your services, and well, that ain't right. And Thelma, well, you been just about the best friend a fella could have. You gave me a place to belong, to play my music and be with folks. I felt comfortable here, and that's all because of you. For a long time now I wanted to do somethin' special for you, but I just never knew what to do, and I couldn't 'ford much. But now I can, so I want you to have this."

He took the envelope from Orris Craven and handed it to Thelma. "This here," he said, "is a—what's that word? A token. Yeah, a token of my 'preciation to both of you. Nothin' I do could ever pay back what y'all have done for me, but it's a start."

Thelma opened the envelope and drew out a sheaf of legal papers. A check fell out and fluttered to the floor, and Bennett reached down to pick it up. "A hundred thousand dollars," he whispered. "Made out to both of us."

Thelma looked at the papers in her hand, and she couldn't believe what she was seeing. "No," she breathed. "Ivory, no."

"Yep." He grinned.

Thelma's eyes swam with tears, and she couldn't speak. Gently Bennett pried the papers out of her grasp and looked at them. "The deed to Ivory's big house," he said softly. "With twenty acres."

"I reckon I'll use some of my money to add onto my cabin," Ivory said. "But I don't need that big old place, and I know how you love it." He leaned down and kissed Thelma on the cheek. "I figgered you could use some of that money to fix the place up, real fine, like it used to be in my Granddaddy Seth's day." He patted her on the shoulder. "Now don't cry, Thelma. I wanted to keep it in the family, and you're the closest family I got."

Thelma threw her arms around his neck and let her tears fall on his bony shoulder. It was too much, far too much, but she didn't have the heart to argue with him. Somehow—she didn't know how—he understood her connection with that old place, her silly dream of being an elegant lady in a magnificent house. And now the dream was coming true—a gift from God and Ivory Brownlee all rolled up in one.

When she got control of herself, Thelma sat back down and took a deep breath. "What do you think, Bennett?"

He was smiling at her with a curious expression. "I think," he said slowly and deliberately, "that if we are going to share a bank account and joint ownership of the Brownlee house, I'd better make an honest woman out of you—and fast."

He reached into his pocket and brought out a small box. "I've been carrying this around for weeks," he murmured, "but with all the activity I never seemed to get a minute alone with you. Maybe this isn't the right time or the right place, but—"

He got down on one knee beside Thelma's chair and took her hand. "I'm an old-fashioned guy," he began, then stopped and grinned sheepishly. "Well, to tell the truth, I'm just *old*. But you know that I love you, second only to God, with all my heart, soul, mind, and strength. I would be honored and blessed beyond measure if you would consent to become my wife."

Thelma started crying again and couldn't seem to stop. Words wouldn't come, and her hand shook as he placed the antique filigree engagement ring on her finger.

"Do I take that as a yes?" Bennett prodded.

She nodded and put her arms around his neck, and as their lips met, everything else faded into the background. After a moment she heard a chorus of hoots and whistles around her, and she felt a wave of heat run up her neck into her cheeks.

"You're blushing, Thelma!" someone said, and everybody laughed and applauded.

Thelma looked around at the dear familiar faces. No, it wasn't the intimate, romantic, private proposal she had envisioned, but it was appropriate. All these people with their differing backgrounds had been forged into a large, loving family—drawn together by war and pain and struggle and hardship into a circle of love that was stronger and more enduring than most ties of blood and kin. She was blessed, all right—blessed with a love beyond anything she had dared to pray for, a family of caring, supportive friends, and now a home that fulfilled all her unspoken dreams.

One by one they came to the table to offer their congratulations and to thank Ivory fervently for his generosity. And at the very last, as the party was ending and people were preparing to leave, Orris Craven stepped forward, took Thelma's hand in his, and kissed it.

"I was right all along," he declared. "You may not be Aurelia Breckinridge, society matron, but you are without a doubt the finest lady I have ever had the pleasure to meet."

43

Love Is Never Lost

The Coltrain Farm
Thanksgiving Day, 1945

"Are we about ready to go?"

Rae looked over her shoulder to see Drew leaning against the doorway of the nursery. "A little patience, if you please. *Your* daughter just spit up all over her new dress, and I had to change her. We still have to get her stuff together, and get the pies—"

He grinned and pulled a diaper bag from behind his back. "All taken care of, milady. The princess's diapers, formula, a change of clothes, and various cleaning items for her messy little habits."

"You're a genius. I love you, you know." She gave him a quick kiss and went back to finish dressing the baby.

"Oh, I deserve a better kiss than that. In addition, the pies are wrapped and in the car. The dogs have been fed. The bed is made, and the cat has been put out."

Rae shook her head and laughed. "We don't have a cat."

"Oh, yes we do. Six of them, in the hayloft of the barn."

"When did that happen?"

"You weren't the only one in labor this month. Evidently a stray wandered up and decided to stay. Gave birth to five beautiful kittens, then got up the next morning and caught two mice."

"Is this some kind of contest? I only gave birth to one, and I don't think I'll be doing any mouse-hunting for a while."

He came and wrapped his arms around her. "Are you feeling up to this, honey?"

Rae leaned her head on Drew's chest. "I'll have to admit the christening party wore me out. I overdid it, I think, for my first day out after the baby was born. But I wouldn't miss this Thanksgiving dinner for anything." She squeezed him around the waist. "I believe I'll just sit back today and let people wait on me."

"You might have some competition for the position as Queen. Don't forget, your cousin, Libba, will be there, too."

Despite her weariness, a surge of anticipation rose in Rae's heart. "I know. I can't wait to see her. And to see the look on Libba's face when she hears the news that Ivory Brownlee is now the wealthiest man in the county."

"He's not the only one." Drew smiled and shook his head. "Amazing, isn't it, what he's done for all of us?"

"He's a sweet and generous man, that much is certain. Makes me aware of what kind of miracles simple faith can accomplish."

"Well, he's given all of us a lot to be thankful for today."

Rae lifted Angelique out of the crib and snuggled her into the crook of one arm. "I'm thankful for the trust fund," she agreed. "But I'm even more thankful for things money can't buy."

"Such as?" His voice took on a low, intimate tone, and Rae looked up to see him gazing at her with an expression of total adoration.

"Such as a husband who loves me and a daughter who gives me so much joy."

Drew pulled them both into a warm embrace and kissed Rae fervently. Then he stepped back and surveyed them with a critical eye. "I wish I had a picture of this moment," he said wistfully. "You both look so beautiful, standing there with the sunlight coming in behind you."

"If we don't get going, it will be moonlight. And that turkey of Thelma's will be nothing more than a bare carcass."

"Ardyce is downstairs with Willie and Owen. We decided to take both cars, in case you get tired and want to come home early."

"I'm going to miss Ardyce when she goes back to Minnesota tomorrow," Rae sighed.

"Me, too. She's been such a help." He twisted his face in a wry grin. "And she really knows how to tell a guy the truth."

Rae handed the baby to Drew and gave him a mock scowl. "You'd better just watch your step, mister. If you fall back into your old habits, I'll have her back down here on the first bus."

Drew kissed Angelique gently on the forehead, and she grabbed his big forefinger with a tiny fist. "I don't think you'll have to worry about that." He gazed lovingly at the child in his arms. "Everything I want is right here."

★ ★ ★

Willie looked around at the friends and family gathered in the Paradise Garden Cafe, and her mind turned over the changes that had taken place since the previous November. Last Thanksgiving Rae was in New Orleans, and Libba was in Memphis trying to find Link. Owen, she thought, was lost to her forever. She had been alone in that big empty house with her father sick in bed and her mother half out of her mind with worry. With no life and no future and not a single thing to be thankful for.

What a difference a year had made! Today she sat beside the man she loved, with his arm around her and his ring on her finger. Rae was home to stay, and the presence of a new child filled the house with warmth and hope. Link was on his feet and doing well in law school, and Libba seemed happier than Willie had ever known her to be. Ivory had watched God meet his needs in miraculous ways and then shared his good fortune with all of them. Thelma and Bennett were preparing to start a new life together. Already they had begun restoration on the Brownlee home, and Willie could see the wonder in Thelma's eyes.

Thelma had confided to Willie that her plan was to give the cafe to Stork and Madge outright as an early Christmas present. It would bring a good income for them when Stork's discharge came through in January, and she and Bennett would help pay for some improvements to the place.

Everyone's dreams, it seemed, were coming true.

Stork and Madge sat at the end of the long table next to Drew and Rae, with Mickey making a huge fuss over his "Bee-bee An-gel." Every now and then, Willie caught Owen's gaze wandering to the children, and a wistful look of wonder filled his expression.

How fortunate she was, to be loved by such a man! Whether he ever regained his memories or not mattered little. His character was still the same, and his heart. He would make a wonderful husband and the best father ever. And, given his warmth and charm and sense of humor, Willie knew that whatever trials they would face, she would never ever be bored.

But occasionally she did question whether or not Owen would be content with his life at the farm. He had plenty to keep him busy, of course, and he was a tireless worker. Yet still she saw him, sometimes, leaning on a hay rake or standing in the doorway of the barn, staring off into the distance as if his mind were a million miles away. Was he grappling with the hidden memories buried deep in the darkness of his soul? Was he thinking of Buddy Ferber, the child who had so captured his heart?

Willie had gotten over being jealous of JoLynn Ferber, the desperate mother who had connived to trick Owen into marrying her. Owen had never loved JoLynn—he had simply tried to do the right thing by her, and thus had let himself be deceived. Buddy, however, was another matter. Clearly, the boy occupied a place in Owen's mind and soul that she could never share. Willie felt small and not a little guilty when that twinge of bitterness gnawed at her, and of course she never said a word to Owen. This was a child, for heaven's sake—a fatherless six-year-old who had adored Owen and wanted him to be his daddy. She should have had compassion for the boy, and love. But whenever Owen got that faraway look, she felt excluded, and no matter how much she sought to change her feelings about the matter, she couldn't seem to break through her resentment.

The light of the candles on the table caught her diamond engagement ring and reflected back a prism of colors, and Willie pushed the unwelcome thoughts away. She should be happy, content—and thankful. And in most ways she was. Time and God would have to take care of the rest.

"Come on, Owen—I know you have room for another piece of pumpkin pie."

Owen looked up to see Thelma Breckinridge standing over him with a pie plate. "Thelma, please. That's the third time you've come around with pie, and I've already had one piece, plus a huge slice of Willie's coconut cake. If I eat another bite, I might explode."

Thelma laughed good-naturedly and plopped the pie down in front of him. "Now, Owen, how often do you get home cooking like this?"

"Every day. Willie's the best cook in the county, don't you know that?"

Thelma pretended to be offended. "You still look like you could use a little more meat on your bones."

Owen laughed. "If I get any more meat on my bones, I'll need a red suit and eight reindeer to go with this beard."

Thelma moved on, and Owen caught a glimpse of Ardyce Hanson slipping toward the door of the cafe. He got up and leaned down to whisper in Willie's ear, "I'll be back in a few minutes. I want to walk off some of this dinner, and I'd like a chance to talk to Ardyce a little before she leaves."

Willie nodded, and Owen followed Ardyce out into the parking lot.

"Getting some fresh air?"

Ardyce turned and smiled at him. "I haven't eaten that much since . . . well, since the last meatball dinner at Syttende Mai."

"Excuse me?" Owen scratched his head.

"Sorry. I forget sometimes that you don't have any memories of life in Scandinavian country. Syttende Mai is the seventeenth of May—Norwegian independence day. Traditionally, they serve meatballs and lefse. The old Norwegians have the philosophy that you eat as many of them as you can as quickly as possible, before they settle like lead weights in your stomach."

"Sounds appetizing. Did you miss any other little rituals by being here at Thanksgiving?"

"I miss the lefse and lutefisk, but I'll get plenty at Christmastime."

"Oh, yeah. Lye-soaked cod. My idea of Christmas dinner." Owen grinned at her, then sobered. "I'm going to miss you, Ardyce. We all are."

She shook her head. "Don't start, please. Norwegians don't cry, and I wouldn't want to be a traitor to my heritage."

"Do you really have to go back tomorrow?"

"I've been gone two months, Owen. Certainly longer than I expected to stay. But I have to admit it's been nice. These people are like—well, like a big family."

"A family whose problems you've seen from the inside."

"But look at how everything has turned out. Rae and Drew have accepted the unique challenges of parenting a Mongoloid child. Drew's father has made a phenomenal change in his life. Willie's wearing your ring. Mr. Brownlee has acquired and given away a fortune. It's been quite a month."

"It's never dull," Owen agreed. "But I get the impression that life in Eden is usually not this dramatic—not every day, anyway."

"You'll be happy here, won't you, Owen? With Willie, I mean?"

"I adore Willie, and you know it."

"Yes, and it's clear she loves you as well. But—"

Owen's stomach knotted. When Ardyce said *but,* something was coming. "But what?"

"I see something in you, Owen. Something that's not quite settled. An expression in your eye sometimes when you think nobody's looking. A sigh." She peered intently at him, and her gaze made him distinctly uneasy. "Do you still think about Buddy Ferber?"

Owen started to deny it, but he couldn't lie to Ardyce. "You were always too perceptive for your own good."

She sat down on the bench outside the cafe and motioned for him to join her. "Do you want to tell me about it?"

He slumped down next to her. "I don't know. There's not much to tell. Willie says I fell in love with him at first sight, and I guess I did. It's just hard to get him out of my mind, though heaven knows I've tried. There was a connection between us, almost as if I were his real father."

"But you weren't."

"What makes a parent, Ardyce? Is it just the joining of an egg and sperm, a combination of genes that results in a life? Or is it love? If I had never known the truth, if I had married JoLynn and taken Buddy as my own son, would I be less than his father because I didn't participate in his creation?"

She motioned for Owen to go on, and he took in a ragged breath. "My mind tells me that I have no obligation to the child, that he is not my son and I need to put him out of my mind and go on and build my life here. My heart tells me different. I'd never give up my relationship with Willie, of course—she is God's gift to me and my first priority. But how do I resolve the conflict? Every time I see Stork with Mickey or Drew holding Angelique, every time I play fetch with Vallie or hold one of those adorable newborn kittens in the barn, I think about Buddy. I don't want to hurt Willie, of course, and I hope that someday we will have children of our own, but in the meantime, how do I rid myself of my feelings for Buddy?"

Ardyce frowned for a minute, obviously thinking about what he had said, then turned to him. "Owen, you loved Charlie Coltrain, right?"

"Sure I did. He was my best friend."

"And you have other friends now?"

"You know I do. Drew and Rae, and Stork and Madge, and Bennett, and you—"

"So you've forgotten all about Charlie?"

"No, of course not. I'll never forget Charlie."

"And you'll always love him?"

"Ardyce, what are you getting at?"

She smiled at him. "The truth that you don't stop loving someone the way you'd turn off a light switch. Just because your life has taken a different turn and Buddy is gone doesn't mean you can't love him—or that your love for him has to interfere with your relationship with Willie and any future children you may have. Don't you see, Owen? You're fighting the wrong battle. You can't simply deny your feelings for Buddy and expect them to go away. You just have to put them in the right perspective. Cherish his memory. Love him. Be happy that you had the chance to know him. Pray for him. Wish the best for him. If you try to suppress that love, it will turn into a dark secret that haunts you. If you welcome the love, it will enrich you. And Willie."

Owen stared at her. "Do you really think so?"

"One thing I've learned about you in the past few months, Owen—you have an enormous capacity for love. Loving Buddy isn't a mistake. Just make sure Willie knows she's first in your heart."

"Willie's always first."

"Then be honest with her about your feelings for the child. You might be surprised—she might come to love him, too, even though she's never met him."

Owen inhaled deeply of the fresh November air tinged with the smell of wood smoke and damp leaves. A huge weight rolled off his heart, and he smiled. "Can you do me a favor when you get home, Ardyce?"

"I'll try."

"You'll probably be seeing JoLynn. Tell her I asked about Buddy, will you? And ask her if it would be all right if I sent him a Christmas present."

"I'll be happy to. And even if she doesn't think it's a good idea, I'll do my best to keep you posted about how the boy is doing."

Owen got up and stretched. "I guess I'll go back in and eat that last piece of pumpkin pie," he said with an exaggerated groan. "Otherwise Thelma will be nagging me for the rest of the day."

"I'll stay out here a little longer." Ardyce rose and gave him a hug, and he saw tears standing in her eyes. "I'm going to miss you, too, Owen. All of you," she whispered in a husky voice.

"None of that, now. You're Norwegian, remember?"

"Uff da! I'd better get back to Minnesota quick, then, before I turn into a gushing southern belle."

"No chance," Owen quipped, trying to hide his own emotion with a joke. "Besides, I wouldn't want you to change. I like you exactly the way you are."

44

Celebrations and Surprises

Paradise Garden Cafe
December 1, 1945

Thelma smiled as she watched Willie Coltrain and Owen Slaughter in the back booth, holding hands across the table and gazing into each other's eyes. If it hadn't been so cute, it would have been downright sickening the way those two mooned over each other like lovestruck teenagers. But then, Thelma didn't reckon she had much room to criticize. She and Bennett were twice the age of these kids, and they—

"Thelma! What are you doing here?"

Thelma jumped and wheeled around. Madge Simpson stood there with her hands on her hips and a dangerous look in her eye.

"I-I was just getting a cup of coffee."

"Well, you're not supposed to be here."

"You mean I'm not welcome in this cafe anymore?" Thelma lifted one eyebrow at Madge. "Well, Miss High-and-Mighty-Business-Owner, I can see I made a big mistake in giving this place to you. Of all the ingratitude—"

Madge poked Thelma in the ribs and giggled. "You know that's not what I mean. I mean you shouldn't be here behind the counter. You should be over there at the best table. I'll bring your coffee to you." She affected a look of disdain. "The elegant Lady Thelma Breckinridge does not pour her own beverage."

"Oh, pooh," Thelma snorted. "The day I'm too elegant to come behind the counter and get my own coffee is the day you'll be carting me off to the sanitarium down at Whitfield."

"That can be arranged." Madge reached behind Thelma, untied her apron, and slipped it off over her head. "And no more of this. Now, go sit."

"The view is better from back here." Thelma pointed to the two lovebirds in the booth.

"I know. They're really cute, aren't they? But I doubt they'd appreciate being spied on."

"Elegant society ladies don't spy," Thelma corrected.

"No, they don't." Madge gave her a playful shove toward a table. "Would you like a doughnut to go with your coffee?"

"I'd like to be treated with a little respect."

"That's exactly what you're getting," Madge returned. "Very little."

"All this abuse, and I suppose you'll want a tip, too?"

"A big one. You can afford it."

"Just wait till Mickey gets old enough to understand all this." Thelma rolled her eyes. "Don't think I won't tell him how his mother abused his poor old grandmother and threw her out of her own cafe. When he grows up and decides to visit me for Christmas instead of his own parents, you'll be sorry."

"I'm sure I will. When that day comes, you have my permission to say, *I told you so.*" Madge brought two cups of coffee and a small platter of doughnuts to the table and sat down with Thelma. "What do you suppose they're doing?" She pointed toward Willie and Owen.

"Who knows? Christmas list, wedding plans. Maybe house renovations."

Madge took a sip of her coffee. "Speaking of renovations, how's the old house coming?"

"That's why I'm here." Thelma shrugged. "They've got the porch reinforced and are starting to paint the outside of the house today. It's a good thing we're having such warm weather. But Bennett insisted I come into town and leave the workers alone. He said they couldn't take another discussion about the right color of paint."

"White is white, isn't it?"

"The white isn't the problem. The trim work is going to be done in gray and burgundy, and I'm afraid they've got it all wrong. I think the gray is too dark and the burgundy is too brown."

"Thelma, they're professionals. They know what they're doing. Have you ever painted a house like that before?"

Thelma leveled a scathing look at her. "That's beside the point. I know what I like."

"It'll be fine. You'll see."

"I suppose." Thelma sighed. "I never knew how frustrating a project like this could be."

"Indeed," Madge said, lifting her chin and looking down her nose. "Good help is so hard to find, isn't it? My, my."

"Oh, stop it. All right, I get the point."

"So tell me about it. What are you doing?"

Thelma grinned. This was her favorite current subject—except for her wedding plans, of course—and she relished the opportunity to talk about it. "Well, the house is in amazingly good shape, given its age and the years of neglect. They built homes to last in those days. No dry rot, no termite damage or other major problems, for which we're thankful. We are putting on a new roof, but except for that and the porch, the rest of the work is pretty much cosmetic. Paint, new wallpaper, stripping and waxing floors, that kind of thing. The curtains are in pretty bad shape, so I'm having most of them replaced, but the rugs are all hand loomed and just need a good cleaning."

"How long will it take?"

"I think Bennett's hired every available craftsman, painter, and carpenter in the county," Thelma chuckled. "The biggest project is the kitchen—he insisted upon having new appliances installed, and they have to come from Memphis. But everything should be done by Christmas. Bennett is going to move in as soon as the painters are done."

"How wonderful for you!" Madge squeezed Thelma's hand. "What a celebration that will be. I can't wait to see it."

"Well, you'll have to wait," Thelma declared firmly. "There'll be no unauthorized tours. I want it all to be finished before anybody gets the first glimpse."

"And that will be—"

"Christmas Day. Everybody will be invited, and it will be a party like you've never seen before."

"Are you sure about this?" Willie asked for the tenth time. "We don't want to rush into anything."

"Rush?" Owen laughed and squeezed her hands. "I want to marry you, Willie—as soon as possible. Before some other fellow comes along and turns your head."

"Don't be absurd."

"All right, then. While you're still under the impression that I'm a great catch."

"That's even more ridiculous."

"I'm not a great catch?"

"You're wonderful, and you know it. Someday you're probably going to get a swelled head because I tell you so often how wonderful you are."

"I promise I won't get conceited if you promise not to stop telling me." He wondered, just briefly, if she knew—really knew—how important she was to him, how much he loved her. People told him that by this time he should be getting cold feet, but his feet were still as warm as his heart. How could he be nervous about something that was so right? The idea of a lifetime commitment didn't frighten him one bit. He was ready to say *I do*. He leaned forward and kissed her hands. "I love you, Willie."

"Owen! What will people say?"

"People will say we're in love," he quipped. But even as he uttered the words, something stirred in him, some nebulous feeling that he couldn't identify. It wasn't bad, exactly, just . . . strange. A vague sense that something was about to happen. Something unexpected.

"How about Christmas Day?"

Willie looked up and blinked at him. "What?"

"Let's get married on Christmas Day," Owen repeated. "It will be beautiful, with all the lights and decorations."

"And you'd never forget our anniversary," Willie added with a cynical smile.

"That, too. But I was thinking more along the lines that you are my greatest gift from God, and it only seems right to celebrate our love on the day we celebrate God's greatest gift to the world."

"Owen, you're such a romantic."

"Is that bad?"

"Of course not." She looked into his eyes as if searching for some kind of confirmation. "All right. Christmas Day. I'm going to wear Mama's wedding dress, so we don't have to worry about that. And we'll keep it simple—just family and friends."

"Wonderful! Will you talk to Thelma and Madge about the reception?"

"Thelma's pretty busy with the house and all—"

Owen shook his head. "She won't be too busy for this. You'll see."

★ ★ ★

At ten minutes to twelve, Madge looked up to see her husband standing in the doorway of the cafe, a wide grin on his face.

"Hi, honey!" He strode into the room and kissed her, sweeping her off her feet and twirling her in a circle. Mickey got down off Thelma's lap and toddled over to him. "Da-Da!"

"Hey, pal—how're you doing?"

"Michael, what has gotten into you? Aren't you supposed to be on duty today?"

"I am on duty," he countered. "Lunch duty. And daddy duty." He picked Mickey up and tickled him in the ribs and was rewarded with a high-pitched squeal aimed directly into his right ear. "We're going to have to figure out a way to teach him about volume," Michael said, plugging his ear with his finger. "How do you get a deaf child to tone it down?"

"You start by not getting him excited right before nap time." Madge scowled at him, then laughed. "Watch."

She turned Mickey's face to hers so he could read her lips. "Say Mama."

"Ma-ma!" he shouted at the top of his lungs, making the sign for *mother* with his pudgy hands.

Madge put a finger to her lips. "Shh. Quiet."

"Ma-ma," he repeated, this time in a whisper.

"Very good. Now, go back to Gramma Thelma. Quietly." He squirmed down from Michael's arms and ran to jump into Thelma's lap.

"Pretty impressive." Michael drew out a chair and sat down at the nearest table. "What does a fellow have to do to get lunch around here?"

"First the fellow has to tell his wife what he's doing off base in the middle of the day."

"Oh, yeah." He reached into his pocket and pulled out a folded sheet of paper, bright canary yellow.

"Michael, what is that?"

"It's an evening of entertainment for us and our friends," he said, holding the paper out in front of her.

USO DANCE, the flyer said in bold black letters. SATURDAY, DECEMBER 15. JOIN LES BROWN AND HIS BAND OF RENOWN FOR A CHRISTMAS DANCE, 7:30–Midnight.

"Les Brown? Here, in Eden? You must be kidding."

"My thoughts exactly. But the major says it's no joke. I thought we'd all go."

"All who?"

"You, me, Owen and Willie, Rae—if she feels like it—and Drew. I called Link from the base, and he says Libba doesn't have to work that weekend. They'll be here. It'll be like old times."

"Old times for whom?" Madge folded her arms and waited.

"Oh. Well, that's right. You weren't here when we were all at the base together. Neither was Drew. And Owen doesn't remember it." He gave her a brilliant smile. "But it'll be fun anyway."

"Willie and Owen are right over there." Madge pointed. "Why don't you ask them?"

She followed Michael over to the booth. "Hey, y'all—Les Brown is going to be playing at the base for a USO dance on the fifteenth. I say we all go together. What about it?"

Willie looked up at Madge with an expression of utter panic on her face, but Owen didn't blink an eye. "Who's Les Brown?" he asked.

"Who's Les Brown?" Michael repeated incredulously, and Madge gave him a poke in the ribs. "Oh, right. You don't remember. He's a bandleader, a famous one, and—"

"Sounds great," Owen said. "But I don't know if I can dance or not."

"Sure you can dance." Michael slapped him on the shoulder. "You and Willie—"

Madge kicked him in the shins, hard, and he gulped.

"You and Willie would make a great couple."

Willie shook her head and shot a warning look in Michael's direction. "I'm not sure that's such a good idea."

"Oh, I don't know," Owen said. "Sounds like fun to me."

Michael turned a triumphant expression on Madge as if to say, *See? I told you it was a great plan.* "All right. Saturday the fifteenth. We'll meet here and go to the base together."

Madge walked back to the counter with Michael dogging her footsteps. When they were out of earshot, she turned on him. "Weren't you listening, Michael? Willie didn't think it was a good idea."

"Willie worries too much. We'll have a wonderful time. And I promise I won't dance with anyone except you."

Madge glared at him. "When we first met, you couldn't dance a lick. Who taught you? And just who, might I ask, did you dance with *last* time?"

"Rae," he answered. "Only she was Mabel back then. And believe me, I didn't enjoy it one bit."

★ ★ ★

Thelma watched as Stork and Madge carried on a heated exchange behind the counter—no doubt concerning Stork's rather pushy invitation to Willie and Owen about the USO dance. Mickey, of course, couldn't hear them, but he was watching with wide eyes.

She turned the little boy's round face toward hers. "Let's go outside, all right, and take a little walk?"

"Ouside!" he repeated, bouncing on her lap. He scrambled down, and she took his hand and headed for the door.

They had only been outside a few minutes when Mickey pointed up the road. "Bus!"

He might not be able to hear, Thelma mused, but there was nothing wrong with his eyesight. Sure enough, the bus was coming, and it veered into the parking lot and pulled to a stop right at the door. "Bus! Bus!" Mickey squealed.

The bus door groaned open, and Monk Lipkin craned his neck and peered down at her. "Hey there, Thelma," he said with a wink. "Who's your little friend?"

"Madge's boy, Mickey. Since when do you drive the Saturday route, Monk?"

Monk shrugged. "Other driver's down with the flu, and I needed the money."

"Can you come in for coffee?"

"Not today, I'm afraid. Got paying customers wanting to get to Grenada. But I do have a delivery for you." He craned his neck and motioned toward the back of the bus. "Come on, kid. This is your stop."

A small boy, perhaps six years old, appeared at Monk's shoulder and stood on the top step. He narrowed his eyes suspiciously at Thelma. "Are you sure this is the right place?" he asked Monk in a timid voice.

"Yep. This is Thelma. She'll make sure you get hooked up with your daddy." Monk grinned at Thelma. "He's come to see his father for Christmas. Take care of him, will you?"

The lad stepped down from the bus and hoisted a knapsack over his shoulder. He watched with a forlorn expression as the bus pulled back onto the highway, then turned to Thelma and removed his cap.

"You can tell me where I can find my father?"

Thelma smiled at him. He was a cute little fellow, with curly blond hair, brown eyes, and a sprinkling of freckles across his nose. The knees of his dungarees were patched, but he was clean and obviously brought up to be polite. She could see a baseball glove poking out of the edge of his knapsack.

"Well, I might be able to, honey, if I knew your name."

"Buddy," the boy said. "My father's name is Owen. Owen Slaughter."

45

Second Blessing

Thelma stared down at the boy. "Did you say *Owen Slaughter?*"

"Yes, ma'am. Please, can you tell me where to find him? I've come all the way from Iowa."

The little guy looked to be on the verge of tears, and Thelma, still clutching Mickey's hand, stooped down to his level. "You came on the bus alone?" The child nodded and swallowed. "You don't have to be afraid. Don't worry, old Thelma's going to take good care of you."

"I'm not scared," the boy said firmly, thrusting out his chin.

"Of course you're not. You're a very brave young man." She stood and took his hand. "This is Mickey," she said. "He's my grandson—well, kind of."

The child seemed to understand what a "kind of" grandmother was, and he smiled briefly. Then his chin began to tremble and his eyes swam with tears. "My gramma died," he said bluntly.

Thelma felt her throat tighten. "I'm very sorry to hear that," she choked out. "Let's go inside, shall we?"

Thelma didn't want to take this boy into the cafe, where Owen and Willie sat planning their wedding. But she didn't know what else to do. Owen hadn't said much about his time in Iowa, except that he had, in his words, *found his direction.* Was this boy Owen's son? And if so, did Willie know about him?

Her stomach churned with tension, and her heart sent up a silent plea for help and wisdom. Everything had been going so well, and now this complication. . . .

But this wasn't just a complication. This was a child—evidently a very troubled child. And somehow Owen was involved. There was nothing to do but face the music and pray that somehow they would find a way to help a little boy who had come halfway across the country on his own.

She pushed the door open and hustled Mickey into his mother's arms. Then, taking a deep breath, she cleared her throat and said, "Excuse me, Owen. There's someone here who wants to see you."

★ ★ ★

Owen and Willie were in deep conversation when Thelma's voice broke in. Owen had his back to the door, and when he looked up, he saw Willie staring past him. Her face had gone utterly white, and her eyes were wide with disbelief.

He turned just in time to see a small figure in a brown jacket take off like a shot, running toward him.

"Owen! Owen!" The child dashed to the booth and flung himself in next to Owen, wrapping his arms around him and burying his face in Owen's chest.

"Buddy?" Owen's breath came in shallow gasps, and for a minute he just hung on. Then he gently pushed the boy back to arm's length and looked into his tear-streaked face. "Buddy, what on earth are you doing here?"

"I know I . . . shouldn't have . . . come," Buddy stammered between sobs. "But I . . . didn't know . . . what else . . . to do."

"It's all right," Owen said soothingly, stroking him on the back. "Take a deep breath. You'll be fine. I'm here." He looked up at Willie over the child's head and murmured, "It's Buddy Ferber. You know, I told you—"

"I gathered as much," she said. "What's he—?"

"You know as much as I do," Owen interrupted. "But we're going to find out."

The boy's sobbing subsided, and Owen settled him firmly on his lap. He motioned for Thelma. "Can you bring us a glass of milk, please?"

Buddy straightened up. "Coke," he said. "Could I have a Coke instead?"

"Coke it is." Obviously glad for something useful to do, Thelma hurried off toward the kitchen.

"All right, Buddy," Owen said when Thelma had brought the Coke and the child had settled down a bit, "now tell me what this is all about. Does your mother know where you are?"

Buddy shook his head vehemently, and his lower lip began to tremble. "I'm going to hell, Owen," he whispered, his tears spilling over again. "I lied, and I stole money, and I'm going to hell."

"You're not going to hell," Owen soothed. "But we'll get to that later. Can you start from the beginning?"

The boy nodded. "My mama ran away," he said, contorting his little face into a scowl. "With *Rudy.*" He spat out the name. "Gramma was taking care of me, and then—then—" He burst into tears.

"Then what, Buddy?"

"Then I got up—yesterday morning, I think. I forget."

"It's all right. What happened when you got up?"

"Gramma was still asleep. I was hungry, so I tried to get her up to make breakfast, but she wouldn't wake up. I shook her and everything. And when I touched her, she was—cold. *Dead.*" His little lip quivered.

"Are you sure she was dead and not just sick?"

He nodded vehemently. "She wasn't breathing. She was all blue, like that naked baby bird I found in the backyard last year. And stiff."

"Then what happened?"

"I took money out of her underwear drawer—I saw where she keeps it. And I walked into town and got on the bus. It was real early. Nobody saw me. And I lied to the bus people and told them I had to go see my father. They were real nice, but it took a long time to get here. I stole my gramma's money, Owen. And I lied—"

He broke down sobbing again, and Owen gazed helplessly at Willie. To his amazement, tears were streaming down her cheeks, and she was looking not at him but at Buddy. She reached out a shaky hand and touched Buddy on the arm.

"Honey," she said softly, "can you look at me?"

Buddy swallowed down his tears and raised his head.

"My name is Willie," she went on. "And I'm—well, a friend of Owen's. We'll help you, sweetheart. Don't worry."

Buddy blinked hard and stared at her. "Willie is a funny name for a girl," he said. "But you're nice."

"Thank you. I think you're nice, too."

"Are they going to put me in jail?" Buddy whispered plaintively.

"For what?"

"I'm just a kid, but I listen to the radio sometimes," he said indignantly. "When somebody gets dead, they find out who did it and put them in jail."

"You didn't kill your grandmother," Owen countered. "Nobody's going to put you in jail." Then a thought struck him, and he peered intently into Buddy's red-rimmed eyes. "How did you know where to find me?"

"My mama told me, after you left, that you had gone to Eden, Mississippi. I 'membered Eden 'cause that was where Adam and Eve lived. In the Bible.

We learned about it in Sunday school. I didn't exactly know where Mississippi was, but I thought it was pretty funny that Eden would be there."

Willie squeezed his hand. "So you got on the bus, told them you wanted to come to Eden, Mississippi, and—"

"And I got here, too," he finished, a look of fierce determination on his narrow little face. Then the expression crumpled. "But I lied again." He pointed at Thelma, who was sitting across the room with Stork and Mickey. "To her." He shook his blond head. "I told her I wasn't scared. But I was."

"I'm sure she'll understand," Owen said. "Right now, we've got to decide what to do about you."

"Can't I stay here with you?" Buddy wrapped his arms tighter around Owen. "My mama's gone, and my gramma's dead, and nobody else cares about me, and—"

Just then the telephone behind the counter rang. Madge answered it, and Owen saw her listening, frowning. She motioned to Thelma, who nodded and came over to Owen. "There's a call for you," she said. "It's Ardyce Hanson. She says it's urgent. Apparently she called home, and Rae told her you and Willie were here."

"I'll take it." Owen set Buddy into the seat and slipped out of the booth. "You stay here with Willie and finish your Coke. Are you hungry?"

Buddy nodded.

"Thelma will fix you up with some lunch. I'll be back in a minute."

He went to the counter and took the receiver from Madge. "Ardyce? It's Owen."

"Owen, we've got problems up here," Ardyce's clipped voice came over the line. "Irene Ferber, JoLynn's mother, died. One of the doctors from our clinic was called down to North Fork. Apparent heart attack—she was still in bed, probably died in her sleep."

"Ardyce—"

"They didn't find her until this morning, when she didn't show up to help the Altar Guild at the church decorate for Advent. JoLynn's out of town—nobody seems to know where—and, I'm sorry to break it to you like this, Owen, but Buddy's missing."

"Ardyce—"

"I knew you'd be upset, but I thought you'd want to know. I'm not sure what I expect you to do about it, except maybe to pray. I—"

"*Ardyce!*"

"What?"

"Buddy's here. Right here, with me. And Willie." Owen turned and glanced over his shoulder. "Eating a cheeseburger, if I'm not mistaken."

"Did you say he was there? In Eden?"

"Yes. He says his mother ran away with some guy named Rudy, and he was staying with his grandmother. When she died, he just panicked, I guess, and got on the bus and ended up here."

"His mother didn't exactly run away, Owen. She eloped."

"Oh."

"Poor little guy. He must have been terrified. Can you keep him there until we straighten this out?"

"Well, yes, but—"

"Hold on a minute, Owen. The doctor just came in, and I want to find out what he knows."

Owen waited, shifting from one foot to the other, hearing muffled sounds in the background as Ardyce talked to someone. He looked back toward the booth. Willie had Buddy on her lap and was pretending to steal his potato chips, and the boy was laughing. This seemed like an appropriate time to pray for God's direction again, so he shut his eyes and tried to concentrate.

"Owen?" Ardyce's voice was low, subdued. Something had happened, and from her tone it didn't sound like good news.

"I'm here."

"The police found JoLynn."

"The *police?*"

"I'm afraid so."

Owen's heart sank. "Well, where is she? In jail?"

"Worse. In the county morgue in Sioux Falls."

Owen could barely breathe, but he managed to get the words out. "What happened?"

"An icy road, apparently. One-car accident, hit a bridge going about eighty. She died at the scene."

"Oh, Ardyce—"

"This Rudy guy was driving. He's in critical condition but alive." She paused, and static crackled over the telephone wires. "He was drunk."

Owen sagged against the counter and held the receiver to his chest. The room spun around him, and he heard, as if from a great distance, Ardyce's voice vibrating against his heart. "Owen? Owen, are you still there?"

He put the telephone back up to his ear. "Yes."

"I'm going to try to find out any other details, and I'll call you later today. Will you be at home?"

"I guess so." Owen took a ragged breath and tried to calm his erratic pulse. "Ardyce? What do I do now?"

"About what?"

"About Buddy, of course. Do I tell him?"

"I don't know. He's had a difficult couple of days, I imagine. It might be better to wait a while. Let him settle down a bit."

"All right. Thanks for letting me know."

"Sorry to spoil your holidays, Owen."

Holidays! Owen had almost forgotten. "Ardyce, Willie and I had planned to get married on Christmas Day, but now . . . well, I just don't know. I'll keep you posted when we untangle this mess a little bit. We'd like you to be here if you can."

"I'll do my best. Give my love to everybody."

All the way to the farm, Buddy sat in the backseat of the convertible and carried on a rambling account of his adventures traveling from North Fork, Iowa, to Eden, Mississippi. "And one time, when we stopped in some little town in Arkansas, this nice lady bought me some lunch at the bus stop diner. Turkey and dressing and mashed potatoes, just like Thanksgiving. And—"

Owen leaned over and squeezed Willie's hand. She had been wonderful, had taken to Buddy immediately and refrained from prodding Owen with questions when he told her they needed to talk. Now she sat quietly with her eyes closed. Probably praying, just as he had been doing nonstop since the word of JoLynn's death had come. But he was no closer to an answer. What on earth was he going to do?

"It's nice here," Buddy commented as they turned onto the gravel road leading to the farm. "Quiet, like at home. But warm."

"Was it really cold in Iowa?" Willie asked, craning around to look at him.

"Uh-huh." He nodded vehemently, then ducked his head sheepishly. "I mean, yes, ma'am."

"You don't have to call me ma'am," she chuckled, giving him a wink. "Willie will do just fine."

"Yes, ma'am—I mean, Willie." Owen glanced in the rearview mirror again and saw Buddy smile. "It's already snowed a lot at home. Does it snow here?"

"Once in a while, but not like you're used to. It's usually not this warm in December."

"I like it," Buddy declared. "I get tired of being cold."

They turned into the driveway of the Coltrain farm, and Vallie came down the slope of the front yard with Curly on her heels, both of them barking and wagging their tails. "We're home," Owen said.

"Vallie!" Buddy bounced up and down in the backseat. "Vallie's here!"

"Of course she is. And I'll bet she remembers you, too."

"Who's the other one?"

"That's Curly," Willie said. "She's my dog—well, our dog."

Buddy stopped bouncing. "Are you guys going to get married?"

Owen stopped the car and leaned over the backseat. "Yes, Buddy, we are."

His little face fell. "Oh." He gathered his knapsack and coat, and when Willie opened the door, he slid out of the seat. "Is it OK if I go play with Vallie?"

"Sure," Owen said. "Her ball is on the porch if you want to play fetch."

The dog came up to Buddy immediately, prancing around him and whining. Buddy knelt down and hugged her, his little body trembling. "Hey, girl," he murmured. "I missed you. Did you miss me?"

Vallie sat down and lifted her paw for a handshake, then jumped up and grabbed the ball off the porch steps. In a flash Buddy was off and running with both dogs.

Owen picked up the boy's coat and knapsack and laid them on the porch. Willie followed him up the steps and sat next to him in the swing.

"Cold?" he asked, putting an arm around her and pulling her close.

"A little. Fifty-nine may be warm to Buddy, but it's chilly when you're just sitting."

"Do you want to go in?"

"No. Let's stay here for a little while. Tell me what happened."

Owen sighed. "That was Ardyce on the phone, as you know. I didn't want to try to explain any of this in front of Buddy." He shook his head. "JoLynn didn't run away. She eloped."

"He seems like a bright boy. He's very sweet and sensitive. Why wouldn't he be able to understand that his mother got married?"

"You like him, don't you?"

Willie smiled and leaned in closer to Owen, her eyes drifting over the yard, where Buddy was throwing the ball for the dogs. "He's a wonderful kid. And a courageous one. Imagine, at that age, finding your grandmother dead and then coming halfway across the country alone on a bus. Not to mention growing up without a father." She shook her head. "He's had a rough time of it."

"It's going to get rougher."

"What do you mean?"

"JoLynn is dead, Willie. This charming guy she was going to marry was driving drunk on an icy road. Skidded into a bridge." He clutched her tighter. "How do I tell him?"

"Maybe we shouldn't just now. Maybe we should wait a while, let him regain his equilibrium."

"That's what Ardyce said."

"Ardyce is a pretty smart cookie," Willie mused. "And she knows people. Does Buddy have any other relatives?"

"I don't know. I think JoLynn mentioned having a sister somewhere—" Owen's heart constricted. How could he give up this boy he loved so much, just when Buddy needed him most? But on the other hand, how could he ask Willie to take on the responsibility for someone else's child? They were about to be married. They needed time, and—

The screen door opened, and Rae poked her head out. "Oh, good. You're back. Ardyce Hanson is on the phone."

Owen got up and went to the door.

"What's going on?" Rae asked. "Ardyce said it was important. And who is the kid?"

"I'll explain later." Owen turned back to Willie. "Can you keep an eye on Buddy until I get back?"

"Of course. And Owen?"

"Yes?"

"Try not to worry. We'll get through this."

Sure we will, Owen thought as he headed for the phone in the hall. *I'm just not sure we'll get through it in one piece.*

Willie sat in the swing and watched Buddy with a heavy heart. How much was a child supposed to be able to endure? And yet he seemed so resilient, playing with Vallie and Curly as if he hadn't a care in the world. He even laughed now and then, and turned to wave at her as he came back up the hill.

She understood now why Owen felt so strongly connected to Buddy, why he had fallen in love with the boy so quickly. It wasn't just because he was polite and well mannered, or because of the charming combination of blond hair, brown eyes, and those freckles across his nose. It was Buddy's vulnerability, an openness of spirit that trusted innately and loved absolutely.

Buddy trusted Owen. He had proved it—if his trust needed proof—by coming halfway across the country to the one person he believed wouldn't let him down. Everyone else had betrayed him, at least in his six-year-old mind. His grandmother had abandoned him by dying, and his mother had run off with some man Buddy clearly *didn't* trust. Who else did he have except Owen, the only man who—even for a brief time—had been a father to him?

And what fate lay in store for this little one now? A state orphanage where he would be thrown in with rough boys and overworked social workers? Being handed off like so much discarded furniture to some distant relative or a foster home? What became of children like Buddy Ferber? Would he grow up to be a cynic, believing in nothing, because life had dealt him such a hard blow at so early an age?

As Willie watched Buddy running with the dogs, she began to pray—for direction for the child; for Owen's hurting, confused soul; for healing; for restoration. And deep within her spirit, a truth crystallized: *I will be Father to the fatherless, and Mother to the motherless. You will no longer be called orphans, for I will lift you up and be your God.*

Willie didn't know if the words were from a Bible verse she had read sometime in the past or simply a truth drawn from the heart of God. But something in her mind rebelled against the thought. It was a nice, spiritual idea that God would be Father to the fatherless, but Jesus didn't have warm arms to wrap around a shivering boy or shoulders to ride him piggyback. A boy like Buddy needed Christ with skin on. Someone he could touch and see and love and trust. Someone who wouldn't let him down.

Willie looked up suddenly to see Owen standing in front of her. His face bore an expression of utter misery, and she could see he had been crying.

"Sit down, sweetheart."

He sat next to her, his shoulders slumping. "That was Ardyce—again."

"What did she say?"

"Buddy has no close relatives—only an aunt and uncle in Chicago. The sister who took care of JoLynn when she was pregnant. She moved from Minneapolis after the baby was born and has had no contact with JoLynn since. According to Ardyce, she helped her sister under duress, didn't approve of her decision to keep the baby, and has no intention of having anything to do with her nephew. Something about the sins of the mother being visited upon the child."

"That's absolute hogwash!" Willie flared. "Buddy is not responsible for what his mother did."

"I know that, and you know that. But just try to convince that self-righteous Bible-thumper of a sister." He sighed. "Buddy won't know the difference. He's never even met the woman. It just makes me so mad when people—"

Willie squeezed his hand gently. "Honey, are we getting off the subject just a bit?"

"Sorry. I guess I'm avoiding telling you the rest of it."

"There's more?"

Owen nodded. "JoLynn left a will—of sorts. Some court-appointed lawyer went out to her house with the police and found it. Handwritten and fairly recent, but apparently legal."

"Did she have anything worth writing a will for? I thought she was pretty poor."

He turned to her, and tears filled his eyes. "She had Buddy."

"Excuse me?"

"She specified in the will that if anything happened to her—" He paused and took a ragged breath. "Willie, I don't know how to say this."

"Just tell me."

"Her will says that she wants *me* to raise Buddy. To adopt him."

"Oh, Owen—"

"I have no legal obligation to do so, of course. If I don't take him, the state will take over and find a home for him, and—"

Willie tried to interrupt, but he raised a hand to silence her and rushed on. "I know this is too much to ask of you. It's completely out of the question. I mean, it'll be nearly a month before we're married, and then—well, I want you to have no doubt, Willie, that you're more important to me than anything else in the world. I won't jeopardize our relationship by—"

"Owen," she said when he took a breath. "Listen to me."

He stopped, a shocked expression on his face.

"This isn't exactly what I had planned when I agreed to marry you," she began carefully. "I sort of figured we would take our time, get adjusted to each other, and then—"

"I know, I know," he cut in. "And we will. I'm not asking you to agree to anything. I just don't know what to do about this situation right now."

"Yes, you do."

Owen stared at her, dumbfounded, and a warmth rose in Willie as she gazed at him. Memory or no memory, this was the finest man she could ever hope to meet, a man whose heart overflowed with so much love and compassion that she had no fear of the well ever running dry. There was plenty of love to go around and a little boy playing in the front yard who desperately needed all the security they had to give him.

"As I was saying," she whispered, "this wasn't what I had planned. But

God's plans are usually a lot better than ours." She put her hands around Owen's face and stroked his beard. "A husband and a son all at once? Yes, we will have some adjustments to make. And so will Buddy. But we'll do just fine—you'll see."

"You mean—?" Owen's voice was so choked with tears that he could barely speak.

"I mean, my darling, that I'm not fool enough to pass up two blessings because I counted on only one."

46

Thelma's Dream

Brownlee Estate
December 10, 1945

"A double wedding?"

"Yes," Thelma said, looking up at Bennett from the desk in the first-floor office. "You don't think it's a good idea?"

"I just thought—well, that a woman always wanted to have her wedding day all to herself, and not have anyone else stealing her thunder. That's why we planned to have our ceremony after the first of the year, isn't it?"

Thelma chuckled. "Honey, I'm so old that most of my thunder has already been stolen. I've waited a long time for you, you know."

He leaned down and kissed her. "Was it worth the wait?"

"Indeed it was. But I don't want to waste any more time. And I certainly don't think it's fair that you get to move in and live here without me."

"You'd rather be living here *with* me and start tongues wagging all over the county?"

"That's not what I meant. It's just that, well, every time I go back to that little apartment, I feel the contrast more and more."

"You're getting spoiled. But I think you can stand it for a few more weeks. Make you appreciate this place—and me—more."

"I appreciate you quite enough as it is. Any more appreciation and you'll be impossible to live with once we do get married. Now, about the wedding."

"If Willie's OK with it, who am I to disagree?"

339

"You're the bridegroom, silly," Thelma quipped. "At least one of them. If you don't remember that, we really do need to have some coaching sessions before this wedding."

"Oh, *I* remember." Bennett pulled a chair up beside her, sat down, and took her in his arms. "If you need to be reminded of my role in all of this, I'll be happy to oblige." He kissed her tenderly and with passion, then sat back. "How was that?"

"Enough to jog a gal's memory, I'd say. Or to distract her from the task at hand."

"Which is—?"

"Finishing these wedding plans, of course. Madge is taking care of the reception, and Ivory will do the music. We still need to decorate. Can you get me a tree—a big one?"

"I've got one all picked out over on the edge of the back pasture. Ivory thinks we can drag it out with his truck, and Drew's going to help me cut it."

"Good. I'll finish up the arrangements with Willie this week, and—"

"What do you mean, 'finish up'?"

Thelma ducked her head. "Well, we sort of—"

"You already had this idea cooked up, didn't you? About the double wedding? Just whose idea was this, anyway?"

"It just happened, Bennett—like spontaneous combustion. Willie and I were at the cafe having coffee, talking about Buddy, about how she and Owen had really wanted to get married on Christmas Day, and things just fell into place."

She paused. "Willie's wearing her mother's wedding dress. I wonder if it will look strange, with me not wearing white as well."

Bennett stared at her as if she had lost her mind. "You're not wearing a white wedding gown? Why on earth not? I know the husband is supposed to stay out of these discussions, not see the bride in her dress until the wedding day, but—"

Thelma held up a hand. How could she explain this? "Bennett, a white wedding gown is—well, a symbol." He gave her a blank look, and she tried again. "Of purity, you know? The blushing bride and all that?"

"So?" Obviously he didn't get it.

"The image doesn't exactly fit me, Bennett. A woman with a past doesn't wear a long white gown."

A flash of anger ran over his handsome features, and he scowled. "A woman with a future does. Never mind about the past."

"Bennett, I can't just flaunt convention like that. Everybody in the county knows what kind of woman I was. It would be the talk of the town for months."

"Let them talk," he snapped. "The more important issue is, do you or do you not believe in God's grace?"

"Pardon me?"

"Whatever happened in your 'past,' as you call it, has been forgiven and wiped clean, years ago. It doesn't make a bit of difference to me what you wear, but before you decide, you might want to rethink your theology just a bit."

"Meaning what?" Thelma frowned at him. What was he getting at?

"Meaning," he said with conviction, "that your 'purity' does not depend upon anything you've done in the past, but what God has done in you in the present. Isaiah said, 'Though your sins be scarlet, they shall be white as snow.' Seems to me your wedding dress should reflect the same measure of grace."

Thelma's heart surged with love for this dear, compassionate man. He believed what he was saying with all his soul. He trusted in her, in what God had done to bring her to new life. In his eyes, she was as unsullied as the purest maiden. She raised her eyebrows at him. "I'll think about it."

"Think hard. And while you're thinking, consider whether *God* would put you in a white gown for the one and only wedding of your life." He smiled slyly.

"No fair bringing God into this argument," she protested. "But I will ponder these things in my heart."

"An appropriate image, if you ask me."

Thelma grinned at him and patted his cheek. "I didn't ask you, darling. Now, can we get back to the original discussion?"

"Which was?"

"Will you be disappointed if we won't have our wedding day all to ourselves?"

He chuckled. "Disappointed to marry you earlier than we planned? Don't be ridiculous. As long as we won't be spending our *honeymoon* with Willie and Owen." He leaned over and looked at her checklist. "By the way, you still haven't told me where you want to go. If we're moving this wedding up, I'll need to make some plans. Have you decided?"

"I have. But I'm not sure it's your idea of a honeymoon."

"London? Paris? Rome?" He squeezed her hand. "Whatever you want, sweetheart."

"Eden, Mississippi."

"What?"

"What I'd like most, believe it or not, is to spend an uninterrupted week with you right here in this house. To cuddle by the fire and drink hot cider, to take long walks in the woods, to sleep late and make outrageously elaborate breakfasts and take the telephone off the hook."

"The telephone isn't even installed yet."

"Fine. Leave it that way until after New Year's."

"Are you sure? We can afford to take a real trip, you know."

"I know. But I'd rather put that off for a while, if you don't mind. Until we get settled." She smiled at him. "Maybe this is hard for you to understand, hon, but all my life I've dreamed of spending just one night in a home like this. And even more, I've dreamed of being loved by someone like you. Now those dreams are coming true, but it's not just one night—it's forever. And I want to begin our forever here, at home. Where we belong. Where we'll always belong . . . together."

"It sounds perfect," Bennett murmured into her ear. "I just have one condition."

"What's that?"

"That you don't expect me to sweep you into my arms and carry you up those stairs the way Rhett Butler did with Scarlett O'Hara. I'm an old man, don't forget, and I'm afraid my back just wouldn't take it."

"Well then, we'll skip the part where you carry me over the threshold," Thelma said. "As long as we don't skip anything else."

★ ★ ★

After Bennett had gone into town to meet Drew at the office, Thelma went outside and walked down toward the river, to the brick patio where Bennett had built a small white gazebo overlooking the water. She sat for a few minutes gazing into the gentle current, then back up toward the house, which glistened in the morning sun like a priceless pearl.

Home. Her home.

Was it possible that after so many years, God had remembered her dreams and brought them to reality? Sometimes she feared it had all been just a figment of her imagination, that she would awaken to find Bennett, the house, all of it—vanishing before her eyes like images in the mist. Yet there it stood, the house, white and glittering against the blue December sky . . . a beacon of hope, a reminder of grace, and a promise of things to come.

So much had happened—to her, to all of them. So many evidences of God's power and mercy, even in the midst of heartache and struggle.

She thought about Willie and Owen. What a fine couple they made, and what exceptional parents they would be to that little six-year-old orphan boy who had arrived out of nowhere to invade their lives! Willie had endured so much in the past couple of years, and she would have been perfectly justified in saying no to the idea of adopting Buddy Ferber. But she had been able to look beyond the inconvenience to the blessing, and Thelma was convinced that she would be richer for it in the long run.

They were all richer—and not just in material ways. God had demonstrated grace and power in all their lives—in Drew and Rae, facing the demands of raising Angelique; in Drew's father, who was making good on his promises to change his ways; in Orris Craven, in herself and Bennett, in little Mickey Simpson. And, of course, in Ivory Brownlee, who had shown them all what it was to live selflessly, to give freely as he had received, with the unwavering faith of a little child.

Christmas was coming—the celebration of the Savior's birth and the joining of two couples in lifelong commitment. An image came to Thelma's mind, of the Babe in the manger, with all their friends and extended family standing there, gazing down in wonder at the Christ child. And she knew without a doubt that Jesus would accept the worship of a simple man like Ivory, a retarded child like Angelique, a deaf boy and an orphan, a man with no memory and a woman with a past. Jesus would welcome them all.

And they would welcome Jesus, too. Welcome the Christ who was born anew in their hearts and lives and relationships. Welcome the Giver of all good gifts, the Restorer of broken lives, the Healer of hearts.

The future held its share of troubles and challenges, no doubt. And yet it held bright promises as well. And through the places of darkness and light, a little Child would lead them.

A child whose name was Emmanuel. God with us.

47

Last Dance at the USO

Camp McCrane, Mississippi
December 15, 1945

Link Winsom pulled to a stop in front of the USO building and turned in the seat toward his wife. "This really brings back memories, doesn't it?"

Libba nodded. "I'll say. I was so nervous that night we met."

"I trust you won't spend this whole evening in the ladies' room the way you did that night."

"It wasn't the whole evening," she protested. "Just—well—a portion of the evening."

He leaned over and took her hand. "I'm glad you finally decided to come out. Otherwise I would never have found out how great you were at jitterbugging."

"I haven't danced in ages," she sighed. "Wonder if I'll still remember how." She looked over at him. "Will you be all right? Your leg, I mean."

Link ran a hand over his knee. There was a time, not so long ago, when he had doubted that he would ever walk again. Now he was negotiating his way around campus, even the tall steps to the law-school building, without a cane. He could drive, could do almost anything he wanted. But jitterbug? He doubted it. He still lived with a good deal of pain, and that kind of movement was bound to give his hip fits. "Maybe we'll just stick with the slow numbers," he said, hoping she wouldn't be too disappointed. "Waltzes, stuff like that."

As usual, she came through for him. "I was hoping you'd say that," she murmured, sliding closer to him. "There's nowhere I'd rather be than in your arms."

Just as he leaned forward to kiss her, a car pulled up on either side of them and a horn sounded. "Guess I'll have to take a rain check," he said. "Looks like the rest of the party is here."

They got out of their car and went over to the blue convertible parked on their right. Owen was driving, with Willie close beside him and Drew and Mabel Rae in the backseat. From the other car, Stork and Madge emerged, holding hands and grinning at each other like teenagers.

"Everybody's here, I see," Stork said, clapping Link on the shoulder. "Glad you could make it, pal."

"I wouldn't miss this for the world, even with a bum hip."

"Oh, that's right," Rae said as she hugged Libba and gave Link a kiss on the cheek. "Will you be able to dance?"

"Not the fast numbers, I don't think," Link said. "But what about you?"

"I'm feeling pretty good—it's been six weeks since Angelique's birth, and Drew has been taking very good care of me. I'll probably try to take it easy, though."

Link smiled at her. She looked good—much happier, more contented. "Maybe we'll have to keep each other company at the table and let Drew jitterbug with Libba."

Libba took his arm, and they walked toward the door. "Is Thelma baby-sitting tonight?"

"Who else?" Rae laughed. "She'll have her hands full with both Mickey and Angelique, but she wouldn't hear of any other arrangements. Buddy can pretty much take care of himself, and he'll play with Mickey. But she'll be glad Bennett agreed to help before the night is over."

Link frowned. "Did I miss something? Who is Buddy?"

Willie tapped him on the shoulder from behind. "Buddy is our six-year-old son—mine and Owen's. Or rather, our soon-to-be son."

"You two work fast, don't you? In case no one informed you, traditionally the wedding comes before the kids." Link shook his head. "And most parents don't hold auditions for the part—they just take what they get."

"It's a long story," Willie chuckled. "One of many. We'll explain it to you once we get inside."

"I certainly hope someone does," Link said. "I think I'm confused."

★ ★ ★

The last time Willie had been inside the USO building on the base of Camp McCrane was the night she and Owen had met. It seemed like a lifetime ago, and the place couldn't have looked more different if she had been picked up and set down in another world. The perimeter of the room was strung with twinkling lights and garland, and an immense Christmas tree stood in the corner behind the bandstand. Tables were adorned with flickering candles and greenery, and the long bar was covered with enough food for an army—an apt image, now that she thought about it. But the army and the war seemed so far away, so removed from the life she now lived. It almost felt as if those days of terror and uncertainty had been a bad dream from which she had finally awakened.

Link and Libba led the way to a couple of tables next to the dance floor. They had come early, certain the place would be packed. Everybody would want to hear Les Brown, and even without the famous band, no one would miss the one Christmas dance of the holiday season. The men pushed the tables together, and they all sat down. Then Stork, who apparently had appointed himself social director for the evening, jumped to his feet again. "I'll get Cokes for everybody." He disappeared before anyone could protest.

Willie sat close to Owen and gazed out over the empty dance floor. What a night that had been, that warm spring evening that marked Libba's meeting with Link and hers with Owen! Libba had barricaded herself in the bathroom, bawling her eyes out and acting like a complete idiot. That poor little puppy, Freddy Sturgis, had nearly had a heart attack when Link confronted him in the parking lot and demanded to be "properly introduced" to Libba. Was it really less than two years ago? So much had happened to change them all, and yet here they were, back again, to mark a new phase in their lives as couples and as friends.

Music began to play—recorded music from the jukebox. Obviously someone didn't want to wait for Les Brown and his Band of Renown to make an appearance but decided to get the party underway immediately. A dozen or so couples drifted onto the dance floor to the strains of "White Christmas." Owen squeezed Willie's shoulder.

"Would you like to dance, sweetheart?"

Suddenly Willie felt her insides begin to flutter with apprehension. So many memories filled this place, tender memories and painful ones. Could she hide those feelings from the man she loved in order to protect him from being hurt? "Well, ah—Stork just went for Cokes. Maybe we should wait until—"

"The drinks will be here when we get back," he insisted. "Come on."

With that he took her hand and urged her to her feet, leading her onto the dance floor and into his arms. Willie closed her eyes and leaned her cheek against the top of his head as they swayed to the music.

"This is nice, isn't it?" he murmured.

"Yes, it is." She relaxed a little, savoring his closeness, his warmth. All during those dark months of his absence, she had longed for a romantic evening like this. And tonight, with the candle glow and the music and the twinkling red-and-green Christmas lights, the place of their first meeting had been transformed into a fantasyland of holiday celebration—and in her mind, a celebration of their love.

"You look beautiful tonight," he said softly as he leaned back and gazed into her eyes. "Somehow I get the feeling that someone did all this just for us."

"It's lovely, isn't it?" She smiled down at him.

"Anywhere with you would be lovely." He sighed and pulled her close. "Just think—in ten days, we'll be getting married."

"Are you nervous?"

Owen shook his head. "Not a bit. Why should I be? I'm marrying the woman of my dreams." He laughed lightly. "Quite literally, in fact."

"And it's all right that we're sharing our special day with Thelma and Bennett? You don't mind a double wedding?"

"Mind? Of course I don't mind. It's a great idea." He spun her around and grinned up at her. "I don't think I thanked you properly for including Buddy in the ceremony."

"Why should you thank me? We needed a ring bearer, and besides, he's part of our family. Of course he should be included."

Owen stopped dancing suddenly and drew her close. She looked deep into his eyes and saw there a look of love that shook her to the core. "I am a blessed man, Willie Coltrain," he murmured. "And you are my greatest blessing."

He lifted his face to hers and leaned in to kiss her, and despite the public nature of their surroundings, she felt no need to resist. Other people milled around them, dancing by on either side, but Willie felt as if they were the only two people on earth. Her arms went around his neck and they stood there with the Christmas lights reflecting on every side.

In the back of her mind, Willie realized that the music had stopped, but still he held on. The jukebox dropped another record, and "People Will Say We're in Love" began to play in the background. Gradually, almost imperceptibly, she felt a subtle change in his embrace, and she tilted her head down to look at him. A strange expression filled his eyes, and his hands began to tremble.

"Owen? Are you all right?"

He said nothing, just stared at her.

"Owen? Come on, let's sit down."

He didn't move.

His behavior was beginning to frighten Willie, and she put both hands on his shoulders. "Owen!"

"We did this before, didn't we?" he demanded, a wild look filling his eyes.

"Did what?"

"Danced, right here. To this song."

Willie closed her eyes and fought back tears. He was right. The first time they danced, it was to this tune from the musical *Oklahoma!* That night so long ago, when she had lost her heart to him.

"Owen—"

"I remember," he breathed. "I saw you across the room, came over to meet you. I had Link's little black book in my pocket, but once I met you I didn't need it anymore. I—"

Suddenly he stopped. "Link! And Stork!"

"Yes." Willie nodded uncertainly. She didn't know if confirming his memories was the right thing to do or not, but she seemed unable to stop herself. "Yes."

"And then we shipped out, and—" He stopped suddenly. "The chateau. Coker. The explosion . . ."

"You remember all that?" Willie began to shake, and she wasn't sure if she was going to be able to stand up much longer. She tried to maneuver him back toward the tables, but he resisted.

"Can we go outside, please?" he gasped. "I think I need some air."

He made a run for the doorway, and Willie followed, with a short detour to the table to retrieve their coats.

"Is something wrong with Owen?" Link asked as she dashed by. "Can we do anything?"

Willie shook her head. "We'll be back—I hope. Just pray."

★ ★ ★

Owen leaned against the side of the car, fighting for breath. His head spun, and his pulse raced. Images crowded to the forefront of his mind, and he was having difficulty imposing any kind of order on the chaos. He saw himself first in a jeep, with Stork and Link running along behind, then in a luxury stateroom on the *Queen Elizabeth*. He could smell the gunpowder, taste the bitterness of the grenade pin clenched between his teeth, feel the heat as the chateau exploded. . . .

He turned to find Willie standing behind him, and he gripped her by the shoulders. "It's true, isn't it? All of it!"

"Is what true?" Willie twisted in his grasp. "Owen, you're hurting me."

He had been holding her more tightly than he had intended, and he let go instantly. "I'm sorry." Then his voice lowered, and he whispered, "I was here."

"Yes."

"I was with Stork and Link and Coker when we shipped out. We couldn't tell you. We—" He stopped as the realization of what he was saying hit him full force.

"Owen, what is it?" She gently reached under his chin and brought his face up so she could look him in the eye.

"I loved you, Willie," he said, feeling a swell of wonder wash over him. "Before, I mean. You were the one."

"The one?"

"The one I've been searching for. The one who kept calling me back." He opened his arms and she came into them, pressing against him as if she would help him remember by sheer force of will.

But he didn't need to be urged. It was all coming back of its own accord now, in a rush—the pain and terror and love and longing that had evaded him for so many months. He remembered his first sight of the mangled car that took his parents' lives. Standing in the bitter cold next to Uncle Earl and Aunt Gert as his mother and father were laid to rest. That frigid February night when he had found Vallie huddled in a snowbank and brought her home. Spending his summers with Cousin Thomas tagging at his heels, and the raft they built to sail on the river.

And he remembered Willie. His first glimpse of her across the dance floor at the USO, in that blue dress with her hair curling around her head like a wild halo. That deep, velvet voice, the one he heard again in his dream, saying, "It's about time you got here. I thought you had forgotten me."

He *had* forgotten. . . .

"Put your coat on, and let's get in the car," Willie was saying. "It's cold out here."

As the music of Les Brown and his Band of Renown swirled around them on the night air, Willie sat huddled next to Owen and listened as he talked—about his family, his childhood growing up in Iowa, his friends, his cousin Thomas. And about painful memories, too—losing his parents, being transferred to Mississippi, facing his fears on the battlefront.

For hours they talked, with Willie sitting beside him, stroking his hand.

"We were out there, dancing—or rather, kissing," he said, ducking his head sheepishly, "and then that record began to play—"

"'People Will Say We're in Love.' We danced to that song a long time ago, that first night we met."

"I know. I *remember.*" Owen looked up at her. "Suddenly something inside me opened up, like a door in a dark hallway swinging open to reveal a lighted room. It was all there, all those memories that had been buried for so long." He sighed. "Willie, I am so sorry."

"For what?"

"For not remembering. It must have been terrible for you, seeing me like that. Why didn't you tell me?"

"We—all of us—had been warned that we shouldn't deliberately try to jog your memory, that it might make things worse for you." She squeezed his hand. "Besides, I didn't want you to come back to me because of some sense of duty. I wanted you to love me."

"And I do." He leaned forward and kissed her, then settled her head against his shoulder.

"It's been strange," she agreed, "to love you and not be able to tell you. But the truth is, I'm glad it worked out this way."

He straightened up and looked at her in disbelief. "You are? Why on earth?"

"Because I know something few women ever experience—the joy of having the man I love fall in love with me not once, but twice."

"Still, it must have been difficult."

"You just don't know. When you shipped out, it was awful not knowing where you were or if you were alive or dead. Then when I got word that you were 'presumed dead,' I tried to let go the best way I knew how. But I don't think my heart ever gave up hoping. When you came back, it was a miracle, like Lazarus being resurrected—except that you didn't know me." The memory of the pain stabbed at her heart, and she let out a ragged sigh. "I've lost you so many times, Owen Slaughter. You'd better mean it when you say *I do,* because I have no intention of going through that again."

"You don't have to worry," he murmured softly. "I'm here to stay."

"Yes, you are," she said. "All of you."

A hand tapped on the window next to Owen's head, and he rolled it down to find Link Winsom's face staring in. "Are y'all all right? We were worried about you. The dance is breaking up, and you missed Les Brown!"

Owen turned to Willie and grinned. "Les Brown," he whispered. "I remember him, too."

Willie craned her neck to look at Link. "We're fine. Just talking."

"Well, you've talked all the way through the dance."

"Let's go back to the cafe, all right? I'm sure Thelma will have coffee and cake waiting. And we've got something to tell you."

Link rolled his eyes. "OK. Drew and Rae can ride with us so you two lovebirds won't be disturbed."

"We'll meet you back at the Paradise Garden."

Owen closed the window and started the car. "Sorry we missed the dance," he said, putting his hand on the gearshift lever and preparing to back out.

Willie covered his hand with her own and looked him in the eye. "I'm not sorry. Not a bit."

"I love you, Willie." He leaned over and kissed her.

"I love you, too," she said, her heart soaring. "Past, present, and future."

48

Till the End of Time

Brownlee Mansion
Christmas Day 1945

Thelma stood at the top of the stairs, adjusting the train of her long white wedding gown and trying to calm the butterflies in her stomach. This was the day she had dreamed of, waited for, prayed for. After all these years, she had no intention of spoiling it by tripping on her dress and ending up in the emergency room. One concussion was quite enough for this year.

On the other side of the landing, Willie Coltrain fidgeted and fussed with her bouquet. She looked up, and Thelma caught her eye and winked. "Are you doing all right?"

"I guess so. You look absolutely beautiful."

"So do you. I take it the grooms got here in one piece."

"I sure hope so. I don't want to go through this again."

"Nervous?" Thelma asked, as if she didn't know.

"Terrified. I have images of falling down the stairs and making my grand entrance headfirst."

Thelma began to laugh, and Willie joined in. Within minutes they were both holding their sides and trying, without success, to regain their composure.

"What's going on up here?" Rae, in a burgundy velvet bridesmaid's dress, came up the steps glaring at them. "Everybody can hear you."

"Sorry." Willie put a hand over her mouth. "Thelma was just trying to get us to relax a little."

"Well, I'd say you're quite relaxed enough." Rae straightened Willie's veil and put a hand to her cheek. "You look wonderful, Willie. Absolutely radiant."

"Are we about ready?" Thelma asked. "My feet are killing me."

"Drew's parents just arrived, and Orris Craven. Back up a few steps, so Madge and Libba and I can get lined up. Ivory's going to start the processional any second."

Just then Libba and Madge appeared, wearing dresses just like Rae's, only in deep blue for Madge and forest green for Libba. "I love this dress," Libba whispered to Willie. "Thank you."

"For what? For not making good on my threat to put you in some horrible billowy ruffled thing?" Willie countered. "After what you made me wear at *your* wedding, I should have put you in a gunnysack."

"And I would have worn it happily," Libba said, coming up the steps to give Willie a kiss on the cheek. She turned to Thelma. "Ooh, you look gorgeous too. Those fellows of yours aren't going to believe their eyes."

Thelma crooked a smile at Libba. "What's she saying, Willie? That we don't look this good all the time?"

Willie opened her mouth to respond, but the opening chords of Ivory's processional cut off her retort.

"That's us," Rae said. "Where's Buddy?"

"I'm right here." The child appeared from behind Madge's skirts, dressed in a miniature gray morning coat and striped trousers.

"Oh, you look adorable!" Libba tousled his blond curls, and he grimaced and turned to Willie for a rescue.

"She means you're very handsome," Willie corrected. "Just like Owen."

Buddy puffed out his little chest and grinned. "I got the rings." He produced a velvet-covered pillow from behind his back, the wedding rings tied on with satin ribbons.

"All right," Rae instructed, "Buddy, you go first—very slowly. Do you remember where to stand?"

He nodded and began to walk solemnly down the stairs, holding the rings out in front of him. Madge fell into step behind him, followed by Libba and Rae.

"This is it," Thelma whispered. "No turning back." She reached out, took Willie's hand, and closed her eyes for a moment. God had been faithful to her—to all of them—and it seemed right to thank the One who had brought this love, this family, into her life. When she looked up again, Willie was gazing at her with shining eyes.

"You deserve this, Thelma," she whispered. "You deserve it all."

"I don't know about deserving," she responded, "but I know who is responsible, and believe me, I will always be thankful."

"New lives beginning on the day of Christ's birth," Willie murmured. "What could be more appropriate?"

★ ★ ★

Owen Slaughter stood at one side of the altar that had been set up in the music parlor and watched as Buddy Ferber made his way solemnly down the aisle to stand at his side. He smiled and winked at the boy, and Buddy's freckled face broke into a grin. The child was healing from his pain and loss, and being involved in this wedding had made him feel truly like a part of the family. No doubt they had a long way to go, but they had begun.

Owen looked around at the parlor decorated in candles and white lights and Christmas greenery. A huge Christmas tree stood across the foyer in the opposite parlor, festooned with garland and sparkling ornaments, with a gold-and-silver angel atop its highest branch. And Ivory's piano! According to Bennett, Thelma had insisted that they get the best repair man in Memphis to come down and refurbish it just for the occasion. Ivory looked so proud, sitting there at the keyboard of the richly inlaid instrument, and when he touched its keys, the sound that poured forth could have been music from heaven. Or maybe Owen just *felt* like he was standing at the gates of glory. He was, after all, waiting to commit his life to the woman he loved.

His eyes wandered over the family and friends seated in the parlor— Drew's father and mother, with Angelique in her grandfather's arms. Ardyce Hanson, holding a squirming Mickey Simpson and seated next to the biggest surprise of this day, Kurt and Leah Sonntag and their daughter, Steffie. Orris Craven. Libba's mother, Olivia, and her Great-Aunt Mag. Bennett's eldest daughter, RuthAnn, and two of her brothers.

His eyes lingered for a moment on Uncle Earl and Aunt Gert. Earl looked a bit uncomfortable in the opulent surroundings, and Gert kept wiping at her eyes. She was crying at his wedding, as his own mother no doubt would have done. A twinge of remorse shot through him at the memory of his parents. He wished they could be here, standing with him. They would have been proud of the man their son had become. And how they would have adored Willie! But the regret was laced with sweetness, for somehow Owen sensed that they knew, and that they did, indeed, offer their blessing on this union.

Owen cut a glance at Bennett and smiled at him, but the man was totally absorbed, his eyes fixed on the foyer that divided the two parlors. Owen craned his neck to look, and saw why.

Thelma Breckinridge descended the staircase in a sweep of white, and turned, her eyes glistening. She did look beautiful, with her hair swept up and small diamond earrings dangling from her ears. The scar inflicted by Beau Laporte had left a slight pucker, a dimple in her cheek that hadn't been there before. Her face fairly glowed, and when she caught sight of Bennett, her knees buckled just a little. Then she righted herself and proceeded down the aisle.

The plan was for Bennett to meet Thelma in front of the altar, take her arm, and escort her to one side while Willie made her entrance. Owen was vaguely aware of movement around him, but he could not for the world have told anyone what was going on. Willie—his Willie—had appeared, and he could barely catch his breath.

She was dressed in her mother's wedding gown, pure white, with pearls sewn into the bodice that captured the candlelight and reflected a soft glow. But he noticed little else about the dress . . . everything faded into the background when he saw her face. She was smiling into his eyes, moving toward him, coming to meet him to exchange vows that would bind them together forever.

Owen's mouth went dry, and his hands began to shake. And suddenly all those memories played over in his mind—memories he thought he had lost forever and memories they had made since he had come back again. Dancing with Willie the first night they met. Hearing that captivating voice whispering in his ear. Seeing the love that radiated from her face. Feeling her hand in his as they sat on the porch swing at dawn. Watching her tenderness with baby Angelique and her wisdom with Buddy. Recalling the sweetness of their first kiss . . .

Christmas Day. A time of love and peace and warm, happy memories. He could hear the angel's declaration ringing in his ears, and for him it signified both the birth of a Savior and the beginning of a new life: *Fear not, for behold I bring you good tidings of great joy.*

Good tidings . . . great joy. Joy such as he had never experienced in his life, past or present. Tidings for a future full of hope and faith and love.

Willie came toward Owen, as she had come in his dreams. But this was no dream. He felt her touch, warm and real, as she reached out to him. And as his hand closed over her outstretched fingers, Owen Slaughter knew he was holding the answer to prayers he had never even dared to pray.

Epilogue

Christmas Eve 1965

She leaned back on the sofa in the parlor and let her eyes go out of focus. The tree looked pretty like this, all shimmery with lights and colors. It was like looking at it through an icicle. Grammy Thelma always made Christmas so nice, with lots of decorations in the big house and wonderful smells like gingerbread and cinnamon-sprinkled sugar cookies and hot chocolate. It was her favorite time of year, and this was her favorite place in the whole wide world.

Her eyes drifted to the topmost branch of the Christmas tree, where a gold-and-silver angel perched. She and Grammy had put the angel up there themselves, the way they did every Christmas. Grammy Thelma told her the angel brought the good news of Jesus' birth in a stable, and even if she didn't quite understand why being born in a stable was such good news, she liked the story anyway. It made her feel all warm inside, because Grammy Thelma reminded her every time that Jesus had been born for girls like her and loved her a whole lot.

The Christmas-tree angel, Grammy had told her years ago, was named Angelique.

Her name.

Angelique looked up at the angel and smiled. It made her feel all dreamy, knowing that an angel had been named after her. Grammy Thelma must love her almost as much as Jesus did.

Angelique loved Christmas. There were presents under the tree with her name on them, and she was pretty sure one of them was a picture book, the kind you could color in with crayons and be—what was that word Mama used? *Cre-a-tive.* Maybe she would get a new box of colors, too, the big kind with real silver and real gold and a sharpener on the back. Mama said she had to wait, though, until everybody else began to open their presents. To be . . . pa-tient. But it was hard to wait, and even though being pa-tient was supposed to be a good thing, a grown-up thing, Angelique always had trouble with that one.

But this year she would try real hard. This was a special Christmas, Mama said, an an-ni-ver-sa-ry for Grammy Thelma and Grampa Bennett and Uncle Owen and Aunt Willie. They had all got married on Christmas Day twenty years ago, right in this house. Angelique was there, Mama told her, but she didn't remember because she was just a baby. Grammy Thelma and Grampa Bennett were getting old, Mama said, and nobody knew how long we would have them with us, so we were going to make this anniversary real special.

Angelique had asked Mama where her grandparents would be going if they weren't here anymore. Mama just got all teary and wouldn't answer, but Angelique knew. Grammy Thelma had told her all about heaven and what happens to people when they die, and Angelique couldn't figure out why everybody seemed so sad about something that sounded so wonderful. When she got a chance, she was going to ask Grammy Thelma if she could come with her and Grampa when they made their trip to heaven. She figured it would be a lot like this big old house all decorated and pretty for Christmas, and she wanted to be there. Forever.

So, because it was a special anniversary, everybody would be here—not just all the family who lived in Eden and usually celebrated Christmas together, but her real grandparents, too, all the way from New Orleans, and Mr. Orris, her Papere Beau's assistant. Her cousin Mickey, who had been away at college, and Buddy, who didn't come home much anymore because he was off studying to be a doctor and was in love with some girl.

Angelique loved her little brother, Beau, and her cousins, but she absolutely adored Buddy and Mickey. They were like big brothers to her. When they were all growing up, Buddy and Mickey never let the other kids make fun of her or tease her, and once Mickey even got a bloody nose fighting with a boy who called her a dummy. Mickey understood. He was different, too. And she missed him a lot when he went away to that special school for kids who couldn't hear.

Buddy was a lot older than she was, and he went off to college when she was only twelve. But he always wrote to her and sent her funny drawings in the mail that made her laugh and not miss him quite so much. And even though she wasn't his *real* sister, he always told her that she was his *first* sister, and that Trudy and Mary Edith would have to wait in line for his attention.

Uncle Owen and Aunt Willie's daughters, Trudy and Mary Edith, were sixteen—just-alike twins who got in trouble at school by fooling people and pretending to be the other one. They laughed a lot and sometimes let her play with them when they were younger, but now all they thought about was boys and clothes and going out on dates, and it was really boring to be around them. Mickey's brother, Chad, had just turned seventeen, and Aunt Libba and Uncle Link's kids, Jim and Penny, lived down in Jackson and only came to Eden once or twice a year. Even her little brother, Beau, wasn't so little anymore. Everybody was growing up, and soon they'd all be leaving home. All except Angelique.

She was going to stay here with Mama and Daddy. At least until she talked Grammy Thelma and Grampa Bennett into taking her to heaven when they went. Mama and Daddy would miss her, she knew, but they would come too, later on, and in the meantime Angelique was pretty sure her grandparents would want her to be with them.

"Bee-bee Angel?"

Even before she turned to look at him, Angelique knew who it was. Only Mickey called her that name, a name Mama said he had used since she was born. She jumped up and threw her arms around his neck, then leaned back to look him in the face. You had to let Mickey see your lips and speak slow so he could understand. "Hey, Mickey," she said. "I missed you."

"I missed you, too." His voice always sounded kind of muffled, like it was coming from someplace deep down inside, and his words weren't always too clear, but Angelique didn't mind. She liked the way his hands danced as he talked, and she had a surprise for him. A real good surprise.

"Merry Christmas, Mickey." She said the words slowly, frowning as she tried to remember the right signs to spell out his name. "I love you." That one was easy, except her fingers bent a little.

"That's wonderful, Angel!" He grinned, then leaned over and kissed her on the cheek. "Thank you."

"It's your Christmas present." Her heart swelled with pride. "Mama and I worked on it real hard."

"You did fine." He steered her back to the sofa and sat down beside her. "Do you know the song 'The First Noel'?"

Angelique nodded. It was one of her favorites.

"OK, you sing it, and I'll teach you the signs."

"No hell, no hell, born is the King of Israel," she sang, watching his hands.

He stopped her. "What are you singing?"

"No hell," she answered hesitantly, confused by the look on his face.

"What do you mean, no hell?"

"It means that because Jesus was born, we don't have to go to hell. No hell, no hell, born is the King of Israel."

Mickey began to laugh. "It's not 'no hell,' Angel," he said gently. "It's *Noel*—it's a French word, I think."

Angelique frowned. "I think *no hell* makes more sense."

"You're probably right," he agreed, still laughing. But Angelique knew he wasn't laughing at her.

★ ★ ★

The ballroom on the second floor of the big house was all decorated and looked like Cinderella's castle. Angelique never quite understood why it was called a ballroom, because she didn't remember any ball games being played there, except for once a long time ago when Aunt Willie's dog, Curly, brought a rubber ball up here and bounced it all the way down the stairs. But Mama said a ball was a kind of dance, and this would be a good place for dancing. Especially tonight.

There were little Christmas trees all around the room, decorated in white lights with cotton snow underneath. Way down at the other end, a big table was set up with pink punch and lots of wonderful things to eat—Aunt Willie's chocolate fudge and cut-out cookies with sprinkles on them and Mama's big coconut cake and some things she couldn't pronounce that looked like frosty stars that Uncle Owen's friend Ardyce the Nurse had sent in a package all the way from Minnesota.

Angelique sat in the window seat and watched. Music was playing, old music—the kind Mama and Daddy liked to dance to. And some man was singing a song about white Christmas in a deep voice that reminded her of her flannel pajamas—all soft and cuddly. Mama and Daddy were dancing to the music, and so were Uncle Owen and Aunt Willie. Grammy Thelma and Grampa Bennett sat in big chairs in front of one of the Christmas trees like the king and queen.

The room was full of people, aunts and uncles and cousins and grandparents. Angelique knew, of course, that they weren't all related by blood, as Grammy Thelma would say. That meant they weren't really kin, but Angelique figured there were all kinds of families in the world, and she felt warm and safe inside just watching them. These were people who loved her, who didn't care if she was slow or looked funny or was clumsy and knocked things over sometimes. She knew what Down's syndrome meant—that was the name they called what she had—and she knew a lot of people would say that she didn't belong because she wasn't normal. But she belonged here.

Grammy Thelma and Grampa Bennett had gotten to their feet and were standing in front of the table with Uncle Owen and Aunt Willie. Aunt Libba stood to one side with two big packages in her hands, and Angelique's daddy stepped up and clapped his hands for attention.

Angelique moved closer, peering over the heads of people in front of her, trying to see.

"Come on, sweetie," a voice behind her said. "Let's get up front."

It was Buddy, tall and handsome, with his curly blond hair and brown eyes. Angelique smiled up at him and whispered, "Where's your girlfriend? I thought Mama said you were in love."

He twisted his face in a grimace and muttered something about everybody knowing everybody's business, then grinned down at her. "Not tonight, Angel. Tonight, you're my best girl." He took her hand and steered her toward the front of the group, and everybody made room for them. At last they stood right next to Mickey in front of Grampa Bennett. Grampa smiled and winked at her.

"Buddy, come up here," her daddy said, motioning with his hand for Buddy to join them.

Buddy leaned down and whispered, "I'll be right back," then went to stand in front. As Daddy talked, Buddy made the signs for Mickey. She liked to watch his hands and felt proud when she knew some of the words.

"Now," Angelique's daddy said, "we all know this is a special night—the eve of Christmas and of the twentieth wedding anniversary for Bennett and Thelma and Owen and Willie." Everybody clapped and cheered. "Libba, do you want to explain these gifts?"

Aunt Libba came up to the table holding one of the big packages, and Uncle Link brought the other one. "You all know that for years I've been friends with Freddy Sturgis—ah, Frederick Gardner Sturgis, the artist."

"You almost married him, you mean," Uncle Michael said, and everybody laughed.

"Ah, but she came to her senses in time to marry me instead." Uncle Link put an arm around her and kissed her on the cheek.

"It's not your anniversary, Link," Uncle Owen said. "Let her get on with it!"

"Anyway," Aunt Libba went on, "Freddy is very busy with his New York showing, but he agreed to take some time off to do a couple of very special projects for some very special people." She handed the big package to Grammy Thelma. "This one is for you, from all of us." She took the second package from Uncle Link and handed it to Buddy. "Since you're the oldest, you get to do the honors for your parents."

Buddy leaned the package against his knees and signed for Mickey while he talked. "Mom and Dad," he said, and Angelique thought he sounded choked up, "you took me in when I was six and gave me the best home a kid could ever know. So I—well, all of us—wanted to give y'all something special to celebrate this day, a remembrance of what a wonderful big family we have here."

He handed the package over to Uncle Owen, stepped back, and took Angelique's hand.

"You first," Grampa Bennett said to Uncle Owen.

Owen and Willie tore the paper off the package. It was a picture, a big one, and they held it up for everybody to see. A painting of the farmhouse, with a bunch of people standing on the porch. Uncle Owen and Aunt Willie with Buddy and the twins, her mama and daddy with a little dark-haired girl in daddy's arms and mama holding a baby. Even Vallie, Owen's dog who died years ago, and Curly and the kitties. Angelique moved closer, and her stomach got all trembly. "It's us," she whispered, pointing. "That's me, when I was just little. And that's you, Buddy."

"It sure is," Buddy whispered. "And you look absolutely beautiful."

"Open yours, Grammy!" Angelique said. This was better than coloring books and crayons. It was like—well, like being famous.

Grammy and Grampa took the wrapping off their package—another painting, but this one was different. It was the front parlor, right here in the house, all decorated for Christmas, and everybody was in it, gathered around the Christmas tree. Mama and Daddy and Angelique's little brother, Beau, Mamere and Papere Laporte, Willie and Owen and their kids, Link and Libba and their two, Aunt Madge and Uncle Michael and Mickey and Chad. Even Uncle Ivory, who had passed on a year ago last spring.

Right in front sat Grammy Thelma, and Grampa Bennett with Angelique in his arms. She was giving him a kiss on the cheek. And high on the top of the tree, the gold-and-silver angel spread her wings and smiled down on all of them.

"It's our family," Angelique said. "Our whole family at Christmas." Then she frowned and looked up at Grammy Thelma. "But where's the baby Jesus? Jesus should be in the picture, too."

"Jesus *is* in the picture," Grammy assured her, giving her a hug. "Just look hard."

Angelique squinted her eyes and looked. Was this like an Easter egg hunt, something hidden for her to find, or like those pictures in her coloring books with birds upside down in the trees? What was she supposed to be looking for?

And then she saw it. They all had their arms around each other, holding hands, touching. All joined together in a circle, with love shining out from all their eyes. And behind them, in a golden glow, lights from the Christmas tree made a big halo that took them all in.

Jesus was there, all right. In their eyes, in their hands, in their hearts. In the love that made them a family, even if they weren't really kin. "Merry Christmas, everybody," she said softly, reaching out with one finger to touch the painting. "Merry Christmas, Jesus."

It was the best family God ever made. And Angelique, slow and clumsy and funny-looking, belonged. Right in the middle of the picture. Right in the middle of the love.